Praise for Sonali Dev

"Dev writes with such rare empathy and humor that I often found myself holding my breath on one page only to be giggling by the next. This is the kind of book you finish with a whole-body, happy sigh and a warm ache in your chest where the characters will live on."

—Emily Henry, *New York Times* bestselling author of *Beach Read* on *Incense and Sensibility*

"Simply put, a masterpiece. Only Sonali Dev could create an achingly beautiful, sob-and-laugh-out-loud, best-banter-ever story of healing, courage, family, and the most magical coincidence ever. Absolutely extraordinary."

—Kristan Higgins, *New York Times* bestselling author on *There's Something About Mira*

"Vivid and deliciously enticing, Dev's storytelling is layered with emotional depth . . . a flavorful harmony of cross-cultural unions, familial love, and an entertaining ensemble of characters that will leave readers with a serious craving for more."

—NPR on *Pride, Prejudice, and Other Flavors*

"This book holds a galaxy of depth in its pages; it is powerful and loving, sensual and layered. Sonali Dev's writing is glorious."

—Christina Lauren, *New York Times* bestselling author on *Incense and Sensibility*

"A truly wonderful and joyous book."

—Jasmine Guillory, *New York Times* bestselling author on *Pride, Prejudice, and Other Flavors*

"A profound, unique talent, Sonali Dev grabs the reader by the heart."

—Kristan Higgins, *New York Times* bestselling author on *Pride, Prejudice, and Other Flavors*

"A cozy cup of chai for the soul."

—*Kirkus Reviews*

"Nuanced and powerful . . . balances the toe-curling romance with high-octane family drama . . . Dev's candor and sensitivity in both story lines set this family-centric romance apart."

—*Publishers Weekly*

"Sonali Dev is a fresh, unique, and wise voice in women's fiction."

—Barbara O'Neal, bestselling author of *The Art of Inheriting Secrets*

"Recommended for Dev's lush descriptions of food, fashion, dancing, college life, romance, and friendship and her sensitive portrayals of infertility, loss, and hope."

—*Library Journal*

"Dev excels at creating multilayered characters faced with the challenge of balancing Indian cultural traditions with modern Western culture, all while tugging on readers' heartstrings."

—*Booklist*

"How do we define love between friends, and how far would we go for that love? Sonali Dev's book peels back one unexpected surprise after another as she blurs the lines between the family we make and the family we are born into, between altruism and selfishness, and between truth and lies."

—Jodi Picoult, #1 *New York Times* bestselling author

"*Lies and Other Love Languages* is a tender and compelling novel about how women navigate their relationships with families, friends, careers, and their pasts. Mallika's disappearance and Rani's emergence set the story on a path of intrigue and revelation. The contrast between Vandy's carefully crafted public persona and her inner turmoil will resonate with many women. This is a story about discovering who we are."

—Balli Kaur Jaswal, internationally bestselling author of *Erotic Stories for Punjabi Widows*

"*Lies and Other Love Languages* is a breathtaking novel that explores the depths of true female friendship, motherly love, marital love, and the challenge of finding your true purpose in life. Sonali Dev pulls the reader as deep as one can go into the hearts of the exceptionally well-drawn, relatable characters. I was emotionally invested from beginning to end, and I can't recommend this gem of a novel highly enough."

—Julianne MacLean, bestselling author of *Beyond the Moonlit Sea*

"*Lies and Other Love Languages* is a gripping mystery cloaked in a rich family drama. It's full of unexpected twists and turns, and Sonali Dev did a masterful job weaving a tangled web of secrets, lies, love, and devotion. I found myself lost in the pages and wonderfully satisfied when the last one was turned."

—Suzanne Redfearn, bestselling author of *In an Instant*

"These Indian American women and their struggles will appeal to readers from every age and culture."

—*The Washington Post*

"An intergenerational tale of self-discovery and the relationships that matter most . . . A cozy cup of chai for the soul."

—*Kirkus Reviews*

"Dev easily gets the reader to root for her well-rounded characters, and the intertwined storylines wrap up with a delightful ending. This effervescent tale is sure to please the author's fans and win her new ones."

—*Publishers Weekly*

"Three generations of Indian American women strive to find what makes them happy in this heartwarming rom-com about the compromises that held them back and how they finally reclaimed their freedom."

—*Booklist* (starred review)

"Dev weaves humor and romance through her tale of three generations of women."

—Audible

"A super-fun, bingeable story about three generations of vibrant women navigating relationships, friendships, mishaps, and ambitions."

—*Ms.*

"I would give this book five stars for the concept alone, but it's Sonali Dev's trademark character depth and beautiful writing that really make *The Vibrant Years* shine. A gorgeous story of evolving female relationships and how love, hilarity, and the bonds between three generations of women help them thrive in even the fiercest winds of change."

—Christina Lauren, *New York Times* bestselling author of *The Soulmate Equation*

"Oh, what a glorious tangle of love, career, the past, and family is *The Vibrant Years*! Sonali Dev writes beautiful prose and complex, delightful characters in this story of rediscovery and girl power for three generations of the Desai women. A delicious treat."

—Kristan Higgins, *New York Times* bestselling author

"A vivid and touching story of the relationships between three women who love each other and their quest to find each other's soulmates. Funny, fast paced, and insightful, *The Vibrant Years* gracefully explores questions of meaning and hope and regret and most of all the love between women. A beautiful book!"

—Barbara O'Neal, bestselling author of *This Place of Wonder*

"I loved this story of three generations of women navigating life, love, and the patriarchy. Sonali Dev's writing is lush and evocative, her characters vibrant with rage, humor, and wisdom."

—Virginia Kantra, *New York Times* bestselling author of *Meg & Jo* and *Beth & Amy*

"Sonali Dev has done it again in this sparkling page-turner about the unbreakable bonds of women and the necessity of forging an authentic path. Three generations of women from one dynamic family band together to navigate each chapter of life, proving that, with the right people by your side, they can all be vibrant years. Dev's storytelling shines!"

—Kristy Woodson Harvey, *New York Times* bestselling author of *The Wedding Veil*

"Just the kind of book I love to get lost in. Great characters, tons of energy, perfect pacing. Sonali Dev absolutely nailed it. Loved it!"

—Susan Elizabeth Phillips, #1 *New York Times* bestselling author

"Dev's characteristic strength at writing relationships between loved ones grounds this larger-than-life plot in a poignant reality . . . Deception and tenderness mingle in this touching story."

—*Kirkus Reviews*

"Bursting with humor, banter, and cringeworthy first dates, Sonali Dev's *The Vibrant Years* is a joyful and fun read, but it's also very much a timely tale about a group of underestimated women demanding respect and embracing their most authentic selves."

—Mindy Kaling

How Simi Got Her Groom Back

OTHER TITLES BY SONALI DEV

There's Something About Mira

Lies and Other Love Languages

The Vibrant Years

The Wedding Setup

The Emma Project

Incense and Sensibility

Recipe for Persuasion

Pride, Prejudice, and Other Flavors

A Distant Heart

A Change of Heart

The Bollywood Bride

A Bollywood Affair

How Simi Got Her Groom Back

A Novel

SONALI DEV

LAKE UNION
PUBLISHING

Published by Lake Union Publishing, Seattle

www.apub.com

EU product safety contact:
Amazon Media EU S. à r.l.
38, avenue John F. Kennedy, L-1855 Luxembourg
amazonpublishing-gpsr@amazon.com

ISBN-13: 9781662524301 (hardcover)
ISBN-13: 9781662524295 (paperback)
ISBN-13: 9781662524288 (digital)

Cover design and illustration by Kimberly Glyder
Cover images: © Grunge Designs, © Foxy Fox / Shutterstock

Printed in the United States of America
First edition

For Janhavi, a real-life heroine if I've ever known one. No book about sisters (especially where the older one is a badass) could ever be dedicated to a better sister. Thank you for teaching me how to live life with main character energy, on your own terms and with fierce grace, always.

ONE

SIMI

My boyfriend drops down on one knee next to the cascading indoor waterfall at Nashville's Gaylord Opryland, and panic grips me.

I've known Prem for just one year, but I've loved him for the entirety of that year and maybe even before that. It's like the idea of him always lived inside me, and when we met, he simply stepped into the love-shaped void waiting there for him.

My palms press into my cheeks, a pose I've seen countless times in movies when a heroine is being proposed to and she's utterly overwhelmed. The expansive glass roof bathes us in evening light. A couple strolling hand in hand over an idyllic bridge stops to stare. A group of women drinking brightly colored cocktails looks on from the redbrick terrace of a bar. One of them points at us.

Don't throw up. Don't throw up.

Prem picks something off the cobbled floor and looks up at my flaming face.

My hands are still frozen against my cheeks. *Great*, now I just look like a moron who finds the sight of him kneeling to pick things up off the floor overwhelming . . . or like I thought he was going to propose.

Can a person die of embarrassment?

His eyes twinkle with amusement as he stands up.

"Simi?" My name does a teasing dance on his tongue.

Instead of leaning into my mortification, he takes my hand and pushes a shiny dime into my palm. "My dad says never pass a fountain without throwing in a coin to make a wish."

Prem's voice always warms in a particular way when he talks about his family and his childhood. It's the thing that most separates us. I have to work hard never to think about my family and childhood because it's too painful.

"You know how lucky this is, right?" A dimple dips into his left cheek as he smiles. "Finding a coin near a fountain means the wish is definitely going to come true."

"Very logical," I say, unable to not smile up at him.

"Go ahead, make a wish." He turns to the fountain excitedly.

"Me? But you're the one who found the coin."

He squeezes my hand, eyes blazing with love. "I'd only ever wish for you to get what you want anyway."

I know it's a corny line, but my insides turn warm and gooey. I hold up the coin. "Why don't we do it together."

He wraps his hand over mine, and we close our eyes and make our wish before tossing the coin into the clear fountain water, where it lands on top of the blanket of wishes already twinkling there.

I look up at him, and he grins down at me, and for one moment what I wished for feels like it's already mine.

Fear prickles in response to my hope, but I shove it away.

"So . . ." he says, studying my face.

I press a finger to his lips. "You can't ask what someone wished for. That makes it not come true."

He gasps, eyes crinkling with laughter. "Tell me my logical Simi isn't superstitious."

"It *is* logical to hedge my bets. If we're doing the wishing, we might as well up the odds of it coming true."

Prem drops a kiss on my forehead, takes my hand, and starts walking. He's trying not to smile. "That's the plan."

Did I really think Prem was going to propose? He did bring me back to the place we came to for our first date. And we've already talked several times about wanting to spend our lives together. We've operated from that place from the very beginning: that this thing between us is forever.

Even so, a proposal would be missing several steps, which must explain the terror I felt, seeing him down on one knee. That's all it was. He hasn't introduced me to his family yet. Maybe that's what he wants to talk about.

"What are you up to, Prem?"

He slides me a glance. "Is it okay if I wait until dinner to tell you? I had this whole thing planned out. Humor me?"

"Of course." If Prem is anything, he's intentional. He takes his own feelings seriously. He also takes my feelings and those of everyone around him seriously. "But if you're planning on breaking up with me, know that I'm fully capable of dumping wine on you and creating a frightful scene."

"So, you're saying wait until after the wine to break up?"

"Definitely. Especially if you like the wine."

He squeezes my hand. "You know I can't imagine life without you, right? I would do anything for you. This is forever, Simi." His eyes glitter with sincerity.

"So, you're saying we can order the good wine."

That makes him grin his wide, eyes-disappearing-into-crescents smile, and my heart fills with an almost unbearable joy.

When I ran away from Mumbai four years ago, at best I'd hoped to find peace and safety. Finding love was a dream I never dared to dream. My past is a poison dart wedged deep inside my chest. It's run with me no matter how hard I've run from it. A year of being loved by Prem, and I've started to feel like I might be able to extract it, to finally be free. But each time I try to take the next step, the fear wins.

Mumbai is a long way from Hochkinsville, Kentucky, where I'm a pediatric nurse. The doctor I work for is married to Prem's sister, which is how we met a year ago. So, technically, I *have* met his family. They just don't know we're together. Suddenly I feel queasy with nervousness. Given that I work for them, the stakes are too high if something goes wrong.

Not only is Prem's brother-in-law my boss, but I also moonlight as a nanny for his sister and Dr. Johnson's triplets. The girls are utterly precious, much like their uncle. Who wouldn't fall in love with a man who can hold his three sleeping nieces on his person while sitting cross-legged without moving for two hours so his exhausted postpartum sister could catch a nap?

Prem and I met on my first day on the job. He'd dropped by his sister's house with the biggest pizza box in existence. I answered the door with a spit-up-soaked burp cloth on my shoulder and a dirty diaper in my hand. We'd just stood there, unable to move at the sight of each other.

Then all three babies had started to cry at once, and we'd jumped into action to rescue their distraught mother. Pizza in the kitchen, diaper in the bin, burp cloth in the laundry. Babies picked up, swaddled, soothed, fed. We'd fought the battle of babies together and won before we even knew each other's names.

Looking back, I'm pretty sure I was already in love with him by the time he introduced himself.

I didn't learn until much later that Prem used to rearrange his entire schedule (he manages his family's chain of twelve pizza franchises across southern Kentucky and northern Tennessee) so he could volunteer to help me babysit his nieces. His family didn't suspect a thing, because no one thinks about it twice when Prem Gupta does something nice for them.

The first time he told me he loved me, we'd just managed to get the triplets to sleep. It had taken two hours of singing, swaddling, rocking, and walking. Prem and I had promptly followed suit and dropped into a bone-tired sleep on the floor of the nursery without even realizing it.

When I opened my eyes, Prem was lying on his side, watching me, our faces inches from each other, the pale-pink Berber carpet pressed into our cheeks.

My first thought had been *God, I hope I'm not drooling.*

My second thought had been *God, he looks hot lying down.*

My third thought had been *God, this silence! It's so beautiful, please don't let the babies wake up.*

That's when he'd said it. "I love you."

It was the barest whisper.

Instead of saying it back, I threw a panicked look at the sleeping girls, without even lifting my head. "You'll wake them," I whispered with true terror.

An entire universe of emotions swirled in his eyes. Heartbreaking disappointment that I'd left his words hanging. Worshipful admiration that I'd thought of the babies first. Abject terror that his screaming nieces might wake up.

The flecks of gold in his eyes brightened and dimmed like a movie screen, and my heart ebbed and flowed with each passing emotion. I scooted close and kissed him.

Everything about us has been backward and upside down, and yet nothing in my life has ever felt so right side up. And easy. The one thing I've learned about life is that easy is the hardest thing to come by.

The kiss didn't come out of the blue. We'd circled each other like delighted larks filled with pheromones for six months. Or like exhausted babysitters seeking out the torture of wrangling three screaming infants just to be with each other because we were so smitten. But it wasn't until four months ago that Prem and I first went on a date.

Between working at Dr. Johnson's practice, and at the hospital, and spending four hours every day helping with the triplets, finding time to go on dates was yet another dream I was not delusional enough to dream. Then one day when the triplets were eight months old, Prem had intercepted me as I left the clinic and informed me that I had the evening off because Preeti, his mother, and his brother's wife were going to spend a girls' night with the babies. Then he'd driven me to Nashville to the Gaylord Opryland for the kind of meal I had only seen actors eat in movies. I found out later that Prem was the one who'd set up the entire girls' night for the women in his family so we could have our first real date.

Now, with the girls a few weeks away from turning one, our love is also about to turn one. And here we are, back at the Gaylord, and something about it feels special.

"Family is the most important thing in my life," Prem says as we settle into our table. For months now, he's been eager to introduce me to his family as his girlfriend. Especially since his family keeps trying to set him up with eligible women so he can settle down.

I wish I could tell him how very different the way we feel about family is. I wish I could tell him how terrifying the idea of meeting his family is to me.

All the wholesomeness that comes with the Guptas is something I've only ever seen in the movies and soap operas I grew up watching. It would be stupid for me to not know that a girl whose mother "settled down" five times with five different men isn't who the Guptas are expecting Prem to bring home.

He reaches across the table, navigating the wineglasses, and knocks one over.

My hand moves faster than my brain to save it. Prem gets clumsy when he's nervous. It's a good thing I have the reflexes of a martial artist, especially under stress. This makes us all the more perfect for each other.

He picks up my hand like he wants the connection to suck up the hurt he sees on my face.

"My family is going to love you, Simi. Preeti already can't live without you."

As her nanny I want to say, but something about that thought makes me sick to my stomach. What am I even doing? I don't know how to do this.

No. I'm not broken. Prem is not getting a raw deal. I know what broken looks like. And I'm neither Ma nor my sister. I swore long ago never to be them. Nonetheless, I can't ignore what this looks like from the outside.

"What if they think I trapped you?"

"You have. You have trapped me quite thoroughly . . . in the greatest amount of happiness I've ever experienced. I never want to be free of this trap. Please tell me you don't doubt how I feel."

"I don't. But we have to be realistic. What if your family sees it differently?"

I hate sounding so pathetic. I'm usually a great proponent of faking strength till you actually feel strong. The first lesson my sister ever taught me was *they will only know what's happening inside you if you're idiot enough to show them.*

"When I said family is the most important thing in my life, I didn't mean just mine." His voice wobbles with emotion. "I meant us, too, Simi, you and me." He taps his chest. "In here you've been my family from the first time I met you. If my family has doubts, I will make their doubts go away. I swear."

I used to be a crier as a child. I've worked hard to put away that part of me, but despite years of practice holding my emotions in check, fat tears roll down my face.

Prem stands, moving his chair next to mine. I look around. This isn't the kind of restaurant where you can just move chairs around willy-nilly. The napkins are folded into fans and swans. A few people turn to look at us, discreetly, of course, because in folded-napkin places, people are classy like that.

Prem wipes my cheeks with the napkin, which feels soft despite its crisp appearance. Naturally he doesn't notice that there is olive oil infused with pepper on the napkin. My cheek stings, but it's so sweet and absurd that my boyfriend just smeared spicy oil on my cheek in the middle of this romantic moment that a laugh hiccups through my tears.

"I'm totally messing everything up," he says when I wipe the oil off my cheek.

"You're not. Everything is perfect. I'm only crying because"—I stroke his jaw—"you keep making me fall more and more in love with you. Tell me what's on your mind, Prem."

"I want us to take the next step." His eyes are fierce with hope. "So, what do you say, Simi Naik . . . You ready to meet my family and go public with me?"

A tangle of emotions clogs my throat. It isn't just that I work for his brother-in-law and I could lose my job if something goes wrong between us. There's also the fact that I'm in the last stages of getting my green card, and losing my job would put an end to the process. I'd have to start it again elsewhere, which could take another ten years, if anyone even employs me without one. Going back to Mumbai is not an option. I will never go back to what awaits me there. I will never again be the person I was there: helpless and dependent.

The person I am now doesn't want Prem because I need him but because I have a right to how happy he makes me. I want all the parts he comes with. I want his cute rom-com life: the doting parents, the indulgent siblings, even the casual way in which they take one another for granted and then whine about it without fear of retribution. A real family. "Okay," I say, pushing past every misgiving. "Let's do it."

The sheer size of his relief makes me feel like an awful person. "I want to tell them before the big birthday party." The triplets' first birthday is going to be one of those two-hundred-guest shindigs that's straight out of a Bollywood movie. "I want you to come to the party as my fiancée."

"Fiancée!" My heart races in my chest. "Aren't we jumping steps?"

"I think I jumped all the steps the first time I saw you, Simi."

Before I can react, our waiter stops by with dessert. Two types of cake, one mousse, and crème brûlée. Another thing that ties Prem and me together is our unfettered love for sugar. Even so, four desserts is overkill, and I restrict myself to one bite of each.

Prem is his usual self, unbothered with anything but the love in his heart. In this moment, his love for sugar.

"Can we please see how meeting your family goes first?" I say.

"Of course. But that's actually not what I wanted to talk to you about." He scoops a forkful of carrot cake and offers it to me. I take the sweet support, because my heart is skittering in panic again. What now?

"Before we make it official, I want to talk to your sister. Ask for your hand properly. I'd like to invite her to the party."

The bite of cake goes straight down the wrong pipe, and I go into a coughing fit.

Prem stands again to come to me, but I stop him with a raised hand. I'm fully capable of stopping myself from choking, and I do.

The way he watches me makes me feel naked. I take a sip of water and force in a breath. The desire to get up and leave is so strong, I grit my teeth against it.

"That's not necessary," I say finally.

I have no idea where my sister is. The last time we spoke, almost a year ago, she sounded like she was in trouble again. I wanted to ask her to come here, but how could I? I have too much to lose now. She promised me she'd take care of things. She made me promise not to look back. That's why I ran. I can't have her bring danger and destruction back into my life now.

"I thought you and your sister were close," Prem says in that way he says everything, as though it's something he cares deeply about, but only if I do too.

I doubt there's anything more complicated on this earth than my relationship with my sister. My earliest memories involve thinking she was my mother. She's just five years older, but she was always more my mother than our mother ever was. Which means I had a mother and she never did.

I have no idea what to do with the person she is now: as sharp as she was soft, as cold as she was warm, as destructive as she was nurturing. None of this matters, because the truth is that I have no idea where she is.

"It's complicated," I say.

"You sound like you miss her."

"I do," I say. I miss her so very much. Even though I don't miss anything about our childhood. Not even the part where I never had to worry about anything because she was there to take care of everything.

Prem looks like he sees the storm inside me. He's plotting to make me happy. It strikes terror in my heart. So much of what keeps my sister and me apart now is exactly this. Her need to rescue me.

The idea of Prem meeting her makes me want to hyperventilate.

"But that doesn't mean I want her back in my life." There's a note of warning in my voice and an entire symphony of terror inside me.

"She's your sister."

"All families aren't created equal, Prem. Some families don't have your best interest at heart." It's not a lie, technically. My family included our mother too. It's the only answer that will keep Prem from going in search of my sister.

"Wasn't she the one who helped you come to America?" He's determined to heal this painful wound he imagines tearing me up.

"It wasn't that simple. I might have said some of that so you didn't have a bad opinion of my family. She's the only family I have left."

"You still love her," he says, as though he's parsed my words and landed on some great insight.

Oh god, he *is* going to try and find her.

"The last time we spoke, she threatened to kill me, Prem!" It comes out with some force. I haven't escaped into lies to save myself in a very long time.

The last thing my sister ever told me rings in my ears. *Someone can only know what happened if we speak of it. If we never say a word, it never happened.*

Lies are the only way I know to protect myself. "And I believed her because she was the one responsible for our mother's death." I double down, but that's not technically a lie either.

Prem reaches across the table, horrified. "Oh baby," he says. He opens his mouth to say more, but I let my tears flow.

"I can't, Prem. I can't talk about it. It's too painful."

That's all it takes. He squeezes my hand. "I'm so sorry. I didn't mean to bring up all this pain for you."

"It's okay. It's important for you to know where the girl you're in love with comes from." It is so not okay. Nothing about this is okay. Prem's reality is so removed from mine, I would have to destroy his view of the world to share my history with him.

"I don't care," he says, eyes filled with generosity. "All I care about is that you're happy and that we're together."

I know him, and I know that he will never again bring up getting in touch with my sister after what I just told him.

"I know you want my family to be part of our life together, but we're going to have to make do with just yours." Finally I get to speak a truth, and it hurts far more than any of the lies.

TWO

RUPI

My clients often cry when I'm done with them. Not because of the pain they feel when I give them what they ask for, but because what I give them is always far, far better than anything they imagined. The lady with silver curls and dark kohl-lined eyes lets out another sob as she slips me a twenty-dollar tip. It's her first time.

A first tattoo is like opening the floodgates to owning your body, claiming your skin, letting yourself flirt with being edgy. The fact that there isn't much space left on my body where my ink hasn't made its mark says all anyone needs to know about me. The client is already talking about the next tattoo she wants. The watercolor I gave her today is a Medusa—the universal symbol of surviving sexual assault. The woman is sixty-seven. Something about the fact that she is only now getting her Medusa makes me want to scream with rage. Rage is how I've always processed sadness.

"Do you have an Instagram page? I'd love to take a picture and tag you," she says. "You're such a great artist. I want everyone to know about you."

"No." I want to laugh. Social media is the surest way to get caught when you're hiding. "I don't do pictures." I don't make eye contact and keep my gaze just over the woman's shoulder, my expression blank.

It works. Her face does the thing I'm hoping for. It registers a hint of sympathy, followed by a flight response. She's identified me as someone who's a little "off." She backs away and leaves.

This is why I love Americans. They respect your space. Or they run from discomfort. Whichever it is, I'll take it. In India, where I grew up, people stop you in the street to point out anything that marks you as different. If you have a scar, they look straight at it and ask how you got it. If they think you're overweight, they offer unsolicited diet tips.

When we were young, my little sister had a severe stammer. Every single person she ever met pointed it out. They either outright imitated it to her face, or they expressed sympathy and provided advice. Simi hated confrontation, so it had fallen on me to tell every single one of those assholes to go to hell and mind their own business.

That's my special skill. I have a full arsenal of weapons to get people to go away. And yet I can't seem to stop being hunted. Perpetually and relentlessly, I've been hunted all my life. That might sound dramatic, but it's true. Unlike my sister, I don't hide from the truth. Only from people.

If you really want to be left alone, stop getting into trouble to seek attention. Those were my mother's go-to lines for me. Our very own bonding words. Parents give us several gifts, but the ones that burrow deepest and stick longest are when they tell us exactly why we're not enough.

As soon as the client leaves, I yank off my mask, then the glasses I don't need and the Chicago Bears cap that makes my scalp sweat. I run my fingers through my short-cropped hair, airing out the sweaty strands and making them stand up in spikes. My arm cramps, and I stretch it out. Medusa took a good six hours of head-down labor.

I push a window open and stick my face out, letting Chicago's famed wind cool me down. I've spent one winter here, and it's the only time in my life that my body felt as cold on the outside as it does on the inside.

Squeezing my eyes shut, I memorize the Medusa I sent out into the world today, her many snake heads alert and ready to strike at any threat. Feminine anger in all its inexhaustible, indomitable, multitudinous glory. Distrustful and alert, with as many fighting heads and watchful eyes as there are threats. In other words, she's every woman I've ever known.

I watch the hordes of tourists and locals walking along Michigan Avenue, with the powder blue lake beyond shimmering all the way to the horizon. Bikes whiz by and dodge pedestrians on paths that crisscross the park. A man with a thick mustache stares up at the building. It's a common sight: tourists and locals alike marveling at the Romanesque-style building constructed in 1887 to be a carriage factory. His gaze stops when it finds mine. My heartbeat slows.

He doesn't know me.

It's just some tourist.

This closet-size room I've been living in for six months is in Chicago's Fine Arts Building. It's often on the list of "hidden gems" that locals share with visiting friends.

The man keeps staring.

I pull away from the window, my heart fluttering against the cage of my ribs. This isn't a residential building. I only live here, in the tattoo studio, because I'm sleeping with my boss . . . Another theme that's become pretty consistent in my life.

When I came to America two years ago, I believed with my whole heart that I was going to break my old patterns. I was going to finally take my mother's advice after her death and stop getting into trouble. I'd made a list of all the things I was going to do differently. The only thing that should have been on that list was learning how to turn invisible.

The only proof that Rupi Naik still exists in this world is the tattoos I've inked into clients, and that's how I want it.

When I got to Chicago, it had been a year and a half since I held a tattoo gun. I hadn't touched one since I fled Mumbai. Then I ran into Matthew on the brown line in Chicago. I was slipping in and out of sleep (the only way I ever sleep), and my flannel shirt had popped a button, exposing the tangled mermaids on my belly. I caught him staring with his startlingly green eyes. When I slipped past him and got off the train, he followed me. My hand was on my penknife, but when he complimented my tattoos, I surprised myself by telling him I'd done them myself. Then he surprised me by offering me a job if I taught him how to ombre a color like that. He threw in a place to stay, because obviously I looked like I didn't have one.

It had been three days since I'd eaten, and I really didn't want to add food theft to my crime repertoire, so I accepted. After spending six months traveling from city to city on buses, trains, and foot, I needed to rest for just a moment.

This wasn't the first time I've found something good after running away. A silver lining, a golden egg, a pot of treasure at the end of a rainbow. So what if the relief is short lived? The gray clouds always return, the goose is impossible to keep alive, and the rainbow inevitably moves as soon as the gold comes into view. That small respite has still always made running away worth the trouble.

When I was a girl, running and hiding meant protecting my sister and myself, but I also got a little addicted to watching the lumbering, drunk asshole we were hiding from lose. Giving those who wanted to hurt us the slip was even better than the high of watching the ink do exactly what I want under human skin and turning it into an inadvertent and unsuspecting canvas.

It's time to give it up again, to run once more.

I pull away from the window and wait in the shadows to see if the man staring up at the building moves on. It takes him a while, but he finally looks away and starts walking. He digs a phone out of his pocket and pulls it to his ear.

I jump into action, my body moving at the speed of my flight response.

I grab my backpack, a hand-me-down from my last boss, Ron Komar.

I'm wearing the only pair of jeans I own and one of the two black Underground Tattoo T-shirts Matthew gave me when I first started here. I cast a glance around the room that's been my home for six months. The place where I got to do what I love. My work is the only thing that I've loved with my whole heart that's loved me back without demanding a price.

I've learned as much from Matthew as he's learned from me. About inking, at least. The sex was absolutely ordinary. Even fifty-year-old Ron Komar had better moves. Now the asshole is back to haunt me. Why don't the dead ever stay dead?

I pull on my shoes. "Running shoes," our mother used to call sneakers. A laugh bursts from me. *Thanks for the laugh, Ma!*

I hook the backpack on my shoulder, and as if on cue, the landline rings. It's the number listed on the internet. If I'm going to run, I should at least know why I'm running. I answer.

"If you're on the run, why would you stand at the window like a call girl in Amsterdam?"

I haven't spoken to her since I came to this country, but I recognize the voice only too well. Tina Komar sounds exactly like she did when she teamed up with her husband to entice me into coming to LA: bright and friendly and high as a kite.

"Return the stuff you stole, or I'm going to have to turn you in to the cops," she says.

"If you were going to turn me in, you would have done it already. But to hire a private investigator to find me is pretty desperate." I thank my lucky stars for taking the documents when I stole her jewelry.

"Just return the stuff you stole from me, damn it!"

The glee I feel at her frustration is a moment of light in the darkness, and I soak it up. "I don't know what you're talking about."

"I'm pretty sure you do."

I go to the cash register and punch in the keys to open the drawer. "Accusing me of stealing and lying is hardly going to get you what you want." I take out every bit of cash. There isn't much. Matthew cleans it out every day. He's obviously been expecting me to run off from the moment I got here. I've never hidden the fact that this is just a pit stop along whatever wretched journey I'm on. I roll up the money and shove it deep into my bra, trying not to think about the fact that it's barely two hundred dollars, including the tip I just got.

"It doesn't have to be this way." Tina changes her tone, attempting some grotesque version of niceness. "We were friends once. One of the pieces you took was my dead mother's bracelet. You can keep that if you want. Just return the file. You have no use for it."

"I can't imagine why you couldn't make it as an actress. You're not half bad." She's actually terrible. "Maybe you can give Hollywood another shot. I hear there are more roles for older women these days. Unless you plan to keep Ron's operation going?"

"You're forcing me to go to the cops."

Despite myself, I groan in frustration. "Stop treating me like I'm stupid, Tina." I consider leaving Matthew a note, but I'm not living the kind of life where I get to say my goodbyes. What's the point, anyway? He was only interested in learning my technique, and he's already gone as far as he can with that. Talent can't be taught.

I put on my mask, cap, and glasses. Time to get out of here. "I think bringing someone to this country under false pretexts and then forcing them to work without pay after taking away their passport might be a bigger crime than whatever lie you're planning to pin on me."

This time her pause is longer. "I wouldn't have to lie. Do you think we don't have cameras in the house?" There's another pause. I'll bet she's wondering if she should offer up my passport, but that would mean admitting to having it. "You are stupider than I thought if you believe Ron could do what he was doing if he was afraid of the cops." Finally she hits her target. Cold sweat breaks across my skin. Of course they've always had the cops in their pockets. "If you're arrested for theft, you'll be deported."

I'm going to be deported even if I'm not arrested for theft, thanks to her and Ron. "I didn't steal anything. You owed me a year and a half of wages."

"Ron took care of you," she has the gall to say.

I want to laugh, but I'm too sick to my stomach to manage it. "I can charge you with trafficking, you know that."

"Is that what we're calling entrapping and sleeping with a married man now?" she throws back.

"And what are we calling a wife aiding her creep husband in cheating a woman into moving to a foreign country so he can take advantage of her?"

"It could be argued that you lured us into bringing you to America and then supporting you at the cost of our reputation and marriage."

"Did I also lure him into taking away my passport and holding me to ransom for it?"

"Stop lying." She sounds tired now. "My mother's bracelet is my only memory of her. To lose that when I'm grieving my husband. Don't you have a heart?"

This time I do laugh. Ron told me exactly where each piece of jewelry had come from and what transgression he was apologizing to his wife for with each one. Ron turned into a storyteller after two Lagavulins. I knew exactly how loving that marriage was. Not that "a loving marriage" isn't the most oxymoronish of oxymorons.

"If you want something from me, threatening me is hardly the way to get it." Not that I can give back the jewelry. I've pawned off all of it, which is probably how the private investigator tracked me. The only thing I have left are those papers. That file is my only leverage.

She sighs a deeply defeated sigh. "Fine. I'm asking nicely. What do you want?"

The last two years of my life back. "For you to leave me alone. Stop siccing private investigators on me, and stop threatening me. I don't owe you shit, but you owe me wages and my passport. Let's talk when you're ready to hand that over."

Another sigh. "Fine. Tell me where to meet you. We'll do an exchange."

Right. She's already told me that the cops are in her pocket and she has me on camera taking her stuff. I send up another thanks for finding the title deed for the restaurant. "I'm not getting anywhere near you. That's never happening. But send me my money and my passport, and we can talk."

This time she laughs. There's no negotiation without trust.

"That's not going to happen until I get that file back first. Aren't you tired? How long can you keep running?"

Oh, the woman has no idea. I've trained for running and hiding since the day I was born.

"Haven't you learned this past year that you will never catch me? Give me what's mine, or leave me alone. Otherwise I'll destroy the thing you're looking for."

I can hear the anger in her pause. "Don't underestimate me, Rupi. I know you're not stupid enough to do that. If that's gone, you have nothing left to protect you. You'll never get to stop running. I know you have nowhere to go."

In that, she's wrong. I do have somewhere to go. I've been avoiding it, but it's time. Time someone protected me for a change. Time someone paid me back for everything I've done for them. I've had enough of being the only one who pays and pays.

"You're right," I say. "Which is exactly why you will never know where to find me."

THREE

SIMI

Can you believe my stupid brother wants to serve pizza at the triplets' birthday!" Preeti Gupta Johnson says.

Preeti is the closest thing to a fairy-tale princess I've ever met in real life. It's not just the fact that she has everything a person could ever want: grace, beauty, and a family that's considered royalty in the community. She also has that inherent diamond-cut strength that only characters in books seem to have, proved by the fact that she was the first Indian child in town to fall in love with and marry a white man. That, too, with minimal drama, from what Prem tells me.

I'm surprised that her brother has chosen to argue with her.

"I don't mean regular off-the-menu pizza. It can be the entertainment, something people can put together themselves. Something that celebrates the family business and the girls," he tries to explain.

Food is Prem's favorite topic, his zone of expertise. He grew up doing homework at his parents' pizza place. He started doing deliveries at sixteen as soon as he had his license. He was managing the staff and the kitchens before he finished high school.

Prem is the only Gupta sibling who never went to college—despite getting into Ross, the business school at the University of Michigan (a tidbit Preeti loves to share). He was about to leave for Ann Arbor when his father had a stroke. Preeti was in college in California, and their oldest brother, Pawan, had just started his MBA at Duke. There was no one else around to run the business that ran the family. So, the youngest Gupta child had derailed his life plan without a second thought.

Prem insists he only ever wanted to work in his parents' business anyway, so it was an easy decision.

"That's actually not a bad idea," Dr. Johnson says recklessly. He once told me getting in the middle of the Gupta siblings meant you had to be prepared to either be ignored or steamrolled.

"What do you think, Simi?" Preeti asks, ignoring her husband. The look she throws Prem is loaded with meaning. "At this point you're practically family." Her gaze slides suggestively between Prem and me, and color kisses the tops of his cheeks.

I focus hard on Anya, Shanya, and Tanya. I guess Preeti and Dr. Johnson didn't have the energy to come up with three names after their birth, so they came up with one and then resorted to rhyming. "I'm sure TASha will be thrilled no matter what you decide."

Prem and I came up with that nickname for the trifecta of cuteness, and now everyone calls them that. I roll a squishy ball to Tanya, who reaches for it with all the concentration her tiny existence is capable of. Shanya has had her fill of tummy time and flips over and gurgles with satisfaction. Anya ignores all the offerings laid out around her and makes her way to her uncle and starts chewing on his knee.

"That's my girl. Look at those teeth." Prem encourages her ambitious undertaking of fitting his rather large kneecap into her tiny mouth.

My heart does the thing it does when Prem is like this—his heart in his eyes as he gazes upon his niece as she uses him for a teething toy. I'm destroyed by the purity of the feeling that fills my heart. I usually avoid his gaze when we're around Preeti and Dr. Johnson. It must be the fact that we're so close to telling them, but I slip up and let our gazes connect for one charged second. An electric spark zaps down my chest into my belly.

Preeti clears her throat, and we both jump.

Preeti's face goes into high alert. Prem picks up Anya with enough nonchalance that his sister has to know he's hamming it. Anya screams in protest, then discovers her uncle's shoulder and starts chewing on it with renewed fervor.

"Why can't we just have regular pizza?" Dr. Johnson says. "It's a first birthday, after all."

Prem slides his brother-in-law an *uh-oh* look.

Preeti looks exasperated. "You married into an Indian family, John. We can't serve pizza at a milestone party! A first birthday party isn't for the girls, it's for the family. We're celebrating life and inviting our community to share in our joy. I can hear my mom now: *Do you want people to think you don't care?*"

"Makes sense," her husband says with a grin that says it makes absolutely no sense.

Preeti turns to her brother again. "We can only do pizza if it's your family version." Her loaded gaze pings from Prem to me again. "Has Simi tried your only-for-loved-ones pizzas yet?"

Indeed I have. Prem loves to experiment with Indian flavors in pizza. Chicken tikka with cumin-infused feta. Saag with crumbled paneer. He even kneads spices into the crust: garlic, chilies, fennel, and caraway seeds. His family thinks it's the most delicious thing ever, but I'm entirely nonexperimental with food. I want Indian food to be Indian food, and I want pizza to taste like pizza. Or I want it to taste like the pizza from the pizza place in Mumbai my sister used to take me to for the rarest special treat. The memory makes an ache gather in my stomach.

Prem's response takes a second too long. He's been really excited about making the announcement about us to his family, but he wants to tell the entire family together so no one feels left out. The plan is to do it this weekend at his mom's weekly Sunday lunch, when the family gathers to watch the latest Hindi film over aloo parathas and rajma rice.

Preeti has asked me to go several times to help with the girls. Fortunately, I work at the pediatric urgent care on Sundays, so I've been able to avoid it. Now the thought of my work life and personal life colliding brings on the usual panic.

I throw a glance at Dr. Johnson. He's studying his phone. There must be an emergency. The room's focus shifts to him. He throws the oddest look at me and stands. "I need to make a call." He leaves the room, but that look stays with me like lingering discomfort.

"So," Preeti says, attention back on Prem and me. Recently she's obviously suspected her brother's feelings for me, but she's never pushed like this before. "Simi, have you tried my brother's wildly delicious desi pizzas or not?"

I say no just as Prem says yes, and Preeti's mood cartwheels from gentle teasing into rampant suspicion. A delighted gleam lights up her eyes.

Fortunately, Tanya is done with the squishy ball and is looking hopefully at me to provide further challenges. I pick her up and kiss her tummy, and she wraps her arms around my head and giggles. Preeti waits, the curiosity on her face showing no sign of fading.

"I only ever see Prem here at your place," I say, setting Tanya on my lap. "I might have tried it when he made it for you."

Prem looks like a deer in headlights. He's realized that his sister has smelled blood and moved in for the kill. If Preeti finds out before his mother or his sister-in-law, he will never be able to live it down.

"It's been a while since Prem made them for us," Preeti says. "Come to think of it, I haven't seen him much except when he's here to help with the girls." She narrows her eyes, giving up on subtlety, and turns to Prem. "And oddly, you only seem to come help when I already have help." Just as her eyes do the slide between us again, Dr. Johnson comes back into the room.

"Can I have a word," he says to me.

My heartbeat speeds up. Did he pick up on Preeti's suspicions? Is he angry? I know dating within the office and hospital is an absolute no-no, but does Prem count?

"Is something wrong?" My voice wobbles as I follow him into the kitchen.

He gives me the most sympathetic of looks. "That depends."

I press my hands into my cheeks. "Oh god."

"Simi, calm down. I'm sorry. I didn't mean to scare you. It's just that we got some paperwork from the USCIS asking for information for your green card application."

My rioting emotions sharpen. This is worse than any drama with Prem. Much worse. The green card process for someone from India is so long and arduous that it's felt like holding my breath ever since I applied two years ago. I'm so close to the stage where all the major hoops are done. I cannot let anything go wrong.

"What kind of paperwork?"

"They need us to prove that we can't find a US citizen to do the job."

"We've been looking for more nursing staff for six months and can't find anyone," I say. "I didn't know we were at that point in the process yet. I would have told you if I'd known. I would never blindside you."

"You didn't blindside me. But you know that I have to handle Karina with care. She isn't a fan of you nannying for us on the side. She thinks there's conflict of interest. She got to the paperwork before I could intercept it. Don't worry, I can handle her. I just wanted you to know. You know I would do anything not to lose you. You're like family."

Dr. Karina Rai is a pain in my behind. To be fair, she's a pain in everyone's behind. She's one of the partners at the practice and a close friend of the Guptas, so she's a pain that isn't going away anytime soon.

"Karina knows we can't lose you."

Karina knows no such thing. She'd be more than happy to lose me. She hates the fact that I'm the girls' nanny. I don't think it's about conflict of interest with my work at the practice. I have the oddest sense that she doesn't like me being in the Gupta circle, as though I'm infiltrating some sort of hallowed space I'm unworthy of.

"Dr. Johnson," I say. "I . . . I just want you to know that I'm very grateful to be able to take care of the girls, but . . ."

He studies me. "Go ahead and say it, Simi. Don't be afraid."

Easy for him to say. How can I not be terrified when my entire life hangs in the balance?

"If Dr. Rai will be less of a problem if I don't nanny for you . . . maybe . . ."

"Do you not want to babysit for us anymore, Simi?"

Gosh, *want* is such a complicated word. "I want nothing more than to spend time with TASha. You know how much I love them. But I can't lose my job at the practice. I've worked really hard to get here."

"I know. Let me talk to Karina. She's not unreasonable. Also Preeti will kill me if you lose your job and have to leave the country." He smiles kindly, oblivious of my racing thoughts.

I force myself to return his smile, and he heads back to the living room.

I don't follow. I need a minute. I've never felt so alone in my life.

It's been four years since I left home. Since I lost Rupi. One mistake, and I had destroyed everything. Ugly memories and the danger that awaits me if I ever go back spin around me.

"Simi?" Prem finds me. One look at my face, and he knows something is wrong.

"Please go back out, Prem. Already Preeti suspects something."

"So? She's going to find out in a few days anyway. What did John say?"

I can't talk about it right now. I haven't slept in almost twenty-four hours. I started the day with a four-hour night shift at the urgent care, then did twelve hours at the clinic, and then I've been here with the triplets.

These work hours aren't a rarity for me. I'm lucky enough to love my work enough that my energy never falters, but right now I feel like I've been squeezed dry from the inside out. The exhaustion is paralyzing. My feelings are all over the place, and I don't want to say something I'll regret.

"Please, Prem. I can't talk about it right now. Can you just go home and let me get the girls in bed? I promise we can talk about it tomorrow."

His pause is barely a breath before he pulls me close and holds me tight. "Don't ever forget how much I love you." Before I can protest, he drops a kiss on my lips. "I'll see you first thing tomorrow." Then with another kiss that melts my knees and breaks my heart, he does as I asked and leaves.

After putting the girls to bed, I head home. I love my apartment. As soon as I step inside, a sense of safety finds me. It's barely five hundred square feet, but it's airy, and sunlight streams in through the windows in the morning. And it's mine. Something I've made for myself, by myself, without anyone's help. I'm surprised at how enormously important that is to me.

I make myself some turmeric milk and take it to my bedroom. My little tropical garden of five planters in the corner seems to brighten at my presence, and I brighten in response. A fern, a palm, a climbing money plant, a rubber plant, and one kadi patta plant that's turned into a veritable tree. I've named them after the five Pandavas from the epic Mahabharata. Yudishthir, Bheem, Arjun, Nakul, and Sahadev. Bheem, obviously, is the kadi patta, which explains why it has grown into a giant. Names have power. Their power comes from their meaning.

Prem's name means "love." My sister Rupi's means "beauty." Both accurate. As for mine, Simi has no meaning in any Indian language as far as I know. I asked Rupi once why my name didn't have a meaning. She's the one who named me. Apparently, it sounded cute, and it just came out when she saw me.

One of Ma's husbands once told me that traditionally it was short for Simran, and that meant "meditating upon the divine," so there was nothing more meaningful than my name. My sister scoffed (scoffing at our parade of stepdads was her favorite thing to do). She said that having a name that had no meaning was like having no blueprint, no predestined purpose. It meant I could be anyone I wanted to be.

Rupi is an artist. Even before she learned how to wield a tattoo gun, she was an artist. She doodled nonstop. But it was her thoughts that were the real art, her own creations. Most people, myself included, take other people's thoughts and internalize them as our own, but my sister was always entirely nonderivative in her thinking. Probably a result of having parented herself.

Rupi is my last thought before I fall asleep.

~

I wake up to my alarm and my doorbell ringing at the same time.

This makes me smile, because only one person knows that I have an alarm set for 6 a.m. every day. Then I remember my conversation with Dr. Johnson, and my smile disappears.

I love that Prem understands my tangled-up need for both space and connection. He's respected my wish to sleep on it, and now I can bet my left kidney that he's standing outside my door.

I push myself out of bed. I'm in my auntie style block print nightie. Prem has never seen me like this, and I'm not ready for him to.

My phone rings.

"Hey. It's me."

"I know. My cell phone told me."

I can hear his smile. "I meant at the door. The person at your door is me."

"I know that too. I'm coming. But you have to close your eyes when you come in so I can change."

I'm standing in front of my closed front door.

"That makes me very curious about what you're wearing." His voice is rough with longing, and I can hear it on my phone and outside my door at once—an echo that wraps around me like the sweetest hug.

"You're going to be very disappointed."

"Never." I hear a bump and imagine him with his forehead against my door. "But I'll close my eyes."

I open the door only a crack. I'm hiding behind it. All he can see is a sliver of my face. "Make yourself comfortable. I'll be just a minute."

With that, I run into the bedroom and put myself together. Brush my teeth, twist my waist-length hair into a bun, cleanse my face. Then finish things up with some tinted moisturizer, a touch of kohl, a dab of lip gloss, and a simple but pretty white eyelet summer dress. When I come out, I find coffee sitting on the kitchen counter.

He walks up to me and pulls me close. There are shadows under his usually bright eyes. It's obvious he hasn't slept well. Guilt grips me, and I squeeze tighter into him. "I'm sorry," I whisper into the soft cotton of his shirt. "I didn't mean to worry you."

He rests his chin on my head. "What happened yesterday? Was it Preeti being nosy? Or did John say something?"

"I don't think Preeti was being nosy, but she definitely suspects something. And, Prem . . . well . . . I don't think I want her to know yet."

His body registers surprise. "I thought you were excited about making things official."

No, he was the one excited about making things official. "Things are already official between the two of us. Aren't they?"

"You know what I mean. We have to tell the family, Simi. I don't want to sneak around anymore. I love you. I want you at Mom's Sunday lunches. I don't want to suffer those awful movies my family picks by myself." He tucks a lock of hair behind my ear. "I feel lost at those family events without you. I feel lonely even when I'm surrounded by my family. I want to be with you all the time."

"I want to be with you all the time too." I pull away and pick up the coffee, hating how my hand trembles.

I hand him his cup and go to the cushions I've scattered on a rug in place of a couch. The sun streams in through the east-facing windows.

"How can we be together all the time if we don't tell people? It's a small town. I'm surprised one of the aunties or uncles hasn't seen us somewhere and taken the news back to my family."

It's not that surprising, because I've made sure that we only meet at Preeti's house while babysitting or here in my apartment. The few times we've met anywhere else have been all the way in Nashville. Even so, this past year I've felt like a bunny crossing the highway, in constant danger of getting hit.

"I work for Dr. Johnson, Prem."

He joins me on the floor. This rug is where I lost my virginity to him. My cheeks warm at the memory.

He wraps an arm around me. I squeeze into him, but it's not enough, so I crawl into his lap.

He strokes my hair. "What did John say?"

I fill him in on how my future hangs on the whims of Dr. Karina Rai.

"It's just paperwork," he says, not registering even a fraction of my panic.

"It's not. They have to advertise the position and interview anyone who applies and provide justification for why they aren't hiring that person." When I applied for the green card, I knew this was part of the process. I just didn't anticipate that one of my bosses would be pissed off about the other boss giving me a side gig as a nanny. I certainly didn't anticipate being in love with a close family member of said boss.

I get up off Prem's lap and start pacing. "I already work for Dr. Johnson outside of the practice. When everyone finds out that I'm involved with you, the optics are going to be terrible. And Dr. Rai already hates me."

"She does not. No one can hate you, Simi."

Hah. If only that were true. He should have seen the loathing on the faces of our neighbors in Mumbai.

"You have to trust me. I'm not being paranoid about her dislike for me. How she feels has a direct impact on my future." I stop in front of him. "I can't go public with our relationship yet. I can't risk everything I've worked so hard for."

Disappointment drains the color from his face. He has eyes that have absolutely no defenses. Lifeboats in a storm. He's destroyed by my words.

Rising up on his knees, he kneels in front of me. "I can't live without you, Simi."

I kneel in front of him, too, and frame his face with my hands. "I'm not breaking up with you, Prem. I can't live without you either." I throw a glance around my apartment. "Why can't we go on like this? Just the two of us in our own world. It won't be forever. Just until I have my green card."

Suddenly his eyes light up.

"Or . . ." His hands squeeze mine. "Or we get married and you don't need your job to get a green card. I'm a citizen. I was born here. You'll get a green card when we get married."

There's so much hope on his face that for a moment my heart leaps with it too. I yank myself back to earth.

"I don't want that to be the reason we get married. I don't want personal gain to be something that taints the start of our marriage. Is that the kind of person you think I am?"

He tips my chin up so I'm looking directly into his eyes. "I think you're the kind of person who works three jobs to support herself. I think you're the kind of person who stays late when TASha are being extra fussy and need you, even when you're so tired you can barely stand. I think you're the kind of person who could give up that job but won't because those girls mean something to you, and because you know Preeti won't trust anyone else. I cannot imagine you ever taking anything from anyone without giving back tenfold."

"Thank you," I whisper. What would he think if he knew how wrong he is?

"How can it taint our relationship if we were going to get married anyway?"

"Don't you see all those things you just said, those are the reasons why I can't marry you right now. I can't be dependent on you for my green card. I have to do this on my own." I know what it feels like to let someone else do everything for me, and I know how that ends up. "I cannot turn our relationship into a transaction. That would destroy me."

He cups my cheek, and there's intense frustration in his eyes, but also pride and respect—two things I've hungered for all my life. "Is it so wrong to take the easy path? Does only struggle make you strong?"

"I don't know. But loving you is the easiest thing I've ever done. I don't want to turn it into a struggle."

The way he looks at me feels like an anchor in a storm. "You're not going to budge on this, are you?"

I hate how disappointed he is. I want us to have a relationship where we both get our way sometimes, and I know that means one of us will be disappointed sometimes. "Can we wait a little bit? Let's see how Dr. Rai reacts to this stage in the green card process. I don't want to give her more ammunition. It's just a matter of a few weeks. Then if all is well, we can tell your family."

He visibly relaxes. "So, we're going to have to sneak around at the birthday party?" He pulls me close and pushes a kiss into the edge of my lips.

"Isn't sneaking around at least a little fun?" Despite the worry gathered inside me, my body loosens and starts to warm.

He smiles against my lips, and it's the most delicious feeling. "I like how much fun it is for you. Maybe you can make my sacrifices worth my while."

"Are you bartering sacrifices for sexual favors?" I nip at his lush lower lip, which I love more than is rational.

"One hundred percent." He stands, picks me up, and takes me to my room, and I realize that relief (and getting my way) really turns me on.

FOUR

RUPI

The bus jerks to a stop with a giant mechanical sigh of relief, and I jolt awake. The first thing that strikes me is the missing weight of my backpack on my chest. I sit up and search the seat next to me, then bend over and look under my seat.

No!

The world stops. Everything stops.

My heart hammers in my ears. This can't be happening. The bus is completely, eerily empty. Not another soul on board, except for the driver. I jump up and grab the overhead luggage rack with both hands and pull myself up, getting a foothold on the seat. My eyes search up and down the empty racks. Rising panic makes it impossible to process what I'm seeing. Emptiness. Nothing but emptiness on either side.

Shit shit *shit*.

Over the past year, I've slept on a lot of public transport. After I left LA, I spent six months going from place to place on trains and buses before I found my way to Chicago. I also grew up in Mumbai. Clutching my belongings for dear life is coded into my DNA. My hyperawareness of my surroundings has always been at peak paranoia levels. I've always slept with my arms wrapped around my backpack, the straps clinging to my shoulders like an insecure baby. How did I let this happen?

I drop to my hands and knees and start crawling around the bus. There's nothing under the seats, except bottles and cans and paper cups lying on their sides. Every last bit of my already paltry worldly possessions is gone. Gone.

Tina's documents, my only leverage, gone.

"Hey lady. This is the last stop," the driver yells back at me. "Time to get off."

I ignore him and check every seat. More nothing. Without those documents, I have nothing.

I run to the front of the bus. "Someone took my backpack." I sound like I'm in the throes of hysteria.

The man rubs his shoulder and looks bored. "Did you check around your seat?"

The urge to run at him and scratch out his eyes grips me, and I wrap my arms around myself. "It's not on the bus. Please. Please. Did you see anyone walk out with a black backpack?"

"Sure," he says. "Everyone. I'm sorry. Listen, I need to empty out the bus." He doesn't sound even a little sorry.

All I have left is the change I shoved into my jeans after buying that last bus ticket.

"You have to get off the bus," the driver says again.

My legs shake as I make myself do as he says. It took me twenty hours to make my way from Chicago to Nashville. Then finding a bus from Nashville to Hochkinsville took almost as much time because I had to wait at the Nashville bus station for a good ten hours. It hadn't helped that I started to feel queasy, achy, and feverish on the bus out of Chicago.

Through it all, I clung to my backpack like my life depended on it. Because it did. When I got on the bus, the exhaustion and the achiness was so bad, my body trembled with it. I had to fight to keep my eyes open. I laid the backpack on the seat next to me for just one second. One second while I settled into my seat.

The next thing I knew, I was waking up with the bag gone.

The driver says something. He's trying to be sympathetic, but what does his sympathy matter now? It's late in the evening, but there's still some light left in the sky. My eyes search for a clock, but the terminal building is barely more than a shack. It's like I took a bus out of Nashville and landed in a dystopian, barely inhabited version of America. I'm fully in character: penniless, my body starving and feverish, and I smell like I've survived an apocalyptic war, in the sewers.

I shake out my empty hands. Everything's gone. All because I was stupid enough to let myself feel cornered by Tina. Why did I even come here? What is the guarantee I'll find Simi? How am I going to find her?

My lost backpack drags at my shoulders like a ghost. I make my way to the decrepit building. Sweat pours down my back. It's like being back in Mumbai at the height of the postmonsoon heat. *October heat* is something every Mumbaikar is intimately familiar with. After months of being pummeled by the pouring rain, the earth releases all the pent-up fire in its belly, wrapping the city in a vise grip of steam. It's inside me now, burning me down.

Simi hated the heat. How has she lived here for four years? Images of Simi as a baby, a toddler, a teenager tumble through me, arms and legs spread like a starfish on the mattress we shared, sheets thrown off, hair wet with sweat. I can smell the top of her head. My baby. How has she survived without me for four years? My heart squeezes with how much I miss her. Then anger drowns me.

Obviously, she's survived much better than I have.

She has an education, a job, an apartment.

It's been over a year since I've stood under a real shower or slept in a real bed. In the studio, I slept on the waiting-area couch and washed in the sink. At least with Ron, the bathrooms and beds were comfortable. Whether it was the hotel rooms he took me to or the apartment he set me up in, everything was comfortable. The man was obsessed with luxury. Clothes and cars and furniture and watches. *I'm a collector. I love beautiful things,* he loved to say. *But you might be the most beautiful of all the things I've ever owned.*

Ron thinking he owned me at least gave me a full belly and a place to sleep. No matter how hard I try, I can't remember why I wanted to get out of there so desperately. When your basic human needs are met, freedom feels deceptively important.

What a laugh Ron would have gotten out of hearing me say that. I still can't believe the asshole was inconsiderate enough to get hit by a drunk driver. Such an irony, given how many times I had to keep him from getting in the driver's seat when he'd had one drink too many. That day he was dead sober. Quite literally.

I hear the sound of laughter—maniacal, barely human. I look around, but there's no one else at the abandoned terminal. Just me. The laughter is mine. My body is shaking with it. It's the saddest sound I've ever heard. I drop into the solitary bench, lean my head back, and let myself laugh, unable to stop.

It goes on and on, until a hand lands on my shoulder. I open my eyes. My face is wet from my laughter, my body sticky with sweat under the sweatshirt. I should take it off before it cooks my flesh.

"Here, you must be hungry." It's a woman in a gray uniform. Not a cop but some sort of ticket agent, probably. She has frizzy gray hair and kind eyes, and it gives her the look of a holy woman like the ones who preach in saffron robes outside temples in India.

The hunger must be making me delirious, because the woman's face changes to the face of one of our neighbors in Mumbai. The one who always glowered at our mother but tried to slip Simi and me bars of Amul chocolate.

I grab the Styrofoam container the woman holds out.

"There's half a burrito in there. Who can eat a whole giant one of those? I haven't touched it. You can have it," she says.

The woman is giving me alms. And I'm taking them. She thinks I'm a beggar. She hands me the box and looks away, as though wretchedness is contagious and spreads through eye contact.

I open the box. The burrito inside, even though it's supposedly only half, is gargantuan. Drool floods my mouth. I take a bite even before I've said thank you.

"Fbonk bou," I say around the explosion of flavors in my mouth.

"You're welcome, honey," she says before walking away.

I should stop her, but I can't stop eating. Hunger is a black hole inside me, sucking everything in. I can't remember the last time I ate. I didn't want to spend my last dollars on something as unimportant as food—not when I needed the money to get to my sister. Simi is capable of feeding me for the rest of my life, even though the only thing she offered me the last time we talked was money to stay away.

Growing up, Simi was everything to me. There isn't a single thing, other than her, that I can remember with any sort of joy. She's the only good thing in all my memories. My one success. And I lost her. I worked hard to lose her.

I pushed her to study, pushed her into the nursing program when I found out how short on nurses the world was. It was the only way I could think of to get her out. I was desperate for her to get away. To be free. I knew I couldn't have freedom myself until she was off my hands. Now here I am.

"You still here, hon?" The burrito woman is back.

The burrito is gone, and I feel ragingly queasy. I always do when I haven't eaten for a while and then shock my system with a cannonball of calories. My body feels so hot, I might be combusting.

"It's not safe to hang around here." The sun has disappeared from the sky. A single lamppost half-heartedly sprinkles us with light. "There's a shelter in town. I could drop you off."

"Is there a hospital in town?" I ask, reaching for my last ray of hope.

"Are you not feeling well?" The concern on her face should restore at least a tiny piece of my faith in humanity, but instead it makes me angry. Why is this woman in a position where she gets to pity me?

"My sister works at the hospital." I hate how proud I sound.

"Sure," the woman says, "but I have some errands to run in Paducah first, and that's one town over. So, if you're okay with that, I'll take you after."

I pull my sweatshirt over my head. The Underground Tattoo T-shirt under it is wet with sweat, but I can breathe again, and I follow her. For the next few hours, the woman drives me all over the place. At least she does it in silence, because not letting on that I'm shivering and feverish is taking all my energy. Finally she drops me off under the porch of what I can only hope is Simi's hospital. How many can there be in this matchbox-size town?

I make my way in, hoping that my face is going to make it easy to find Simi. My sister and I have almost identical faces, albeit very different body types, a fact our mother loved to remark upon. *One of my girls is a bat, and the other is a ball.* That was our mother—as unfailingly cruel as she was neglectful.

I'm five feet six—a good four inches taller than Simi—and I've always been nothing but skin and bones even though I'm the one who can eat an entire pizza by myself and still have room for a milkshake.

Simi, on the other hand, has never cared about food. I spent hours trying to feed her as a child, but Simi would rather do anything else than eat. How my sister always looked like a curvy little children's doll is anyone's guess. The only other difference between us is our hair. Simi has our mother's lush locks that cascade down to her waist. She was always terrified of scissors going anywhere near her head, and I made sure they never did.

I oiled and braided her hair every morning and every night. It was so thick and long that my hands hurt, but I loved it. Taking care of it had filled me with purpose and satisfaction.

My own hair, on the other hand, is barely there. Simi insisted it was because I never let it grow out and constantly experimented with it, but it was a chicken-and-egg situation. I had to keep cutting it because it grew out wispy and ratty. Truth was, the scar I hid beneath it hurt when it grew out.

Other than the body types and hair, we look like identical twins. The same medium-brown skin, neither light enough for what the aunties called "fair" nor dark enough for them to call "dusky." The same neither small nor big nose. The same little too-wide and pouty mouth we'd inherited from our mom and the same heavy-lidded hazel eyes that slanted up at the edges that are the only thing I remember about our father, a man Simi never met.

I find a young male nurse at the information desk, tell him I'm Simi's sister, and ask for her.

"You look just like Nurse Naik," he says, blinking in surprise. "But she isn't here today."

"Can you tell me where I can find her?"

"During the week, she usually works at Dr. Johnson's clinic."

My head hurts so badly, it feels like it's going to explode. My belly and my legs aren't that far behind. I lean on the counter between us. "How far is that from here? Can you write the directions down for me? My phone was stolen."

"On no. Do you want me to call the cops?"

Gosh no! The last thing on earth I want is for anyone to call the cops. Ever. I smile my most helpless smile. "I just need to get to my sister." It's become a chant in my head. I need to get to my sister.

"It's past nine, the clinic is closed. Did you want me to call Simi for you?"

Finally we're getting somewhere. "That would be incredibly helpful." I try to keep the desperation out of my voice and cling to the counter to keep from sliding to the floor. My belly churns.

The guy calls Simi and puts it on speaker. We wait for her to answer. After a few rings, the call goes to voicemail.

Come on. Can I please catch a break? Please?

"Can you try one more time, please?" Keeping the edge of panic out of my voice is getting harder.

The guy calls again. Nothing.

"Can you try her landline?" I ask. If she has one, the hospital she works at should have it.

"Do you have the number? It's not on file."

The string wrapped around me, which has been holding me together, snaps. I give up on pretense and lean limply against the counter. My insides are fully churning now. The ugliest burrito-laced belch pushes into my mouth, and I gag. I should never have eaten that stupid thing.

The guy steps around the counter and comes to me. "Hey, listen, are you okay?" He squeezes my shoulder. "You know what, give me a minute. Let me check something." He goes back behind the desk and taps his keyboard. "We have an emergency number listed for her, and I think this counts as one. Let me call that, okay."

I want to hug the guy, but my stomach is cramping, and I wrap my arms around myself instead.

He dials, and the person answers on the first ring.

"Hello, this is Tom from St. Joe's. I'm looking for Simi . . . No, nothing is wrong . . . Well . . . Her sister is here, looking for her."

There's the longest pause, during which my heart spins and slides between hope and desolation as reactions pop on this Tom person's face.

The fact that the spasms in my belly have turned into an unholy agony doesn't help.

This might be the worst day of my life, which is saying something.

Just as Tom is getting somewhere with the person at the other end, the most brutal jolt of pain rips through my stomach.

"I need a restroom. Right now," I say to Tom.

He's obviously seen enough of these situations and runs with me to a door that is blessedly close by. I run into the bathroom so fast that my brain must've been left behind. I barely slam the door shut when things fly out of me in all directions, and my insides spin like they're whirling around the eye of a particularly nasty storm. As though the diarrhea isn't bad enough, vomit spurts out of me. I have no idea how long I stay in there, having my insides emptied out. A knock on the door breaks through my misery.

"You okay in there?"

Define *okay*.

The urge to laugh grips me. Along with the urge to start crying. Which is a skill I've never developed. My belly does another threatening dance, reminding me that I can do neither without horrible consequences. Another startlingly painful cramp grips my belly. For the first time I realize that whatever this is, I might not survive it.

How many times can I beg the universe for a break? How many?

"I'm fine," I say, but my throat is so raw that the lie doesn't make it all the way out. "I'm fine." I force myself to try again, making the lie louder.

"I'm sorry." There's genuine regret in his voice. I hate when people apologize for things that aren't their fault. "Do you need help coming out?" he says.

What the hell, Tom? Can't a girl even die in peace?

"Just washing my hands," I say, using whatever energy I can dredge up to scrub my hands with soap.

"Hang on, I'm going to get someone to help you."

Holy fuck. I'm in a hospital. If I don't get myself together, they're going to treat me. I cannot let that happen. I have no paperwork, and I'm not supposed to be in the country.

Cops. Immigration. Deportation. It all flashes like police car lights in my racing mind.

Nope.

Not today, you assholes.

I make my way out of the bathroom.

"Tom! Wait!" How I have the energy to chase after him, I don't know, but I grab his arm. "I'm fine. Really."

Obviously he doesn't believe me, but he stops.

"I just need my sister." And a hot shower. And a new life.

"Tom? Hey . . ." A round-faced Indian man jogs up to us. "Holy shit," he says when his gaze lands on me. He presses his hand into his mouth, an inordinately overwrought reaction. "Wow."

Granted, I look like I've just crawled out of a swamp, but is the horror really necessary?

My smell must have reached him by now, because he winces and lets out another "Wow!"

I decide then and there that I will kill this man, whoever he is, if I ever hear him say the word *wow* again.

"You look just like her," he says. "But completely different." That declaration is accompanied by a quick scan of my hair and clothes. Another wince. It must be the pain that shoots through my back and wraps tight around my belly, but the urge to kill the guy returns full force.

"You are?" God bless Tom for thinking of all the important questions.

"Prem Gupta. We just spoke. I'm . . . um . . . Simi's friend."

He blushes like a freaking pomegranate when he says the word *friend*. Also, what the hell? Who names their son Prem in this day and age? It's like calling your son Lover, only more simpering.

As if to punish me for that mean thought, another cramp twists my insides, and bile shoots up my throat. I swallow it back. I need to get out of this place before Tom remembers his threat to get help.

"Thanks, Tom. We'll leave now." I grab Lover Gupta by the arm. "You were very kind. Thank you."

I start walking toward the exit.

"You sure you don't want to see a doctor?" Tom calls after me.

Go away, I want to scream. But I raise a hand, shake my head, and keep walking.

Well, thank god for Prem Gupta, because I couldn't have walked out of that hospital without someone to hang on to. If he gets me out of here, I might reconsider killing him.

"You don't look very good. You sure you don't need to go back in there?"

"Where's my sister?" My stomach gurgles angrily. If I soil myself in front of this stranger, I am never ever going to forgive the universe.

"She's babysitting my nieces."

"Why didn't she answer her phone?"

"She keeps her phone on silent when she naps with the babies."

Simi is napping? My life is over, and my princess of a sister is asleep? Great shitballs, I'm going to throw up again.

The next thing I know, I vomit all over Prem Gupta's shoes. How is there anything left inside me after the mayhem in the bathroom?

"Oh god," he says eloquently, looking like he's going to throw up himself. "I'm taking you back inside. You don't look good."

If he says that one more time, I'm going to make the effort to throw up on him again.

"You're burning up. You need a doctor."

Where did Simi find such an astute man?

I tighten my grip on his arm with every ounce of strength I have left. "We are not going back into that hospital." The world spins. Darkness pushes into my vision. "Just take me to my sister. Please."

"Listen, didi, um, I don't think—"

I yank on his arm. "If you take me back in there, I will kill you with my bare hands." The guy's face swings close, then away, then ripples like water. "Promise me." My voice is a croak, a sob, and a scream all rolled into one. "Just promise me you won't take me back in there." I shake him by the arm. Or I think I do, because everything is starting to dissolve around me. "Promise me. Please," I whimper.

"Okay okay," he says. "Fine. Just hang on. Stay with me."

Relief floods through me. I cling to those words as his face fades and everything goes black.

FIVE

SIMI

The last thing I expected to see when I got to the hospital was my indomitable sister lying in the critical care unit, her face covered with an oxygen mask and tubes connecting her to all sorts of machines. She's even thinner than I remember. It looks almost like there's no body under the sheets attached to her ghostly pale face.

"She's going to be okay," Prem says.

He has no way of knowing that. "I don't think she's ever been okay a day in her life," I say, because right now none of my usual filters, the ones that separate words into speakable and unspeakable, are working.

His arm around me tightens.

It should be comforting, but I don't think I remember what comfort feels like.

"They said it's not serious."

"Then why the hell is she in critical care, Prem? I'm a nurse. They don't put anyone in the CCU without it being bloody serious!" I pull away and start pacing.

"Simi?" He tries to follow me but trips over his own feet and stumbles.

I grab his arm and steady him. "I'm sorry," I say, not wanting to apologize. Not wanting anyone here right now. Because no one needs to witness how I'm going to shake my sister until her bones rattle when she wakes up.

What the hell, Rupi? Why can't you let me live in peace? I came five thousand miles to get away from your drama!

My thoughts are so unfair, they fill me with shame. Her face the last time I saw her spins in my head. We said such ugly things. I knew what she was doing. Rupi pushes people away as a matter of habit, but that day she'd pushed hard. Because she wanted to get me to safety. Her love is forged from iron. I don't know anyone else who would do the things she's done for me. It's all too intense with her.

As with the rest of our lives, that last fight went exactly the way Rupi wanted it to: with her taking care of everything, with her making saying goodbye easier for me.

If something happens to her, what am I going to do?

Too many memories rush through my brain. The times she pulled me close when I cried, fed me when I was hungry, even though it meant pretending she was full when she hadn't eaten, when she squeezed her palms into my ears so I wouldn't hear the screaming fights that usually started a few months after a new stepfather came into our lives.

What do you think Ma is looking for? I asked her after our mother had introduced us to the last in the Parade of Dads.

The perfect punishment, Rupi said. By that time, the Rupi I grew up with was already gone. She was particularly upset about Glen, Husband Number Four. I, on the other hand, had to admit he was my favorite of the lot. Unlike the others, he didn't make my skin crawl or make me shake with terror. Rupi loathed him. She refused to be in the same room as him. He never pushed her, never lectured her to be nicer like every other person in her life. I never understood how she was so resistant to his kindness. Losing him had felt like the extinguishing of all hope.

Punishment for what? I asked.

Us. For Dad leaving us behind. We are how she gets to punish him.

It was the one thing Abha Naik did a great job at: punishing us to punish Husband Number One, the father I never met. He left her with nothing but the roof over our heads. Every day she went to work, cooking in people's homes, then came back with the weight of her rage and made his daughters pay. And Rupi bore the brunt of it.

"Tell me what happened," I ask Prem again as we walk to the waiting area.

"I rushed over as soon as Tom called. When I got here, she was in bad shape. You didn't answer your phone, so I called Preeti."

"I know all that." When Preeti woke me from my nap with the girls and told me it was an emergency, I was in the car headed to the hospital the moment the words *your sister* left her mouth. "What happened after you met her?"

"Not much." He looks away, breaking eye contact for a quick second the way he only does when he's nervous. "It was barely a few minutes before she fainted."

"What did she say to you?"

"She looked really sick, and, well . . . um . . ." His fingers fidget.

I take his hand and squeeze reassuringly when what I want is to scream *Just say it!*

"She looked . . . She looked destitute . . . like she'd been living on the streets." That can't be true. My heart squeezes. "It was clear that she was really sick."

I press a hand to my chest, wanting to quell the restlessness raging there.

"I tried to get her to see someone in the hospital, but she dragged me outside. She seemed, I don't know . . . scared. She didn't want to be at the hospital. She was desperate to leave. Then she fainted, and I didn't know what to do but to carry her in here."

This is bad. There's only one reason why Rupi is scared to be in a hospital, and I've been doing my best to avoid talking to her about it for the past two years.

More secrets on top of secrets. All the things she's made me swear never to speak of. *The only way to keep a secret is to never say the words out loud. To never even think them.*

"Are you angry with me, Simi? Did I do something wrong?"

I hate that he asks me that. Not because a person should know for themselves when they do something wrong and not rely on someone else to tell them, but because I made him feel like this, lost and guilty, when none of this is his fault. It's Rupi's fault. Of course, it's mine, too, but as always, it's her taking the actions and making the choices with everyone else being left feeling lost and guilty about it.

"You did nothing wrong. Of course you had to bring her into the hospital. You could hardly leave her passed out in the parking lot." Obviously she needed a hospital, given that she's currently in critical care.

My god. My sister, my only living relative, is in critical care.

Just as the enormity of that sinks in, a nurse walks up to us. My insides go cold. I imagine the very worst news. She's gone. She has six months to live. She's going to be stuck in this vegetative state for the foreseeable future.

"She just woke up, and her vitals are looking good," the nurse says. "Her blood pressure and heart rate fell too low and weren't stabilizing, so we had to monitor her. She's okay now. They're moving her to a regular room. They're going to keep giving her fluids and electrolytes. Once she keeps some food down, they'll let you take her home. Just a nasty bacterial infection from something she ate."

My legs buckle in relief. Prem holds me up. "Thank you." I lean into him. "Can I see her?"

"Of course. I'll take you to her room. Oh, and we need ID and insurance information to get her registration completed."

"Someone stole her bag," Prem says. "She didn't have ID on her when I brought her in."

"Okay. We'll need something, at least a Social Security number and emergency contact information. But we can wait until you've seen her," the nurse says. "No rush." She leads us to Rupi's room and leaves us at the door.

Rupi blinks when she sees me. For one second her exhausted eyes brighten with heartbreaking relief. Time stops. Then rushes back into her eyes as rage as she comes back to the present. "Who brought me here?" she demands, trying to sit up.

I rush to her side and try to get her to lie down again, touching my sister for the first time in five years. "Hold on, Rupi. Calm down." It's funny that those are my first words to her.

"What the hell is wrong with that guy?" Prem is standing behind me, and Rupi glares at him like she's going to strangle him with the tubes from her IV.

She pushes me away and sits up and starts pulling at the electrodes stuck to her chest and yanks at her IV.

I still her hands. "Stop. You'll hurt yourself. Stop being so dramatic. You're not Ma!"

She freezes. "That's below the belt."

"It would be if you were not being totally unreasonable right now. You can't just start yanking out your IV. The darned thing goes inside your vein. You're not in a soap opera!" It's such a nonsensical thing for me to have to say out loud that a laugh spurts out of me.

A smile breaks on her gaunt face.

For one brief second, we're back in a different time. A time when laughter saved us.

This is not that time.

"You were just in the CCU," I say, every hint of laughter gone. "You almost had a cardiac episode from your electrolytes falling too low. What the hell is wrong with you? How long did you go without eating?"

The laughter is gone from her, too, replaced by her go-to emotion: disdain. Tinged with something new: a hint of what has to be panic. "Stop being jealous of my skinniness for just one second, and listen to me. I need to leave this hospital right now. I cannot be here."

"Why?" I ask, though I already suspect the answer. I need to know exactly how bad things are.

She gives me her best sneer, then throws one at Prem. "Because places like this need paperwork. Do I look like I have any paperwork on me?"

"They don't need it this second. We can get your paperwork later."

"Hah," she says. "Get it from where?"

"From your home."

"Home?" There's an edge of hysteria in her tone. "You mean my mansion on the Gold Coast? Sorry, I had to put that on the market because"—here her voice turns to a hiss—"I just love having nowhere to go!"

"Hold on," I say, sliding a glance at Prem, whose gaze is bouncing between the two of us in utter confusion. "What are you saying right now?"

"What the hell do you think I'm saying, Einstein?" Her angry eyes shoot rage lasers at me. "All I own in the world is lying on this damned bed. And that includes any paperwork."

So, I was right.

Oh god.

"Don't give me that look," she says. "Don't make this about you. This isn't a poor-Simi moment. It wouldn't have come to this if this *friend* of yours hadn't broken his promise. It's his damn fault."

Prem makes a strangled sound.

"Rupi, please!" I say. "This is Prem. He's . . ." I hate the term *boyfriend*. It sounds so childish, like we're playing house or like we're off to prom. *Partner* is for people far cooler than I'll ever be. I want to say *the man I love*, but it sounds absurd and nothing at all like it should. "He's my boyfriend," I say.

"How cute," she hisses. "You found yourself a boy who doesn't keep his word. Why am I not surprised?"

"You fainted," Prem says to her, not unkindly. Then he looks at me. "I had no choice."

She snarls at him. "I was clear about what you needed to do *before* I fainted. You had the choice to listen!"

"Stop it, Rupi," I say. "It's not his fault."

"Oh my god. You sound just like Ma!"

"Don't ever fucking say that to me!"

"But it's okay for you to say it?"

Prem's eyes have gone round as saucers. He's never heard me swear. I feel like we just leaped out of a Disney movie and crash-landed into a Tarantino film.

Rupi ignores him and turns to me. "Stop glaring at me like a soap opera mother-in-law, and help me get this IV off."

"I can't do that."

"Really? What do they teach you in nursing school, how to milk cows?"

"Can you be quiet for one minute and let me think."

"Oh, I think that might take more than a minute."

"My god, Rupi. Stop talking!"

For a moment, everyone is quiet. But she's right. I seem to be unable to think. My brain is racing around like the mice that used to get into our kitchen and not know how to get out. One of our stepdads liked to smash them with a frying pan while we watched.

I start pacing. What happens when someone who's applied for a green card is caught harboring an illegal relative? Does it make you an accomplice in a crime? Holy shit. I'm going to be deported. We're both going to be deported. If they send us back to India, I'll lose everything.

"Do you at least have a Social Security number?" I ask after taking a breath.

"No. But I can make one up," she says without a hint of irony.

"Oh god. How many times have you done that already?"

"I love your faith in me, but never before has an idiot disregarded my wishes and admitted me into a hospital against my will, so the opportunity never came up."

"You literally passed out in front of him. What did you expect him to do, leave you there to die? Stop being mean to him."

Before I can say more, there's a knock on the door.

Two women dressed in scrubs walk in. I've never seen one of them before, and she's carrying a clipboard with forms. The other one makes my heart stop.

Holy.

Bloody.

Shit.

It's Anagha Rai, Dr. Karina Rai's daughter. A monstrous pain starts to push behind my eyes. Anagha is a dietitian at the hospital. Her eyes skim past me like I'm invisible and light up when they land on Prem.

"Prem!" she says breathlessly, batting her eyelash extensions so hard, I'm afraid she'll be airborne soon.

"Hi, Anagha."

They hug as though they haven't seen each other in years.

I can feel Rupi's eyes on me. My urge to leave the room is so overwhelming, it's a miracle I don't teleport out of here from sheer will.

"What are you doing here?" Anagha asks Prem instead of introducing herself to the patient first like a professional.

"I brought her in," Prem says, stepping close to me and pointing at Rupi. "How are your parents?"

A side conversation starts where Anagha fills Prem in on the health, well-being, and general schedule of her extended family.

At least the woman with the clipboard introduces herself. "I'm Sheena. I take care of registration and billing. We're missing some information on your chart."

I love how she worded that. Good job, Sheena. Behind Sheena's head, Rupi glares accusingly at me, but it's the panic that lurks behind the glare that jumps out at me.

"What information do you need?" I ask, buying time. Why on earth did I put Prem down as my emergency contact?

"If you give me your ID, I can get most of what I need," Sheena says, holding out her hand to Rupi.

"My bag was stolen on my way here. My driver's license was in there," Rupi says. Rupi doesn't drive.

Sheena gasps dramatically. "You were robbed? I'm so sorry. That's terrible."

Everyone who works at a hospital is trained to commiserate with patients. Sheena obviously trained well.

"Do you have a picture of your ID on your phone? That would work too."

"My phone was also stolen." Rupi hams up the tragedy, big sad eyes dripping with helplessness.

She's moved from a flight response to a fight response. I can see the cogs in her brain turning ferociously. I've seen this more times than I can count. She's in a corner, and the corner is folding in on her. I was usually in the corner behind her, with her arms shielding me. The thing that scares me now is that she always got us out of the corner, no matter what it took.

"Okay, then let's start with your insurance information, your Social Security number, and your address," Sheena says with the calm of a monk and the focus of a shark.

Rupi starts coughing. I go to her. Prem hands her a glass of water. Her eyes are watering.

Anagha stands there like a statue. Sheena waits with her shark-monk patience.

"I don't have health insurance or an address," Rupi says finally, but she doesn't stop there. "*Yet.* I quit my job and, um . . ." She looks around the room, the desperation for a solution dilating her pupils and darkening her hazel eyes. That's when her gaze settles on Prem. An expression too close to relief floods her face. It sparks terror in my heart. Rupi reaches out her hand to Prem.

To his credit, he takes it and tries to compensate for his confusion with a smile.

Rupi gives him the most angelic of smiles in return. "But I will have both when Prem and I get married and he puts me on his insurance." A loud ringing starts in my ears. "Until then, you just have to send us the bill so we can take care of it. Right, honey?"

Sheena blinks. She obviously had no idea they were together. Well, same here, lady.

Next to me, Anagha slaps a hand to her mouth and gasps. Her lips form the word *Prem!* but my hearing is still nowhere to be found. Her gaze slips from Rupi to Prem, then pings back from Prem to Rupi, and then gets stuck in that loop. Back and forth. Back and forth. Commiserating with her shock was not on my bingo card today, but here we are. "You got engaged?"

Prem looks at me. All of me feels frozen. I've never fainted in my life, but now feels like a great time to give it a shot.

"Congratulations," Anagha says, finding her manners like a right proper lady. Her voice is a little too high pitched, but at least it brings my hearing back. She throws her arms around Prem. Can she please stop doing that?

"Thanks." Prem pats her back. I feel like someone just shoved me off a cliff and I'm hanging by a wiry branch growing on the edge.

"It's been such a whirlwind courtship," Rupi says. *Great!* She's doing our bit where we slip into the soap operas of our childhood to help us navigate real life. She manages to sound exactly as coy and chirpy as the heroines in every one we ever watched. "We barely had a chance to catch our breath." Her chest heaves bashfully—another skill picked up breath for breath from the heroines of our childhood. "That's probably how all this happened." She waves a hand around the room, eyes wistful and sparkling at once. "With all the excitement of seeing him, I totally forgot to eat, and then I think I ate something bad. It must've been that burrito we got in Nashville, right, honey? Good thing you didn't eat any."

"Good thing," Prem says. The glance he slides my way cries *help!* He struggles to conceal his shock while also trying to gauge how I want him to play it.

Hell if I know, *honey*.

"Where's her ring, Prem?" Anagha asks. Why is she still batting her lashes when she knows he's an engaged man?

Oh dear.

"I'm Indian," Rupi says to Anagha in her sweetest voice. The *and unlike you, I haven't forgotten that, witch* remains unsaid. I want to groan. Rupi has that look she gets when she's getting ready to charge at someone and knock them over.

"Sorry?" Anagha takes a step away from Prem.

"Where I come from, engagement rings are only exchanged in the presence of family, no?" Now Rupi is exaggerating her accent. She makes a bashful face. "Prem might be American, but he gets that. How can you not love a man like that?"

Prem makes an impressive effort not to wince and pats the hand Rupi is gripping him with.

"We still need some information," Sheena says.

Rupi returns her attention to Sheena. "I'll have to apply for a replacement passport. In the meantime, will Prem and my sister's contact information work?" She lets out a giant yawn that's so well executed, even I believe that she's ready to fall asleep.

The worshipfulness with which Rupi looks at Prem is so real, it almost makes me jealous, which is absurd, because I can also feel her loathing for him. It's going to be impossible to convince her that this isn't his fault.

"Sure." Sheena looks a little lost. There's nothing on her script to help her deal with newly engaged bliss covering up for missing patient information. "Thanks. We'll use that as the billing address."

Sheena doesn't care about anything else. I give her my address, and she leaves. The problem is Anagha. She's still here, disappointment making her fight hard to hold the smile on her face.

"Have you guys set a date yet? I'll bet your mother is excited for another wedding, Prem. The last in the family." She turns to Rupi with all the regret in the world burning in her eyes. "Prem's mother is the sweetest person on earth. You're going to love her."

"I know I will," Rupi says sweetly. "It's going to be love at first sight. Just like with Prem."

"Love at first sight," Prem repeats. "We haven't set a date yet. Everything happened so fast. We weren't planning on it, but one look at Simi, and I just knew this was it."

My cheeks warm.

"Simi? You mean Rupi," Anagha says, suspicion folding between her brows.

"Huh?" Prem says, waving his arm and knocking over a cup of water from the table next to him. Naturally, I catch it mid-fall. "Rupi," he says a little too loudly. "That's what I said. Rupi. I met Rupi, and I knew. When you know, you know, you know? With Rupi I knew. Rupi. Rupi and I knew."

God, can he stop saying Rupi? Actually can he just stop saying anything.

"Yes, it's true. I knew," Rupi says angelically. "I don't usually like people that fast. In fact, I hate people. People-ing is the worst. Except Prem, of course. Love him. Love you, honey." She winks at Prem. "But when strangers talk to me, I just want them to leave." She mimics Anagha's eyelash batting.

Anagha does not take the hint. "I thought he said Simi. And I was like, 'Who's Simi?'" She smacks her forehead. She hasn't looked at me once. It's like I'm not even in the room.

"Prem did say Rupi. You must've heard Simi because that's my sister's name. She's the one who introduced Prem and me. Everyone should have a sister like that, no? Maybe you thought you heard her name because you meant to say hi to her since you work together and all, and she's been here this entire time."

Anagha finally looks at me. She can't seem to settle on a response.

"Oh, have you two not met? Well, this is Simi," Rupi says, then turns with utter boredom to Anagha. "And this is . . ." Another yawn. "What did you say your name was?"

"Anagha. Anagha Rai. Prem and I grew up together. We used to be best friends."

"In fifth grade," Prem says and drops his phone. When he bends to pick it up, he knocks over the garbage bin.

I hand him the phone and help him straighten the bin.

"I think I need rest," Rupi says. "Did you need something, Anita?"

"Anagha," Anagha says.

"Yes, of course. Did you need something?"

It takes her a moment, but she finally seems to remember why she's here. "I'm the dietitian on duty. I was here because Rupi's blood tests show mineral and vitamin deficiencies. I recommend you take these supplements." She pulls out some sheets of paper from her folder and puts them on the bed. "There's also some recommended foods to include in your diet on there. I'll let you get some rest. Let me know if you have questions. Prem has my number. And, well . . . I'll see both of you at the triplets' birthday party. Sorry, I'll see all three of you there. You're still their nanny, right?"

"I am," I say and watch as something like amusement floods her eyes, if amusement can be ugly.

"Well, it was nice seeing you, Prem." She's about to hug him again, but Rupi clears her throat aggressively, and she stops in her tracks.

Then she nods quickly at the room in general and leaves. Even before she's all the way out the door, she has her phone out.

SIX

RUPI

"What the hell was that?" Simi hisses, shutting the door a little too quietly after the cranky dietitian leaves in a snit.

If it were me, I would have made sure the door hit her ass when I slammed it shut. Alas, I'm laid up in this damn bed because of the idiot Simi calls her boyfriend.

"Why don't you ask *him* that?" I hiss back and point at him.

He's looking at Simi as though he needs her to tell him what to do. What the hell is my sister doing with this rasgulla? He's a dead ringer for a cheeseball that fell into a bowl of sugar syrup and rolled around in it.

If I weren't so livid with him, I might have wanted to poke a finger into his squishy middle to see if he squirts syrup in my eye.

Simi raises both arms in exasperation. The gesture is such a throwback to our mother that I almost gasp. "Why would I ask him anything? You're the one who just lied. To someone in my workplace. In front of someone who knows Prem's family and my boss." She presses a hand to her forehead and looks at him. "My god. Anagha is going to tell everyone, isn't she?"

Her rasgulla makes a pathetic sound. "Phones across Hochkinsville have to be lighting up right now."

They look at each other as though this is some sort of cataclysmic disaster. Has Simi forgotten where we grew up? If the opinion of neighbors mattered even a little bit, Simi and I would never have survived. Being shamed and pointed at when we left our home was part of our daily existence. Who is this woman, and what has she done with my sister?

"What the hell kind of name is Hochkinsville anyway? It sounds like a place where everyone has the same disease," I say.

"Really?" my sister snaps. "How does the name of this town matter right now?"

"I mean, it needed to be said."

Rasgulla cracks a smile. Then swallows it back quickly the moment Simi catches sight of it, and returns to gawking at her as though she has all the answers.

"None of what you say ever needs to be said, Rupi. Most certainly not what you said when those women were here. How do you think it's going to look when the truth comes out?"

Even before she left India, my sister had stopped being as worshipful of me as she'd been when we were younger. But I'm not liking her tone one bit.

"The whole point is to not let the truth come out, isn't it? Why would I lie if telling the truth were an option? What did you expect me to do, tell them that I'm here illegally and this guy here"—my gaze slices to this Prem—"just threw me under a speeding train?"

"He did nothing of the sort."

"Hello? Have you not been listening? I begged him not to bring me in here. He made a promise." I would not have fainted if he hadn't made that promise.

"He didn't know, Rupi!"

My god, she's turned into our mother. Every instance of Abha Naik choosing a man over us burns through my mind.

"But you do! You know I wouldn't be here unless I had nowhere else to go. Or have you conveniently forgotten your life before you met him? I can remind you since you're so into telling the truth these days. Or do you think he can't handle it?"

That shuts her up. If that stupid burrito hadn't soured my belly into a cesspool, this would've done it.

"I love Simi. I don't care what happened before we met, no matter what she chooses to share with me." Great, now the rasgulla wants to add his two cents when he knows nothing about anything.

I'm about to tell him to shut up, but Simi cuts me off. "You can say whatever you want in front of him. You already pulled him into your mess." Her chin is raised, and she's obviously counting on the fact that I'll say nothing.

She's right. I'm the one who taught her the rules of silence. I'm not about to break them myself. I would never say what both of us swore never to say. But what I can say needs to be said.

"Fine. Then here's the truth. What do you think would have happened if I told them that I have no paperwork because some assholes brought me into the country to work for them for nothing and then took my passport away so I'd be trapped? I was a captive. For a year." Until I found a way to free myself. Or a way had found me. "And I've been on the run for the year after that."

Simi presses a hand to her mouth. *Now* she looks sorry. I don't need her pity.

"And what will your Romeo think if he knew that I begged for your help and you turned me away?"

The blood drains from Simi's face. "That's not true. Why do you always have to alter the way you remember things to suit your needs? You just showed up here in America one fine day all excited to be here, working for this man. I told you not to fall for it. I told you how it would end and that I wouldn't be able to help you when it did." Despite the coldness of her tone, she looks like I've kicked her in the ribs.

This. This particular face is responsible for ruining my life. I've always done everything I could to keep her from looking like this: lost, heartbroken, terrified. To hell with that.

"You're so right," I say. "You did tell me that I should not have come to America. Thank you! Such wise advice. You escaped. You got a fresh start, but I should have stayed there, stuck for eternity." *Paying for your mistakes.* I hate that I can't make myself say that part.

"That's not what I meant." But there's no conviction in her voice. Tears fill her eyes and trickle down her cheeks. Tears have always sat on her lash line, ready to spill over. She hasn't changed one bit.

Prem puts his arm around her. "It's okay," he says.

"How the hell would you know what's okay and what isn't?" I say.

He gapes at me like he has no idea what to do. From everything I've seen thus far, that seems to be his entire personality.

"Don't talk to him like that," Simi says on a giant sniff, but she can't inject any force into it.

Another look passes between them. "I'll wait outside. Call if you need help."

Is he suggesting I would hurt Simi? I can't believe she doesn't correct him. I'm where I am because not hurting Simi was more important to me than not hurting myself. Obviously the same can't be said for his precious Simi.

She squeezes his hand, and they let go an inch at a time, as if in slow motion. He's leaving for the corridor, not going off to war, for shit's sake. How can I not scoff?

Simi turns on me, tired eyes narrowed. "You're being incredibly cruel right now."

"I'm the one being cruel? Are you not seeing me lying here? It isn't cruelty, it's self-preservation. It's a concept we're both quite familiar with."

Simi squeezes her temples. She looks like she has a million things to say, but she's weighing each one to come up with the exact right thing to make all of this, and me, go away quickly.

"Ask me what you want to ask me, Simi."

"And what do you think that is?"

"Why I'm here."

"Tell me, then."

"Because I thought when it came down to it, I had you. But I was wrong."

She looks like I've slapped her. "Of course you have me. But I have a life to protect now, Rupi. You have to respect that."

It's my turn to feel like she's slapped me. "Really? Do tell me about protecting things, little sister." I feel heartsick. "Why don't you teach me what that's like: fighting for yourself. Because I was so damn tied up, protecting my little sister, that I never got to build a life to protect. Maybe while you're at it also teach me how to walk away and let someone else take care of everything for you."

Simi pales. Her eyes—eyes that I once watched like a compass to gauge my own success and failure—fill with guilt, but she shoves it all away. "You were the one who insisted I leave India. You practically pushed me out. You said you wanted to live and you couldn't until you had me out of your hair."

It's funny how complicated sacrifice is. I might be a poster child for mixed-up intentions, but I'm not stupid. I know exactly what I've done for my sister, no matter what it cost me, no matter how much she hated it. I know that she wouldn't be where she is without my sacrificing everything. And here she is, remembering it all backward.

"Now who's altering the way she remembers things to suit her needs? Do you really believe I took the fall for you because I wanted you out of my hair?"

She balks to hear me say the words, but it's the truth. When I made the choice, I didn't hesitate for even a moment. Clearly, sacrificing myself was a duty I took on so wholly that I never let Simi learn what it meant. Simi obviously only cares about Simi.

"I don't believe I have to say this, but I did what I did to make it easy for you to leave. Because you've never done a hard thing in your life."

That hits hard, too, but I can also see her defensiveness rise like armor. "And now that I have the things you wanted for me . . . safety, a better life . . . you want to take them away?"

"No, I don't. I want you to have that forever. How can you question that? But don't I also deserve some safety, a semblance of a life, too?" I have never, before this moment, thought about it this way. What have I ever done but fight and claw for everything? Why don't I deserve what Simi has? What Tina has. What Ron and Matthew and the whole wide world have. Dignity. Ease. Safety.

"If you really want those things, your choices have to reflect that, Rupi." She says it quietly, as though she's imparting some deep insight.

Well, isn't that precious?

"You're right. I should have picked different choices from the array of choices life presented me with." I press a finger to my temple and make a thinking sound when what I want is to break into hysterical laughter. "Just to satisfy my curiosity, can you name one choice—*real choice*—that would suggest I want my life to be like this?"

Simi has that look again, like she's waded into the wrong pond and it's made of quicksand.

"I'm not the one who . . ." Thankfully she doesn't say the words, because that much I've taught her well. The only way you can get away with a crime is if you never speak of it to anyone.

She doesn't need to say the words for me to know what she was about to say. That she wasn't the one who insisted we flee the scene and leave someone to die, if the bastard wasn't already dead. But that's just idiotic. I didn't raise her so she could go to jail because our mother had a talent for picking assholes.

It's easy to talk about making choices when you have them.

"I know that choice was mine," I say. "Which is why the consequences were mine. And god knows I've borne them alone."

This time it's like I've pulled the ground from beneath her. I don't want her to feel guilty. That's not why I'm here.

"I didn't ask you to bear the consequences, Rupi. You never gave me a choice."

I'm so darned tired. She's right. I didn't give her a choice. She thinks she wanted those choices, but she doesn't realize that would have meant both of us having no good choices instead of only one of us. I was already broken enough to absorb the blow but not strong enough to watch my sister break.

When Vivek, our mother's last husband, fell and hit his head after attacking Simi, she called me in a panic. I got her out of there. No one saw us. Vivek didn't survive, and two days later a cop showed up at our door. He showed us the CCTV footage of Simi entering the room where they found Vivek dead. It was two weeks before Simi was supposed to leave for Kentucky. Even if we could prove that it was an accident, an investigation would have meant her not being able to leave the country. It would have meant her losing an opportunity we'd both worked all our lives for.

Fortunately, the cop had no interest in an investigation. Unfortunately, he wanted to be compensated for the hard work of deleting the footage. His first choice for compensation was cash. An amount so high, it meant his second choice for compensation was the only choice. He let us decide which one of us would give him what he wanted.

Simi wanted to find a lawyer, report the cop, get justice. Simi was too naive by half. While she tried to come up with a solution, I went to the guy and got rid of the problem by giving him what he wanted.

Except it never works that way, does it?

"What happened after I left?" my sister asks, her voice breaking like she already knows the answer is going to be as unbearable as the memory.

"What do you think? He didn't destroy the footage."

"Oh my god, Rupi. Why didn't you tell me?" She sits down next to me, and despite everything, the vise around my chest loosens.

"Because you were eight thousand miles away. And because we swore never to breathe a word about it."

Simi presses her hand to her mouth. "Tell me what happened. Please."

"He kept telling me he was going to destroy the evidence once he got bored with me." So, I waited for that to happen while I distracted myself with caring for our ungrateful mother, who was no less vicious in her dying days than she was in her living days. "After Ma died, he started pressuring me to sell the flat and give him money, getting angrier and angrier when I didn't. I even sold some of Ma's jewelry and paid him off. But he was impossible to get rid of. That's when Ron and Tina showed up. It felt like a chance for escape." I watch Simi as shame wraps around her. "What choice do you think I should have made?"

"I didn't know any of this." Her eyes are filled with pain, and my heart squeezes, which in turn makes me angry.

"What would you have done if you knew? You know now, and all you want is for me to go away. As always, you're like iron filings at the wrong end of a magnet, scooting away from the problem. I get that you're terrified of bursting this pretty bubble you've built, but I didn't come here to blow up your precious life. That man you were siding with against your own sister, he's the one who put us in this position. He said he was your friend, so I trusted him. I trusted that he would not bring me into the hospital."

Simi looks angry again. Unsurprising, given that coming face-to-face with your own failings is infuriating. I should know.

"Everything you did for me, you did without me asking for it," she says. "Even with the cop, you made that choice for me. How was I supposed to do anything? Look at everything I've done when you weren't here, insisting on doing it all so you could control everything?"

Wow, so this is the thanks I get. "Okay, fantastic. You have control now. I don't see you rushing to help."

"Of course I'll help. But you have to let me think. Blowing up your life at every turn is not the only way to do something, Rupi. Self-destructive action is not better than inaction. Building a life means controlling your rage and leashing your impulses. It's work. More work than doing the first thing that pops in your head."

The thing popping in my head right now is pure, unadulterated rage and disappointment. "Fine. So, sit there and think about how to save your own ass. I'll figure my own shit out. The way I've always done."

Simi makes the most frustrated sound. "Fine. Then tell me. What do you want? You want me to remove your IV? Help you run away and maybe lose my job over it? No, wait, how about I go out there and back up your lie. Tell them, yes, she's getting married to Prem Gupta. Then what? They let you just walk out of here because you're marrying someone with insurance? That's not how insurance works, Rupi. Or maybe I bring Prem in here and force him to marry you. Boom. Done. You're safe. No one can throw you out of the country. No more running. No more worrying. All your problems gone!"

I push myself up to sitting. My heart is racing in a whole new way. "You know, that's the only decent idea you've had thus far. Let's do it. Call your rasgulla in. You're so sure he loves you. Let's put him to the test. See how far he'll go for love."

For the first time in my life, my sister looks at me with true loathing. Great, she's let a man become more important than herself and her family. Now, where have I seen that before?

I lie back down. "No? Don't feel like testing out what love means? I didn't think so. Because that would mean actually understanding what love means. I don't want your damn boyfriend, Simi. What I want is for you to care about what happens to me. I am so incredibly tired of being alone. Tell me something, do you remember feeling alone even for a minute when we were growing up? We were so alone. The most fragile, unprotected beings on this earth, but put your damn hand on your heart and tell me if you ever felt alone. Do you know why that is? Because I never let you. Do you think it was easy? When I, myself, was a child?"

Simi looks like I just crushed her, again. Which feels too much like being crushed myself, again. I don't want that. I don't want to care when Simi looks like this.

I let out the sigh that's trapped so deep inside, it drains me on its way out. "Truth is, I didn't feel alone either. Because I never let myself think about myself as separate from you. When you left, I felt like someone ripped off parts of me. Maybe that's why I'm here. Because for one moment, I want to feel whole again. Of course I don't want you to destroy the life you built. I just want you to take me into that life for one blessed moment and keep me safe until I can feel strong again. Do you know how hard it is for me to ask for your help? But I came because you are my very last hope. The edge of my cliff. And you don't care. You're just another person who doesn't give a shit about anyone but yourself. You're worse than Ma."

"Please stop saying that." All these years later, that's still the worst thing we can say to each other.

All our lives we've had to teach ourselves that there are other ways to be, choices to make so our life looks nothing like our mother's. We've had to ask ourselves *what would Abha Naik do?* and do the exact opposite.

Then help me. Think about me I want to say, but I can't bring myself to beg more than I already have. "It stings, because it's true," I say instead.

Simi's head snaps up. "What about you? Do you think you've escaped Ma? You're exactly like her too. With your eyes on the next easy way out."

I sit up again, and my head swims. I feel insubstantial, like the spinning in my head might make me float away. "Easy way out?" How can I not laugh at that? "You know what, go to hell. I don't want your help. Forget I asked. I survived without you before. I'll survive again. Seriously. Go. Get out. I don't want you here. I don't want you, Simi."

SEVEN

SIMI

"What do you mean, she's gone?" I ask as Sheena runs up to Prem and me in the hospital cafeteria.

"I mean we went into her room, and she was no longer there," Sheena snaps, as though I'm the one who's run away from the hospital and not my sister.

"Did someone discharge her?" I'm already jogging toward Rupi's room, my heart outracing me.

"Of course not." Sheena pants on my heels.

I run up the wide staircase. A doctor dodges me to get out of my way and snaps something at me that I don't hear. Doctors here tend to expect their path to clear before them like the parting ocean.

I ignore him and keep running, imagining Rupi yanking out her own IV and stumbling out of the room. I imagine her passed out somewhere. She has critically serious bacterial food poisoning. What if she goes into electrolyte shock? Or worse, it induces cardiac arrest. It's more common than people think.

My already raging panic doubles when we reach her floor and find two uniformed policemen standing there. "Did someone call the cops?"

"No," Sheena says, studying my terrified face. "But maybe they can help."

"No!" I squeak too loudly. The cops are here for someone else. I better calm down, or I'm going to do something stupid.

"No need to bother them," Prem says quickly. "She's probably just gone looking for a restroom?"

Sheena throws him an exasperated look. "Why didn't she call a nurse to take her? How could you leave her alone like that?"

Prem and I exchange confused glances before it strikes us both at once: In Sheena's head, Prem is Rupi's fiancé.

Prem drops my hand like it's turned hot. I hadn't even realized we were holding hands.

"It's going to be okay," I say, patting his shoulder as though comforting him. "We'll find her. Don't worry."

We pass the cops and make our way to Rupi's room. The bed is disheveled, but the plastic bag with her clothes is still there.

Where are you, Rupi?

The deep sadness in her eyes when she told me to go away has been sitting on my heart like a boulder, but now it flattens me.

Every single word she said was true. Every single word I said was unfair.

"She's got to be in the hospital somewhere," Prem says.

My aching heart fills with gratitude. He's helping me. Even when he has no idea what's going on, he's in my corner.

I am so incredibly tired of being alone.

Tears spring into my eyes. I swipe them away. I want to be angry with her for the terror that's racing through me. She raised me. She was fearless every time she threw herself in front of me to protect me. If not for whatever happened in California, she wouldn't even have looked my way for fear of hurting me.

In return, I turned away from her.

For the past four years, I've ignored her existence to survive. But I've always known she's there—a twin soul who knows me fully. I've always known that if I ever needed help, all it would take to summon her was to reach out.

She hasn't had that. I've never given her that.

"We'll find her," Prem says, rubbing my back. Sheena can go to hell. Your sister's fiancé can comfort you if he wants.

"Just give me a little time to find her," I say to Sheena.

I don't know what she sees in my face, but she nods.

I make my way back to the cafeteria. Prem follows me silently.

I go straight to the vending machine and start selecting things: nut bars, cheese-and-cracker sandwiches, chips, candy. I fill my hands with them, then grab an orange soda. It's her favorite.

I take it to my Honda Civic, dump the snacks on the back seat, and get in the driver's seat.

Prem gets in next to me.

"Are we running away?" he says.

I want to smile. I really do, but I can't. "She doesn't have money, so she's walking." When she's sick and starving.

Memories of her feeding me and pretending she'd already eaten fill me.

"She can't be moving too fast right now." Although I know that Rupi's stubbornness gives her supernatural strength. I try not to think about the time she broke open a door when one of our stepfathers locked us in a room, and the time she climbed out our balcony with me on her back when she wasn't even twelve.

Fortunately, there's only one road that leads out of the hospital. We drive past parking lots and doctor's practices. At the end of the street, I turn right on a whim, my eyes scanning everything.

Prem is doing the same, but I can tell he's filled with questions that he's holding in.

"She couldn't have walked more than two miles in this much time, even if she were perfectly healthy. In two miles we'll turn around and go the other way." Working things out logically is how I handle a crisis.

"She could have turned off into one of the side streets," he says.

"She hasn't." I know she'll stay on this street because she knows I will come looking for her. "Ask me what you want to ask me," I say. Might as well get this out.

Before he can respond, his gaze catches on a slight figure walking along the sidewalk. I slow down, but it's a young boy. He turns and glares at us, daring us to approach him. When we drive away, he flips us off.

"You told me your sister threatened to kill you," Prem says. "Now we're driving around, trying to find her."

How did I forget about that conversation? But everything that happened before Rupi showed up seems ages ago. Prem bringing up marriage feels decades ago. Can I even remember the person I was when I sat at that table, stretching the truth?

I make a U-turn. "It wasn't that simple." There are advantages to being the kind of person who documents every fact she skews to save her ass. "She did threaten me, but she wasn't actually going to take my life."

He doesn't point out how absurd I sound. He scans our surroundings, looking for my sister. "You also said she took your mother's life."

"No, I said she was responsible for our mother's death." We're driving in the opposite direction now, and the setting sun is blinding me as I search the sidewalks. "That wasn't a lie, but I might have spun the truth a little."

For the first time since we met, I can't find worshipful devotion in the way Prem is looking at me.

Let's put him to the test. See how far he'll go for love.

Caring for Ma was another thing Rupi got stuck doing for the both of us. "Rupi had to be the one to take our mother off life support. I wasn't there to help."

He reaches over and squeezes my hand. The worshipfulness in his eyes might have dimmed, but he's here, and everything about him says that he wants to be.

For one second, I want to tell him everything. Pour it all out. But I have to focus on finding my sister.

Please, please let her be okay. Let me find her, and I'll do everything to make sure she's safe. Please.

I chant the word as we drive down the blessedly uncrowded street. The memory of running around our building shouting *Anyone seen Rupi? Anyone seen my sister?* comes back to me.

"I think I see her." Prem sits up.

My gaze follows his, hope rising too fast. I struggle to manage it, even as the chant of *please please please* hits a crescendo in my head.

A figure in scrubs is sitting hunched up against the wall of a strip mall, her slight body curved into itself.

I swerve the car into the parking lot, grab the snacks, and run to her.

"Rupi." I squat in front of her. I don't think I've ever felt such a disorienting volume of relief or guilt in my life. Then again, those are the two emotions that are never far when I'm anywhere near my sister.

It takes her a whole half minute to look up at me. "Go away."

I shove the orange soda at her. "I got you Fanta."

"Is it poisoned?" Her chest is heaving. She wouldn't have dropped here unless she was out of every bit of energy. The scrubs she stole from the hospital are wet with sweat. She's shaking.

She takes the bottle and gulps it down too fast. Then presses a palm against her sternum as though trying to keep from bringing it back up.

I hand her the snacks.

"I don't need your charity."

"You can pay for it. I'm keeping a list."

She snatches the packet and tears it open. "Of course you're going to charge your own sister for plastic snacks."

"You're not supposed to eat the packaging."

She almost cracks a smile, but then she narrows her eyes. "Why are you here?"

"To take you back to the hospital."

"You're really going to hand your sister over to the authorities to save your job?"

"Don't give me ideas."

Finally, she huffs out a laugh.

"Can you please get in the car? We can figure out what to do next together."

"No, thank you."

"Rupi, I know that I've been missing. That I abandoned you. That you've sacrificed everything for me all my life. I get that. But can you trust me? I'm not going to let anyone hurt you."

"Why do you want to help suddenly? What's changed?"

I throw a look Prem's way. His face is shuttered. "Can we talk about that later? Right now, we need to get you back inside the hospital before Sheena calls someone."

"And then what? What happens when I can't pay the bill and they call the authorities?"

"That's not going to happen. The hospital treats people even when they don't have paperwork, and they don't report people for it."

"Yes, but those people don't look like they were born in a different country." She runs her fingers through her hair and winces. There's a splotch of dried blood on the back of her hand from the IV.

"You were in critical care. I need you to be checked out before they release you. We'll figure everything else out."

She's looking at me a little differently now. It's my day to change minds and influence people, I guess. "What happens when someone can't pay their bill?"

"They hound you with collection calls. But we don't have to worry about that. I'll figure out a way to pay." I do work three jobs. I have loans and rent, and this wasn't in my budget spreadsheet, but my sister is sitting on pavement, and suddenly nothing else matters.

"If you don't come back to the hospital, they'll be compelled to report you as missing." I know that's what she wants to avoid above all.

"What happens after the hospital?"

"Then we go home and figure things out," I reassure her.

"I don't have a home."

"You do now. Come on." I stand.

After the longest pause in the history of pauses, she takes my hand and stands.

In the car, Rupi eats her way through fifty dollars of vending machine snacks. She's always been able to do this: survive on nothing, then eat five thousand calories at a go.

My survival technique might be The Ostrich—avoidance—but hers is The Camel—famine survival.

As we get out of the car, I cast a nervous glance around the parking lot. St. Joe's is a small hospital, and there's a very high probability of someone recognizing me.

Rupi is wearing scrubs, but even in those she's entirely too striking. Tall and long limbed, with dramatic cheekbones and eyebrows and a jaw that can make plastic surgeons weep. Tattoos cover her left arm. There are a lot of new ones that I haven't seen before, a psychedelic sleeve coming all the way down to her wrist.

Before I can figure out how to sneak her back in, she walks past me and into the hospital. Prem and I race behind her as she strides past registration to the stairs with all the confidence of someone who works here.

"You take the elevators and make sure the coast is clear," she throws at us and continues up the stairs. It's three floors up. I try not to worry about her blood pressure as Prem and I take the elevator.

The first person we see when we get out is Sheena. Of course it is. Behind her, I see Rupi start to emerge up the stairs.

"Hey, Sheena!" I call out without thinking. She turns to me just as Rupi comes into view.

Sheena walks up to us. Behind her, Rupi slips calmly into her room, unseen.

"Did you guys find her?"

I burst into laughter. I don't even know how I'm doing it, but it spurts out of me. I can't remember which movie this was from, but I'm the heroine cracking up after she's played a prank on the hero.

"It's the funniest story," I say.

Sheena looks as confused as I'm feeling.

"I told you she must have gone looking for a restroom," I say. "She got lost. And before she found a restroom, she peed herself." I'm laughing like I've come unhinged. "They had pumped her so full of fluids. Obviously she was dying of embarrassment. Imagine your fiancé witnessing that."

Prem looks at me like he has no idea who I am, but he goes along with whatever it is I'm doing. "I can't believe she was embarrassed," he says. Then his eyes fill with meaning. "Love means seeing each other at your worst."

I give another bizarre laugh. "Well, mission accomplished." I turn to Sheena. "Someone needs to help clean up. Prem can show you where it is."

"Of course," she says.

Prem leads Sheena away, and I run to the storage area and grab a gown and IV kit before going to Rupi.

She's passed out on her bed. I give her shoulder a nudge. "You okay?"

"Define okay," she says, eyes still closed.

I help her out of bed. "Let's get you changed. You never left the hospital. Got it?"

She grunts, but she lets me get her into the gown. Her body is darned near skeletal, and my heart clenches.

"I need to get the IV back in." I push her on the bed and thank the big fat veins we're both blessed with. That bottle of orange soda was truly an inspired choice.

I have the IV in her in under a minute. I did graduate top of my class.

I tape everything in place (also in record time). Just as I'm tossing everything in the garbage, I hear Prem speaking unusually loudly in the corridor. He's warning me that they're near.

"Someone must've cleaned up before we got there. But thank you for helping me."

I drop into the chair next to the bed and take Rupi's hand. "By the way, you went looking for a restroom and peed yourself."

"What!" I can feel her body getting ready to sit up, but there's a knock on the door, and she closes her eyes and pretends to be dead to the world.

They come in to find me stroking Rupi's forehead. The poignancy is so overdone, I feel like I missed my calling in the world of soaps.

Prem looks at me with his heart in his eyes, and I glare at him. He quickly turns the look on Rupi and pats her, but distracted as he is, instead of her leg he ends up patting her crotch. Her eyes spring open.

Horrified, he pulls his hand back. Color floods his cheeks.

"When do you think Rupi will be discharged?" I ask a little too loudly to keep both me and Rupi from bursting into untimely laughter.

"Hopefully soon," Sheena says in a tone that suggests she cannot wait to be rid of us. *I hear you, babe.* "Were you able to get her Social Security number?"

All the laughter in the world dies inside me. It's been barely an hour since she asked last. "It's going to be a while before we can get any of that," I say. "Remember she was robbed. She has nothing backed up. We'll have to apply for replacements for all of it. But you have my contact information."

She lets out a sigh. "That should work for now. Let me check if we need anything else before we let you go. Oh, and we had to call the cops when she went missing and we couldn't find any of you."

EIGHT

SIMI

Rupi sits up the second Sheena leaves. "Congratulations! You've basically handed me over to the cops."

"You're the one who ran away. How are you blaming me for this?" I say.

She looks lost, then glares at Prem with the heat of a thousand suns. "None of this would have happened if he hadn't broken his promise and dragged me in here." She's never letting this go.

"And you shouldn't have told them you were engaged to him," I snap. "This is a small town, everyone knows him. Now we're all stuck." I can't believe Prem is stuck in this mess because of me. How is he still here?

"You can always tell them I lied. If they arrest me and deport me, so be it."

She knows very well I can't let that happen. Not when I know what's waiting for her in Mumbai.

Before I can respond, Prem's phone rings.

"It's my mom," he says.

Wow. Anagha works fast.

He doesn't answer. "I already have twenty texts on the family group chat. I haven't opened them, but I can't ignore them much longer."

He never ignores his family. The fact that he isn't immediately responding is probably going to cause them to send out a search party soon.

"Can't you tell them you're busy and you'll call when you're free?"

"That would mean I looked at my texts. And that would mean I know that they know that I got engaged without even telling them that I'm dating someone."

I open and close my mouth.

"I have to tell them the truth, Simi."

"I know." My brain is racing. My sister is staring into the distance, jaw clenched, steeling herself against what she's expecting, which is the cops coming for her.

Prem reaches for his phone.

"Actually, can I talk to you outside for a minute first?" My voice wobbles.

He looks scared, and I hate it. "Sure."

I follow him into the empty corridor.

"Let's go to the cafeteria," he says.

I throw a glance at Rupi's door. "I can't. I can't leave her again."

I realize that I don't mean that just for now. Ignoring my sister's existence was possible when she wasn't near me. Leaving her for the first time was devastating. It hurt so much, I built thick scabs around it. Now that she's here and I can see what she's been through, what she bore for me, I just can't. I don't know how I'm ever going to forgive myself. Sending her back to India by herself is impossible.

"Is it such a bad idea?" I say, turning to him. He's all I have. All Rupi and I both have.

You're so sure he loves you. Let's put him to the test.

"What?" There's an ocean of tentativeness in his voice.

"Marriage."

We're standing face-to-face, alone in this clinically clean passageway, the fluorescent lighting making everything too visible. Unforgiving. There's no place to hide under lights like these.

"Not even a little bit," Prem says. "Marriage is a great idea. That's what I've been trying to tell you. I wish we were already married. In my heart"—he touches his chest in that way that turns me inside out—"I'm already married to you."

"I'm not talking about you and me." It's a good thing there's a whole foot between us. If I were touching him right now, I might not have been able to say the words.

The shock on his face is like physically being shoved away. "Come on, Simi."

I have to take a breath. My heart feels like there's a truck parked on it. "I know it sounds ridiculous. Don't you think I know that? But if you give it a moment's thought, you'll see that it's the only possible way out of this situation." I've searched and searched for another solution, and there's no other way.

His hand goes to his forehead. He squeezes his temples. His eyes search up and down the empty corridor. He's looking for escape, for help.

"Your sister could go back to India."

"She can't. Her life is in danger if she goes back." Because of me. The face of the cop who'd come after us flashes clear as day in my head: tobacco-stained teeth, back hair sticking out from behind his collar, bulging predator eyes. Bile churns in my stomach at the thought of him touching Rupi.

"She can't get on a plane without a passport." I have no idea what happens when you're in the US illegally and get caught. "Do you want her to be thrown in jail? Is that what you want?" I know how unfair I'm being. That only makes me angrier. I have no one else to turn to. Rupi and I have never had anyone to turn to. What about that is fair?

A frown is pinched between his brows. This is it. He's the best thing that ever happened to me, and it's about to be over. Rupi was right, after all.

"She won't be arrested," he says as though he has any idea how these things work. He was born here, and like every immigrant child born here, he's never had to give any real thought to what it took for him to be here. “My friend Saj is an immigration attorney. Let’s ask him. His whole life is about helping people harmed by the system. He can help us.”

“Can your friend guarantee she stays here? The only way to guarantee that she stays is marriage. Will Saj marry her? She can’t go back to India, Prem. Didn’t you hear me? She is in danger there.” The kind of danger Prem can’t even comprehend, because he’s been safe all his life.

Suddenly, it strikes me that there’s no way that Rupi left without making the cop pay for what he did. Knowing Rupi, it’s got to be bad. Whatever happened in California has got to be bad too.

Prem looks up at the ceiling. He can’t believe what I’m saying. I can’t either. Suddenly I know without a doubt that it is this or losing my sister forever. “Prem, look at me. Do you think I would ever suggest this if there were any other option?”

“This is not an option, either, Simi. How can you think it is?”

And there it is.

See, your rasgulla failed, Rupi says in my ear.

I step back as though he’s pushed me away. “You’re right. I don’t know what I was thinking.” I turn around and start walking. I can’t believe what I just asked of him. I can’t be here right now. I can’t be around him.

“Simi,” he calls after me. “Hold on.” He catches up with me. “What is going on here? When your sister lied in front of Anagha, you looked like you were going to blow a fuse. Now you want me to marry her? I don’t know what is happening. Ever since your sister got here, it’s like I don’t even recognize you.”

His words rip me to shreds. They gouge out every bit of fear I’ve always had about us. I never was who he thought I was. And now that I’ve shown him who I am, he doesn’t know me.

“I’m the woman you professed to love. I’m that same Simi. Nothing has changed, except you’re seeing me in the context of my own life, not in the context of your and your family’s life.”

Until I say it, I've never thought this, but suddenly it's clear to me. Today, in this one day, Prem has seen more of me—the old me, the one I was before I came to America—than he has in the year we've been together.

Before he can respond, his phone rings again. "It's my mom again." He disconnects the call. Almost immediately it rings again. He disconnects again.

"I'm texting to let my family know I'm okay and I'll call them soon. I have to."

I nod. I hate Anagha from the core of my being right now.

As soon as he sends the text, the phone rings again. "It's Preeti."

I forgot about Preeti and Dr. Johnson. I can't think about what this means for my job yet.

We're silent for a long moment. All the while, Prem's phone pings nonstop. With a groan, he turns it off.

"Do you really feel that way?" he says finally. "Do you really feel like I see you only in the context of my own life?"

"It's not how I feel, Prem. It's a fact. You met me in your sister's home, taking care of your nieces. Ninety percent of the time we've spent together has been in your sister's home. I work for your brother-in-law. I live in your town. You have no idea who I am outside of your life." Ever since I met Prem, I've never considered a life without him in it. Now I try to, and my chest aches. "I'm sorry that your first glimpse of me as myself has been such an ugly disaster."

For the first time since we started this conversation, he touches me. He cups my cheek. My entire body leans into his touch.

"It's not ugly. Just a disaster." He smiles. When I don't smile back, he gets serious again. "But you're right, I've never seen you like this."

"Your life revolves around your family. Why is me needing to take care of my sister so different? I'm the same person. Other than the fact that I need your help, desperately, nothing has changed."

"Nothing has changed? You're asking me to marry your sister. I would have to lie to my family, lie to everyone I know."

"What if this were your sister? What if you had to marry someone else to save Preeti's life?"

"That's an absurd comparison. This is completely different. You're asking me to commit a crime."

"How is it a crime? You'll actually be marrying her. The marriage would be legal. It's the only way to get her to stay here. To not be deported. You were willing to do it with me, marry me so I could get a green card."

"I'm in love with you, Simi. How is that the same thing?"

"Do you think every couple who gets married loves each other? Love has nothing to do with the legality of marriage." It's not like I don't see how ridiculous my arguments are, but every word I'm saying is also true.

"You're right. But intention does. We were going to get married because we love each other. Our intention was not to get married so you could get a green card and stay in the country. That's fraud."

"Actually that's exactly what you suggested." I know what he's saying makes perfect sense, but in one way the distinction is also absurd. "Plenty of married people don't love each other. That doesn't make their marriage illegal."

"My god, Simi, how is that relevant?" He runs his hand through his hair again, leaving trails in the thick curls.

"What I'm saying is that you did want me to get a green card that way."

"And you refused. It's one of the many reasons I love you. I can't imagine you doing anything unethical or dishonest. Now you want me to do something that involves lying to everyone I know and dishonoring our love."

I look around to make sure we're alone and step close to him. I press a hand into his chest. His heart is racing. "Prem, I've never felt like anyone belongs to me. Until you. Do you know how hard it is for me to ask anyone for anything? And yet I'm asking you, because you've given me that. From the day we met, you've given me all of you. I can only ask because I honor our love that much." Saying those words is terrifying, but every one of them is true. This truth is all I have.

He grips my hand like a man drowning. He's in pain, but he's holding me like he'll never let go. Hope rises inside me.

"I haven't told you about my childhood because it would break your heart." Rupi is right; there are no good choices, and it's too late to not tell him the whole truth. "Rupi was five years old when I was born, and she raised me. Our father left when my mother got pregnant with me. Her husbands came and went through a revolving door. You can't imagine what our world was like. No one played with us in the neighborhood or at school. The other kids weren't even allowed to talk to us. We were constantly attacked and mocked. That was still easier than being at home. I survived it because Rupi protected me. Who you see standing here before you, the person you profess to love . . . I wouldn't be that person if she hadn't paid for it with her own life and her own future." And I had forsaken her. "I cannot turn away from her again."

"I can't, Simi. I'll do anything for you, but don't ask for this."

"There's more. At least hear me out. The reason she can't go back is because of something I did. Our mother was sick for the last few years of her life. The nurse who gave her dialysis was her last husband. He knew exactly how much longer she was going to live when they got married. He also knew that she owned a flat in Andheri. Rupi noticed that Ma was deteriorating really fast since she met him. Rupi was always paranoid, suspicious of everyone and everything. It's how she kept us safe.

"But after she said it, I investigated the meds he was giving her. I had just graduated nursing school, and I realized that he was giving her enough of a drug to essentially poison her. I confronted him. Things didn't go well. He attacked me. I pushed him off me, and he hit his head and passed out. I called Rupi. We decided to leave him there without getting help, and he died. It was an accident, but we were sure no one would believe us. We thought no one had seen us, but then a cop showed up with some CCTV footage and started blackmailing us."

I'm crying again, but Prem doesn't move to wipe my tears, and that hurts. He looks like I've rammed into him with a truck.

"I had already been admitted into the fellowship program here. I would have lost everything if I'd been arrested. Basically, Rupi gave him what he wanted. And . . . and it wasn't money, because we didn't have any. She made it possible for me to be here. But the cop never stopped blackmailing her. Leaving Mumbai was her only chance to escape. She's in this situation because of me. I have to help her. Please."

"My god, Simi." He steps away. He looks horrified. "How could you hide all this from me?"

Betrayal slices me in half. I turn away from him, my face flaming with shame. I just showed him everything, all the truth I had. And he pulled away.

"Maybe," I say, bitterness coating my tongue, "I hid it because I knew it would make you pull away." I start walking again. I've left my sister alone for too long. I need to get her out of here and figure out what to do next.

"Simi," he calls after me. "I'm not pulling away. I just need a moment to digest it all."

I stop, but I can't make myself turn to him. "Fine."

"What does that mean?"

"It means take your time. Sorry I asked for your help. I don't know what I was thinking. I'll figure it out." The way Rupi always figured things out for me.

"What about us?"

"I don't know, Prem. I can't think about that right now." I can't wrap my head around what I just did. I laid everything out in front of him. I know what I'm asking is too much. I think a part of me knew it was impossible. Prem was never going to do it. No one would. Yet all I can think is that Rupi was right. Prem didn't come through.

NINE

RUPI

Simi looks like her heart has been ripped out of her chest. The last time I saw my sister look like this was after our mother told us that Glen had liver failure and had a few weeks left to live.

Glen Sequiera was Husband Number Four. The man who taught me how to wield a tattoo gun.

Tattoos deface the body. That's what Husband Number Three loved to say. Well, maybe they weren't actually husbands. Our mother simply announced herself married to the string of men who came and lived with us, and no one ever went looking for a marriage certificate. This I had found to be true of most things in life. People only went looking for the truth if it served them. Otherwise looking the other way was the easier option.

Back then, it never struck me to not believe her, either, even though Simi and I never actually attended any of the weddings.

Weddings are a waste of hard-earned money, Ma loved to say. *That's what courthouses are for. If you want to live with someone you love, why do you have to pay a priest and feed a bunch of relatives who you never see when a free meal isn't in the picture?*

Sadly, my mother was often right. Especially when it came to seeing the world in all its dismal and bitter glory. Ma was a sieve for catching life's ugliest bits. I would be delusional if I didn't recognize that it was a skill I had inherited in its entirety. Or maybe there were only ugly bits. Maybe the beautiful bits you saw in other people's sieves were a lie to keep us all restless like fish on a hook, unable to let go even if it meant you couldn't breathe.

This is why the beauty of ink under skin meant so much. It was beauty in an unexpected place. It was the human form subverted. Not that I was thinking any of those things when I first got inked. It was the first time in my life that running away led me to something serendipitous.

Mom's Husband Number Three made the declaration about tattoos defacing bodies when Glen moved in to the flat below us. And Glen, whose memory still makes my throat choke with tears, was inked all the way up and down his incredibly beautiful arms. I can no longer remember why I ran away that day, but I sneaked into the back of the building and hid in the nook that looked into Glen's studio room. He saw me hiding (and spying on him working) and invited me in.

He taught me everything I know about tattoos. My first and last guru. The only ink I carry on my body that I haven't put there myself is the trident Glen inked on my inner thigh. I can still feel the back of his hand stroking between my legs as the ink pierced my skin. There is no way to ink that high up on the thigh without touching someone there. When Glen asked me where I wanted my first tattoo, that was the spot I chose.

So, yes, Glen taught me more than just how to use a tattoo gun. I was fourteen years old, a fact he didn't learn until much later. He let me ink him back. In all my years, I've never seen work more beautiful than what Glen could do. And an artist like that letting me, a novice, a child everyone else treated as worthless and strange, mark him permanently changed my life. I would have let him do anything. I wanted him to.

When my mother found out, she was livid. About the tattoo, of course. The rest I never shared with anyone. Obviously Ma hadn't noticed my feelings. A woman with two little girls has to willfully block out many things when she lets so many men into her home. Not that Ma would have cared if she did know how I felt about Glen. She cared little about anything other than herself, her carousel of husbands, and getting back at our father for accusing her of cheating on him and then abandoning her for it.

The only reason Ma saw the tuberose I put on my own bicep under Glen's careful guidance was that I let her. It was the first tattoo I gave myself. The thrill of her finding out was too much to stop and consider the consequences.

Ma marched down our building's worn wooden steps to make sure Glen knew exactly what she thought about him teaching a fourteen-year-old how to give herself a tattoo. They had a screaming match all the neighbors heard. Six months later, Glen became Husband Number Four.

I didn't care. It wasn't like I loved him or anything. All I knew was that I carried him in my art, in the ink that flowed from my gun. Nothing in the world mattered more than that. Everything and everyone other than the ink you shot under skin was temporary. Even at fourteen, I knew two things for sure: Marriage and love had nothing to do with each other, and both those things were the surest way to destroy your life.

Seeing my sister's heartbroken face now is even more proof. Obviously the rasgulla hadn't lived up to all she'd made him out to be. People seldom do.

My anger at Glen and Ma helped me survive the blow of his death. By then, I'd already stopped feeling things enough to let them hurt, but Simi never did learn that skill.

Glen was the closest thing Simi had to a father. Losing him was the first time I wasn't able to protect my sister from hurt. I had to watch every day for two weeks while Simi sat by Glen's bed. I, on the other hand, never went into his room. Not once. I waited outside for Simi. I knew he asked for me, but I didn't go in to see him. Not until after he was gone. Ma wasn't the only one who could carry a grudge to the grave.

Simi looks just like that again. Like she needs to do something to stop time, to turn it around, but she doesn't know how.

"How bad is what you did to Ron's family?" Simi asks, trying to reason and calculate her way out of this.

"How does that matter?"

"When was the last time you gave a straight answer to a question?"

"When there's a straight question, I'll give a straight answer."

"What was crooked about my question?" Simi asks, her tone innocent. There was a time when I could tell if Simi's innocence was an act to get something she wanted, or more likely, if she was avoiding something. I can't seem to tell anymore.

"The whole thing," I say, restlessness gripping me. "There's nothing straightforward about that whole situation, so expecting an answer that's straightforward is absurd."

"Fair. So, give me the twisted version."

"To what end?" I say. "Ron's dead. His wife hates me. Until yesterday, I had leverage to get her to return my passport. But now, the leverage is gone and all I have is my name on a computer that's going to get immigration knocking on my door."

Obviously she doesn't like the answer she demanded.

"Can we talk her into giving us the passport?"

I have to laugh at that. "All we'll achieve is giving away my current location. You already know you can't convince anyone to do anything unless they stand to gain something from it. I'm guessing your rasgulla didn't let you squeeze the syrup out of him."

"Please stop calling him that."

"But it's such a delicious metaphor. He's all soft and sweet, but there's no spine inside, is there?"

"That's not true. Prem is a rock, not just for me but for everyone who knows him."

Right. I want to yawn. "So, he's going to help us, then?"

Simi squeezes her forehead. "It's not that simple."

"Now who's not giving a straight answer to a straight question."

Before Simi can respond, there's a knock on the door and a nurse comes in.

"How are we feeling?" she says with all the chirpiness of someone who has to ask that question twenty times a day.

"I'm ready to go ho— Well, I'm ready to be discharged. What are my chances?"

"Your vitals look good, and you've kept your last meal down, so let's get a urine sample, and then if you're not dehydrated anymore, we can get you on your way. Who's taking you home today?" Is this really happening? I tamp down the hope that rises inside me.

"I am," Simi says. "I'm her sister."

"No way!" the nurse says with a wink. "Does anyone not immediately get that when they see the two of you together?"

Simi and the nurse start chatting about all the ways in which Simi and I look similar and different. Then the nurse walks me to a bathroom (evidently word of my "getting lost" has traveled), where I produce a urine sample while she waits outside.

Once the nurse has dunked a paper strip into the sample, she declares me good to go. I'm lightheaded with relief as she gets my IV off. Just as she tapes a bandage on, another knock sounds. The door is already open, and I watch with utter horror as two cops enter the room: a gorgeous petite woman with dark eyes and the curliest lashes I've ever seen, and a completely bald giant of a man with beefy shoulders that make his swinging arms look like he doesn't quite know what to do with them.

The officers introduce themselves, but my ears are ringing, and I miss their names. This is the moment that's been chasing me ever since I landed in this country and the immigration officer asked why I was here. "I'm visiting a friend," I said and told myself it wasn't a lie.

Ron did a great job pretending to be my friend. Or maybe he was my friend. If friends took away your passport, didn't pay you for your work, and only put a roof over your head when you slept with them.

Great, all this reminiscing meant I missed what the officers said about why they were here.

"Sorry," Simi says to them, giving my shoulder a gentle shake. "She's been pretty disoriented. Rupi, hey, the officers want to ask you a few questions, okay?"

I nod, playing up my exhaustion. My sad-stoic face has gotten me out of many a jam.

"We heard you went missing this afternoon," the lady officer says, her gaze hovering somewhere between empathetic and alert.

"She got lost looking for a restroom," my sister says. "It was a misunderstanding."

The cops exchange glances.

"You were also robbed?" the curly-lashed one asks.

"Yes," a voice that's much deeper than mine says just as I say it too.

Simi's rasgulla rolls into the room.

He walks straight to me and takes my hand. "She fell asleep on the bus, and someone took everything she was traveling with. What a horrible way to welcome someone to Kentucky. After all the nice things I'd told her about our beautiful state."

"And you are?"

He reaches over and shakes their hands. "Prem Gupta, Rupi's fiancé."

"Congratulations," both the cops say at once.

"Don't I know you from somewhere?" the lady officer says.

"Well, my family owns all the Dominic's Pizza places in southern Kentucky and northern Tennessee." I hadn't noticed until this minute that the guy has a heavy southern drawl. Or maybe he's suddenly leaning hard into it.

I've always had the urge to laugh when an Indian person opens their mouth and an American drawl comes out, but this is even more comical.

"Oh my god, I love Dominic's," she says, brightening. "The honey barbecue chicken. How do you get the chicken to taste like that?"

"It's marinated in orange juice overnight. My mother's recipe to tenderize chicken breasts for chicken curry."

"I have to try that. My chicken breasts always get dry. I love chicken curry."

The beefy officer clears his throat, evidently uninterested in sharing his opinion on chicken curry.

"How long have you two been engaged?" he asks.

"A week." Prem attempts smitten eyes at me. I know I should be grateful, but I can't push away the urge to poke at his middle.

"How did you meet?" The curly-lashed cop's tone is friendly.

"Simi introduced us," the rasgulla says.

My heart races even as I smile.

"That's me. I'm her sister." Simi pops in, smiling her most angelic smile.

Simi explains how she works as a nanny for Prem's sister. Together they spin an impressive tale about how Prem met me when he visited Chicago a few months ago. Apparently, we'd talked for three months, and Prem had convinced me to move to Hochkinsville.

Is it usual for the officers to be carrying out a full-fledged inquisition like this for a stolen backpack?

"Is it okay if we take down some information, and then you can come into the station and file a report about the lost paperwork?"

"Can we choose not to report the theft?" Prem asks.

"Well, filing a police report will help when you apply for new documents. But you can speak to a lawyer about the details. We're here to help."

"Thank you," Prem says, taking the notepad Officer Curly Lashes holds out.

I watch in horror as he fills out the information that means the cops know where to find me and hands it back. And with that, the nurse announces that I'm free to walk out of the hospital.

TEN

SIMI

As we leave the hospital, we run right into a very angry blockade of three Indian women in Dominic's Pizza polos over jeans: Preeti; Prem's mom, Tanuja; and his sister-in-law, Chandni.

"What on earth is going on, Prem?" his mom demands, her silver bob catching the harsh afternoon sun.

I've spent the past year avoiding two of these three women. Whenever they visited Preeti and the triplets, I made the effort to disappear into the furniture or into other parts of the house. Fortunately, Preeti much prefers going over to the Gupta house to having them over because it's the only true break she gets, so I've only had to deal with the situation a couple of times in the past year. I'm not sure why I've avoided them so assiduously, but it probably had to do with not wanting them to see me as the nanny. I wanted them to know me as the woman Prem loves. Now here we are.

"Holy shit," Prem says. He grabs Rupi's wheelchair from the ward assistant who's helping us and spins it around, but it's too late for escape.

"Really?" Preeti shouts after him, chasing him down.

With a groan, he processes the fact that there's no getting away and turns back around. He's making such an effort not to look at me that I feel the pull deep under the surface of my skin.

"Why are you not answering our calls?" his sister-in-law demands in the tone of someone who's grabbed a misbehaving child's ear.

"It's obvious why he's avoiding us, now, isn't it?" his mother says, looking at Rupi, who waves sadly, doing an astonishingly good impression of a wounded kitten.

"Simi!" Preeti says, noticing me amid all the chaos. "What are you doing here?" She brightens. "Now it makes sense. You two are the ones engaged?"

In that instant I love Preeti as much as I've ever loved Prem.

I shake my head and pretend surprise. *Me? Engaged to Prem? How preposterous!* "I'm here because Rupi is my sister."

Preeti throws a glance at Rupi, and a tornado of confusion spins into abject disappointment on her face. For a moment I think she's going to lean over and squeeze my hand, but she throws a glance at Prem and controls herself.

"Can we wait until Rupi is better before we do this?" Prem says in a pained tone. "She's very sick. We're in a hospital, for the love of god!"

As though planted here by the director of this nonsensical farce we all find ourselves in, an older couple walks up to the hospital entrance we're currently blocking. The man is supporting a bent-over woman. The lady throws off the man's arm when she sees Prem. She limps right up to him and grabs his arm. "My love!" she says with so much feeling, it's like she's inside me. "You're here. Oh thank god!" She tries to lay her head on Prem's chest.

Prem throws the man a look that's half confusion, half apology. What is it with all these women wanting him suddenly?

The man tries to tug her away. "April, not this again," he says with the kind of exhaustion that I feel deeply. So deeply.

April grips Prem's hand with renewed desperation. "But I can't leave him. I just found him again." She sounds so sad, everyone looks suspended between horror and laughter.

"Move along, Mr. and Mrs. Bigly." The ward assistant regains control of Rupi's wheelchair and directs the couple through the hospital doors.

The sound of a guffaw gets everyone's attention. Rupi is laughing so hard, tears run down her cheeks. Just as the others start to crack, she turns her laugh into a cough, then lets the cough rise in slow, delicate bursts. She had no respiratory symptoms until now, but as her cough turns into choking, even I believe she's in respiratory distress.

Prem squats in front of her. "You okay?" Dear god, our acting condition has infected him.

She catches her breath with some difficulty. "I'm fine," she rasps in the most self-sacrificing tone. "I'm sorry. Can we just get out of here, please?"

Great idea. We need to leave before someone else shows up and tries to claim Prem as theirs.

Prem folds his arms across his chest and turns to his family. "This is not the place for any of this. We're causing a scene."

"I never wanted to cause a scene." Rupi makes the saddest eyes, and her audience deflates visibly.

Causes a scene should be Rupi's middle name, the warning label she comes with.

Prem, who is impressing me (and scaring the heck out of me) with his performance, glares daggers at his family.

The three women step back guiltily.

"The car is right there. I'll get it," I say and sprint to my car, seriously considering driving away from this mess forever.

I pull up to the curb and help Prem help Rupi into the front seat and catch her amused wink. Not for the first time today, I want to strangle my sister.

Prem tosses his keys at Preeti. "I'm going to Simi's place with Rupi. Can you take my car home?"

"We're not going anywhere," Chandni says. "Not without answers."

"You will have answers when I come home after dropping them off," Prem says with a finality I've never heard in his voice before.

"Fine, but you're not going anywhere until you've introduced us. What is wrong with you?" his mom demands. Each woman has a hand on her hip. Obviously, they are not impressed by the finality in his voice.

"Mamma, right now she's not herself. She needs rest. I want to do it later, when she's better. Can you trust me, please," Prem throws out the counterdemand. Has Prem always been this resourceful? I can't say that I don't like it.

"Dear Krishna, is she pregnant? Is that why you had to rush into this?" His mother looks at Rupi with whole new eyes.

I glare at Rupi to not get ideas. Her hand stops on its way to her concavely flat belly, and she gives me the slightest shrug. How can she be enjoying this?

"Can you please not embarrass me in front of her?" Prem says, and I know that the *her* is not Rupi. It's the first thing that's come out of him in this exchange that's sincere. "I told you, I'll answer all your questions when I get home." He notices his mother's expression, and his face softens. "Don't worry, I'm not going to be a father just yet."

His mother doesn't look quite as relieved as she should, and it's my turn to blush, not that anyone is paying me any mind. Prem's family is obviously eager for him to get on with baby making. And I just set everything back a whole heck of a lot.

I have no idea why Prem changed his mind and decided to help us. I pull out of the parking lot, noting gratefully that we're not being followed by Prem's family.

"What the hell happens now, Simi?" Prem is the first to speak.

"Don't talk to my sister like that," Rupi says.

"Don't talk to him like that," I say. "We do need to know what happens next."

"What do you think happens?" Rupi says. "There's only one of two things that can happen. Either he follows through and we get married. Or those cops report me."

"My god, Rupi. Do you realize what you're demanding of us?" I say.

"You think I want to marry him, or anyone else? You think I have any interest in taking away your little playing-house fantasy? Please come up with another solution, because I will one hundred percent take it."

I open my mouth, then shut it again, but instead of responding to Rupi, I catch Prem's eye in the rearview mirror. "Why did you say what you said to those cops? I thought you didn't want to be part of this?"

"Of course I don't want to be part of this. Because *this* is absolutely bananas. But I saw the cops go into the room, and I didn't know what else to do."

"You should have stayed out of it," I say, trying not to let bitterness, which I know is unfair, seep into my voice. "Now you're involved with the cops!"

"I wish you'd just let me run away," Rupi says, and I don't know if she's being sincere or dramatic.

"You should never have done that! If you hadn't pulled that stunt, the hospital wouldn't have had to involve the cops." I squeeze my temples. The unholy headache pushing out from the center of my head is like a ticking bomb. Dehydration. I grab the bottle of water in my cup holder and down half of it. "And don't blame Prem for taking you into the hospital again. You fainted."

"You think I wanted to faint?" Rupi asks, and my heart does another tight and painful squeeze. I've never known Rupi to be able to sleep—really sleep. She doesn't trust anyone enough to let go of consciousness fully. Far as I know, she's been awake her entire life, aware even in sleep.

I turn to Prem. "How are you going to get out of this?"

"I'm not. I just lied to the police and my family." I watch in the rearview mirror as he types something into his phone. "So, I guess we're doing this."

I sit up. Is he serious? I try to meet his eyes, but he's furiously studying something on his phone. "What are you looking at?" I ask.

"I'm googling how to get married in Kentucky without ID." His brows draw together as he reads. "Did you say you have absolutely no paperwork, Rupi didi?" he asks absently, eyes on his screen.

A horrified peel of laughter spurts out of Rupi. "Oh my god, can you not be creepy and call me *didi* when we're talking about getting married?"

He colors. "It's not going to be a real marriage," he says. "It's just until we can make sure you're safe. Then we're getting divorced, and Simi and I are getting married." His eyes, filled with questions, meet mine in the mirror. He's asking me if he's gotten that right.

Hearing it laid out like that makes me nervous and reassures me at the same time. Are we really doing this? Can we all go to jail if we're caught? Am I risking my own deportation to prevent my sister's?

"Shouldn't we talk to a lawyer first?" I ask.

"I'm sending Saj—my immigration-lawyer friend—a text right now."

"What are you telling him?"

"That I want to get married to Rupi and she has no legal status and no paperwork."

Both Rupi and I turn to him in unison.

"He's a lawyer. He's also Chandni's brother. He's family. He's not going to tell anyone. There's attorney-client privilege and family loyalty."

"What if he tells Chandni?" I ask. "She's more his family than you are."

"He won't. That's not how lawyers operate. Also, we've been best friends since grade school, and god knows I've kept enough of his secrets."

"What kind of secrets?" I say. I've heard about Saj but never met him.

"Let's just say Saj had more fun when we were growing up than I did," Prem says.

Rupi huffs out a groan. "Great. He sounds totally responsible."

"He is," Prem says. "And brilliant. He'll know how to help us." He scans his phone some more. "What kind of visa were you on?"

"A tourist visa, which you can't work on. But it was valid for ten years."

"So, technically you are not illegally here. You just worked illegally and there's no paper trail," I say, hope rising.

"I wasn't supposed to stay more than three months, based on the passport stamp, but I'm not sure what that means legally," Rupi says, but she looks the tiniest bit hopeful too.

"Okay, we have to be present to get a marriage license in the state of Kentucky. And there's no waiting period," Prem says.

"So, let's go to the courthouse, then," Rupi says.

"They need a government-issued photo ID," Prem says.

"Is there no way to create a fake ID? They show that in the movies all the time," Rupi says.

"I think we're trying to get you to be here legally, not trying to do more illegal things," I say.

Before any of us can say more, Prem's phone buzzes.

"Hey, man," he says. Then laughs. "I was just about to call you." I can hear the voice on the other side of the call, but the words are not clearly discernible. "Well, it's a little more complicated than that." Another pause. "I think it's better to discuss it in person . . . You are? That's great. Thanks. No, not the house. Let me send you an address. We're almost there."

A few *okays* follow before he hangs up and we pull into my apartment parking spot.

I know the timing is all wrong, but something inside me flutters with excitement. My sister is going to see my home. It's the first home I've lived in without her. Even when I picked it out, she was the one I was thinking about. She was the one I most wanted to show it to. Now she's here.

I see the column of her throat bob with a swallow. I run around the front of my car to open her door. The fact that she doesn't have a bag or even a purse hits me hard. She's always had the barest minimal needs, but the reality of her earthly possessions being the clothes on her body is a lot. Growing up, she owned two salwar kameezes. One pair of jeans and some T-shirts that Glen had bought us. She only wore those for lack of choice.

It's not like either of us could have thrown away clothes that weren't in tatters. Every piece of clothing I've ever bought sits in my little closet. When you've experienced having nothing, you don't get rid of things when you do have them.

The musty smell of the boxboard cupboard we shared as girls fills my head. The memory brings with it an unbearable onslaught of emotions, so much pain and fear, but also the safety of my sister's presence. I haven't let myself feel any of it in so long. I open the door for Rupi and try to give her my hand. She doesn't take it.

I want to turn to Prem, but he's standing a few feet away from me. There's an odd stiffness to him. A coldness I've never seen before. It's like I've broken something between us. But he's still here.

Rupi pulls herself out of the car on unsteady feet. I try to meet Prem's eyes, but he avoids my gaze.

I lead her to my nondescript wooden front door with its faded varnish. I use the keys to let us in. I steel myself for her to say something harsh, to flick her whip, to yank me down to earth. But one step into my little apartment, and her eyes soften into wide, bright pools of emotion. Everything I'm feeling in my heart is in her eyes.

Her gaze travels from the tiny open kitchen to the living room with a rug with some pillows standing in for a couch. She walks across the narrow space and into the bedroom, where there is real furniture, a bed with a bright sheet set covered in yellow flowers, and my little potted garden.

"What are their names?" she asks.

I have to fight the tears that rush into my eyes. "There's five of them, so I named them for the Pandavas."

"Of course." She steps closer and touches the leaves. "Let me guess. Bheem," she says, stroking the giant kadi patta.

I want to wrap my arms around her, but I no longer know how.

Growing up, we used to covet our neighbor's lush balcony plants. Then one day when we were walking along one of the office buildings near our home, Rupi noticed a gardener planting some yellow-and-red crotons. She squared her shoulders and walked up to him and asked if she could have one.

"Sure, little girl," he said and gave her a generous cutting. He also grabbed her hand and smiled at her, completely ignoring me hiding behind her.

Rupi smiled back and licked her lips. The man was so surprised, his grip loosened. Taking advantage, Rupi snatched her hand away and broke into a run, dragging me along, screaming, "Go die, you letchy bastard" over her shoulder.

As we ran home, I was terrified that he'd give us chase, but Rupi was fearless. She understood the power of a public place. When we got home, unfollowed, we fished an oilcan out of the dump behind our building. Together we washed it out and made a hole in its bottom. Then I helped her fill the can with dirt from the unpaved strip edging the road. We stuck the pink-and-yellow cutting into the soil and stared at it for a long time.

Rupi watered it every day. She collected the skins from the copious amounts of bananas our mother ate and soaked them to use the water to fertilize Rukhmini. By the time I left Mumbai, Rukhmini had climbed all the way up the metal grille enclosing the balcony of our flat. A living wall of the most beautifully colored leaves that we made together. Even now, when I think about the home that had sheltered me for the first twenty years of my life, the thing I see in my mind's eye is that thick wall of leaves.

"Did you want to have a shower and freshen up?" I ask, watching her watch my garden of Pandavas.

"The soil is a little dry. You aren't watering them enough."

I don't respond. I don't want the gruff criticism to make me smile, but it does.

"You should soak banana skins in the water a few times a week."

"I do, didi," I say, and it snaps her out of the trance. I catch the same memories that just rose up inside me in her eyes.

"Good," she says. "I know how you rich people like to waste money on buying fertilizer in the store."

"Not that rich yet," I say, and she looks around and harrumphs as though I just said the shallowest, most materialistic thing ever.

I probably did, because now that she's here and she's seen the tiny little world I've built, it suddenly feels enough.

ELEVEN

RUPI

The hot spray of the shower hitting me might be the best feeling I've ever experienced in my entire life. I want to open my mouth and drink in the comfort. I want my pores to gape like a colander and rain on my parched insides. There's shampoo—real lathering shampoo. It's been so long since I've felt lather against my scalp. In Matthew's studio's powder room, I used a washcloth and hand soap in the sink through the winter. In the summer, I discovered the public showers by North Beach and walked there to partake. But those showers had nothing on this.

I practically scrape off the surface of my scalp with the force of my scrubbing. I avoid the scar across the back of my head, even as it tightens with sensation and memories. I ignore everything but the relief of soap and water against my body. Rubbing and rubbing until my skin pinkens and turns raw. The ink on my arms and thighs brightens. My signature watercolor style has the versatility of an amphibian. The fire lilies that bloom through the flames blaze to life, the fire and petals indistinguishable. Flowers that can grow only on the ashes of an inferno—the destruction and the beauty separates and rejoins—the canvas of my body speaking to me and for me.

This is the reason I love my work so much. Tattoos are the only permanent gift you can give yourself. A freezing in time. A moment immortalized on the only thing that stays with you forever: your physical being. Apparently there are monks in the Himalayas who spend days creating intricate masterpieces with colored sand, and then when the art is complete, they sweep away their labor. A practice to reinforce that nothing is permanent; that life is about the journey, not the destination; that attachment brings with it sorrow and moves you away from peace.

Tattoos are the opposite. Tattoos help you hold on. The point isn't the doing—it's the after, which fully erases what came before. Tattoos make you a new you. The attachment is only to yourself. If you don't even own your own self, you own nothing.

I study the many jars and bottles lined up in the corner shelves of Simi's bathroom. Sugar scrub. I know my sister isn't snacking on her beauty products, but imagining it makes me smile, nonetheless. Simi's always been obsessed with sugar. Probably my fault, because it was a simple comfort I always tried to provide. Swiping money from Ma and the stepclowns to buy Simi treats was even more entertaining than the TV we loved so much.

But what about you, didi, Simi always asked. *Don't you like chocolate?*

I'm already too sweet, Chipku. You'll get a toothache if I get any sweeter, since you're always stuck to me.

Why didn't anyone tell you until you were too old that attachment was a bad thing? That it caused the kind of pain that could kill you piece by piece.

For the first twenty-five years of my life, I believed that the tighter I was connected to my sister, the better our chance of survival. It was impossible to imagine existing without her. Turns out I was right. Look at the mess I made of my life after I lost her.

After my luxurious shower, I step into the bedroom with its forest of tropical plants and fluffy bed. Simi said to help myself to whatever clothes I need. She even took away my old clothes so I wouldn't be able to wear them again. There are advantages and disadvantages to being known so well.

When Simi gave me a quick tour, she showed me her closet. It was like a tiny room all on its own. Probably half the size of our room growing up. I remember running a hand over the neat piles of clothes and stopping on a soft black T-shirt. Now it calls my name. I walk to the closet door and pull it open.

A man stands across the room.

Before I register I've opened the wrong door, he turns to me.

Instead of gasping in shock, or apologizing and turning away, he just stands there, eyes widening ever so slightly. He makes no other movement as my towel starts slipping down my body. He waits to see what I will do. Watching him is like watching time slow.

I've always had this thing inside me—this person who takes over when I'm faced with strange situations. *Real Rupi.* That's who I've always thought of this other person as. Real Rupi likes to watch things unfold. She likes to toss water in smoking-hot oil to see what might happen. She's an observer, never a participant, on the outside of destruction, waiting to see how far it will go. Real Rupi lets the towel fall.

The man blinks. His eyes follow the towel as it descends my body and pools around my ankles. Without lingering any more than that, he looks back at my eyes. That's it.

I can't be sure if it's been one second or one minute since I opened the door, thinking it was the closet. I push the door shut without picking up the towel. His eyes remain locked with mine. There's nothing in them. Not any of the things I've always seen in eyes when they take me in. When he disappears behind the door, I'm acutely aware of two things. That the man had the darkest, most dangerous eyes of anyone I've ever met, and he saw all of me without showing me anything of himself.

TWELVE

RUPI

"This is my friend Saj," Prem says. "He's an immigration attorney. He has some questions for you."

"I'll bet he does," I say, hating that I don't want to meet the man's gaze, which shows no memory of our meeting minutes ago.

How did I get the door to the closet wrong? Who the hell thought putting a regular door on a closet was a good idea?

This man, Saj, doesn't react. I'm not sure if he's heard me.

He's tall and as dark skinned as Simi's rasgulla is light skinned. His brows are slashes across his forehead, and his jaw is an almost perfect square trapping gaunt hollows. There are shadows under his eyes. He looks like the angel of death. That's probably why he became an immigration lawyer. No one but the most desperate would work with someone who looks like this. I expect a scar to be running down his cheek, but his skin is smooth and unmarred, which makes me inexplicably angry. The fact that he's making my anger pop to the surface like this makes me even angrier.

"So, what do you think?" Saj asks, taking me by surprise. His voice is the exact opposite of the rest of him: warm and nonthreatening.

"About what?" I say.

"He has some questions, Rupi. He's the lawyer who's going to help with your visa," Simi explains in a voice used to talk to children. She's pouring chai into four mismatched cups.

I focus on the smell of ginger, cardamom, and black tea steeped in milk. It's been so long since this aroma brightened my senses that my legs feel weak. I want to reach out and lean on the kitchen counter, but my audience already sees me as helpless, and I've had about enough of that.

I pick up the biggest of the four cups and take it to the pillows laid out on the floor. "Of course I'll answer his questions. It's not like I have a choice."

He's obviously good at keeping secrets since Simi and Prem don't have the slightest clue that he just saw me stark naked, and as far as he's concerned, I'm the woman his friend wants to marry. I'm getting not a clue of what he thinks about any of that.

The three of them join me on the floor with their own cups.

"So, tell me about your situation," Saj says, taking a sip.

"My situation is that I have no papers or proof of who I am. The only evidence that I exist is that I'm sitting here. I own absolutely nothing other than the clothes on my bare body." I pause, but there's not even a flicker of a reaction to my allusion to nakedness. "Actually, these are my sister's, so I own nothing more than what's under them."

Still nothing. "The more significant thing is how that came about." He crosses his legs and takes the posture of the Buddha. There's a legal pad sitting next to him that he's brought to the party. "How did you lose everything?"

I try not to laugh but fail. I throw a look at Simi. "Where would we start? When I was born, or when you were born? Or when you left to come to America?"

Honestly I can barely remember life before our mother had Simi. My only tangible memory from before that is our father leaving after telling our very pregnant mother that he knew Simi wasn't his. *If they aren't yours, then why are they mine?* That was Ma's response. Another memory ripples inside me like a tremor in my heart: waking up at night to soothe and feed newborn Simi, who slept pressed against me, and thinking, *You are mine.*

"Why don't you start with how you came to America?" Saj says, picking up the pad.

"Sure." So, I start there. "Soon after our mother died, I met this American couple, Ron and Tina. They were visiting Mumbai, and they came into the restaurant in Andheri where I worked as a hostess. Tina was impressed with my tattoos. When I told her I'd done them myself, she was blown away."

I pause for Saj to react to the fact that I'm a tattoo artist. He doesn't.

So, I go on. "I gave Tina the address of the parlor I worked at. It was common for customers at the restaurant to ask about my tattoos and want them. Tina and Ron showed up at the parlor. Tina wanted an Om on her butt."

Simi and Prem narrow their eyes. The Om is a sacred Hindu symbol. The butt, obviously, isn't the best location for sacred symbols.

Saj shows the first flash of amusement. "You refused."

"At first. But then they offered me enough money that it would have been idiotic to refuse. So, I gave her the Om she desired. I simply mirror imaged it, so it wasn't an Om at all. Obviously neither Tina nor Ron noticed."

Simi grins with satisfaction. Saj's eyes return to being inscrutable.

"Tina loved it so much that she wanted Ron to get a matching one. So, I did another reverse Om at the center of an elaborate mandala on another butt cheek. The money was more than I made at the restaurant in six months. After a week spent inking their butts, they adopted me as their local friend and asked me to show them around Mumbai."

Growing up, I barely saw much of Mumbai outside our neighborhood. Even the restaurant and the tattoo parlor weren't too far from our flat. I never had a desire to fly the nest. Not because I loved the nest but because, given what the nest was like, I had little hope for the rest of the world. Whatever little I knew about safety, it was in that flat, which was the most darkly ironic thing ever. But I did know I had to get my sister out.

After Simi left, the dead thing inside me had died a little more. Whatever there was in that flat that held me tightened around me. But Ron and Tina were relentless, and with everything else going on with the blackmailing cop, I forced myself out of my bubble. Prem and Saj don't need to know any of this, and Simi already does, so I restrict my narrative to the relevant parts.

"Ron and Tina were friendly and generous. It wasn't something I had any experience with. It was easy enough to show them around Mumbai and satisfy their hunger for local flavor. By the end of that second week, I had an offer to go back to LA with them. They owned a restaurant and said I would be a perfect hostess."

I remember wondering how it could possibly be that easy. It had taken a lot of money and years of planning to get Simi to America. Simi's initial effusive daily emails had trickled to one a week after the first year, then pretty much dried up to one every few weeks. I hadn't allowed myself to miss my sister until the idea that I might actually be able to see her again presented itself.

None of that is relevant, either, so I just tell them that I refused the offer.

Saj asks his first question. "Why?"

"Because trusting people I'd known for just a few weeks was stupid." And yet it was so tempting.

Saj nods for me to go on.

"Ron was surprisingly disappointed." Which, now that I think about it, might have shrunk the size of Tina's disappointment a little. I didn't notice anything but affection between them back then. "Ron tried hard to change my mind, offered me money, a ticket, an apartment when I got to LA. He even went with me to the passport office and got me an expedited passport. Then he took me to the US consulate and got me to apply for a tourist visa. He paid all the fees. I was shocked when my visa came through."

The day I got the visa was the first time escape felt like a real possibility. Until then I didn't dare to believe anything Ron offered. The blackmailing cop breathing down my neck was becoming more and more unbearable.

"I still didn't think I could leave. Ron didn't pressure me more and left with a promise to send money and a ticket if I changed my mind."

"How did your mother die?" Saj asks, interrupting my thoughts.

I've been avoiding Simi's eyes, but now my gaze strays to her. I want to tell him that this has no relevance to the case, but something tells me to tread carefully. He can't suspect that I'm withholding anything.

"Kidney failure."

"This was before your sister left India?"

I very badly want to ask where he's going with this, but I don't. "Yes, she got sick before Simi left but died after she left."

"So, you cared for your mother yourself? What about your dad?"

"Our dad left before I was born," Simi says, speaking for the first time. "When Rupi was four. Our mother was . . ." She throws a wary look Prem's way, and I realize she hasn't told Prem about our childhood. "She was married four times after that. Her last husband died a little before she did."

"How?"

"How what?" I snap, unable to stop myself.

"How did her last husband die?" he elaborates calmly.

I force myself to reflect his calm. "He was found dead at work. He fell and hit his head."

"Hmm," Saj says. "This was before Simi left?"

"Yes," Simi says before I snap again and ask what he's digging for.

"How did your mother meet him?"

It's becoming impossible to not sound defensive. "He was her dialysis nurse."

"So, he was her primary caregiver."

"No, I was." I was always the one to take care of Ma, even before she got sick. The only husband who ever did it was Glen. Vivek, who made it to Husband Number Five just in time to poison a dying woman for her flat, was no Glen.

"Simi, you're a nurse, aren't you?" Saj asks.

Simi nods.

"And you got your nursing training in India? Was that influenced by your stepfather?"

I don't know what this guy is trying to get at with these questions, but I don't think I want him to be my lawyer anymore. Then again, maybe I need someone exactly like him.

"No," Simi says. "I was already done with my nursing program and was working on my licensing exams when our mother met him."

"Okay, so, when you left India, your mother was sick?"

"Yes, she was already in a coma with no hope of recovery. And my training program here in Kentucky was starting."

"She had an opportunity," I say. "She had to take it. We knew our mother was never waking up. There was no reason for Simi to stay."

"So, you're the one who insisted she take the opportunity?"

"I encouraged her to take it, yes."

"How long after Simi left did your mother die?"

"Six months."

"I'm sorry," Saj says. Even his sympathy is robotic.

Simi thanks him.

"And how long after that did you meet Ron?"

"A year and a half after Simi left. A year after our mom died."

He notes something on his legal pad, which he's been scribbling on off and on. "So, what changed your mind about taking Ron up on his offer?"

"I'm not sure," I say, pushing away the darkness of the memories of that time. "I think it was between the shock of actually getting the visa, a feeling of loneliness, and the hope of seeing my sister again."

"That must have been quite the reunion," Saj says. "Meeting your sister after two years."

"I never did get to meet her. Not until now."

"Why?"

"Because of what happened when I got to LA."

"Tell me what happened," Saj says, his spear-sharp pencil hovering over his legal pad. The page is already covered in neat, methodical writing.

"I'm getting to it," I say. Then I take a breath and tell them the rest.

Ron picked me up from the airport by himself. Tina was nowhere in sight. In fact, in the year that I lived in LA and worked at the restaurant, I saw Tina only a couple of times, and she ignored me completely both times. At first, I wondered if I got it wrong and that Tina wasn't Ron's wife but just someone he had traveled with. Turns out Tina was, indeed, the wife. When I asked Ron, he told me to ignore her and said she'd only been that happy in India because she'd been on vacation and high, which, according to Ron, was her general state.

Ron took me from the airport to a hotel, where he tried to kiss me. It was something he'd never before done. I was surprised, but when I told him I was tired (I wasn't. I was super excited and nervous), he backed off.

Then he took me to a McDonald's for dinner and bought me a chicken sandwich, fries, an apple pie, and a huge milkshake. He said he'd already eaten and watched me eat the entire thing.

After that he dropped me off at a hotel, where despite not thinking I was tired, I fell into a half-awake sleep with the door dead bolted. At the front of my mind, I still believed the fairy tale I wove for myself: that friends, a job, and a safe life awaited me in America, along with my sister. But somewhere at the very back of my mind, the truth lurked. I knew the moment I saw the expression on Ron's face when I pulled away from his kiss that I had made a mistake. That life would always be as I'd known it. Just sinkholes and land mines.

From then on, things unfolded in the most bad-movie, predictable manner. I might as well have been an actress in a horror film who followed the scream into the dark forest instead of running in the opposite direction. Ron tried again the next morning to come in for a kiss, but when I pulled away for a second time, he asked me to pack and took me to the restaurant.

Curry, Ron's Indian restaurant, was a dimly lit, seedy joint with velvet curtains, cheap bronze statuettes, and some twenty tables covered in red-and-gold chintz tablecloths. It was nothing like the fancy eatery he described in India. The food was cooked mostly by Jesús and his two assistants from Mexico. Indian students worked as servers in the evenings and weekends. The employees were all polite with me but skittish. Apparently, I was not the first "girlfriend" Ron had installed to "keep an eye" on the employees.

Some of the waitstaff consisted of pretty young South Asian girls dressed in very tight sequined cholis over very tight embroidered skirts. They all wore long braided black-hair wigs, lined their eyes with dark kohl, had nose rings, and wore bindis. They were always assigned to a particular kind of table of raucous, heavily drinking men. The girls often left when the men left.

They barely ever spoke to the other employees. In turn, we ignored them too. Basically everyone ignored everyone. That was the culture at Curry, and it was so potent that within days of getting there, I became just as skittish and suspicious as everyone else. Not that I hadn't already been those things before I got there.

We all did our jobs. Served the drunk crowd that showed up for dinner starting at 7 p.m. and then stayed until 2 a.m., leaving behind so much filth that the two servers and I took four hours to wash the beer-sticky floors, tables, and utensils. Jesús cleaned the kitchen and put away the leftovers, which would be used for the lunch take-out orders the next day.

No one questioned how a place this wretched stayed so busy. It certainly wasn't the food. Even so, I saw, smelled, served, and packed so much butter chicken, dal makhani, and saag paneer that if I never see those dishes again in my lifetime, I'll be okay. Even now the memory makes me want to bring up my tea.

There were a couple of rooms above the restaurant, and Ron gave me one with a mattress on the floor to live in. I think Jesús and a few of the other staff lived in the other room. I never asked. The culture of silence that permeated the staff was absolute. No one even made eye contact. Everyone obviously lived in terror of deportation and being arrested.

Ron had taken my passport for "safekeeping" the day I got in. When he left me at the restaurant, he warned me not to leave the premises or tell anyone anything about myself, because I was not legally allowed to work there. He promised not to tell anyone that he was paying me in room and board. Apparently not needing to pay rent or pay for food was a deal anyone in my situation would kill for.

After two months of working twenty-hour days, seven days a week, and never leaving the dingy restaurant, and not seeing Ron, I started to fear that I was never getting out of this situation. At the end of two months, he showed up to give me the promised tour of LA.

As we drove around LA, I let him kiss me and touch me, and I made sure I liked it. What I didn't like was that smelly, bug-infested room above the restaurant and the idea of ever having to wear those cholis and skirts. Ron told me he had an apartment in Koreatown that I was going to love. I told him how lucky I felt that he thought that.

He was right. I did love his apartment. It had real furniture and sunlight. If navigating Ron's vile breath and sweaty body while having sex was the price for it, then it wasn't that high a price. He only visited the apartment a few times a week, and his visits came with a trip to the grocery store.

Those ten months were the most peaceful months of my life. I worked—turns out Ron owned another restaurant, Tikka, where he moved me—and slept in a clean bed and let Ron talk about himself and allowed him access to my body. Fortunately listening to him talk about himself was much more frequent than the other part of the job.

I never asked about Tina, but after a few scotches, complaining about his wife took up as much weight as talking about himself. Her materialism, her constant need for validation, her laziness. He was always buying her happiness, with jewelry and bags and clothes and fillers. One weekend when Tina was in Cancún with her girlfriends, Ron took me to the home he shared with her. A McMansion in Palos Verdes with a pool and palm trees.

We had sex on Tina and Ron's bed. It was the most vigorous Ron had ever been. When he showed me Tina's closet, I wanted to throw up. There were more shoes and bags and clothes than I'd ever seen in a store. He showed me her jewelry, describing the indiscretions (his) and tantrums (hers) that went with each piece.

He knew I wouldn't touch any of it. He knew I had nowhere to run to if I stole something. He knew me as well as any owner knew his caged birds.

I missed Simi terribly, but that was not a life I wanted her to see me in. Ron sure as hell wasn't getting anywhere near her.

I played the role to perfection. So much so that Ron swore he was never letting me go. I never asked for a thing, never talked about myself, and listened with rapt interest. I kept the apartment spotless—much cleaner and tidier than when he first moved me there. I had no curiosity about any of the shady goings-on at Curry or about how Tikka stayed in business with barely any customers. I didn't care. So long as I had a roof over my head and food to eat, and no cops knocking on my door, what did I care?

The vacation ended when Ron was hit by a drunk driver. I was at the restaurant when I found out from Jesús. He'd also been moved to Tikka a few months after me. Together, the two of us removed all the cash from the register—a total of $2,000 and change. We split it, and then he packed up and left, which meant I had to do the same. When I got to the apartment, I saw that Tina and a couple of her cronies had already made it there and were having the locks changed.

I turned around and made my way to Ron and Tina's home. I'd memorized the code Ron used to open the front door. I searched the house for my passport but had no luck. So, I made my way to Ron's closet and picked up a backpack, a Lakers hat, and a pair of diamond cuff links. I picked out the pieces of jewelry from Tina's stash that seemed to have the largest diamonds. Then I helped myself to a few pairs of her jeans and T-shirts, some snacks from the pantry, and a pair of sneakers that amazingly fit perfectly, then went to the bus station. For the next six months, I traversed the country on trains and buses until I found myself on a CTA train in Chicago, where I met Matthew.

Obviously, I give them the PG-13 version of the story. Not that one needs much of an imagination to fill in the NC-18 parts. I don't mention the blackmailing cop in Mumbai or taking the documents from Ron's closet. That information is a little more than I want to reveal.

When I finish, the room is so quiet, I can separate the sound of each person's breathing.

Simi and her rasgulla have tears in their eyes. Usually sympathy makes me sick to my stomach, but Simi looks like she's in enough pain that I'm the one who feels sympathy for her.

Saj's eyes are as flat and opaque as the black granite in Ron's kitchen.

"Any more questions?" I ask him.

"Several, but first you should know that you were trafficked into the country." A blast of hot rage slips into his eyes, but he leashes it. "We can put Tina away, get you justice. Will you be okay pressing charges?"

This time the laugh that bursts from me is so loud, it makes my breath hiccup. "Justice?" I say. How cute. "Can you bring Ron back from the dead and have him pay? Even if you could, he was actually the one person who at least gave me something in return for what he took from me. That's more than anyone else has ever done. All I want is to not have to go back to India. Can you make that happen? That's all the justice I want."

THIRTEEN

SIMI

I knew ring shopping for my sister's engagement to my boyfriend wasn't going to be easy, but the stab of pain I feel is still shockingly intense.

It doesn't help that Prem is refusing to meet my eyes, and Rupi is in full nonchalance mode. It's always been her best defense.

"Are they completely out of their minds?" Rupi says, not bothering to lower her voice so as not to ruin the moment for the other customers. "Do people actually walk around with a year's rent on their finger? Why? For what possible reason?"

The salesperson clears his throat. "It's a celebration of your love," he says, forcing a smile. "Because you're worth it, ma'am." It's a sentiment his face fights hard to commiserate with.

Rupi is unimpressed with his effort. "I'm worth a colorless stone that looks like broken glass?"

He looks at Prem, half sympathy, half cry for help.

Another wasted effort. Prem looks like he isn't even here.

Saj waits a beat for Prem to say something, then jumps to his rescue. "It's a stone Prem wants to get you because he wants people to know how much he loves you." Saj is here because he needs pictures of the engagement. Yesterday, after Rupi gave us her story and issued Saj a challenge, Saj left with a promise to come back with a plan. Today, he came back with ring shopping as the first order of business.

Rupi balks. "Do people in this town have vision issues? Can they not see a smaller stone?" This is the hill she's choosing to die on right now?

Saj looks confused. "No, but a bigger diamond makes a bigger statement. I think Prem wants to make a big statement. Right, Prem?"

"Right," Prem says, and if Saj hears the despondency in it, he doesn't react.

"It's the way they do it here," I say, because Rupi is looking at me like she's lost her ability to understand the world. "It will strengthen our case," I add in a whisper.

"Fine, then why don't you pick out one you like," she says so casually that it's obvious she doesn't have any idea how much I'm hurting.

Prem looks like someone just stuck a knife in his chest. "Simi will not be the one picking out this ring," he says, looking at me like the sight of me in pain is destroying him.

I want to go to him, but I stay by my sister's side. "I don't mind," I say. I need to get this over with. I point at a simple band setting with a pea-size diamond.

Rupi looks at the price tag and turns a few shades paler. "There is no way. Why can't we buy a fake one? Don't they have those cubic zirconia?"

Once again Saj waits for Prem to say something. He doesn't. So, Saj says it himself. "Prem's mom and my sister will know it's a fake in a second."

"Do they have magic eyes?" Rupi says.

"Just buy the damn thing," Prem says.

"Why, thank you, honey," Rupi snaps.

The salesperson looks from Rupi to Prem.

"It's been a long few days," I say apologetically. "We'll take this one."

The one-and-a-half carat lab-made diamond is big enough to make sure everyone believes in the authenticity of this fake relationship.

Rupi is not wrong. The price tag is preposterous. I can't let Prem pay for this. He's going to fight me on it, but I have to pay him back. Not in the store, of course. Here, I stand by and let him do the honors. That receipt is going to be evidence for the USCIS.

"Congratulations." The salesperson shakes Prem's hand, and we leave the man to enjoy his relief at getting rid of us.

"Let's get a picture," Saj says.

Prem slides the ring on Rupi's finger right there outside the store as Saj captures the moment.

I feel like someone is stripping the skin off my body.

Prem refuses to look at me. There are tears in his eyes. He looks shaken by the moment, and Saj's pictures take that fact and feed it perfectly into the fiction we're creating.

Saj squeezes his shoulder. "No need to be shy, Prem. Some PDA will only help your case."

Rupi and Prem hug. Saj takes another picture.

That's when it strikes me that Saj doesn't know about Prem and me. He thinks Prem really is with Rupi.

It stings. I have no right to feel this way. I'm the one who chose to keep our relationship secret. Prem was respecting my wishes when he didn't tell anyone about us. Not even his best friend. And now I've all but forced Prem into this arrangement with Rupi. I know the love isn't in the ring, it's in what Prem is doing for me, but my brain refuses to process any of that.

Rupi stands there, performing for the camera. My clothes hang on her body, and the food poisoning has painted shadows under her eyes. I can barely recognize her eyes anymore. All the warmth is gone, burned away by an angry fire.

For years I've felt like I'm hiking up a mountain without rest. My nursing program in Mumbai involved attending school and working long hours at the hospital for three years, then studying for my licensing exams while working and applying for jobs in the US, then taking the NCLEX and going through my pediatric fellowship, all while moving across the world, and then working three jobs to pay off the loans I took to get here. But when I heard what Rupi has been through, every bit of the sense of achievement I felt disappeared. All I feel is shame.

Prem and Saj haven't asked me why I didn't bother to help my sister or how I didn't figure out something was wrong for two years. I can't stop asking myself that question. How could I have failed her so badly? Granted, Rupi never let me know she needed help, but in my heart I knew. I never pushed because I was too afraid of the truth. I feel as small as a dust mite and far more harmful. I don't know who I'm more angry with: me or her.

Rupi and Prem smile into each other's faces as they pose. I try not to be sick. Not that anyone will notice if I am.

I'm still in shock that she poured out her entire story in front of Saj and Prem. Saj is really good at his job if she trusted him so easily. He has one of those larger-than-life presences. I'm almost afraid of him. Maybe that's it. Rupi hates being intimidated. Maybe she was trying to intimidate him with her truth.

Saj finishes taking pictures and congratulates Prem and Rupi. I want to do it, too, but the words won't come out.

Prem's gaze finally slides to me, and I want to crumple to the floor. There's so much pain there but also a challenge.

When we left my apartment this morning, I took him aside and asked if he was sure he wanted to do this.

I'm absolutely sure I don't want to do this. But I also can't think of another way to help you help your sister. I'm doing this for you, Simi. You have to promise to remember that. This will only ever be a marriage on paper.

God, I hope he meant that. I love my sister, but I also know how superior she is to me in every way, and the idea of Prem seeing that and then choosing her makes my heart feel like it's being ripped down the middle.

If we were in a rom-com, that's what would happen. Prem and Rupi would fall in love.

What if that happens? a voice inside me keeps asking. Am I tempting fate? Am I taking my relationship for granted? The answer to both those questions is yes, but the question I don't have an answer to yet is, Will this push things too far to ever recover what Prem and I had?

They're going to get married. *Legally married.* Every movie I've ever watched with this plot insists that there is sanctity, magic to that bond. It develops into love even when it doesn't start out as such.

Then again there's my mother, who refuted that theory over and over. Marriage was just something you could do with as many people as you wished, for whatever reason you wished.

The way Prem looks at me, I know he can see the storm churning inside me. It's churning inside him too.

My sister watches him watching me and rolls her eyes. Despite what Prem is doing for her, Rupi can't seem to stand him. I just don't understand it.

I feel an intense surge of anger, and I can't bear it. I turn away from them and walk to Saj's car and get into the back seat. I need a moment. In under a minute, Prem gets in next to me. I can't look at him right now.

Rupi and Saj get in the front. Saj turns to Prem, but before he can say anything, Prem says, "Just drive, please."

The moment Saj starts driving, Prem grabs my face and kisses the heck out of me.

For a moment no one else exists in the car. Nothing else exists in the world. I love this man so much, all of me hurts.

I'm doing this for you. It's like his hands on my face, his tongue in my mouth, are screaming the words. *I can't lose you over this.*

Saj clears his throat.

I break our kiss and lean my forehead against Prem's. He's still holding my face. His face is wet.

"Okay, then," Saj says. "I did not see that coming."

Well, he knows about Prem and me now.

"As your lawyer I feel obliged to warn you that you should never do that in public again," Saj says. "I think you left something out."

No one responds.

"This is fucked up, Prem," Saj says finally.

"Did you not know they're in *luurve*?" Rupi says with the most heartless callousness.

Prem's eyes are squeezed shut. He's refusing to let go of me. I guess Rupi's dislike for him is not one sided.

"All he told me yesterday is that he needs to marry you to make sure you stay in the country," Saj says, piecing the mess together. "And there was some urgency because you were hospitalized and there were cops involved."

"And you assumed he was in love with me."

"We haven't exactly had the time to sort through everything. You okay back there, Prem?"

A laugh that sounds more like a sob escapes Prem.

"Just great," Rupi says. "He's not going to be able to follow through. I should have known."

"Rupi!" I say. "Can you give him a break, please."

"Whatever is going on, we have to figure it out fast, because once I file those papers with the USCIS, there's no going back," Saj says.

"So, you'll still help us?" I ask.

For a while he doesn't respond. Then he throws a look at Prem over his shoulder. "Prem? You're going to involve your parents, your family. What are you planning to tell them?"

Prem looks at me.

The idea of facing his family right now is unbearable to me. I can't imagine how he's feeling.

I've taken the day off at the clinic, but I have to be at Preeti's for the triplets this afternoon. I'm surprised Preeti isn't blowing up my phone. She's probably feeling guilty about whatever betrayal she imagines her brother inflicted on me.

"How is it anyone's business if we sign a piece of paper or not?" Rupi says. "Why can't we all just go about our lives the way we always have?" She waves a hand at Prem and me. "You continue to do whatever it is you two do together. I find something to do around here that pays my bills. Then when they give me a green card, we get divorced and you marry him. Why does it have to be more complicated than that?"

"That's not how this works," Saj says. "You'll only get a provisional green card when you get married, and only if you're able to convince the government that your marriage is real. This is just the first step. For the next two years you have to convince the United States immigration control that you did not get married only for a green card. You have to prove to them that it's a real marriage. You only get a permanent green card after that."

"Wait!" I say. "Did you say *two years*?"

"Oh god," Prem says.

"Yes, the green card will be provisional for two years," Saj says. "If you get divorced before that, or if they suspect your marriage isn't real, the green card will be revoked, and you'll have to leave the country."

Finally Rupi looks concerned. "Why do they care? What is a real marriage anyway? Isn't every marriage a marriage because a piece of paper says so? How does one even prove that a marriage is real? Do they crawl in bed with you to make sure there is sex involved? Does the government run around making sure all married couples are really *married*?"

"No," Saj says. "But those people aren't getting the huge privilege of a United States residency out of their union. And yes, you do need to state under oath that your marriage is a real and healthy marriage before you even get a provisional green card."

"Healthy marriage?" Rupi says with disdain. "Isn't that an oxymoron? Do they scan your heart to see if it pumps daisies when you're with your spouse?"

"I'm not a fan of marriage either. But I don't make the laws, and I'm certainly not the one who will be impacted if I can't convince them."

I like this guy.

Rupi doesn't respond.

"What kind of proof are we talking about?" I say.

Saj looks at me in the rearview mirror, and his eyes are filled with sympathy. I hate nothing more than being pitied.

"There will be a team of experts assigned to assess the authenticity of the relationship." He throws a look Rupi's way. "We'll have to provide proof of your courtship. There will be interviews with the two of you and also with family, friends, workplace colleagues. Which means you have to convince everyone that you're in love and you intend to spend the rest of your lives together."

"Two years?" Prem repeats the words like they're a death sentence. "What happens if we can't prove it? What happens if we're found out?"

"She will be deported and probably banned from ever entering the United States again. And you can be fined or even go to jail."

"And my family? Can they get in trouble?"

"Well, that's not an easy answer. You should know that if you've decided to do this"—he doesn't say the words *commit fraud*, but he manages to communicate exactly that—"then you are putting the people who know your real reasons for doing it in danger of legal action."

"Oh god," Prem says. "Can they really get in trouble if they know?"

I never considered that involving Prem's family in this might put them in danger.

"If your case is held in review, then yes. Given the problems with her visa status, chances are they'll suspect that you're marrying for a green card and we'll need to provide statements from friends and family as additional evidence. In which case, them lying can amount to immigration fraud."

"There's absolutely no way that I can let that happen," Prem says.

"What happens if he backs out now?" Rupi says, and every hint of amusement is gone from her.

"The first thing I'm going to do is initiate the process to petition for the extension of your tourist visa. If it goes through, you'll get, at best, a month before you have to leave the country."

"And at worst, they'll deny it and deport me immediately."

"Yes."

"I'm not leaving," she says.

I can practically see the plans to run away forming in her head.

"There's always the option of making the case that you were trafficked and seeking asylum," Saj says.

"Can you stop with that?" Rupi says. "I was not forced to sleep with anyone. I lived with this man for close to a year. There is no way to prove that he forced me. I'm one hundred percent at fault here, legally. Even I know that. I don't want to talk about it anymore. But I cannot go back."

"You can if I go with you," I say. "We'll figure it out together."

"Don't be ridiculous, Simi," Rupi says. "That's not happening."

Prem finally speaks. "You're not going anywhere." His eyes burn into mine, every promise he's ever made to me shining there. "She's not going back either. We're getting married. Tell us what we have to do, Saj."

Saj pulls into a McDonald's parking lot and turns to Prem.

"Don't ask me if I'm sure," Prem says. "I am. But my family can't get hurt."

Saj nods. "It's a good thing that you have a good lawyer, then. I will make sure they don't get hurt. But I can only do that if we come up with a strategy and follow it to a T."

"And how do we do that?" I ask.

"We do it by sticking as close to the truth as we can. Which means you have to tell me the whole truth first. No more half truths and assumptions."

So, we sit there in Saj's super-fancy Mercedes and tell him everything that we left out yesterday, which comes down to the fact that I basically forced Prem to do this when he'd never even met my sister before. Then we let Saj tell us exactly how we're going to handle this, which comes down to the fact that we have to convince Prem's family and this entire town that the man I love and the sister who raised me are madly in love.

FOURTEEN

RUPI

If I believed that the United States Citizenship and Immigration Service was my greatest challenge, I was entirely wrong. That is going to be a walk in the park compared to the rasgulla's family.

It's disturbing how very much like the rasgulla the rest of them are. Each one of them is soft and cuddly and gives off the most annoying unbridled joy. No wonder their faces are so rounded—it's all that smiling. The cheek muscles must get quite the workout.

Even now when their golden son is springing a tattooed stranger on them, they're fighting the good fight to keep on smiling. Which doesn't mean every smile isn't uncomfortable as heck. Unless I'm projecting, because, wow, I've never felt this uncomfortable in my entire life.

The idea of all of them under one roof being super cheery all the time is exhausting. The brothers live in the house they grew up in with their parents, the way families traditionally used to in India. It's still a common practice there but much rarer than it used to be in generations past. You know where it isn't uncommon? In Indian soap operas. Those are still obsessed with joint families (so much scope for delicious drama).

This one is lined up at the wide front door under a brick portico held up by two massive columns. Around us, rows of neatly manicured topiaries look on at the spectacle.

A woman I recognize from the hospital holds a silver platter with an oil lamp.

Prem groans. "Mamma, can we not do this right now?"

"Did I say that to you when you went off and got engaged without telling anyone?" his mother says.

She has a point.

She beckons us to the threshold and rotates the aarti platter around our faces, touches the haldi and kumkum powders to our foreheads, sprinkles rice grains over us.

Her eyes are filled with focus. She's actually putting devotion into blessing the arrival of her prospective daughter-in-law into the home. I'm not a person who believes in rituals, or in anything really, but the expression on her face is so serene and filled with faith that even I can't come up with something snarky to think.

I search the faces lined up behind Prem's mother, looking for Simi. Simi left a little before us to go to Prem's sister's house. She was supposed to come over to this house with his sister and her family and meet us, but I don't see her.

Saj isn't here either. After handing out a long list of dos and don'ts, he left us to our own devices, which I hate to admit is a bit nerve racking.

Prem and I drove here in silence. Thank god the guy has it bad for my sister. For a moment there, I was sure I was going to have to find a way to disappear again. I'm not sure yet how long his bravado or his smitten-ness will last, but I'm not overwhelmed with confidence. I just need to get the marriage certificate signed so he can't change his mind.

His mother puts a piece of mithai in his mouth and then in mine too. "May having you join our family bring you and us good fortune and abundance," she says. There's an odd, determined kindness in her tone. Like she's not happy with how we've done this, but she refuses to be a bitch about it.

Saj's rumbly authoritative voice lingers in my ear. *If the family believes your relationship is real, then we have a fighting chance that everyone else will.*

I manufacture a demure smile, inspired by every soap heroine ever, and thank her.

When we step over the threshold and enter the house, everyone claps.

His mother gives Prem a look that makes him lean over and touch her feet.

I really don't want to. It's a common Indian practice, but I've never touched anyone's feet in my life. Our mother was many things, but the thing she was most proud of being was an iconoclast. She loved to announce how she didn't believe in nonsense like society's rules and rituals. We only ever saw people touching their elders' feet for blessings on TV, which was our real parent and guide for the entirety of our childhood.

I lean over and touch Prem's mother's feet the way I've seen it done on TV. She puts the aarti platter down on a console table and pulls me up (much like they do on TV). "You don't have to touch your mother-in-law's feet, beta. You just have to be honest with her."

Okay, then, the family talks about themselves in third person. I have the uncontrollable urge to laugh and run. It's official. I just walked into a true-to-life Hindi soap opera in the middle of small-town southern Kentucky, duly populated with sari-clad, bejeweled women, a grand mansion, family business, and a fake marriage.

I give her an innocent, wide-eyed smile.

The grand entrance foyer we're standing in rises two floors above us and has a chandelier that's fully on brand with the soap theme. It's just the sort of thing that can be used to kill someone off by tampering with it so it crashes on the hapless victim. Which genius came up with the idea of suspending sharp glass overhead anyway?

I step aside and out of its path—better safe than sorry—and encounter a whole line of overdressed people.

A hugging mob descends upon us.

Pawan, Prem's brother (even more soft bellied, creamy skinned, and teddy bearish than Prem): "We have so much to talk about, bro, but congratulations!"

Chandni, Pawan's wife (huge boobs, big hair, wide mouth, and an embroidered lehnga most Bollywood heroines would find too heavy even for their own wedding): "You owe me a new sari for the engagement and an extra one for keeping it secret, but congratulations!"

Dolly, Prem's mother's friend (crying actual tears and also in the kind of sari that might suggest there is an actual wedding in progress): "I've changed his diapers, did you know? But congratulations!"

Dwai, Dolly's husband (shockingly in a simple white kurta) remains silent as he hugs Prem, then me, so I have no idea if he has changed Prem's diapers or not.

Next come two women who help take care of Prem's father, who for some reason are also crying.

"Let's go say hello to Papa first," Prem's mother says, leading us past the receiving line through the most ornately decorated room I've ever been in. There's a sweeping staircase with carved wood balusters. Carved inlaid panels cover the wall, surrounding a huge fireplace with a mantel that's, you guessed it, heavily carved.

Parts that aren't covered in carved wood are covered in carpets. The Kashmiri kind. Intricate patterns of bright reds, blues, and greens freely mix together in motifs that range from peacocks to parrots and urns and towers. It's like a tattoo sleeve come to life in decor form.

She leads us to a bedroom that is exactly what I expected after all that harem-esque splendor. A heavily upholstered bed with a red velvet skirt, a tufted red velvet headboard, and red velvet curtains hanging from a valanced canopy. Gold cord edges everything.

Instead of the sheik of the harem, a frail man sits propped up on the bed against red silk pillows and bolsters. He looks almost like someone put an age filter on Prem and Pawan. He moves his head ever so slowly and looks at me.

"Pankaj, look who's here. Our Prem's future bride," Prem's mother says.

Pankaj's facial muscles barely move, but his eyes smile. He makes a sound, and Prem goes to him and wraps his arms around his father. He holds on for such a long time I could swear the boy is crying. His father lifts his arm, and his mother presses her husband's hand against Prem's back and holds it there.

Despite myself, my throat constricts. Come on! Look at this room! This is a comedy, not a tearjerker. But I do press my hands together in a namaste.

Pankaj's eyes smile brighter. One is slightly more focused than the other. It takes him an effort, but he lifts his arm just the slightest bit from the bed, and his thumb pops up from a loose fist as his eyes dance at his son. It takes me a moment to realize that he's giving us a thumbs-up. Then he pats the bed.

"Baba wants you to sit by him," Prem says, moving out of my way.

I sit.

It takes him another moment, but he lifts his right hand and touches it to his left arm, which seems to be entirely immobile.

He makes a sound that I don't understand.

Prem's mother looks at my arm. "He wants to see your tattoos." She's been avoiding looking at them this entire time.

I'm wearing one of Simi's salwar kameezes. My arms are longer than my sister's, and the sleeves stop part of the way down my forearm, exposing the part of me that makes so many people balk. I hold out my arm and pull up the sleeve past my elbow.

He studies it with the softest eyes and makes a sound that's something like *fife*.

His wife slides me a look. "He thinks they're nice," she says, only slightly grudgingly.

His eyes twinkle, and he makes a twisting motion with his hand. He's either asking me where I got them from or when or why.

"I started getting them when I was eighteen," I say, unable to tell the truth.

He twists his hand again.

"Most of them were done in Mumbai."

He gives me another thumbs-up sign, then very slowly he moves his hand to his chest.

I'm not sure if it's the tattoos or the mention of Mumbai that makes him touch his heart, but I say, "Thank you."

Just then the doorbell chirps and echoes through the house.

"The girls are here!" Prem's mother says, and veritable stars burst in his father's eyes.

Even Prem smiles a genuine smile for the first time.

Prem, his mother, his brother, his brother's wife, and the entire jingbang lot (who I hadn't realized had followed us into the room) file out to welcome what I'm assuming are the babies Simi babysits. I stay sitting on the bed, and Pankaj gives me another lopsided smile.

A startlingly handsome white man walks in with one baby on each arm behind a woman who was part of the ambush at the hospital. She, too, looks like a model and carries the third baby. I assume that's Preeti—Prem's sister, the babies' mother, and my sister's employer.

Behind them Simi trails in, arms filled with diaper bags.

Prem takes the bags from her and looks at her as though the sight of her is at once too tragic and too joyful to bear.

Simi ignores him. Her jaw is tightly clenched. She's going to wear off her tooth enamel if she doesn't loosen up.

The babies, who are unsurprisingly cute and surprisingly loud for creatures who can't talk yet, are deposited on the bed and promptly crawl all over their grandfather.

The man is so frail, I want to ask if that's safe, but no one else seems the least bit concerned.

For the next half hour pandemonium ensues. Everyone hugs everyone, and the party moves to the living room.

A huge quilt is put down over the peacock-splattered rug, and the triplets are let loose. Prem and his brother carry their father and deposit him with utmost gentleness against a mattress seat on the floor, where the girls can crawl to him.

Everyone else sets about bringing an absurd amount of food into the room and setting it on a sideboard and then dropping down on the floor or the extensive expanse of the sectional couch.

After a stiff hug when she got here, Simi has avoided meeting my eyes. The rest of them seem determined not to bring up the engagement-ring-shaped elephant in the room. It's like their son getting engaged to a stranger happens every day.

Prem's mom hands me a plate with a samosa, dhokla, bhajjias, and green and red chutney. The smell hits me hard. After the food poisoning, food smells have been making me gag.

One look at my face, and she pulls it back and smacks her head. "Oh no. Your stomach. I knew you wouldn't be able to eat any of this."

Why thank you, Mom-in-law.

"I'm fine." I try to take the plate from her out of politeness. I really need the woman to like me.

She hides it behind her back, as though I'm five and reaching for too much cake. "I'm an idiot. I did make you some khichdi and forgot all about it. Too much excitement, no?" She starts to walk away.

"That's not necessary. Truly." I follow her, trying not to think about how the mention of khichdi is making me drool.

"Come come," she says, "I want you to see the kitchen anyway." Suddenly she stops in her tracks and turns to me. "I don't mean that in a mean mother-in-law way. You don't have to do anything in the kitchen if you don't want to. We have people, and I love to cook. Chandni and Preeti hate to cook. But Prem and Pawan love it. It's all okay. Everything, everything is okay."

Are we still talking about cooking?

I have no idea how to respond, because I think she's trying to convince herself more than me. So, I say the first thing that pops into my head. "Thank you for being so nice. I know this was not what you were expecting for Prem." I hate to admit it, but she really is trying.

She looks at me with some surprise. *Oh,* her face says, *I was not expecting to have an honest conversation today.*

"Why do you say that?" she says, then sighs. "Never mind. Of course we didn't expect it to happen like this. But that doesn't mean there is anything the matter with you." She throws a quick glance at my tattoos, then seems embarrassed to have done it. "I just wish . . . well . . . My children don't usually hide things from me."

Her son hasn't told her about Simi. Not that I'm about to correct her. Prem did, however, under Saj's direction, drop something about my visa issues to them before he brought me here.

"It wasn't him. I was the one who was scared of how you would react. Because . . . well . . ." I give her my best sad eyes. "I have some issues I'm dealing with. But Prem . . . well, he thought you'd understand."

"Oh yes." She looks around the gigantic empty kitchen. "Prem was saying there might be some"—she lowers her voice—"immigration stuff."

"Yes," I say, and inexplicably my voice lowers too. "I don't know how much Prem has told you, but can I be honest?"

"Of course." Her eyes sparkle at the prospect of learning something about the stranger her son has brought home.

"The only way I can stay in the country is if I marry Prem. And I didn't want to put that pressure on our relationship."

Her eyes fill with understanding, and regret, and the slightest bit of doubt. She might have the most transparent face of anyone I've ever met. "Ah, and I can't imagine that my son would listen to that."

"You know Prem," I say worshipfully. "Is it okay if we wait for him to explain the rest?"

"Of course. I didn't mean to turn this into an interrogation. I just meant to feed you." She takes the lid off a pot on the stove. "I hope Prem and you will trust us in the future." Hurt flashes in her face, but she covers it up with a determined smile and sets about ladling some soft khichdi into a bowl. "I'm not like other mothers. That's what everyone says." She blushes like a happy light bulb, and my heart does something weird. "One must be open minded in today's day and age, no?"

She drops a healthy dollop of ghee on the khichdi and holds it out to me.

The gentle buttery aroma wafts up my nose and around me and wraps me tight. I can't remember the last time the smell of food soothed me. Of all the mortifying things, my mouth fills with drool, and tears clog my throat.

"Beta?" She squeezes my shoulder. "Did I say something?"

I shake my head. I've never been so embarrassed in my life. "Sorry," I say. I never apologize, and I want to take it back. But something just opened up inside me that I can't control. I think I'm just hungry. God, I'm so very hungry.

She pushes me into a barstool at the oversize island and places the bowl in front of me. "Eat."

I do. After what is days, but really a year, or maybe a lifetime, I eat. It's the best thing I've ever eaten. The lentils and rice are perfectly cooked into a soothing, perfectly seasoned porridge. The ghee and the salt dance on my tongue. My heart sings. My belly screams with long-awaited satisfaction.

She refills my bowl and hands me a glass of thin churned buttermilk. It's spiced with cumin, ginger, and cilantro, and forget Prem—I think I was born to marry this woman.

Just as I'm scarfing down the second bowl of magical khichdi, the other daughter-in-law walks in, followed by Preeti.

At this point, if the immigration people walk in, I wouldn't break a sweat. I'd ask them to wait until I'm done.

"Are you still sick?" Preeti asks, looking at my bowl.

"Obviously," Chandni says. "Why else would she be eating bland khichdi when there's so much good food?" She finishes up the samosa on her plate with relish.

This khichdi is better than any samosa anywhere, but I'm too lost in it to argue the case.

For a while they go off into the merits of samosas over khichdi, then Tanuja clears her throat. "Girls," she says to the two grown-ass women, "at least ask Rupi how she's doing or if she needs anything."

"Omigosh, of course," one says as they both drop into the stools on either side of me. The first order of business is my engagement ring, which has been feeling like a ten-ton abscess on my finger. Much gushing happens, which explains why the horrendous experience at the diamond store was necessary. Then just as suddenly, they fall into a cascade of questions.

"How did you get food poisoning? What a nightmare."

"And where did you meet Prem? Was it through Simi?"

"Had you seen each other before? Or was it all online? Oh no, were you sick when you saw him for the first time? How mortifying."

"How long have you known each other?"

The questions flow, but they don't pause for answers.

"I see him every day. I have no idea how I missed it." That from his sister.

"Well, I live in the same house as him." That from his sister-in-law. "I should've guessed. Actually, to be honest, I was quite sure the boy was in love. You met last year, didn't you? Around the time the triplets were born. Prem totally changed then. Became bouncy and chatty and just generally sweet as hell. Not that Prem was ever not sweet."

"He's the sweetest," Preeti says. "And yes, I noticed the change a year ago too. I guess he didn't say anything because of the immigration stuff."

"How did you end up in this situation with the visa?"

I'm not sure which of them that last question comes from, but after that the two of them go silent. It's as though all that chattering was orchestrated to get to that last question.

I look at their eager, waiting faces.

Saj already made Prem, Simi, and me practice our story, so I'm ready. I'm also adept at leaning into stories to save my ass. My soon-to-be mother-in-law hands me a glass of water, and the lies stick in my throat.

Just then Prem rolls into the room, looking like the world has ended. I swear to god, that boy is not winning an Oscar anytime soon.

He walks up to me, probably forced out here by a pleading look from Simi. "You feeling okay?" he asks, looking at the wiped-clean bowl in front of me.

"This might be the best khichdi I've ever eaten in my life." Why am I telling him the truth?

"Let me get you more," his mother says.

"No, please. I don't think there's space for another morsel inside me, but this is the most I've been able to eat in days. Thank you."

"You need some flesh on those bones," she says and then stops guiltily. "Sorry, we aren't supposed to say anything about weight these days, no? My girls will kill me." Sure enough, her "girls" widen their eyes at her. "Sorry, all I'm saying is that food poisoning weakens the body, you need to get some nourishment. There, better?"

"It's okay. Really," I say, feeling that weird warmth in my chest again.

"What a lovely girl, Prem," she says. "You could definitely have told me about her. I only want you all to be happy. Now I'm just sad that you didn't trust me."

"It's not that at all," both Prem and I say together, and the three women make an "awwww" sound and burst into delighted giggles.

"How adorable you two are," Chandni says.

"They are, aren't they?" Prem's mom says. "You know what? You should make a portrait of them as a wedding present, Chandni."

"Are you an artist?" I ask.

"She is!" her mother-in-law says proudly.

"I'd love to make them a portrait. They can hang it in their room," Chandni says.

Our room?

Prem looks like death would be a better alternative to sharing a room with me. Well, likewise, rasgulla.

"I don't think Rupi likes portraits," Prem says a little too loudly. His face is all flushed. Apparently, I'm not worthy of Chandni's art.

"I'd love a portrait," I say.

"Perfect. We can talk about how to gather your material later," Chandni says.

Material?

Prem looks like he's going to explode with something I can't identify. "We should talk about a wedding date," he says.

"Oh yes," his mother says. "We have a wedding to plan!"

Now we're getting somewhere, Tanuja.

"Like I said before, there are some legal issues," Prem says, looking at his fingernails and then at me. It's the moment of truth. "We're going to have to do it soon."

Tanuja seems to sense the worry gathered inside her son. Not surprising, given how terrible he is at hiding his feelings. She puts a hand on his shoulder. "Well, I don't believe in long engagements anyway. How soon is soon? And how bad is it?"

So, he tells them. It's the ultrasanitized, Saj-approved version of how I came to lose my visa status. With hardly any untruths but with many an omission.

I came to America to work at the restaurant at the invitation of the owner, who I met in India. Instead of converting my visa to a work permit as promised, the restaurant owner took away my passport and blackmailed me into working for almost no pay. Finally, when he died in an accident, I escaped and went to Chicago, where I found a job in a tattoo studio.

After this part the untruths get a little thicker on the ground: When Prem visited Chicago six months ago, Simi gave him my number, and he called me. We connected immediately, but I was too scared to get into a relationship, given my situation. But we couldn't let each other go, so we talked on the phone for six months and fell in love. Then Tina found me again and threatened to deport me if I didn't go back. That's when Prem decided we should just go ahead and get married.

All the truly heinous parts aren't even in the story, but all three of them look like they've been knocked off their feet by the injustice of it. Their eyes shimmer with unshed tears. Must be nice, to be hurt so easily.

"We'd better hurry up, then?" Tanuja says. "The girls' birthday is in a few weeks. Let's do it right after that."

They start discussing the details of the wedding. At the Gaylord in Nashville, obviously, just like the other two kids. They'll have to call in some favors because it's such short notice. Some cousin will get Prem's and my clothes made in time. Food, the guest list, even the priest is discussed as though my visa-shaped trouble is already a distant memory.

"Prem, beta," Tanuja says when they've fixed all my problems just like that. "Why haven't you shown Rupi your room yet?" And we've circled back to the room. Prem looks like someone just placed his neck in a guillotine. "Come on, let's show her where she'll be living after you're married."

FIFTEEN

SIMI

"You okay?" my sister asks, coming up to me as I mix formula into bottles.

"Peachy," I say. I can't get the measures wrong. The girls have sensitive stomachs, and the right blend of two formula brands keeps them from getting gassy.

I take the three bottles to the quilt, where the girls are eagerly waiting for me, and hand them each a bottle. They roll over and start to feed themselves.

I've been here by myself for the past hour while my sister was being fawned over in the kitchen. The rest of the party is with Prem's father.

If you asked anyone in the house to take a head count, every single one of them would skip me. I don't exist. Except maybe for TASha and Prem.

I smile sweetly at Rupi and hope like hell that no one can see the steam coming out of my ears.

"Are you going to be this pissy for the entirety of the next two years?" my sister asks, and I want to shake her.

How can she be so comfortable, no, downright heartless, about this? I'm still in shock that this is going to go on for two years. I don't think I can get through this if she's going to be so mean about it. And I don't feel like I can give her a free pass for having a defense mechanism anymore. "At least I have reason to be pissy. You're being pissy when everything is going your way."

"Going my way?" she says with an incredulous laugh. "You're right. This is what I've wanted all my life." She throws a look at the beautifully carved mantel. "All this delicious normalcy. Like a damn Karan Johar film! In fact, shut up and let me enjoy it for a moment." She closes her eyes and takes a deep, mocking breath.

I want to strangle her with one of the silk ties holding back the drapes. "What is it that you actually want, Rupi? What is it that you've wanted all your life?" I ask with some exasperation. "Do you even know?"

She looks taken aback, and my heart twists. Then she does what she always does: She laughs as though I've asked her to eat cake if she's starving. "Honestly? Your safety, and mine. In that order. I haven't thought about much more than wanting to survive. It must be nice to have the luxury to sit around, thinking about what you want from life." She presses a finger to her temple and gets all dramatic. "Who am I? Why am I on this earth? Let me figure out my purpose while everyone around me takes care of me."

"That's not fair."

"You think?"

I hate that shame fills me. I want to apologize.

Shanya gets to almost the end of her bottle, tosses it away, and rolls over, ready to crawl off and explore the world.

I roll her back and put the bottle back in her mouth. She likes me to feed her the last bit and chugs away with satisfaction. The look she throws me over her bottle is the best thing that's happened to me today.

"That was her plan all along, wasn't it?" my sister asks, studying Shanya.

"It's her routine, yes."

"That's strange." Something in her eyes softens. For the first time since she got here, I see the sister who raised me. "You did that too. You liked me to coax you to finish up the last bit."

I look at Anya. "That is strange. Anya needs me to put a hand on her forehead so she can fall asleep. Just the way you used to do for me."

That seems to shake her. "You know you just work for these girls, right?" she says. "If you're not careful, it's going to hurt like a bitch when they don't need you anymore."

"The way it hurt when I left."

"Stop being an idiot. You're my blood. It's not the same thing." She strokes the flames on her forearm, her restlessness leashed in that action I haven't seen in so long. "How do you even tell them apart? They look exactly the same."

I stroke Shanya's cheek. She's not just someone I work for. She's Shanya, Prem's niece. I'm going to be her aunt someday.

"Actually they look completely different to me and have entirely different personalities," I say. "Tanya is my focused doer. Shanya is the peaceful one, satisfied and happy to be taken care of. Anya is the explorer, always seeking what isn't easily available."

Sure enough Anya finishes her bottle, tosses it as far as she can, and heads to Tanya. I reach over with one hand and grab her before she grabs Tanya's bottle.

"Another routine?" Rupi asks, but a grudging smile slips into her eyes. "I actually like this feisty one."

The feisty one screams to be let go.

"I'll put you down if you go get me the blocks," I say into Anya's ear.

She crawls away at record speed.

"Did they name the girls in their sleep?" Rupi says, watching them. "This might be the laziest naming of children I've ever seen."

"Like Rupi and Simi are any better," I say a little too defensively. "Our names aren't even full names, they're just parts of names."

"Well, if Mom was anything, she was disinterested in anything to do with us. But the hot doc and Preeti seem to be like those parents in commercials. I would expect more care. Anya, Tanya, Shanya sounds like they could only bother with one name and then just rhyme."

I've had this exact same thought, but it didn't sound so unkind in my head. "They are. Dr. Johnson and Preeti are model parents." The kind of parents these beautiful girls deserve. The kind of parents we deserved.

"Dr. Johnson?" Rupi says. "The man is called John Johnson? Maybe lazy naming is a family tradition."

I want to smile, but my face refuses.

Prem walks into the room, his mom, Chandni, and Preeti trailing right behind. "Ready?" he says.

Preeti's been avoiding meeting my eyes.

Her brother, on the other hand, can't be looking at me like this. I'm also only surviving this because he is.

Rupi stands, and Prem's mom squeezes her arm.

"Auntie and Prem want to show me our room," Rupi says, sounding so demure I'm caught between laughing and throwing up.

Our room.

I press a hand to my chest, where the words pierce like a poisoned spear. "That's just lovely," I say. "Go ahead. I'll wait here with the girls."

"Rupi wants you to be there. That's why she came to get you," Chandni says. "I can watch the girls. I haven't had TASha time in too long." She joins them on the quilt, and they head toward her with glee.

"You saw them yesterday," Preeti says, not the slightest complaint in her voice. "You go with your sister, Simi. John must be poking and prodding Baba and lecturing him about his physical therapy. It's time for a rescue mission."

Rupi may never have had the time to think about what she wanted from life. But this is all I've ever wanted: this kind of "delicious normalcy" that I only ever saw on the TV screen that was our sustenance growing up. I dreamed every night of those families, with me inside them, part of them.

Since meeting Prem, I've worked hard to not think about how close I am to the reality of it. Only now I'm not.

"Come on, Simi," Prem says, and I hope no one else hears what I hear in his tone. Exhaustion. Exhaustion my entire being echoes.

"Will Rupi be moving here with you?" I ask, unable to help myself.

He looks like I just sliced another knife into him.

"That is the way we've done it in our family for generations. Sons bring daughters-in-law into the home," Prem's mother says. "It's natural for you to be anxious that your sister will be living with her in-laws. It's become such an old-fashioned thing to do these days. But don't worry, we do it in a very modern way. We'll take very good care of her. Ask Chandni, it's not all torture."

"Oh, is that what you want me to tell her?" Chandni says to her mother-in-law. "I am very happy," she says in the most robotic tone, as though she's being forced, but her eyes are twinkling with laughter.

"Blink twice if you need help," Preeti says, laughing.

"I love living here. There's always company in the house, but there's also a lot of space and freedom. We try to have dinners together as a family, and honestly we end up hanging out a lot, but often I'm too busy to see anyone all day. I get ample time for my art."

"And ample raw material," Preeti mumbles.

Chandni makes a face at her, but her eyes are still laughing. "You better believe it," she says. "This family sheds hair like golden retrievers."

Rupi looks confused.

"And obviously, caring for Pankaj after the stroke is entirely different with a full house," Prem's mom says. "For the first few weeks, all three kids were here, but then it was just me and Prem." His mother looks at Prem like the sun shines out of him, and I work hard not to tear up. "Now with a full house, Pankaj always has company. I can leave the house when I want because there's always a family member here with him, and we don't have to leave him alone with his caregivers. All his life Pankaj did nothing but care for us. This is the least we can do."

Tears spill from Prem's eyes. I want to go to him, but I throw Rupi a look, and she places a hand on his shoulder and pats him like he's a puppy.

Which ends up looking like she's being strong for him. Great!

The family beams approvingly through their tears.

"It actually works wonderfully," Chandni says. "My sons, Neel and Nathan, always have someone to drive them around and help with homework. I've never needed childcare even though Pawan and I work full-time at Dominic's." She squeezes Rupi's arm. "Rupi, I think you'll really like it here. Khichdi whenever you want it." She winks.

My heart is racing. I can't think of a single thing worse than having to survive my sister living in this house. Now is the time to say something. To stop this.

"Let's do it! Let's show you your room," Prem's mom says.

Rupi will be sharing a room with Prem. Of course she will. The reality of this is way worse than I could have imagined.

I don't know how I make my way up the curving staircase behind the three of them, every step adding more deadweight to my body.

A huge open space lined with built-in shelves and big leather couches greets us. A massive TV screen hangs on one wall.

"This is the TV room," Prem says. "It's where we used to do movie Sundays. Now we just do them in Mamma and Baba's room, so Baba can be comfortable." He's talking directly to me.

Rupi clears her throat, and he turns to her as though she's holding a gun to his head.

The walls are lined with photographs. Each one of the kids posing alone at every age and an endless number of family pictures with all of them posing together.

The phrase "delicious normalcy" starts to play inside my head in an endless loop.

Delicious normalcy.

Delicious normalcy.

Delicious normalcy.

My sister watches me as though the chant is playing in her head as well.

She did refuse to come up here and see the room without me. She thought about me without even trying to think about me, which is such a Rupi move, it makes everything worse.

Prem's mom keeps a running commentary going for every picture. "Prem was in fifth grade here . . . This is our trip to Yosemite National Park when Prem got lost in the visitor center . . . This is Prem going out on his first pizza delivery . . ."

Rupi is giving a masterful performance of listening with full focus. Prem's eyes keep straying to me. His mom hasn't noticed, because her focus is entirely on Rupi. I feel his gaze boring into me. I feel sadness come off him in waves. This was important to him: my first time in his home, sharing his childhood and life. It was important to me too. I saved it up like a special treat I wanted to unwrap only when the time was right. I waited too long, and the treat spoiled before I got to it.

"And this is Prem's and your room," Tanuja says in the tone usually accompanied by drumrolls. She's still looking at Rupi. Prem is still looking at me.

Rupi grabs my hand. "I'm so excited," she says, pulling me along. She pushes me and Prem in front of her and into the room together.

Tanuja is behind Rupi and can't see Prem squeezing my hand like a drowning man as we cross the threshold.

Once we're inside, I pull away.

Prem doesn't let go easily.

The room is steeped in one of my favorite smells. Prem. Soapy and sudsy like his cologne, and I have to admit, the slightest undertone of cheesy pizza dough. The bed is covered in a thick midnight blue quilt. Midnight blue pillows, a midnight blue rug, a midnight blue accent wall, and dark-cherry furniture. It's him, but his family's version of him. Prince Prem, the youngest.

Who's bringing home a princess. Who will be sharing his bed. Will she? There's a couch by a bay window. In the soap operas we grew up on, if there was a couch in a married couple's room, one of them was going to be sleeping on it. They always made up. They always got together in the end.

My gaze goes to the throw wrapped around the base of his bed. A gray-and-maroon crocheted throw that doesn't match anything. I made it for him last Christmas because he told me that his family had always done Christmas gifts under a Christmas tree. Their family's way of making the children feel like they belonged here.

"There's an en suite bathroom in all four master bedrooms," Tanuja says. "We custom built the house and made sure all three kids would always have a place to stay. So what if Preeti and John don't live here? So what if daughters, unlike sons, are supposed to move out after marriage? This is her home too. We don't treat our daughter any different than our son."

This family is almost like a family someone might design to make someone with no family feel like shit. They're everything Rupi and I missed out on wrapped up in gold brocade with a diamond cherry on top.

Tanuja takes Rupi into the bathroom. Prem looks at me as though he wants to throw me on that bed and hold me for the rest of his life.

"You use the throw," I say.

"Of course I do. It's the most precious thing to me in this house. I love you, Simi."

I shush him. "Don't," I say. "She'll hear you."

He squeezes his eyes shut and leans his head back. He doesn't argue or tell me he doesn't care.

Is that what I want him to do?

I can hear Rupi asking all sorts of questions. She's keeping Prem's mom in the bathroom as long as she can. Prem and I stand there and gaze at each other. I want to kiss him. I want to say *thank you* and *sorry* and *why did you agree to this?* But I just stand there.

He steps closer and reaches for me, his hand going to the nape of my neck and bringing me to him, just as the two of them come out of the bathroom.

We pull apart so fast, Prem spins around and stumbles into the desk.

My heart feels like it might have stopped beating.

His mother has eyes only for Rupi, who's doing a great job blocking her view. "So, Rupi, beta, what do you think?"

"It's beautiful. The room, the whole house, it's better than any place I've ever lived in."

There's an odd note in my sister's voice, and I search her face for buried scorn.

I find none. My god, Prem's mom is not the only one with stars in her eyes. Rupi actually likes Prem's mother too.

"It's your home now," Tanuja says.

It's almost bizarre how lovely Tanuja is. Usually a person like that would freak Rupi out, but she's looking like she's found proof that Santa Claus exists.

A chill runs down my spine.

"Actually, since we've just met you and we're having to rush into the wedding, why don't you just move in now? We have a guest bedroom, and we can all get to know each other."

Prem knocks over a picture frame. I save it before it crashes to the ground.

"That's really nice of you," Rupi says, so calmly I want to shake her. "But it's been a long time since my sister and I have seen each other. I was hoping to live with her for a little while."

Prem's mother seems to notice me for the first time. "Doesn't Simi live right here in town? She's always welcome to come and stay in the house whenever she wants. Simi, you know this is going to be your sister's home and you are welcome here anytime, correct?"

"Thank you," I say. "That's very generous of you."

She pats my cheek and studies me for a long while. Prem has her eyes, alight with kindness and love. For no reason at all my heart fills with hope. She sees something in my face. She knows.

Suddenly her eyes brighten even more. "You're such a pretty girl. Are you single?"

"Ma!" Prem says.

"Umm," I say. "I'm not married."

"Perfect," she says and rubs her hands together. "I think I know just the boy for you. He'll be at the triplets' birthday party. I think I have a plan to make you even more part of the family."

SIXTEEN

RUPI

I don't want to come inside," Simi says, pouting exactly the way she did when she was two. "You're the one they want to take shopping, not me."

"Tell me something, does self-sacrificing sulking ever work?" I ask. Because she's been acting a little too much like a long-suffering lamb headed to the slaughter. "It's on brand, but what are you hoping to achieve?"

She pulls into the sweeping driveway of the Gupta house. It's been a week since our first visit, and Simi's driven me here every morning on her way to work so I can hang out with the Guptas and participate in their Get to Know the Fiancée Plan. She turns to me with all sorts of accusation dripping from her eyes. "I'm hoping to not waste my time fighting you on what you want."

"Why is it so hard for you to see that this is not what I want? What I want is to not have to go back to Mumbai. Even now, if you come up with a better plan, we can stop all this." Truth is, it's a lot—all this Gupta syrupiness. I'm at risk of going into sugar shock.

Simi scoffs. I don't have any interest in deconstructing that scoff.

"It's a matter of two years, Simi! After that, this is your life and your home, not mine. I don't want it."

"But I do! And we have no way of knowing what will happen in two years. How can you expect me not to be sad?"

I squeeze my temples. "What good has being sad ever gotten us? Don't you think getting out of your feelings and thinking would be smarter? Whatever you think is going to happen in two years will be worse if you choose to disappear and hide. Let them see you. That way when Prem and I break up, they'll be glad you're around to pick up the pieces."

"My god, I can't believe you've thought all this through," she says with some horror.

I hadn't until this minute, but it feels like the most obvious plan of action. I'm going to have to move into the house once we're married because our dark overlord of law, Saj, thinks it will make our case stronger. In case a site interview comes up, living under the same roof will make it easier with so many witnesses to our love. That doesn't mean I want to.

"The real question is, Why haven't you thought this through? One of us has to do more than just sulk." I didn't even consider taking Tanuja up on her offer and moving in immediately. I was actually excited about living with Simi after so long until I realized it wasn't mutual. She's never home. And when she is, she's only interested in giving me the silent treatment.

"It's amazing to me that you keep saying I'm doing nothing when I am actually handing over my entire life to you," she says.

"It's amazing to me that you keep saying that you're handing over your life to me and then doing nothing to actually back up this grand sacrifice. Why can't you help make this work in a way that both of us can live with? Why is that always my job? It's not like I want you to give up all your power and look to me for all the answers all the time."

Another scoff.

"What the hell, Simi? Stop scoffing like a horse, and say what you're thinking."

"From the day I was born, I've had to give up all my power to you. That's how you operate!"

Wow. "It's no longer the day you were born, though, is it? You're twenty-six. You can move the hell on." *You ingrate.*

"I have!" And the pout is back. "I thought I had."

"Until I showed up again." I absolutely hate feeling sad, and I will not do it now.

She looks sad enough for the both of us, and guilty and miserable, and I hate that even more. "I'm happy you're here."

"Is that why you've been avoiding spending any time in your home when I'm there?"

"When are you ever there? You're here at the house all the time." And there it is. The crux of her pain.

"Because you're never home. And I'm helping with the party."

"What do you think I'm doing? I've been helping Preeti prepare for the triplets' big day. After working my other two jobs."

The girl does work more than I've seen anyone work. I guess she did grow up when I wasn't there to "take away all her power." A memory of a baby Simi following me around and letting me do everything for her fills me. *Chipku.* That was my nickname for her. It essentially means "sticky."

"Oh, so you haven't been avoiding me," I say. "And you haven't been avoiding Prem?" The rasgulla has been sulking even more than Simi. I haven't seen much of him either. What a match made in heaven they are.

"Prem is a very busy person," Simi says, her tone wretchedly unsuccessful in covering anything up. "He runs twelve pizza restaurants."

I'm aware. The family loves nothing more than to tell me how Prem runs the operations of their pizza empire. His brother, Pawan, runs the financial and marketing end of the business, and Chandni handles quality. Another perfect, Guptaesque symphony.

"There's always a fire to put out somewhere," Simi says.

Sometimes literally. "No kidding," I say. "I imagine he's been setting some of those fires, given that they've only been happening in the most faraway of the restaurants. It's the perfect excuse for him to stay away from home."

Simi looks appalled at this most obvious observation. "Prem would never do that." At least her indignation is less pathetic than her self-pity.

I hate to admit that I've been grateful that he isn't around much.

Before I can respond, two twin tornadoes fly across the driveway at us. My heart does the oddest flutter at the arrival of Chandni and Pawan's eight- and ten-year-old boys.

I get out of the car, and Neel and Nathan race at me, then stop six inches before their bodies crash into mine and stare up at me with the most excited puppy dog eyes.

I pull them into quick hugs. They smell terrible, like sweaty soccer equipment, but also sweet and sticky, like boxed juice.

"Be patient," I whisper as they bounce on their heels. "You have to be strategic when it comes to surprises."

This deep philosophy makes them get adorably serious.

I sniff the air around them and make a face. "I think showers might be needed before we can work on secret projects."

"Man!" they both groan. "Do we have to?" But they run off, racing at first and then throwing a look over their shoulders at me and slowing down.

Their mom walks up to me and gives me the warmest hug. "Whatever magic you've been using on the two monsters, please don't stop."

Simi gets out of the car, looking miserable as ever, and Chandni waves at her, one arm still around me.

"They're adorable," I say, and Chandni rolls her eyes.

"They are tornadoes, and until you came along, they spun around the house all day long, leaving mayhem in their wake." There's so much gratitude on her face, I want to shake her.

The family's strategy for dealing with N&N's astounding quantities of energy has been to enroll them in every available activity. They play every seasonal sport, which means they currently play soccer (hence the vile stench), learn musical instruments (that they're terrible at), take math classes and writing classes (that they have minimal interest in), and are part of the Indian drama club that puts up plays from the Indian epics (that's a good one, and watching them practice is probably the most fun I've had in a very long time).

By any yardstick, that's an absurd number of activities. It only seems to make them more hyperactive than calm them down. By some stroke of luck, when they first met me a week ago, they were terrified of me. I think it's the tattoos and the spiky hair, and maybe a little bit the resting bitch face I'm rather proud of. Basically, unlike everyone else in their orbit, I didn't cower when they spun around in their energetic way. I simply offered to teach them how to "make" tattoos (it's our surprise project).

They each now have a sketchbook in which they're practicing drawing tattoos. Because, of course, they have to be good on paper before they can touch skin. It's the rules. The rest of the family isn't allowed to see what's in the sketchbooks, but yesterday when they sat down with me and drew for two hours straight, their mother broke down and sobbed.

Now the family thinks I have some sort of magical powers. There's something very wrong with this family. They're completely unaware of my motives. How people this gullible and generous built an empire, I will never know.

Simi is about to say bye and leave when Chandni mentions that Prem is inside, and Simi changes her mind.

Chandni leads us into the house, where I'm greeted like a conquering hero by Tanuja.

"I made khichdi," she says, throwing a knowing glance at Prem, whose sad-sack face just brightened when we entered.

At this point all I care about is that there's khichdi.

Prem and Simi lock eyes as though there's no one else in the room, and someone clears their throat behind me.

The hair on my arms perks up in a breezy little dance. Only because I'm not a fan of someone approaching me from behind.

"Saj," Simi says. "I didn't realize you would be here."

Me neither.

"I needed to talk to Prem and Rupi about some paperwork."

"Okay to eat some khichdi first?" I say without turning around to face him.

Fully on brand, I get no response.

I dig into the khichdi. Tanuja has made it for me every day since that first day.

The family settles around the island, where Prem is drinking coffee. He drinks it black (yuck), something I cannot reconcile with his rasgulla personality.

Chandni informs Tanuja that the boys have gone off to take showers without a fuss, and Tanuja looks like she wants to pull out the aarti plate and spin it around my face in worship again.

"I can't remember the last time we didn't have to bodily force those boys into the shower." She squeezes my shoulders in a sideways hug. "I don't know how you do it, beta."

"I didn't do anything, Auntie," I say around a mouthful. "I just asked them to smell each other."

She laughs. "It's time to stop this Auntie-Shantie business, don't you think? You're calling me Mamma from now on."

Prem drops his cup, spilling coffee across the island. Simi springs up and starts mopping it with paper towels. She looks like she's going to cry.

"Let me get that," Prem's mamma says.

"It's okay. I got it, *Auntie*," Simi says, all the longing in the world hanging by that word.

Come on, Simi, have some self-respect.

Obviously, her hopes are dashed. Tanuja turns to me. "So, it's Mamma from now on."

"Thanks, Mamma," I say, and she grins happily and goes off to check on her husband.

I reach over and pat Simi's hand, but she yanks it away. "I'm fine," she snaps.

Good. I shrug and go back to my khichdi.

I don't care to look at the judgment in Prem's and Saj's eyes, so I turn to Chandni, the only person here to whom I'm a hero instead of a villain.

Chandni looks excited. "So, I've been thinking about the portrait I want to make for you and Prem as a wedding present."

"That's so sweet," I say, and I mean it. "I'm excited about that."

"You are?" Saj says, his Dark Shadow eyes not quite as shuttered as I'm used to when they slide from his sister to me.

"Why would I not be? Everyone has told me that she makes the most beautiful art."

"She does." What is that I hear in the deep rumble of his voice? "She makes the most beautiful art with human hair."

The khichdi gives a push up my gullet. Mr. Dark Shadow meets my bewildered eyes with the briefest twinkle and promptly goes back to being dark and shadowy.

Chandni beams. "I use all sorts of organic material for art. But yes, human hair is my favorite medium. Very versatile," she says with perfect seriousness.

"Tell us more," Simi says, brightening.

So, Chandni does tell us. In detail. Apparently collecting shed hair is involved.

"It's so lovely that both you and Rupi are artists. Isn't that just serendipitous?" I catch a sparkle in Simi's eyes for the first time since I came into town.

"It is!" Chandni says. "And we both work with human material."

Simi squeaks to keep her laugh inside.

"Why don't you show her some of your work," Saj says. And there it is again: the slightest amused glint in his eyes. But I can't be sure which one of us he's teasing—his sister or me.

Chandni points to what looks like a sketch of a tornado over a town, hung on the wall above the dining table. It's not half bad. But it's still a whole lot of human hair hanging out in a kitchen.

"It's lovely," I say, dying but hiding it as stoically as I can.

Saj gets all shuttered again and sips his coffee. Also black. And so much more on brand.

"That's Mamma's hair. I gathered it from her brush over a year." Again, Chandni says this with all seriousness.

I suppress another shudder. I knew it. All this wholesomeness was a little too good to be true.

My gaze meets Simi's, and we quickly look away, because she looks like she's going to explode too.

"Mamma and I think a portrait of Prem and you together would be perfect. I can start gathering your hair today. Do you shed a lot?"

Twin laughs spurt out of Simi and me, and we both turn them into coughs.

Chandni is looking at me with such sincerity, I guess this is really happening.

"Umm. Not really." Everyone here has longer hair than me, and it's a whole heck of a lot thicker too. "I barely have any hair, so it would take a lot of time to collect." Aaaand, I'm really considering the merits of gathering my shed hair for her. "Can you use Simi's instead? She has more than enough to spare."

Simi widens her eyes at me. "That's not necessary." I haven't seen her eyes shine like this in too long.

The Dark Shadow speaks. "I mean, it's the same DNA."

Even Prem lets a grin escape.

"Sorry, Simi, I can't use your hair for their portrait. That would be compromising my artistic integrity." Chandni is still 100 percent serious. "But collect it for me, and I can use it for my landscapes."

"Thank you," Simi squeaks around another suppressed laugh, and Prem looks at her like the sun just came out. And for one moment, the world feels okay.

SEVENTEEN

SIMI

Who knew that a bizarre choice of art medium is what would thaw my relationship with my sister? I guess Rupi is right—the world does need art. So what if shed human hair is involved. It's fitting because our truce feels like it's hanging by a hair. On one hand, it's become hard for me to think about Prem without wanting to double over in pain at the thought of them together. On the other hand, having Rupi in my home is like having a lost piece of myself restored.

Rupi is making chai when I walk into my kitchen. The déjà vu is powerful, and my brain shuffles past all the Rupis of my childhood before it lands on the thirty-one-year-old one in front of me.

Her eyes light up when they catch sight of me, then they get all guarded again. "I got you something," she says, pointing to a shopping bag on the floor. "But I don't want you to take it the wrong way."

"That's an ominous thing to say when you give someone a present." I pick up the bag and bounce it in my hand. It has some weight.

"Well, you haven't exactly been generous with judging my intentions lately."

Is she really trying to start a fight while giving me a present? There's no way I'm taking the bait. We get only an hour in the mornings before I have to go to work. As always, I'll drop her off at the Gupta house on my way to the clinic for another day of pampering, and one of the Guptas will bring her home. She'll be asleep before I get back. I wonder if she's noticed that she's sleeping through the night now.

"What is it?" I ask instead of addressing her accusation.

Instead of digging in her heels, she smiles. "Art made from nail clippings," she says, eyes sparkling.

"Please don't give Chandni that idea," I say on a groan and return her smile.

"Open it." She looks so nervous, my heart squeezes.

It's a set of six matching cups embossed with glittery dresses and shoes. "I love them!" I say. "You didn't have to do this." I don't know where she got the money from, but I can't ask.

"I know I didn't have to." She reads my mind and sticks up her chin. "Prem's mom's friend Dolly Auntie gave me a gift card. Apparently, engagement gifts are a thing. I figured you were the one who had a right to that money anyway, so." She goes back to the chai boiling on the stove and turns it off. "They just . . . they were just so you."

"They are!" I say, holding a beautiful cup with both hands and pressing it to my chest. "Thank you."

"It's not for cuddling." Her tone is reprimanding, but she's smiling. "Let's inaugurate them?"

I wash the cups, and she strains chai into them.

We bump into each other as we navigate my tiny kitchen, and it makes us both laugh. It strikes me that we are in *my* kitchen, but it feels like ours. Sharing space with her is different from sharing space with anyone else on earth. Every space I'm in will always also be hers.

"This is nice," I say.

Before she can respond, her phone pings on the breakfast bar. She doesn't notice.

I got her a phone last week, but she wasn't exactly happy, and she's terrible at using it. I lean over and look at it. The screen is covered in notifications.

"Rupi, your phone is filled with missed calls and unread texts. Don't you check it when you wake up?"

"I'll check it later."

"It's not a landline with an answering machine. You're supposed to have it on you and respond in real time."

"Who says?" she asks. "Why?"

"I don't know, it's a cell phone. That's the expectation." I have to laugh at the expression on her face. "You're the only person on earth I know who's managed to escape the phone-addiction epidemic."

She rolls her eyes. "Yay poverty! I guess." She narrows her eyes at me as soon as she says it. "That was a joke. Don't get all pouty and sad. You know I hate feeling like something is controlling me. Who wants to be tied up with a leash all the time?"

"Apparently, all of humanity." I pick up her phone. There are five missed calls from Prem. That ugly knife that's been lodged in my belly twists.

Rupi reads my face. "Is it Prem? What does he want?"

How should I know? It's not like the missed calls are on my phone. I hand it to her.

She reads the message. "I think you might want to run in and get dressed. Prem and the dark overlord are on their way."

Right on cue, the doorbell chimes.

"Go," Rupi says, knowing I won't open the door in my pajamas. She's wearing sweatpants and a tank top, her usual black on black setting off the bright colors inked into her arm.

When I come back out in my scrubs, showered and presentable, I'm greeted by the sight of Rupi signing papers.

When she's done, she hands them over to Saj.

"Can you please give it some thought," Saj says.

"No," Rupi says.

Prem looks exhausted. His eyes get all puffy when he hasn't been sleeping. The combination of longing and exhaustion in them makes me want to buckle at the knees. How can he look at me like this and be so distant at the same time?

"What's going on?" I ask.

"Nothing," Rupi says. "Saj and Prem were just leaving."

"What does Saj want you to think about?"

"It doesn't matter," Rupi says. "I've already told all of you that I'm not interested in going after Tina." She turns to Saj. "You're going to have to prove these two right about how good you are at your job and get me a new passport without bringing Tina into it."

Saj doesn't look happy, but he takes the papers and starts to leave.

Prem doesn't move. "Can we talk for a minute?" he says to me.

I'm going to be late for work, but I haven't had a moment alone with him in weeks.

"Rupi, can you walk me to my car, please?" Saj says, making Rupi sigh.

"Only if you promise not to bring Tina up."

Saj grunts.

"And if you promise not to be so cheery."

Instead of responding, he holds the door open for her, and she flounces out.

Prem and I are alone. He's sitting on the rug where we've made out so many times. Despite everything else I'm feeling, longing tugs at my belly and pulls me toward him. I don't move. "I can't be late for work." It's the last thing I want to say, but it's also the truth.

"I know." He sounds like a stranger. "Why did you transfer that money to me?" He's obviously feeling none of the things I am. He's completely shut me out.

"It's a lot of money. And she's my sister."

"I'm the one engaged to her. I should be the one to buy the ring."

"If it were a real engagement."

"We're getting married, Simi. You're the one who wanted this."

That's his answer? Not that it isn't a real engagement? "You know I didn't have a choice, Prem." *That doesn't mean I want to lose you.* Why am I not able to say that part?

The way he's looking at me, there's a demand in his eyes, a plea even. Why can't I read it?

"What more do you want from me, Simi?" he says finally.

It feels like he just bodily shoved me away. He's right. How can I want anything more from him after what he's already given?

"I want you to let me pay for the ring." That much I have to do.

He looks disappointed and frustrated. All these new feelings in his eyes. "You paid the hospital bill too. It's a lot. Let me help you." And now there's pity too.

Between the ring and the bills, I've pretty much emptied out my bank account. It's still a lot less than my sister has given up for me.

"You are helping me. You are doing more than anyone should ever have to."

"I don't want your gratitude, Simi!" He stands and comes to me. "Let me at least pay the damn bills."

"And I don't want your charity, Prem!"

He steps back. "You're calling my love charity?"

I step closer to him. "You're saying the only way you know how to love me is by helping me."

"That's not fair," he says. Or his eyes say it. But that's what I hear. Neither one of us is saying any of the things we want to say or need to say.

Maybe we no longer know how. I know I don't want to hear the things I see in his eyes. That I have asked for too much. That I am using him.

"Don't do this, Simi," he says.

"I have to," I say, but I'm not sure he's talking about the bills.

My phone chimes. I'm going to be late for work. Karina's patient is my first appointment. "We need to talk, Prem. But I have to go right now."

"I know," he says, but he doesn't move. "I miss you, Simi."

And just like that, everything else disappears.

I step closer. If I touch him, I won't be able to pull away again. "I miss you too," I say and cup his cheek.

That's it. That's all it takes. He grabs me. His hands in my hair, his mouth on my mouth. His hungry body pressed against mine. He kisses me like it's the last time we'll ever kiss. Like the first time we ever kissed. Everything I am is in that kiss, and he takes it.

My phone chimes again. Then chimes again. I pull away and stumble back. Leaving him is like tearing myself in half. There's an ache deep in my belly, in my heart, between my legs. There's a ravenous hunger in my soul.

His eyes are dilated with that same hunger. He looks destroyed, unable to speak.

"It's Karina," I say, looking at the name on my phone that strikes terror in my heart.

My finger is shaking when I answer. My heated body feels like it's been dunked in ice.

"Do you think a patient appointment is a casual suggestion?" Karina's voice says on the phone.

"I'm sorry," I say. "I'm on my way. The first appointment isn't for twenty minutes."

"Oh, so you plan on getting here with the patient? What about reviewing cases and supplies inventory?"

"Dr. Rai, I already sent you a report for both of those. I took care of it."

"You're opening patient records at home. That's a HIPAA violation. Do you think rules don't apply to you?"

"I did it before I left work yesterday."

"Do you think I have time to butt heads with you first thing in the morning? If this is your attitude, don't bother to show up for work today. I'm sure we can find someone else."

She hangs up on me, leaving me unable to breathe.

Prem comes to me, but I step back. "Don't," I choke out. "I have to go."

"Simi, at least tell me what's going on. Is Karina Auntie being a problem again? Let's call John."

"No!" This is not Prem's problem to solve. I don't want to be Prem's problem to solve. His cause to save. His burden. It's the very last thing I wanted to be to him. "I can handle it myself."

I grab my purse and keys and open the door to find Rupi sitting on my front step. Shit, I forgot about dropping her off at the Guptas'.

"Go," Prem whispers behind me, still standing where I left him. "I'll take Rupi home."

I run to the car. I don't know what hurts more: the fact that he just saved me again or how much I hate the idea of him taking her home.

EIGHTEEN

RUPI

It's finally the day of the triplets' party, also known as the event that has kept my sister and me too busy to think about much else. I've been at the Gupta house every day, having my mind blown by the details involved in putting together a celebration of this magnitude. The entire family has been on its toes for weeks, and I've been dragged into the very eye of the storm of action items.

Honestly, it feels like this party has kept all Hochkinsville on its toes. What seems to be the entire town has shown up at the Gupta house to help bring it all together today. Or, at least, the entire Indian population of the town, along with the neighbors and all the employees at the twelve restaurant locations.

Setup teams have been working tirelessly since the wee hours of the morning. Hundreds of pink and silver balloons have been filled from helium tanks to build a gigantic arch. Folding tables have been set up with satin tablecloths. Some two hundred chairs have been wrapped with silver chintz and tied with pink silk bows. Centerpieces are being put together with fresh pink lilies and sprays of goldenrods (Preeti refused to use the silk flowers an auntie brought over).

A group of high schoolers, directed by some adults, are installing a stage with wooden crates brought in from someone's attic. Things that have already been installed include a sound system with AV and mic, a bouncy house, and carnival games like basketball tosses and bag throws. It's all being done by friends and employees, and the Guptas didn't have to ask anyone for help. All those people are simply contributing to the Guptas' great celebration because they are loved and respected that much in the community.

Some forty-odd people have driven or flown in from out of town. The Guptas have rented out their friend's motel for their guests. Chandni and Pawan are in charge of taking food and chai to the motel for the guests and arranging transportation when needed.

After all the gossip (thanks to Anagha) about how Prem went behind the family's back and got engaged, Tanuja is determined to make sure everyone knows that I've been embraced by the family. She gave Prem and me the very visible job of coordinating the decorations and setup at home and keeping the volunteering hordes well fed. I never expected to see, let alone warm up, so many samosas and dhoklas in my life. Nor did I ever expect to make so much chai. I've been boiling the darned thing all day using Mamma's exacting recipe. The chai is on par with her khichdi, and so long as I get my fix of both, I'm not going to complain about all this smiling I have to do every time someone congratulates Prem on how beautiful I am, while avoiding looking at my tattoos.

It's actually quite the lucky break to have all these witnesses to our relationship. Take that, USCIS!

I am also tasked with keeping Neel and Nathan occupied. They are by far my favorite characters in this play I find myself in the middle of. What's not to love about two adorable boys following me around and listening to everything I say as though it's gospel? Last week we planted a vegetable patch. They seem to share my love of growing things, because I swear they've spent hours tending to that piece of earth, watering and fertilizing and staring unblinkingly at the sprouting saplings to see if they can catch them growing.

Today I have them finishing up their huge undertaking of making thank-you cards for the guests. They've chosen to draw anime characters (which I know nothing about but which they are obsessed with and have been tutoring me about) using felt-tip pens and colored pencils. Turns out two hundred cards can keep two young boys occupied for days on end. Especially when they want to create their life's work.

Prem has kept up a steady supply of their favorite blueberry lemonade and pizza dough chips (which he makes specially for them). The rest of the community isn't allowed in their studio (their grandfather's room, because he loves watching them work), because the cards are a surprise. This was kinda genius of me, because it also means Baba will get some rest before the afternoon festivities, and he doesn't have to visit with all the people walking in and out of the house. No one in the family wants to be rude enough to draw boundaries and ask visitors to leave him alone. Because if your last name is Gupta and you get caught being "not nice," you have to hand in your Gupta card.

By noon, after spending the morning setting up, the gathered town finally leaves to get dressed. I check in on the boys in Baba's room. Baba's eyes light up when he sees me, even though I've been in and out of the room all day. He beckons me to sit by him on the bed, as though I'm the one who needs rest. We watch in silence as N&N finish up the last of the cards, then show us every one of their two hundred drawings.

"These are fantastic," I say, and my heart fills with an odd sensation. It's alarmingly close to what I feel when I see my own work.

The boys look like they're going to burst with pride. Baba's eyes fill with tears, and they throw their arms around him and hold on. His gaze finds me, and there's something in it that makes me step back and clap my hands to get the boys to move. We all need to get dressed. They put the cards in the shoeboxes we decorated with their grandmother's old scarf and hot glue, squeeze hugs into me, and run off.

I'm about to leave, too, when Baba stops me with one of his sounds.

"Do you need something, Baba?"

He moves his head to look at two silk kurtas laid out on his bed.

"Are those for the party?"

The barest nod is followed by the twitch of a hand. He wants me to help him decide which one to wear.

"Have you not decided what you're wearing?"

He raises his chin. *What do you think?* his eyes ask.

I pick up both options and hold them up against him. His pale-brown skin and amber eyes make the royal blue really pop. The gray is too drab.

"This one definitely," I say, and he grins and gives a thumbs-up.

~

Every single one of the guests is dressed as though this is a wedding and not a birthday. If I dare to verbalize this (the blasphemy!), I would be told that it was no ordinary birthday but the first birthday of miracle babies. Mamma filled me in on how Preeti was told that she had, at best, a 10 percent chance of getting pregnant and carrying a baby to term. Having said that, she also told me that all first birthdays are celebrated with similar glee in the community.

Naturally I didn't tell her that I only knew Simi's and my birthdays because I saw them on our birth certificates when I had to take them into school for something. Our mother didn't believe in nonsense like birthdays. *What's wrong with the days on which you weren't born?*

It's a question I feel fairly confident no one will ever be asking these three unbelievably adorable, albeit very sleepy, little girls. The crowd of two hundred watches with wonder as they very generously let their mom, dad, and grandma guide their hands on ribbon-adorned child-safe knives to slice into cakes iced in pink, sage, and lavender buttercream and covered in miniature sugar work decorations of their favorite things: cars, puzzles, books, teddy bears, and musical notes. The cakes are understated yet fancy, a reflection of Preeti and John. It's what makes the couple stand out in the kitschy, earthy, gaudy splendor that is the Guptas' Hochkinsville community.

Simi is standing next to the girls, watching them with guarded eyes. I can feel her struggling hard to hold in her proud tears. She loves these girls so much, but her body language is reserved. Subservient, even. She behaves like a servant around these people. This makes me livid.

I focus my anger on Prem. How dare he let her feel this way? He's looking even more like a rasgulla than usual in a white silk kurta. Since we're outdoors and it's still bright, he's able to wear sunglasses, which means he's probably all teary under those. I get that marrying me when his sights were set on Simi is like getting thorns when he wanted a rose, but can he please stop crying and help her deal with this?

As soon as the girls have "cut" the cakes and the crowd has belted out an unabashedly tuneless rendition of "Happy Birthday," Mamma brings me a slice of cake, feeds some into my mouth, and hands me the plate. I've been standing next to Baba in his wheelchair. He looks delighted at the sight of the cake, and I feed a spoonful into his mouth. He beckons me close, and when I lean over, he drops a kiss on my cheek. Mamma kisses my other cheek, sandwiching me between them. Something painful constricts my heart. I want to pull away, but I can't move.

I wait for them to pull away and straighten up, feeling strangely suffocated, only to find Simi watching me. She looks like I just murdered her puppy.

Come on!

I thought we were making progress, but since that day Prem and Saj brought me those papers to sign, she's been entirely swallowed up by a dark cloud.

Mamma takes the wheelchair, and they head off to lead the guests to the food laid out on the other side of the patio. The aroma has been hanging in the air enticingly for the past half hour, and everyone rushes toward the buffet in a hungry mob.

Across the mob, I see Simi's face go from heartbreak to terror. Anagha and an older woman walk up to her, and she struggles to smile at them.

This has to be Dr. Karina Rai, Anagha's mother and the boss who's been making life hell for Simi. Where is Prem? Why has he left her alone?

I weave through the stampeding hordes and make my way toward her.

"Can I get you something, Dr. Rai?" I hear Simi say in a sickeningly simpering tone.

"I'll take a chai," the woman says dismissively, without bothering to look at Simi.

Simi runs off to fetch the demanded chai. I stop behind a potted fern, because the conversation that follows fills me with enough rage that I have to stop and breathe. And eavesdrop.

"Why is she dressed up like a guest?" Karina says to her daughter. "She's the nanny. It's tacky."

"Because she thinks she's family now," Anagha says. "Prem's with that trashy sister of hers, remember?"

"What is wrong with the Guptas?" Karina says. "I thought they had some sense. I should have warned Tanuja. I could see the girl was trying to worm her way into their family. I knew it when she played the Indian card to get the nanny job. These new immigrants make us all look bad. When we came to America, we worked hard. We didn't just take shortcuts."

Working three jobs is a shortcut? How has Simi not poisoned this witch's chai yet?

Simi comes back with two cups and hands them to the two women. She's all big empty eyes and blank smile. It's her nervous face.

"Thanks for giving me another chance, Dr. Rai," Simi says. "I promise I won't let you down." She needs to not just let the woman down but shove her to the floor and stand on her neck.

The woman doesn't respond. She just makes a huffing sound as though Simi can't possibly disappoint her more than she already has.

"I was waiting for the party. I couldn't leave Preeti and Dr. Johnson in the lurch until that was done. I'll take care of it this week."

"I mean, it's your life. I only care about the practice. I think our patients deserve nurses who put them first."

"I do." Simi swallows. "I will. Can you please tell me when the papers will be signed?"

"Our lawyers are looking at them. I'll keep you posted." With that, the nasty witches saunter away, leaving my sister in their wake.

My anger makes it hard for me to see straight. My entire body feels hot with it. I emerge from behind the fern. "What the hell, Simi!" I say.

She blinks up at me. We're back in our building in Mumbai, with children dancing around her, calling her "motorcycle" and screaming stuttering sounds into her face. Before I beat the shit out of them.

"Did you need something?" she asks.

"Yes, I need you to start standing up to bullies."

"Sorry?"

"You should be. For letting those women treat you like that."

"She's my boss," Simi says.

"So?"

"So, she's within her rights to fire me for not doing my job well."

"Are you not doing your job well?"

She raises her chin. "I'm the best nurse they have."

"I know! How is it you grew up with bullies and you still can't recognize them?"

"Just because I can recognize them doesn't mean I magically have their power," she snaps and wrings her hands like a helpless waif.

I pull her hands apart and hold them steady. "When you got done with your nursing course, you had three job offers in three different countries. Have you forgotten that? And that was before you had four years of experience. What is wrong with you? What's the point of having power if you're not going to use it?"

"Use it how? By blowing up the only choice I have at this time?"

"How do you know that? You've said yourself that they've been looking for nurses for a year and found no one. You know you'll get another job in a minute. Call her bluff."

Her gaze burns angrily into mine. She scoffs out a laugh. "I cannot restart the green card process elsewhere. It takes too long. My job is my only path to a green card right now." She doesn't say "thanks to you," but it simmers in her voice.

Now it's my turn to scoff. "Way to go with the guilt trip. But I know choices, and this job isn't your only choice. Even if it were, the other doctors at the practice aren't stupid. They're never going to let you go. Karina is yanking you around by a chain because you're letting her. That's how bullies work. If you kneel to her now, you'll never stop kneeling. You love those girls. They need you. Why would you give up on them because this woman gets off on seeing you miserable?"

"Who wants to see her miserable?" Mamma walks up to us. And lo and behold, on her heels follows our friendly neighborhood lawyer man.

He's wearing a black-on-black kurta, much like me, and it irritates me more than it should.

"Everything all right, Simi?" he asks with such gentleness, his whole dark-angel vibe trembles at the threat.

He slides me a look. The next time someone looks at me like I'm stabbing pins into my sister, I'm going to actually stab them.

"Just some work stuff," Simi says.

"No work talk. We're here to have fun," Prem's mom says and looks from Saj to Simi with the most excited smile. "I saw that day that you two know each other already."

"We do," Simi says. "He's Rupi's lawyer. Prem introduced us."

"So, you know he's a lawyer." Mamma's eyes do a happy dance. "And you're a pediatric nurse. Both professions where you help people. Isn't that perfect?"

Oh! Saj is the "nice boy" she's been wanting to set Simi up with. I press a hand to my mouth to keep from laughing.

Simi and Saj look like they've just figured it out too.

As if on cue, in walks Prem.

"Oh hey, Prem," I say. "Just in time."

"For what?" Prem asks.

"What do you think?" Tanuja says. "Now that you're getting married, don't you think your friend should also settle down? And Simi is also single."

Prem's mouth falls open. The man should never travel to a place with flies. "Mamma, please. You're embarrassing them."

She looks appalled at the accusation. "Well, that wasn't what I was trying to do. I just think they would make such a cute couple. Look at them."

Prem glares at her.

She ignores him and pats Saj's arm and throws Simi a commiserating grin. "What's the harm in going out and getting to know each other?"

Simi blushes, and Saj remains as impressively unmoved as ever.

"Look at them being all shy," Tanuja says to me. "Rupi, aren't nice boys hard to find these days? You tell your sister. I get a feeling she listens to you."

"Simi knows her mind," I say.

"You're right, everyone should know their mind. I'm so proud of you girls these days. Anyway, as the people closest to the bride and groom, they're going to have to work closely together on planning your wedding. So, they will have no choice but to get to know each other. We're going to need all hands on deck if we want to pull this off in two months."

"Two months?" Simi says. "You guys set a date?"

Prem and I look at each other. The family decided on a date two days ago. We're getting married in two months. I haven't told Simi yet. Obviously, Prem hasn't either.

Simi's expression is the exact reason why we haven't.

"Yes, didn't your sister tell you?" Tanuja says.

"She did," Simi says, betrayal-filled eyes fixed on me, not even a glance spared for Prem. "But sometimes Rupi likes to yank my chain around just for fun, so I wasn't sure if she meant it." Did she just compare me to that bully Karina?

The look she gives me tells me that she did exactly that. Then she shakes my hand as though we're meeting for the first time. "Congratulations, didi. Everything you've always wanted is about to be yours."

NINETEEN

SIMI

This is the first time in my life I'm attending the fabled Gupta Sunday movie lunch.

Now that I'm the bahu's sister, I'm family, and I *have* to be here. I almost didn't come. I don't want to be around either Prem or Rupi. I can't believe they didn't tell me about the wedding date. When I confronted Rupi, her reaction was predictably unrepentant. *Is it really that hard to understand? For one, where was the time? You were so busy with the birthday, and we didn't want to ruin something you were that excited about. Also, if you were in our position, wouldn't you avoid that conversation too?*

The thing that's been stuck under my skin like a splinter for a week is the fact that she said "we." Since when are Prem and she a *we*?

When I talked to Prem, he was so filled with remorse, I couldn't be angry with him. All I wanted to ask him was if he also thought of himself and Rupi as a *we*. I didn't, of course. He's been so miserable because of me, I can't get myself to make things worse for him.

Not that it matters. It's not like I get to see him anymore. Prem's been gone all week to Nashville for another work emergency. I don't know what he's going to do to escape his home, and me, once the new location they've opened is running smoothly and he's done with all the repairs he's decided to take on since Rupi showed up. His family thinks he's being extra responsible now that he's getting married.

As for me, the gaping hole inside me from his missing presence has turned into a constant and unbearable ache. Not seeing him at all is only slightly worse than seeing him with Rupi and having his family fawn over them like newborn puppies.

I watch him across the kitchen as he deftly presses and shapes the pizza dough on the stone. Instead of the aloo parathas that I was looking forward to, we're having chicken tikka pizza. Prem is experimenting with his pizzas again, god bless him. The timer buzzes, and he pulls a pizza out of the oven. The kitchen fills with the smell of Indian spices mixing unappetizingly with cheese and pizza dough. He holds it up to me and I clap, making him smile.

One of my favorite things about Prem used to be how easily he smiled. Lately seeing a smile on his face has become so rare and so forced that my heart breaks with guilt every time I see him work to manufacture one. I did this. I created this bizarre situation and stole every bit of joy from the happiest, most undemanding man on earth.

"How have N&N not attacked the kitchen yet with you making family pizza?" Chandni asks. She's standing next to me at the kitchen island, where we're both slicing cucumbers, tomatoes, and onions for raita.

The whole family has now taken to using Rupi's nickname for Neel and Nathan: N&N.

"They're with their favorite chachi in Baba's room," Pawan says, stirring the chai he's making. Next to him, his mother sprinkles spices over the rajma she's making.

"Is it my imagination or has your father's health improved since Rupi came into the family?" his mother says, adding cream to the Dutch oven. Then she throws a look at Chandni. "You're doing such a great job with the salad, beta. No one chops vegetables like your wife, Pawan."

"Thanks, Mamma, but you don't have to placate me every time you say nice things about Rupi," Chandni says. "I happen to agree with you.

Baba is spending a lot more time awake. And please, N&N have been sitting in one place for such long periods of time, Pawan and I checked their temperature a few times last week to make sure they weren't sick. They're fine. Just obsessed with whatever surprise project Rupi's got them working on."

"Rupi has been spending a lot of time on that. Simi, beta, do you know what this surprise is?" Prem's mom says.

I startle, not expecting to be pulled into the conversation.

All this while I've been waiting for them to include me, and now that they've asked me a question, all I do is open and close my mouth like a hapless goldfish.

Prem dives to my rescue. "I think Rupi wants Simi to be surprised, too, Mamma." Unless he's diving to Rupi's rescue. Has she told him what the surprise is?

"Rupi just focuses really hard when she works on anything. If she's working on something with the boys, she's going to get fully preoccupied with that and forget everything else. She's always been like that." I finally find my voice, and a painful memory slides into my brain. Rupi reading up everything she possibly could about overcoming a stammer. Her talking to teachers. Then spending years relentlessly making me work on breathing and voice exercises. She even took me to a speech therapist and painted a mural in her clinic to pay for it.

Pawan pours out the chai and hands cups around. "She's taken over most of Baba's care. With Mamma preoccupied with the party and now the wedding, and the rest of us busy with the new store, Rupi has picked up all the slack with Baba. Last week she was asking the physical therapist all sorts of questions to understand his exercises, and I think she's doubled his movement."

Prem's mom gets teary eyed. "I think she's been researching some new therapies that one of John's neurologist friends is working on. She was talking his ears off about it at the party." She wipes her tears away with a finger. "Truly, what a gift she is." She squeezes Prem's shoulder, then pulls him close. "You chose well, beta. You chose fast and with secrecy, but you did choose well. May you two be together until eternity."

Pain seeps through my body as though my bones are being crushed. Will this ever get easier?

Prem slides me a look, and for the first time I see anger and accusation and a whole heck of a lot of worry there.

I can't be here anymore. I excuse myself to check how far Preeti and her family are and step out onto the deck. The heavy blanket of heat that engulfs me feels a little too much like Mumbai.

Prem follows me out. I should have known.

Meeting his gaze is like being pushed off my feet. I press a hand into the railing for support.

There is so much restlessness inside him, I don't know what to do with it.

"Prem, please," I say, because I don't know what else to say. I'm imagining another kiss, him unable to bear the distance we have to keep from each other.

"They're going to get hurt." That's what he opens with.

"Who?"

He points at the house and looks at me like he can't believe how clueless I'm being.

"Your family?" I feel disoriented. The anger in his eyes takes over. It fills the way he's looking at me.

"Yes." It's a strangled whisper. "They're getting too attached to Rupi. How are we going to end this?"

"Oh my god. Are you telling me you can't leave her?"

"Simi! What is wrong with you? I'm saying this is not going to end well. And it's not just my family. Rupi is also getting too attached."

That I laugh at. He's bought into the act like the rest of them. This is what the Naik sisters do. We make people believe things about us.

"It's all an act," I say.

Before he can answer, a scream emanates from the house. We rush back inside to hear another bellow come from Prem's parents' room.

Everyone drops what they're doing and runs toward it. Every worst-case scenario grips me. Wasn't Rupi with Prem's father?

"Mom, Dad, everyone, come see!" Neel and Nathan run at us, whooping and spinning around like fireworks gone rogue.

I almost topple over one of them.

"Come! Come!" one of them yells. "Grampy has a surprise!"

Fresh panic grips me. Oh, Rupi, what did you do now?

I follow the family into the room, hearing the horrified squeals as they enter one by one.

Prem's dad is sitting propped up in his bed as usual, but something is very different. He's wearing a sleeveless undershirt over his pajamas. And one of his arms is completely covered in tattoos.

I almost faint.

"Pankaj!" Prem's mom gasps. "Your arm!"

Nathan and Neel spin around and through everyone and finally land on Rupi, wrapping their arms around her from either side. She has the strangest, most strangled expression on her face. The boys squeeze against her with unbridled joy.

Chipku.

It's the one unbroken, untainted memory from my childhood. Clinging to my sister, hanging from her waist. It's the safest place I've ever known. She never pulled away. Not once.

She gathers both boys into herself absently and watches the room for reactions with guarded eyes.

"We did it. Daadi, Mom, Dad! We gave Grampy tattoos!"

"You did that? How?" Chandni looks halfway between horrified and disbelieving.

How? With what? When? Why? Questions fly around the room. No one's quite sure how angry to be and with whom.

Then suddenly everyone stops.

Prem's baba is smiling. His eyes are twinkling. Only one side of his face moves, but his smile is wide and incredible.

"You like it?" Prem's mom says with surprise.

He gives the slightest nod and makes a happy sound.

"You asked them to do it?"

He gives another nod.

Then he lifts his arm. A few inches, but he lifts it.

His wife goes to him, sits on his bed, and takes his arm.

"Did it not hurt?"

Neel and Nathan pull away from Rupi and double over with laughter. "Omigod, Daadi thinks they're real!" They smack palms in a high five and run to their grandparents. Jumping, somewhat gently, onto the bed. "They're transport!"

We all turn to Rupi.

"They mean transfer. They're transfer tattoos. Like a sticker. They're temporary."

"Yes, they're transferrr," the boys repeat.

"My god, you scared us!" Their grandmother is the first to burst into laughter. "They look so real! Did you do these?"

"Yes!" Neel yells.

"No, Neel," Nathan says. "Not by ourselves. Ruchi helped."

Ruchi?

"They combined Rupi and Chachi and came up with Ruchi," Chandni explains.

"This is fantastic, boys," their father says. "How much time did it take?"

Everyone moves to hover over Prem's dad and studies his arm with utter awe.

It's intricate and vivid. Colors edged with sharp black lines. Snakes and butterflies in a thicket of leaves and flowers. There's even a tiger, black stripes over orange fur, fierce eyes and sharp teeth. It's truly beautiful.

"Did they really do this?" Chandni asks.

"We did, we did." The boys point at each one of the motifs that make up the connected monolithic pattern. They run to the desk and bring two sketchbooks that are filled with practice drawings. Pages and pages filled with rough sketches of each of the motifs. For the three weeks Rupi's known them, she's had them drawing and drawing. Their pride bounces off the pages and explodes into stardust that fills the room.

Their mother is in tears. Their grandmother pulls them close and kisses their heads over and over, and they wrap their arms around her and stay still.

"You like it, Daadi?" Two sets of eyes beg their grandmother unabashedly for praise.

In response, Tanuja picks up her husband's arm like it's the most precious thing on earth and drops a kiss on the patterns across his forearm. "I love it!"

"Grampy wanted them. We showed him our sketchbooks, and he wanted them."

"Pankaj, I didn't know you liked tattoos," Prem's mom says with the sweetest coyness.

Her husband's eyes glitter naughtily, and he gives another nod.

"I wish I'd known. I would have gotten one for you when I was young and foxy."

He makes another head motion, his lips quirk, and his eyes shine in a whole different way. He makes a long sound.

"Come on! Now? I'm sixty-five. It's too late." Is she blushing?

Finally Rupi speaks. "It's never too late. I mean. Technically. If one wants it. I'm not saying you should get one."

"You should get one, Mamma," Prem says.

Really?

"Oy hoy, look at him. We all know how much you love them. Now you want everyone in the family to get them too?"

"Not everyone," Prem says, cheeks turning pink with embarrassment. "Just you if you want one."

She smacks his shoulder. "Stop being silly. But this is great."

He looks at me. *See?* his worried eyes say.

"Can we make you some? Please please? Ruchi, can we make them for everyone?"

N&N fly back to Rupi and start spinning around her like tops.

She ruffles their hair. "Only if they want them. What did I tell you about the magic of tattoos?"

"That the magic comes from people wanting them. You cannot do anything to anyone else's body that they don't want." They parrot the words with utmost sincerity.

The room fills with silence.

"I'm sorry. It's just—" Rupi says.

"Oh, Rupi, that's so beautiful. Thank you." Is Chandni crying again? I mean, that's a pretty important thing to teach little boys, but Rupi, can you stop?

My sister is watching me, and my thoughts have to be showing on my face, because she has that hurt, cold look again. *I don't care what you think,* her eyes tell me.

The fawning goes on for a while, then Preeti, Dr. Johnson, and the girls arrive, which feels like such a relief I want to cry. I squeeze the girls to myself. *Look, children love me too!*

Prem is right; his family stands no chance. Which means this ugly, horrible feeling that's been burning through me is jealousy. Rupi has also been right all along. I'm jealous of my sister.

I. Am. Jealous. Of. My. Sister.

I've been struggling to fathom the fact that my sister has everything I've ever wanted. When, really, she has nothing at all other than her spirit and her heart. And I'm jealous of her. I'm jealous of her for the things that sustained me through life.

Just as I'm reeling from that, Saj arrives and is immediately accosted by his nephews before he can say hello to anyone else. They drag him to their grandfather. Saj makes the requisite impressed sounds when they show him their artwork.

"There's Chacha's tandoori chicken pizza!" the boys announce.

"And you've held everyone up for lunch." Saj's sister gives him an affectionate slap on the arm. "How can you never be on time?"

"Don't say that! He's a good boy," Prem's mom says, leading us back to the kitchen. "And you already know he's a lawyer," she says directly to me, taking my hand. Great. She's not going to let this go. "And you're such a beautiful girl. Isn't she so beautiful?" She throws the question out to the room in general.

They respond with a chorus of enthused agreement.

Rupi grins. "She is," she says quietly. "She's the most beautiful girl on earth. And she's a beautiful person too."

"See, that's what I'm saying," Tanuja says. "Saj, did you think about what I said that day?" And if that's not clear enough, she clarifies it further. "Did you ask her out yet? Enough of all this single life."

Saj gives her a patient look. "I did think about it, Auntie-ji. And I quite like the single life. Not that I don't agree that Simi is lovely." He throws a look Prem's way.

Prem isn't in the mood to help him out right now. He looks neither angry nor sad, just deeply exhausted. As though this situation has gotten so bizarre, he's out of reactions.

"See! He thinks you're lovely, Simi. Look at him, so handsome. Is he not handsome?" She turns to Rupi this time. "Rupi, tell your sister how handsome he is."

Rupi looks up into Saj's face and studies it with full bald-faced focus. It's impressive how he doesn't shrink away from her scrutiny. "Simi, he's very handsome," she says drily. "In that angel-of-death, hired-assassin sort of way."

Saj gives her a dark look.

Tanuja puts a hand on her hip and regards Saj. "You know what, you're right. Such a smart girl. I think it's the tattoo artist in you. You see things. There's something dashingly dangerous, no?" She waves a hand around his face. To his credit, he follows the motion with more amusement than anything else. "Also rich and single! It's a miracle no one has swooped him up."

"I mean, someone did," Saj says. "I was married."

This is news to me, but Prem's mom makes a *pish* sound.

"Not anymore," she says. "And it wasn't for long. Just a few minutes, it felt like."

"It was three years, Auntie-ji."

"That's a few minutes in lifetime terms, no?"

"In that, you are correct."

"And it doesn't count, because she was terrible," she says directly to me.

This makes Saj huff out a laugh. "She wasn't terrible."

"See, such a good person. Who protects a woman who hurt him and took all his money?"

He gives a good-natured shake of his head. "She didn't take all my money. Divorce is expensive." For some reason, he looks at Rupi when he says this. Then seems to realize this and turns back to Prem's mom. "And there's always hurt on both sides when a marriage breaks."

Rupi's smile is equal parts mockery and delight. She presses a hand into her hip and matches Tanuja's pose. "Forget how hot he is, Simi. He's basically the Dalai Lama. You should totally go out with him."

TWENTY

RUPI

I'm going to put the girls down for a nap," my sister says after we've spent two hours stuffing our faces with a house full of Guptas.

The baby Simi is carrying squeezes her cheeks with both hands and presses her sleepy face into Simi's.

"I know, baby girl," Simi says. "Almost time for ninni. You've been so good. I'm so proud of you." The words toss me back in time. Only it's a baby Simi in my arms. I'm not much more than a baby myself, but I feel just as old as I am right this minute. I've only ever felt this old—at once stunted and ancient.

I can't believe she's actually thinking about giving up the girls because of that awful boss.

"You need help with them?" I ask and take a baby from John, who follows the rest of the family to the living room, where everyone is discussing which movie to watch.

The baby I'm carrying (I still can't tell them apart) screams as though I'm murdering her.

Simi takes her from me, completely at ease with a baby in each arm. The ungrateful drama queen quiets instantly and squeezes into Simi and away from me.

"I'm guessing the Resignation-of-Submission hasn't happened yet?" I say.

Simi and the two babies glare at me. It's like having a Trimurti, a three-headed statue of the mythical gods, shoot eye lasers at me.

Ever since Simi found out about the wedding date being set, she's been walking around as though the knife I slid into her back is stuck there. I've tried to smooth out her feathers. I did her laundry and ironed her scrubs. I deep cleaned her fridge, and I've made chai every morning. The way she's looking at me right now means the peace accord I've been proposing has been soundly rejected.

I take the third baby out of her high chair. This one also screams and reaches for Simi with both arms.

Fortunately, our mopey knight in shining armor hears the yelling and arrives to save the day.

I hand the baby over to Prem.

"I need to feed the babies before nap time," Simi says to Prem and walks off as though my presence is unbearable. Prem, carrying the now magically silent baby, follows.

I hate that I follow them.

Have these two forgotten that they were on board with this scheme when we set off on it? I've tried my best to make this comfortable for everyone. Is it my fault that Prem's family takes getting to know their future daughter-in-law seriously? It's not like I want to be here all the time. It's not like I have any road map for what to do with a family of veritable golden retrievers.

I've spent a lot of time trying to put Simi's mind at rest. Well, telling her she's being absurd by being jealous should have put her mind at rest.

I follow them into Preeti's room.

"It's a bit ridiculous that you won't talk to me," I say, pulling the door shut behind me.

"Don't raise your voice around the girls," Simi says.

"I'm practically whispering. Also, if raised voices were harmful to babies, you and I wouldn't be standing here."

She groans from the depth of her being. Prem and she start changing diapers with such deftness, they might as well be doing it one handed and blindfolded. Show-offs! *I cleaned your bum when I was five!* I want to say. But discretion is the better part of valor and all that.

When they're done, they lay the girls down and hand them their bottles. All three exhausted babies drain the bottles in minutes and pass out.

"If you weren't on board, you should never have agreed to this," I whisper-hiss when the babies' eyes are good and closed. "Now you're having second thoughts? What do you think I'm supposed to do?"

"I don't know, Rupi. Stop working so hard to deceive everybody," my sister says.

"The whole damn point is to deceive everybody," I say.

"This is my family," Prem says.

"Really? I thought I had walked into some random house off the street and was hanging out with random people like Goldi-effing-locks."

Simi narrows her eyes at me. "Stop it! Don't act like you don't always do this."

"Do what?" But the answer is in her eyes. "You think I manipulate people into liking me to get my way."

She shrugs.

"Of course I do that! I've had to do it. It's called survival. Who doesn't use charm to get what they want?"

"You were supposed to . . . never mind. Just forget it."

"I was supposed to what? What was I supposed to do, Simi? Tell me, so I can do whatever it is I'm supposed to do to get you to stop trying to sabotage me."

"You're not supposed to hurt them." This from Prem.

"Hurt them?" My heart clenches. "Did I do something to hurt them? Did they say that?" Do I sound needy? I absolutely do not. I don't do needy.

"See!" Prem says to Simi, and they both look like they've caught me plotting murder.

"If they like you so much, they're going to be heartbroken when we separate," Prem says, but he doesn't sound half as mean as my sister.

Oh, now I get it. This has nothing to do with Prem, so I turn to my sister. "You don't want them to like me. Not only do you not want them to like me, you're surprised that they do. You think if someone likes me, I'm going to use it to hurt them. Nice, Simi. At least this guy gets to judge me because he doesn't want his family to get hurt. What about you? When do you start caring about me being hurt?"

"Really?" Simi says. "You're getting married to the man I love *because* I don't want you to be hurt. You want to think about that for a moment?"

"All I've done for the past month is think about that, Simi. What you've done for me is incredible. You've saved me." There, I've said it. "But I love how you keep forgetting that the reason I'm in this position in the first place is because of you. I had to leave India because of something you did, and because I had to find a way to get you out of trouble." To hell with not saying words.

She gasps. Nice. Now she cares.

"Before you tell me again how I didn't give you a choice, let me remind you that to me the only choice was not letting you get hurt. That's all that was going through my head. It's called love. So, no, I'm not sitting here looking for ways to hurt people."

"That's not what we meant," Simi says, and I want to shake the guilt off her face.

That's exactly what they meant. I don't care anymore. If I can't count on my own sister to give a shit about me except to make some sort of grand gesture and then rub it in my face, how can I expect these strangers to be any different? I don't care about any of them.

"Never mind. You're right. Everything I'm doing is calculated, and all I care about is getting through these two years. It's actually a shock they're buying it." I look at Prem. "Then again, it's not a shock. They're just like you. Not one of you has a spine or sense of self-preservation. I'm screwing everyone over, and look at how they're lapping it up."

They look at me with twin horrified expressions, and I can't stand to be around them anymore. I can't believe I let all this absurd normalcy lull me. What have I gotten myself into? The familiar sense of being cornered constricts my lungs.

"Don't worry. I get the assignment now. I'm not allowed to like anyone—not my skill set anyway. Most importantly, I'm not allowed to let anyone like me. I'm supposed to be a rag doll, one that can't ever possibly hurt anyone. Also, Simi, if I'm a good enough actress to get them to like me enough to give you a stomachache, then I guess when I hand him back to you, I'll be just as good at getting them to hate me. So, you can breathe easy, *Chipku*!"

I storm out of there.

I can't go back down, because the lower floor is teeming with Guptas, and I can't be around that anymore. I make my way to the guest room, where I've spent a few nights when Simi had a night shift and Mamma insisted. I'm livid at myself for thinking this could work. For getting carried away. For something I can't even put my finger on. I'm livid. Period.

"Hey," a rumbly voice calls behind me, and I stop in my tracks. Saj is the absolute last person I want to see right now.

I feel like I've been following his instructions to a T, for all the good it's done me.

"What do you want from me now?" I wipe my eyes on the cuffs of the stupid salwar kameez Mamma bought me and turn to him.

"Excuse me?" He's in a black linen button-down that seems custom tailored to his lean body. For some reason, the image of him in his black Indian kurta from the party flashes in my mind. Black has always been my clothing preference, but it fits his assassin vibe so much better.

"I'm sorry. Ignore that. I guess you should consult with your bestie before you give me instructions on how to behave with his precious family."

"Ah, trouble in paradise. Did you expect there not to be?"

I open the door to the guest room and go inside. "We can't talk out here, someone might hear."

He follows me. "Did you and your sister fight again?"

How can I not laugh at that? "I mean, can you find me sisters who wouldn't be fighting in this situation? Actually, who else would ever get into this situation?"

"Actually, what's going on here isn't that uncommon. Which is why it's hard to get away with."

"So, what you're saying is that you assist in committing immigration fraud on a regular basis." I ignore the fact that he did not know when he took the case that Prem and I weren't really together. Though once he found out, it's not like he walked away from it.

"No. I personally have never had a case like this, but one of my lawyer friends had one where a couple got their citizenship perfectly legally. Then they got a divorce, went to their home country, married each other's siblings, and brought them back on spousal green cards. They stayed married for two years until the siblings got green cards, then got divorced and remarried the person they were originally married to."

"And here I was thinking I had an original idea."

"Sorry. Not even a little original. Quite common, in fact."

"Well. Turns out the quite common idea is a dud around here. It's dead upon arrival."

"I thought it was going well," he says with no emotion whatsoever. "My sister seems thrilled with you. You've had quite the impact on Neel and Nathan. You tamed my untamable nephews in a week, I'm told."

"It took me a day, actually. I think the problem might have been just that: that everyone's been treating them like little demons in need of taming, not little boys filled with curious energy."

He looks taken aback at that. It's so subtle, I could be imagining it. "You only say that because you didn't see them growing up."

"No, I'm only saying that because it's what my mom liked to call me. A little demon that she wished someone would tame." I hate that my throat tightens around those words. Even more, I hate that I let something like that slip. To him, of all people. All this deadly normalcy is making me idiotic.

He goes back to studying me without any expression at all. Maybe he has one of those conditions where he can't process other people's emotions.

"Not that I care. They can treat the boys however they like. It's not my problem."

There's a long pause (another one of his specialties), then he pulls his wallet out of his pocket and retrieves a folded card from it. He unfolds it to reveal two brightly colored, big-eyed figures hugging a tall figure in black. He keeps the thank-you card N&N made for him in his wallet?

"Ever since the party, everyone is treating the boys like they're gifted artists. It's quite beautiful what they've done with these cards."

The cards his nephews made for the guests *are* beautiful, and thinking about them makes my heart do something I refuse to analyze. I can appreciate art without being a blubbering mess about it. "They're okay, I guess."

He cracks what might be a smile. I can't be sure, because there's no previous benchmark to go by, but it's definitely a possibility.

"Simi still having a hard time?"

I don't want him talking shit about my sister.

"This." I make a circle around the room with my hand. "This was her dream, not mine." I meet his dark-as-death gaze. "What will it take to abort mission?"

He blinks in shock. Wow, a smile and shock. Maybe the rusty robot face got some WD-40 today. "As in?"

"As in, all this syrupy wholesomeness was never what I wanted. Now that I've tried it on for size, I don't think I can deal with it for two years. What's the exit strategy?"

"Jail," he says easily. "Or a fine. Definitely deportation."

At least I can count on him for answers.

"Probably for both you and Prem, if they suspect a conspiracy."

"Ah, a silver lining then!"

He makes a sound. I could bet good money it's a laugh (also no previous benchmarks to go by).

"Has anyone ever made you laugh before?" I say with some wonder. "I feel quite victorious."

"You should. There are contests. Medals. No one's ever won."

A joke. My head just exploded. "So, if they made it an Olympic sport, I'd be a gold medalist?"

"You'd be in the running, yes."

Is the man attempting charm? Suddenly I want to know why his wife left him.

There's always hurt on both sides when a marriage breaks.

"My point is, you can't change course now. Too many people would get hurt."

"You're a lawyer, what do you care about people getting hurt? Aren't you guys supposed to suck on the blood of people's hurt?"

He raises a brow but sidesteps the bait. "Prem is my best friend. We've been friends since elementary school. Long before our siblings married and we became family."

"Congratulations?" I say. "I want to say I'm surprised, but opposites attract and all that. You with your robotic stiffness and him with all that soft spinelessness."

"Wow."

"What?"

"The man is doing probably the most generous thing it is possible to do for love for your sister, and you're calling him spineless."

"I mean, if you really think about it . . . he would have said no if he could stand up to my sister." I shrug my shoulders.

I didn't think it was possible, but he stiffens even more. "You do realize what you're saying is totally fucked up, correct?"

"It isn't what I'm saying that's fucked up, it's the situation. It's ironic and unfortunate that I find myself in a situation where the thing that makes the man completely wrong for my sister also benefits me."

He looks at me weird. He has this way of hearing things unsaid and seeing things unshown. He knows nothing about me, except, of course, how I look stark naked, a fact he seems to have deleted from his hard drive (and it's about time I did as well). And yet, I know I'm going to absolutely hate what's about to come out of his mouth.

"Ah, so you hate him because you know he's going to hurt your sister," he says in a stage whisper, totally breaking character. "Now I get it."

I want him to go back to being a robot. I don't respond.

He pauses long enough to make me uncomfortable. It's a cheap trick that doesn't work on me. I'm perfectly at ease, thank you very much.

"Fine, I'll bite. What is it you think you got?"

"That it's not him you hate at all. It's all the men who came before him. You just think he's them. And no matter what he does, you see them and not him. Because no matter who it is, she's going to get hurt."

"Wow, you should quit lawyer-ing and start therapy-ing. Two whole professions made just for people like you."

"You mean for robots like me."

I raise my chin. "*Ah*, you do get it, after all."

"Prem is probably the finest human being I know. Except maybe for the rest of his family. They're good people, Rupi."

"Great. You, too, ha?"

Suddenly his black-on-black eyes are all expressive, because I can see them fill with sympathy—my least favorite thing to find in people's eyes. "Me, too, what?" he whispers.

"You, too, are trembling in fear of me sinking my evil talons into the lovely Guptas. Well, you're right, all of you." I don't care who I hurt so long as I can save myself.

Another long, deliberate pause. I want to throw it in his face and walk away.

"Not even close," he says in the quietest voice, and it strikes me like a punch to the gut that the thing in his eyes isn't sympathy. It's gentleness. "That's not what I meant at all. I meant they really are good people, and they won't hurt you if you let yourself love them."

TWENTY-ONE

SIMI

This past month has been no cakewalk, but standing outside Dr. Johnson's office feels even harder. Too unfair.

I try not to think about my sister's words. *That's how bullies work. If you kneel to her now, you'll never stop kneeling.*

I wish I could talk to Rupi about what I'm about to do. But Rupi and I have been stuck in a seesaw of silent treatments. It's currently her turn to hand it out and mine to be at the receiving end.

I hate how hard Prem's family liking her hit me.

I'm not sure what exactly I expected, but it wasn't this endless fawning. I don't even know why I'm surprised or why it bothers me so much. It's not like I wanted them to dislike her, and the truth is that for all her prickliness, no one ever does once they know her. My sister has always been unfailingly endearing to anyone with half a brain and any heart at all. She's always acted like it's a part she plays, like she does it on purpose for gain—the making people like her. I've never noticed until now that it might be because she's terrified of actually being liked and even more terrified of liking others.

It's been three days, and the hurt in her eyes over what I said at the Sunday lunch hasn't stopped haunting me. But I was hurting so much, and seeing her so oblivious of it really messed with my head.

She might be right about the fact that I'm responsible for her being in this situation, but she is absolutely wrong about how I should handle Karina. Sure, she's a bully, but she's a bully who has me exactly where she wants me. She knows exactly what I have to lose. And I'll do anything not to lose it.

I take a breath and walk into Dr. Johnson's office. A huge framed canvas of TASha on the wall greets me and breaks my heart.

It's cowardly of me to do this in the office without Preeti here, but things have been a little awkward between Preeti and me recently. She seems to sense my feelings for Prem, and her guilt at having "encouraged" me when he wasn't interested hangs between us, unspoken.

It's a good thing that the girls are supposed to start spending a few hours a day in day care this week to get better socialized. Maybe it was time to cut my hours with them down anyway.

Instead of beating around the bush, I come right out and tell Dr. Johnson that they need to find someone else to help with the girls. "With my sister getting married, I want to spend more time with her, and there's a lot to be done before the wedding." I've rehearsed and re-rehearsed the words over and over, but it still hurts to say them.

He stands and comes around his desk. "Is this about the green card paperwork? Did Karina say something to you again?"

I shake my head. If he gets in the middle of it, that will only make Karina even more mad. "It's just a matter of not having enough hours in the day. I'm feeling too stretched thin. I don't want my work at the practice to suffer."

"Simi, you're the best nurse we have. Dr. Cline and Dr. Ung both think so. And Dr. Rai knows it too."

"I really need your help with this, Dr. Johnson. Please."

"I'm guessing you haven't talked to Preeti about it yet."

"I will. But can you talk to her first and explain?"

He studies me, his expression deliberately neutral. "Can you do me a favor? Can you stay until TASha have transitioned into day care? After that, we'll look for someone else."

"Of course. Thank you so much. I can't tell you how much I appreciate it."

He gives me a half-hearted smile. "Also, let's not tell Preeti just yet. She's already not doing well with the girls starting day care."

I'm not either. I want to keep the girls at home and not expose them to the big, wide world just yet. "I understand."

He looks as relieved as I am to have bought some time. I can tell Dr. Rai that it's done, and we can get things going on the paperwork.

I make my way to her office and find she's left for the day.

I should feel lighter, but I don't. I keep seeing visions of my sister punching the children in our neighborhood for teasing me.

Just as I'm getting ready to leave work and wondering if I should try to pick Rupi up a little early today, she calls.

"I was just thinking about you," I say before I can stop myself.

"Well, if you were wondering how to get rid of me, you're out of luck."

So much for sisterly bonding. "I'm done with work early. I was wondering if you wanted to hang out."

"In that case, you're in luck. The angel of death and the rasgulla have decided to drag me to your place of work. We're almost there."

I was not expecting that. "Prem's with you?" I say, not even caring how pathetic I sound.

I can hear her eye roll.

"Yes, he got tired of setting fires at his restaurants and decided to come home. Meet us at the hospital cafeteria. We're almost there."

When they get there, I'm already waiting, because I no longer care about appearing desperate to see Prem. He looks as exhausted as ever.

"Hi," he says, walking right up to me and not stopping until our bodies are almost touching.

"Get a room," my sister mumbles as she passes us and plonks herself at a table in a far corner.

Every time I want to soften toward her, she pisses me off. *Can you have some respect for my relationship?* I want to scream. I don't, of course. I quietly follow with Prem and Saj and join her.

"To what do I owe this pleasure?" I ask after we've grabbed our drinks of choice.

Rupi throws Saj an icy look that makes me wonder what he did to make her angry. "We're all wondering the same thing. Maybe Mamma convinced him to ask you out and he's done enjoying the single life."

"Not quite yet," Saj says in the calmest voice. "And lovely as you are, Simi, I don't think we need yet another complication."

"Word," Rupi says on one of her particularly mean scoffs. I guess I'm not the only one she's frozen out.

"You called this meeting?" I ask Saj, because it's impossible to engage with Rupi when she's like this.

He nods. His eyes are watching Rupi. "Looks like we have no choice but to reach out to Tina Komar and make an appeal for Rupi's passport after all."

Rupi freezes over her ice coffee, which means this is the first she's hearing of it too. "Wow, this again?" she says, working hard to sound bored. "In case it didn't register the last fifteen times I said it: Tina will not return my passport." There's absolutely no emotion in her voice, and dead coldness in her eyes. She turns to Prem. "I thought you said he's a good lawyer."

"I am," Saj says with even less emotion. "Which is why I know that we have to do this. Not having a physical passport is going to add a year to the process since we don't have any other documentation."

"My god," Prem and I say together and with enough emotion to make up for Saj and Rupi.

I squeeze my temples. This cannot be happening. "Another year on top of the two years they have to be married?" I absolutely cannot imagine going through this for three years.

"Yes," Saj says a little more kindly. "Unless Rupi lets me contact Tina."

I don't think I can breathe. My lungs constrict, and I gasp for breath. I can feel all the blood in my body rushing to my face.

Prem rubs my back. The horror on his face makes everything worse. My sister sits there and watches me struggle to take in a breath, her face frozen in a mask.

Saj brings me a glass of water. I take a sip and hand the rest to Prem.

I want to hold him. I want him to hold me. I miss him so much, I don't think I can bear it.

I force myself to slow my breathing, to calm down.

"There is no way we can do this for three years," I say. I have not a single doubt that Prem and I will not survive it. We're already stretched at the seams to tearing.

"You have to let Saj contact Tina for your passport," Prem says to Rupi. "Please."

She throws a look of loathing at Saj. As though Prem begging is his fault, and she's never going to forgive him for it. Then she turns to Prem again. "They have me on camera taking thousands of dollars' worth of stuff. Do you want cops to show up at your door and arrest your fiancée? Because the moment Tina knows where to find me, that will happen." She rubs her arms and throws him a look that unleashes all her rage. "But that would solve all your problems, wouldn't it?"

"If I wanted you to end up in jail, I wouldn't be doing any of this," Prem says with surprising heat.

Rupi blinks as though she was not expecting him to respond.

He looks at Saj for help.

Prem shouldn't have to solve this by himself. "What if Saj can figure out a way to make sure that doesn't happen?" I say, because there has to be a way out.

"I know you both think that Saj has some sort of magic wand, but I know what his strategy is, and I've already said I'm not going after Tina for trafficking."

"But why?" I ask. "What happened to standing up to bullies?" It's the one thing Rupi has always been obsessed with. It's why she'd never forgive me if she knew I'd just resigned. No one cares more deeply about justice than she does. She may not admit it, but the reason we both survived our childhood was because Rupi knew when something was wrong and she never sat by and let it happen without doing something. Her not wanting to go after Tina makes no sense.

"Really?" she says. "You want to talk to me about standing up to bullies? Does that mean you're not going to roll over for Karina?"

"Don't you think me rolling over for Karina becomes even more imperative if you insist on stretching this out even longer?"

For the first time, she shrinks back. "I can't," she says.

Suddenly I know there's something she isn't telling us. "Why the hell not?"

"Because I can't throw everyone who works at Curry and Tikka under the bus, okay! Not without knowing how this will impact them."

Saj is watching her with the most intense look. "Are you saying that if we could do this without hurting the other employees, you'd be okay with it?"

Rupi leans into his space. Just like that, she's done with the shrinking. "You can't. That's not how these things work. I was there. I know. It's not a simple situation for anyone who's stuck there." A world of anguish passes in her eyes even as she fights it.

He swallows, but he doesn't look away. He's about to open his mouth when she raises her hand and stops him. "Don't you dare say that you know. You don't. You don't know what it's like to have to make that choice. Even calling it a choice is sick. It took some of those people risking their lives to get there and be stuck in that wretched situation. You don't know what's waiting for them outside. It's very likely that it's far worse." Her hand is pressed in a fist into her chest. "You don't know what that fear feels like." Her voice cracks, and she looks enraged at the indignity, but she refuses to look away.

For a moment they stare at each other, breathing hard.

"You're right," he says finally, keeping his voice flat, as though he knows that if he lets any sympathy slip, it will destroy her. "I don't know how it feels to be in that situation. But you do. You got out of it. You know how that feels too."

"But I'm not all the way out of it. I'm hanging by a thread. I'm dependent on the generosity of my sister and Prem. And you."

This time he leans away, giving her space. "If this doesn't work, would you go back there?"

"Of course not."

"Then let's give the others a way out too." His voice is so soft. He looks at her hand like he's going to pick it up, but her glare stops him. "I promise I will not let any of the victims get hurt."

She groans and looks up at the ceiling and does what she always does when she doesn't know what else to do: She laughs. "You can't. And it's not just that." Her gaze slides to Prem. She takes a breath. This is not easy for her. I want to go to her, but no one can touch her right now. "Your family . . ." Her jaw works. "They've been gullible enough to buy all of this, but that doesn't mean they won't change their minds if . . . well, they can still change their minds, and I can't afford for them to."

My heart squeezes. She doesn't want Prem's family to know what happened to her in LA. She doesn't want them to see her as a victim. She doesn't want them to know what she did to not be one.

"You're not to blame for what Tina and Ron did." Prem's the one who says what we're all thinking, and Rupi looks at him funny. "My family won't change their mind about you over that."

Another, even sadder laugh escapes her. "You might be right. But I don't feel like taking a chance on my freedom based on that. I mean you—" Her gaze moves from Prem to me and lands like a slap. "Even my sister. You both promised to help, and you keep trying to get out of it. Forgive me if I don't trust your family to stand by me after knowing me for just weeks."

"We're not backing out, Rupi," I say. "We're trying to help you."

"But you want to back out!"

Of course I do. Who would want this? When I agreed to it, I didn't know it would be two years. And now it could be three? Would I have let this happen if I'd known? Truth is, yes, I still would have. I wish I didn't have to make that choice. But Rupi is not the only one for whom letting her sister get hurt isn't a choice. That's the real reason we are here. I just haven't had the guts to commit all the way. I've been waiting for Rupi to do that for me—to do all the work that comes with a hard choice.

I meet her fierce gaze with my own. "I'm not going to, though. That's the part that matters."

Whatever she sees in my face makes her response stick in her throat.

I'm not above using her very rare state of speechlessness. "That doesn't mean we don't take every opportunity to not stretch this out. Especially when a solution is available."

"But it's not available," she says again.

"Then let's figure out a way to make it. You're afraid that if we call Tina, she'll track you to Hochkinsville. What if I go there and do it?"

Rupi grabs my hand. "You are not going anywhere near that place!" Every bit of her emotionless mask drops off her face. "Those people cannot find you."

"What the hell, Rupi! You're afraid for me, what about you? Can you let me decide what risks I want to take? I'm not a child anymore."

Her gaze moves from Saj to Prem and then back to me. "You are acting like one, though. Your own green card is in jeopardy because of that witch."

Saj looks at me. "You're having trouble with your green card?"

"Karina's not signing my papers."

"Let me take a look at what's happening, and I'll take care of it," Saj says, jaw set. "Karina Auntie was friends with my mom."

Rupi practically snarls at him. "Just like you'll take care of not letting Tina have me arrested and thrown out of the country?"

"Yes, exactly like that." How is Saj not even a little bit intimidated by her? "Because we have laws."

"And you also have people who can manipulate them."

Saj shrugs. "Sure. But now you have someone who can manipulate them on your behalf."

For a second, she stares at him as though she believes it.

He meets her gaze unflinchingly.

"If I get Simi's processing moving, will you let me contact Tina?"

"Are you negotiating with me about my sister's life?"

"That's a little dramatic, don't you think?"

"That's a little manipulative, don't you think? Why is this so important to you?"

"Every case is important to me." He takes a breath and slides a quick glance my way. "And I'll help Simi anyway. Whether or not you agree to go after Tina."

Rupi smiles the most evil smile. "Maybe you can take Anagha out. Karina should do anything you want in return."

He narrows his eyes at her, but his lips quirk the slightest bit. "Sure. I'll let Karina and Tanuja Auntie fight over me for Anagha and Simi. Can I go see Tina, please?"

"We have to at least try, Rupi," I say.

"Do you know Saj has never lost a case?" Prem says.

"There's always a first time," Rupi says.

"This won't be it," Saj says with a remarkable amount of confidence, and patience.

Rupi rubs her arms. Her thumbs trace the lines of her tattoos. "I can't believe you're ganging up on me with them," she throws at me.

"One has to do whatever it takes to survive. You're the one who taught me that."

"I did not teach you to be stupid."

"It would be stupid not to follow the easiest path," Saj says. "Without a passport or a birth certificate or a Social Security card, we have to gather evidence for where you were these past two years. I tried to get past it, but they won't allow it. Not without extensive background checks, and they're going to find out about your time in LA anyway. The only way to not have this defeat us before we've even started is to get the passport from her. I will not let her hurt you, Rupi. I'm your lawyer. You have to trust me."

She studies him for so long, I almost lose hope. He refuses to look away. Finally she sighs. Her shoulders droop and then come back up in attack mode. "But Simi cannot go anywhere near LA."

"Shouldn't Simi be the one to make that decision?" Prem says, and damn the audience, I lean over and squeeze his hand.

To no one's surprise, Rupi rolls her eyes, but she doesn't bite his head off, and that feels like out-and-out approval.

"She won't have to," Saj says.

Rupi turns to him. "Good. And I'm only agreeing to let you threaten Tina to get my passport, not to letting you go after whatever operation they're running."

"That's the plan," Saj says. "For now."

TWENTY-TWO

RUPI

My wedding is just about a month and a half away, and I have now been a fixture in the Gupta landscape for two months. One thing I'll say is that time flies in the Gupta home.

After my sister all but warned me not to hurt Prem's family by getting too close to them, I figured the easiest way to distance myself without losing my chance at freedom was to spend time with Prem's father. The man needs company, and I want to avoid it. I get that I'm using his illness, but hey, even my own sister thinks I'm a leech.

It has turned out to be the worst and best sort of bad decision.

At first, when I started spending time in Baba's room, there was this strange sensation that filled me up. It was like a hit of something heady and intangible that I kept coming back for. I had never experienced it in my life before, so it took me a while to put a word on it. I think what I've been experiencing might be peace.

I can breathe. My vision doesn't dart here and there, looking for danger. For all his frailness, there's a solidity to Baba, a substantialness to his spirit. He is fully present and entirely undemanding. No one has ever been so interested in my art. No one has ever been so comfortable with my silence. No one has ever been so on board with all my plans concerning him.

I twist and turn his limbs the way his physical therapist showed me. I can tell it hurts, but he smiles through it. I breathe with him, holding his nostrils in alternating patterns. I read to him, which has gotten me back into reading. I used to read like a beast in school, but then I lost my taste for it, because the books made me either too sad or too hopeful, and I didn't have time for either.

We're reading a book Preeti thought I'd love because of the protagonist, a female scientist in the 1950s who has no patience for the world's bullshit. It's filling me with anger but also making me laugh. I've never known rage to be so delightful. It's amazing how books make us feel our own feelings as someone else's. I've avoided myself for so very long, it's therapeutic to see myself in a book's character. For some reason, the book makes Baba cry, too, but when I offer to switch to a different book, he absolutely refuses to let me.

The family comes and goes. They tease and hug and provide anecdotes about their long, hardworking days. They think I spend so much time here because I can't get a job while I'm waiting for my green card.

I've borrowed Baba's old bike. He was an avid biker before the stroke. He biked some twenty miles every day from restaurant to restaurant. Mamma says he loved that bike as much as he loves his family, but none of his kids wanted it. Until now.

I love it too. Suddenly I have freedom. I bike from Simi's apartment to the house every morning now, so she doesn't have to drive me. Simi gave me a credit card, which I wanted to throw in her face, but really, not having a penny is limiting.

I still didn't use it for a while. There's really nothing I need. Mamma and Simi both took me shopping on separate occasions, and now I own clothes and shoes and even a little backpack for my bike rides here. Then one day I brought Baba some nankhatai cookies Simi baked, and he got so excited that I realized he loves gifts.

Now I stop at the grocery store on my way and bring him a little something every day. Candy, cookies, oddly flavored chips. He is technically Simi's father-in-law, so I feel completely valid spending her money on him.

Simi keeps trying to buy me things. Clothes and bags and makeup. I leave it all unused, hoping she'll return it. I hate how things make me feel. Weighed down.

I know she's trying to make amends for accusing me of being a callous user of the Guptas, but I'm not sure she was too far off the mark. Nonetheless, not having to fight with her all the time is nice. I guess the strategy of locking myself up with Baba so I can't hurt anyone else works for her. I don't care, because it works for me too. I quite like this peace thing. And no one ever makes me feel like I shouldn't be here.

Except my mother, who shows up in the room every so often and looks at me the way she always looked at me, like she wishes I wasn't here. She stands in the corner and watches as I push Baba's knee into his belly.

He groans in pain.

"Sorry," I say. "I'll be more gentle."

He shakes his head. *Keep going,* his eyes say.

But I stop, and my mom gives me a knowing smile. *Wimp.*

I pull the covers over Baba and put a hand on his head. "Sleep," I say. "We'll do more later."

He's tired enough that his eyes flutter shut.

Ma doesn't like that. She sneers.

I do see that I'm the one who's putting her inside this room, and I have to be the one to let her go.

It's one of the many things I've learned from Baba. He never turns away any healing he's offered. Not medicine, not exercise, not any time anyone wants to spend with him. He is wide open to help. He values it, feels fully deserving of it.

Maybe I'm deserving of it too. His body is as sick as my mind feels, but it's me who has to do what I can to help heal it.

Saj's unsolicited insights notwithstanding, I am only interested in helping myself. I am most certainly not in danger of liking these people.

Fine. I'm quite in danger. In fact, the danger might have fully overtaken me. A family's love may be the world's most powerful force.

I hate that Saj's annoying voice has gotten stuck inside my head.

They won't hurt you if you let yourself love them.

He's dead wrong. It's going to hurt like a bitch. It already does.

Even the part where I can't talk to Simi anymore. Not without feeling like I've stolen from her. It was much better when I didn't know these people, so I didn't know what I'd taken from her. She no longer looks at me like I have everything she wants, but now that I know how having all that feels, I can't bear to have her witness it.

All I want is to stay here with Baba and read. We're almost done with this book, and we have our next one picked out. I'm dying to know what happens next, but Baba is fast asleep.

I pick up my phone to check on Simi. She usually texts throughout the day. Difficult patients, Karina drama, hospital politics. I pretend not to care, but she's so entrenched in her life, it fills my heart. If I was the child my mother wanted to tame, Simi was the child our mother barely knew existed. That's probably why Simi only existed in her own mind through my eyes. Seeing her like this, so present and complete in her own world, is so deeply satisfying it makes me smile.

There's no text from Simi, but there's one from Saj.

Saj: Going to LA today.

I am aware, I text back. I want to stop him. I wish I hadn't agreed to this, but Simi is right. We have to do what we can to get through this as fast as we can.

Saj: Thanks for agreeing to this.

Rupi: Did I have a choice?

Three blue dots dance on the screen. Then stop, then dance again.

If you say you always have a choice I might have to kill you, I type before I can stop myself.

Only a robot would say that to you. And I'm human, Rupi. His text lands on my screen, and the strangest electric spark splits through me. Then: Also, I like being alive.

I refuse to smile.

He waits for a few seconds, then the blue dots start to dance again.

Thanks for trusting me, he types finally.

Something tells me this is what he wanted to say in the first place. The reason he texted.

Do I?

I cannot start to depend on people. What is wrong with me?

Just do your job and get my passport back. That's all I can think of to say.

His silence is longer this time, and for a while I think he won't respond to my rudeness, but he does. You got it.

I put my phone away and start pacing the room. Baba is still asleep. I pace until the restlessness eases, then I sit back down and lay my head on the edge of his bed. Before I know it, I slip into sleep.

I dream about my sister.

Clinging to me. Scared. Unable to protect herself.

I see a man put a hand on her shoulder. Something about the way his thumb moves, stroking over the tiny curve, makes fear prickle down my spine. She's five years old. I pull her away. Take her away. I tell my mother. She tells me to stop trying to ruin her life with my imagination. I hear another man outside the door. I've learned to bolt it shut. My mother asks me why. I make up a story about monsters. About hearing voices in my head. I let her think I'm crazy, because it scares her and it scares the men. I realize I like scaring people. It keeps them away. But at least Simi is safe. I don't let her get hurt. Simi is never scared of me. She knows it's for her. She knows.

I startle when a hand lands on my shoulder.

"Rupi, beta, it's okay." It's a voice that's grown to soothe me. I relax and feel deeply embarrassed at having jumped out of sleep with such terror.

"It's going to be okay," she says, her Mamma face burning over Ma's face, and I realize my own face is wet. I've cried through my dream.

Mortified, I jump up and leave the room.

I go to the guest room. I wash my face, scrubbing at my skin. The rock on my finger flashes under the lights. The ring has gotten snugger on my finger, and sometimes I forget it's there. It no longer feels too heavy to bear. There are no hollows in my cheeks, no shadows under my eyes. There is a gold chain around my neck, and there are little gold tops in my ears. There's a line of embroidery around the neck of my blouse. Gifts from Simi, and Prem's family.

I no longer look destitute.

My hair has grown out, and that, of all things, makes my heartbeat speed up. I need a haircut.

I pick up the phone, and my fingers dial the only person I can speak to right now. I've never been nervous talking to her before.

"Rupi?" she says, worried.

"I still can't believe your phone tells you who's calling. Isn't it funny what's happened to our world?"

"It is. It is very funny what's happened to our world." Simi's voice is quiet, but there's so much relief in it.

"Can you take me for a haircut?" I ask before I change my mind.

I expect her to be at work. To be busy. To ask me to wait while she looks for an opening in her schedule.

"I have a hair person. Let me call her."

Just like that, she gets an appointment. I want to bike there, but she insists on coming to get me. Apparently, we have to take the freeway there, and my helpless bike isn't allowed on there with all the monstrous trucks. She happens to have the afternoon off because one of the doctors is out this week and one of the PAs called in sick and they had to cancel their appointments.

"I was going to call and see if you wanted to hang out anyway. I'm so glad you called," she says as we drive away from the house. It's been an age since I've heard her be cheerful, and I hate that my defenses go up.

"Thanks," I say, and the word feels strange on my tongue.

The surprise on her face makes me smile. I don't think I've ever thanked her in my life.

"Have I never said thanks to you?" I say.

She stops at a light. "I don't think so." She says it with a smile. "Have I? I didn't realize siblings are supposed to do that."

I think the Gupta siblings do it all the time.

Her face says she just had the same thought.

"I think we're supposed to say it for the small stuff," I say. "A ride. A glass of water. Borrowed clothes. I think the big stuff is outside the scope of thank-yous."

"Makes sense. Some sacrifices are too big for thank-yous."

I don't know how to respond to that.

We drive in silence until we get to a parking lot, then she leads me into a salon. It's completely empty, which is a relief.

A gorgeous girl with purple hair is chewing gum and reading on her phone on a couch. When she sees us, she spits her gum into a trash can and comes to us.

She gives Simi a hug. "Sims! So good to see you. Who is this beauty? You cloned yourself, yes?"

Simi introduces me to Suzanna, and I explain what I want. Which is to take it all off. I don't know what it is about my hair, but I hate it. I want it all off. I'm surprised I haven't woken up one day and shaved my head. I haven't had the urge in a while. Now I really want to.

"I'm not shaving your head," purple-haired Suzanna says. "It's already too short. I'll shape it up. Trim it. I've been trimming Simi's hair for, what, four years now. The girl refuses to let me put any layers in it. Funny that I have to convince one sister to keep it and the other one to take some of it off! Are you two like that about everything?"

"Pretty much," I say just as Simi says, "Not really."

Then she covers up the awkwardness that follows with "You can't show up the month before your wedding with a bald head, Rupi."

I picture it. Mamma, Chandni, Pawan, Preeti all with their jaws dropped open but not wanting to be hurtful. Then there's Neel and Nathan. What would it be like for them? To see my bald head with the ugly scar splitting the back of my head. And Baba. Would he care? He might worry. They all might.

I do this every time. I come this close to exposing it and then back away. Suzanna runs a comb through my hair, scraping right across the scar.

Despite myself, I wince.

"I'm sorry," she says. "I'll be more careful." She doesn't ask questions or remark on the scar, if she sees it. I have no idea how visible it is with hair. It's been an age since I held up a mirror and looked at it. She finishes up the trim, then flips it all out with a dryer.

"You look like an eighties pop star," Simi says in a whisper.

She pays for me, and we get back in the car.

"Can I ask you a question?" she asks.

I've been avoiding her eyes since the wince. "It's never a good sign when someone asks that before they ask a question. We've just made peace. You sure you want to disrupt it?"

"No," she says quietly. "I would do anything to never disrupt the peace with you." She merges the car into traffic, and the ease with which she does it is so badass, something shifts inside me. I don't drive. I've never had a car. My baby sister isn't a baby anymore.

"Fine, ask me."

It takes her a long time, but she finally looks over at me. "You still have the scar?"

How can she possibly remember? She was four years old.

"I think the memory of that much blood is one of those childhood memories that sticks." She answers the question I didn't ask.

"I do still have it." The memory of the rain hits me, making the world beyond it invisible.

The only thing I can see other than the rain is my sister's hand in mine. She's holding on with all her might. All I know is that I can't let her hand go, no matter what. The streets around the school have already turned into gushing rivulets. The water reaches Simi's knees. She's pressed against me, and I can feel her body trembling with cold. All the other children were picked up from school. The rickshaw driver who usually brings us to school and takes us home with the other kids from our building didn't let us on the rickshaw today. He's been warning us for weeks that he will have to stop letting us ride until he's paid. Our mother ignored my pleas to pay him. Despite the rain, he leaves us behind because he gave our spots to other children. There's no place for us.

I remember waiting. I remember knowing no one was coming. I remember knowing that our mother wouldn't care if we didn't go home. I remember walking the two miles home through rain so violent, even Mumbai was deserted. I remember falling and hitting my head. I remember never letting go of my sister's hand.

"Does it still hurt?" Simi's voice brings me back to the present.

"I'm not sure." I don't know if it's pain or sensitivity or just the sting of memories. I reach back and touch it. It's wider than it should be because it was never sewed up. A wound never treated. I'd hacked off my hair, then washed out the gash myself and pressed a cloth to it to stem the blood. For months my hair stuck in the scab and pulled, making it take years to heal.

"Thanks," my sister says.

"For what?"

"For not letting go."

TWENTY-THREE

SIMI

What I remember about the day my sister brought me home in the rainstorm is knowing I was safe. Even when she fell, even when blood gushed from the back of her head and turned pink as it mixed with the rain and streamed down her white school uniform, I knew she would get us home.

I so badly want to be that for her.

She slept in today. Whatever happened at Suzanna's hair place yesterday seems to have taken the stuffing out of Rupi. She's sleeping a lot. Given that sleep is probably the most healing of our bodily functions, my heart fills with something harshly hopeful, watching her. Her body is rolled up, folded into itself. Her delicate bones poke out against fine skin. The points of her elbows, the angle of her jaw, the ridges on her wrists, the wings of her collarbones. How someone so seemingly fragile gives out such a sense of power, I will never know.

"If you're planning to strangle me in my sleep, let me tell you, I'm stronger than I look," she says with her eyes still closed.

"Curses, foiled," I say, quoting a comic book from our childhood, and she smiles with her eyes still closed. "I brought you chai."

She pulls herself up to sitting before opening her eyes and taking the cup. She takes a long sip, then a deeply satisfied sigh leaves her body. "Okay, spit it out, what do you want?"

"Why do you think I want something?"

She holds up the cup. "Chai in bed?" Points at my face. "The fact that I know that face. Either you want something or you're hiding something."

I try to imagine her reaction if she finds out that I quit the nannying gig because of Karina. I feel her future disappointment like a body blow. I think about how she let Saj go to Tina, despite her fear.

"How do you do it?" I say. "How are you not scared?"

"Maybe being scared is a choice I never had. I've always had to act before I could let fear set in. It's always been a race toward not losing something important."

All her choices run in my mind. Suddenly they make sense.

"Will you tell me something?" I say, and she nods. "What happened in India before you left?"

She looks up from her cup and meets my gaze. "I've already told you what happened."

"You haven't told me what you did to the blackmailing cop before you left."

"What makes you think I did something to him?"

"Let me think," I say and point at her face. "The fact that I know that face."

She looks impressed, and it makes me feel a little too victorious.

After draining her cup, she puts it down on the nightstand. "Get me a brush."

I grab a hairbrush from the bathroom and sit down in front of her.

She starts brushing my hair. The perfect pressure and pull against my scalp is so comforting, it melts my muscles. "Ron gave me a cell phone before he left. I used it to record the cop blackmailing me. Before leaving for America, I sent the video to three people: his boss, that journalist who lived in our building, and the cop's wife."

I spin around, not caring that my hair tangles in the brush. "Rupi! That's brilliant!"

She smacks my shoulder for interrupting her brushing. "Pretty sure it was more stupid than brilliant, but it felt good."

"Well, I hope they hung him," I say. "By his privates. So, what happened after that?"

She goes silent for a beat. "I didn't wait around to find out. He probably handed in that CCTV footage, and we might be wanted by the law. Even if he didn't, he probably wormed his way out of it and is hunting me all over Mumbai."

"At the very least, his wife had to have killed him, right?"

Rupi puts the brush away and starts pulling my hair into a French braid. The familiar confidence with which her fingers part and tug digs up all the things that have been pushing us apart and threads them back together. "I wouldn't hold my breath. He was probably making enough in bribes that the wife had a life she didn't want to give up. Who kills a goose that lays golden eggs even if the goose preys on another gander? Doesn't matter anyway, he's no longer our problem."

She pulls the end of the braid into a hair tie and gives me a nudge. "I need to hop into the shower, and you'll be late if you don't head out soon."

I get off the bed and study my braid in the mirror. "How do you get it to look this good?"

"Because I'm an artist," she says and goes into the bathroom, but then she pops her head out again. "Simi, I'm really proud of you for standing up to that witch," she says. "Those girls need you, and you need them. I'm so glad you didn't give in." With that, she disappears behind the closed door, leaving a yawning hole of shame inside me.

When I get to the office, the first thing I see is a young woman in a pantsuit leaving Dr. Rai's office. I know without asking what is going on, but I ask Mary at the front desk anyway. She tells me Dr. Rai had some nurses in for an interview today.

This has happened before. I refuse to be afraid.

For the rest of the morning, I don't have the time to be afraid. It's patient after patient. Five walk-ins on top of the appointments. Broken bones and stitches and an endless number of shots. By the time I sit down with my sandwich in the lunchroom, I feel like I haven't taken a breath all day.

I check my phone. Nothing from Prem. I can't think about the distance between us right now. Rupi's out shopping for wedding clothes with Prem's mother. There's a text from Saj, checking if my papers have been signed and offering his help again.

Who am I kidding? I'm not Rupi. I'm terrified. If I have to go back to India now, the police probably have the CCTV footage of me walking into the room where a man died.

Without thinking about it, I open the browser on my phone and type the cop's name into the search box.

Within seconds his ugly face pops up on the screen. Bulbous nose, thick mustache covering his upper lip, multiple chins, bulging frog eyes. A shiver starts from the back of my neck and crawls down my spine to my toes. The memory of his tobacco-laced breath and his violating gaze flashes to life in my head. The picture is from an article in *The Times of India*.

"Subinspector PK Sharma Listed Among COVID Deaths in Yerawada Jail."

I drop my phone. Sweat beads on my forehead and drips down my back. Sweat stains paint my scrubs at my armpits.

I breathe through the nausea that grips me.

The asshole is dead. He was in jail. I pick the phone up again with shaking hands and start reading.

Turns out the man had been blackmailing people with CCTV footage from various crime sites for years. Then I see the name I've been dreading: Rupi Naik. She's listed as one of the victims. The recording of him blackmailing her is public. It has millions of hits. How the hell have I missed all this?

Because I've avoided everyone and everything I left behind.

Everyone at home knows what Rupi had to do. Every unsavory name our neighbors ever called us rings in my ears.

My finger hovers over the social media app I've curated to avoid everyone from our old life in Mumbai. I navigate to the group where all the gossips from the neighborhood gather online to spill scalding tea. Entering the cop's name into the search on the group page yields a post from a year ago when the man died. There are a hundred and seventy comments. Rupi is the topic of almost every comment.

My skin feels hot with rage when I exit the app.

These people . . . They were the people Rupi stood up to. A single warrior against a crowd intent on stoning her to death with their shame stones. With me hiding behind her.

Dr. Rai walks into the break room and stops when she sees me. "We're short staffed, and you're on your phone here," she says.

I'm literally on my lunch break at 4 p.m. I turn to face her. "Did you get a chance to sign my papers yet, Dr. Rai?" I ask instead of acknowledging her comment.

She looks bored. "I told you I'm having our lawyers look at it."

"That's not what Dr. Johnson said."

She's taken aback at being contradicted. "Well, obviously John would say that."

Now she's bad-mouthing Dr. Johnson? Something inside me snaps. "Brianna works for the senior center after hours. Marquis works at the hospice. All the other nurses in the practice have other jobs. There's no conflict of interest, and it's perfectly legal for me to work outside of the clinic."

She folds her arms across her chest. "They don't let it impact their work."

"I don't, either, and you know it. The only difference between them and me is that they don't need a green card and you can't lord that over them."

She gasps. It's the most satisfying thing I've experienced in a very long time.

"If you're going to fire me, fire me, so I can apply elsewhere. Recruiters have been reaching out to me for years. I don't want to take their calls, but I will if I have to. I need those papers signed today. And I'm not quitting babysitting for the triplets. Let me know what you decide."

Her mouth is still hanging open when I leave the break room and make my way to Dr. Johnson's office. It's empty. He's probably with a patient, so I wait. In about five minutes he comes back, Dr. Rai a step behind him.

"Simi," he says, "everything all right?"

"No, Dr. Johnson. But it will be. Can I change my mind about babysitting? I don't want to quit."

"Of course." He practically bounces on his heels. "I knew you'd see sense. That's great news!"

"Thanks. Also, can you please make sure my paperwork is signed? Saj Rawal is my new lawyer. If you have questions about the paperwork, please let him know."

TWENTY-FOUR

RUPI

If I was stupid enough to think that the Gupta world was all roses and rainbows, I was absolutely right but also a little bit wrong. The real wedding preparations for my fake marriage are the special kind of awkward adventure I am absolutely not equipped for. Today is the day we go shopping for my wedding dress. Given a lifetime spent learning how to pretend, this should be easy, but I'm filled with terror.

The only silver lining is that it's just Mamma and me.

I could not be more thrilled about the family opening their thirteenth location. Bless them for working so hard, because I absolutely cannot imagine having to do this with an audience.

I try not to think about how horribly I miss my own work. I doodle and draw with N&N, but I want to wield ink with the kind of desperation I absolutely cannot let myself feel right now.

"I wish your sister could be with us when we do this. Should we have waited for when Simi was free?" Mamma says.

"I wish she was here, too, but her schedule is impossible." Simi and I might have managed to get a nice truce going, but she is absolutely not ready to shop for a wedding dress with me.

We ring the doorbell of a little blue-siding-covered house. This is our last hope. Prem's mom tried to get the designer in India who made the clothes for the weddings of her two older children, but the timing is too tight. It's wedding season in India, and it's apparently impossible to even get anyone worth their salt on the phone. So, one of the aunties suggested this woman in Nashville who runs a wedding-clothes business out of her home.

A woman approximately Mamma's age opens the door. She's in a hot-pink salwar kameez with heavy gold embroidery. She greets Mamma with the utmost warmth. Then her gaze falls on me, and she falters somewhat.

I'm wearing black jeans and a black T-shirt. The clothes of my soul. If I never had to wear anything else in my life, I'd be perfectly happy. If anyone ever cared about what the bride actually wants, this is what I'd get married in.

The woman, who introduces herself as Bina, slides a bug-eyed gaze at my tattoos and my hair.

"Where's the bride?" she asks, taking us into a sitting room where bridal ghaghras are hanging on a trolley. There's a tufted couch and snacks set out on a coffee table along with a teapot and cups.

"This is Rupi, my daughter-in-law," Mamma says, completely clueless about whatever is going on in the woman's head. As for me, I've seen that look too many times to miss it. Usually I hunger for it. The look is discomfort, and making people uncomfortable has always been immensely satisfying. Today, it exhausts me.

"She will wear ghaghras and all?" Bina asks Mamma, as though I'm not standing right there and as though she can't picture my biker-chic vibe in anything as feminine as a ghaghra.

"Of course," Mamma says. "She wants something pastel, delicate, like her."

"Yes, of course." Bina is obviously unconvinced and seeks solace in offering us chai. "We might have some ones with long sleeves. But not many."

Mamma looks confused. "I don't think she wants long sleeves. It's barely fall. Is that what's in style right now? Tell Bina what you're looking for, beta."

"Something that shows off my tattoos," I say, biting into a too-spicy samosa, which isn't half bad.

Bina looks like she might explode into a confetti of little Binas. She emits a syrupy laugh. "But for bridal, that will not look good. Correct?" She makes the appeal directly to Tanuja.

"Do you think so?" Mamma looks at me. I can't quite tell if she's figured out what's going on yet.

"I mean, it's your son's wedding. You can decide," the woman says.

"Actually, it's Rupi's wedding. She will decide."

"Of course." Bina titters out that syrupy laugh again. "You're very modern. So nice to see."

"I am," Tanuja says. "Everyone says that."

Bina produces a syrupy smile to match the laugh and points at the hanging dresses. "Would the bride like me to find something for her to try?"

No, thank you. The bride would rather not pay you for anything, you judgy woman. But Mamma's eyes light up at the sight of the ghaghras, so I shut up and nod.

"How about this one?" Mamma picks up a pale-pink net piece with crystals on it. The blouse has tiny cap sleeves.

"Oh, lovely color. Hold on, I might have another piece in pink." The woman rushes off and finds us a much brighter pink. I'm not even a little surprised that it has sleeves all the way down to the wrists. Tenacious, this one.

I ignore her offering and find myself a pale-green piece with in-cut sleeves that will show off the desert rose on my shoulders nicely. "I think I'll try this one."

"It's gorgeous," Prem's mom says.

The woman smiles uncomfortably.

I go to the makeshift trial room made out of curtains and pull the heavily embroidered thing on. The blouse hangs on me, and I have to hold the ghaghra to keep it from sliding right off. But the colors pick up the greens and blues on my arm. It's almost like my tattoos are an extension of the dress. If the person who's going to make an absurd amount of money for it didn't disgust me, this dress might be perfect.

"Oh, Rupi, beta, that's just beautiful," Mamma says, almost tearing up when I step out. "You have the most gorgeous arms." She pats my cheek. "Do you like it?"

I shrug. "It doesn't fit."

"Can you take this one in to her size?" she asks Bina, who's shifting on her feet like a rusty nail is stuck in her shoe. I think I want to put one in there before we leave.

"I'm not sure. There's too much embroidery for alterations, I don't think it's possible."

"She's right," I say. "I think it will lose its charm if it's taken in."

"That is not true at all," Mamma says and studies Bina like she's a boot caught on a fishhook. For a moment she says nothing more, but the moment doesn't last. "Is there something bothering you, Bina?"

I should have known. If I've learned anything about Tanuja Gupta, it's that she always intends to hold her peace, but the peace never cooperates.

She stares Bina down until the woman breaks like a cookie in hot tea.

"No no. Not bothering. It's just . . . I have very traditional clients. I do very traditional brides. I will . . . I can do the taking in. Just don't tell anyone where you got it from. If you put pictures on social media and all that, it's okay to not tag."

"That's so sweet of you," Mamma says. "Isn't that so sweet, Rupi?"

"It's very sweet," I say, and what the hell, I take another samosa. This is about to become fun.

"See, such a kind girl. You're insulting her, and she's calling you sweet. But I think she's right. Taking it in would make it lose its charm."

The way she says that last part makes me stuff the remaining samosa in my face with glee.

"Please don't be upset," Bina says. "I have to take care of my clients. Business is hard enough."

"Ah, business, yes. Did you know that my husband and I run twelve—well, thirteen soon—pizza places in Kentucky and Tennessee?" She pauses to let that sink in. "When we opened our first one, people said the restaurant business was too tough. A hard business. But you know what? We were blessed, and it never was. Do you know why?"

Mamma waits, and Bina, whose face seems to have shrunk to half its size, shakes her head.

"We followed two rules." Mamma counts off on her fingers. "One, we always serve only the best, freshest pizza. That's the obvious one. But the other one is more important. We've always welcomed every single person who stepped into our restaurant with open arms and treated every single customer exactly the same."

She turns to me. "Go change, beta, we've seen all we need to see." She's not done with Bina, though. "My father sold mithai in a little shop in Nagpur. He believed he did god's work by feeding people sweet things. If a person in rags was ahead in line to buy his sweets and someone stepped out of a fancy car and tried to cut ahead, do you know who he served first?"

She doesn't give Bina the answer, but I'm pretty sure she doesn't need to.

"He always said you can't come at business from a place of fear," she goes on. "You have to come at it from a place of service. We were looking to buy at least fifteen dresses from you. It's our youngest child's wedding, the last in the family, so obviously there will be many functions, and we're a large family. Alas, we're going to have to find someone else."

That's what finally makes Bina's eyes widen with regret. "You're misunderstanding me. I'll alter the dress, all the dresses. You don't have to find anyone else."

I'm back in my jeans and shirt. I hand her the hanger with the tag facing her. Five hundred times fifteen is a lot of money.

"Oh, but we do. Thanks for your time. I hope you'll follow the wedding on social media."

I grab another samosa before we saunter out of there. I want to grab two, but I'm not a monster. As we step into the sunshine, I feel like a warrior princess riding home victorious—or more like her sidekick.

Mamma looks at the samosa in my hand. "Are they that good?" This is my third vengeance samosa.

I split it down the middle and hand her half. She takes a bite and concedes grudgingly.

"Terrible people serving good food is one of life's great tragedies," she says when we get in the car. "I'm so sorry."

"Why are you sorry? That was awesome!"

"You think so? Maybe I said too much."

"I thought you said just enough."

She smiles and starts driving. "I hope you'll ignore her. You are a very sweet girl. Appearances can be so deceptive." As soon as she says it, she realizes how that came out. "Sorry, that came out mean. I meant it as a compliment."

I laugh. No one has ever accused me of being sweet in my life. "It wasn't even a little mean. Just honest. And I know exactly what you mean."

"I feel terrible. This was supposed to be a special day."

"It is. It's the best day. Please don't feel bad. People have always judged me before knowing me." I slide her a look. I remember her discomfort the first time she saw me. "They just don't usually change their mind so easily. And they're definitely not so lovely to me when they do."

She throws her head back and laughs. "Thank you. Remember to tell my son that you think I'm lovely. And my other kids too."

I lean toward her in my seat and say in a stage whisper, "I think they already think you're the best thing since cotton candy."

She takes my hand and drops a kiss on it. "I'm so glad my Prem found you. I think you might end up being the best kind of girl for him."

How can I not laugh at that?

Which makes her frown. "You think I'm just being nice?"

"Aren't you?"

"Rupi, beta, are you joking?" She takes a breath, because her voice chokes with emotion. "Pankaj fed himself the other day. That would not have ever happened without you."

Baba had lifted a potato chip to his mouth by himself. It had taken him a full minute and herculean effort and focus, but he'd done it. "That's all him, not me."

"Of course. And Neel and Nathan, that's not you either."

"Oh, their cuteness is totally all me." I roll my eyes, because my stupid voice is choking up too.

"If I'm being honest, I didn't think my Prem would do something like this. I mean he's stubborn as heck. I'm not at all surprised that he didn't care about your paperwork. He'll do anything for love. I'm sure he would have even followed you to India if things didn't work out. All my children have minds of their own. It's just that I always . . . never mind."

"Say it. I won't take offense. I promise."

"Well, I just always saw him with a much more conventional girl."

Again, I can't help but laugh.

"Go ahead, laugh at me. But I mean conventional only on the outside. I always knew he'd find someone strong as steel on the inside but also filled with so much love and generosity."

God, she has no idea. That's exactly the kind of girl her son is in love with. "It's amazing how well you know your children." The way our mother knew us was as "the tall one and the short one," or maybe she knew more and she wished she didn't.

"Which mother doesn't?"

It's a good thing she's driving, because I don't want her perceptive eyes on me.

"He surprised me, but not like Preeti. Did you know Preeti just showed up at a Diwali party with this boy with blond hair and blue eyes? Your baba and I considered leaving them there and running away from our own party. Can you imagine the gossip?"

She goes off into spot-on imitations of all the horrified reactions from their friends, and I can't stop laughing.

"But look at them now," I say. "They're the it-couple of the community."

"That they are," she says with all the pride in the world.

"How did you make peace with it? With your daughter choosing someone so different from who you had in mind for her?"

"Have you seen my grandchildren? I would forgive John anything after giving me those girls." She's laughing, but she turns to me with an indecipherable expression. "Can I tell you the truth? Just for your ears. Only because no one has ever asked me such an impudent question so casually."

I did indeed. What she doesn't know is that no one has ever made me feel comfortable enough to ask such a question before. "I'm a vault," I say, making a locked-lips gesture.

"Don't I know that? My son hid your relationship from us because of how private you are, remember? Again, that's an observation, not a criticism. Actually that's not true, it's a little bit of a criticism too."

"I don't mind. Honest criticism is so much better than dishonest politeness."

She squeezes my hand again. "I'm not going to tell my friends how lucky I am that Prem met you. I don't want their envy to cast an evil eye on our good luck."

I press a hand into my chest, unable to respond to that. "You were telling me something," I remind her.

"Ah, yes. I was answering your nosy question. Ever since Preeti was little, once she set her sights on something, she could never let it go. I used to try to deny her things every once in a while, just to teach her how to deal with disappointment, but it never worked. The only chance I ever had of deterring her from anything she'd set her sights on was by appealing to her power of reasoning and logic. But hers is better than mine anyway, so I can't remember ever succeeding.

"When she sat her father and me down and told us she had decided to marry John, I admit I could not imagine a worse fate for our family. This girl, who loves her ghaghras and jhumkas and who needs her chai to be just right and who I can't even get to eat pizza unless it has Indian spices in it. My girl, who grew up dancing kathak and having crushes on Shah Rukh Khan and Hrithik Roshan, I could not believe that she thought that a man who had no idea what dal was could ever understand her. I mean, the boy is a looker and all. And a doctor. But still, looks and money only take you into a relationship, they certainly don't keep you there."

"What changed your mind?"

"It's the oddest thing. When John met us, he seemed so nervous, almost terrified of us. It reminded me of how terrified I was when I first came to this country as a new bride. I was stressed about everything. Not being able to speak the language, not looking anything like the locals, not knowing how to dress, not understanding the rules and the culture. I was so lonely and afraid of everything. The first six months, I just walked around with my head hurting and my belly cramping.

"Then one day your baba took me to the beach, and there I saw all these people lying by the ocean half naked, eating ice cream and throwing balls, and I thought: They don't care what I think of them. They don't even know I'm here. What if it didn't matter where I had come from and how I got here. What if all that mattered was what I did with what was happening right now. That was it. I ran into the water in my jeans, and the strangest thing happened. Joy filled me. I felt happy for the first time since I said goodbye to my family. For the first time, I was inside myself and not inside everyone around me, and I stopped wondering what they saw and stopped worrying about what they thought.

"When I saw Preeti and John happy, I figured, whatever is going to happen in their relationship is going to happen. They're happy today, and that's the only thing that's actually real. So, I ran into the water again. I gave myself up to that moment."

By the time she's done, we're home.

I find myself squeezing my arms around myself. I only know tears are streaming down my cheeks because Mamma pulls up her dupatta and wipes them.

I can't remember the last time I cried. I'm mortified.

"Arrey, what did I say to make you cry?" But her eyes are moist as well.

"No one has ever told me anything like that about themselves before." The words slip out before I can stop them.

She's been so open and honest with me, how can I not be the same? Except I'm not. My very presence here with her is a lie. Just as I've started to find myself, I've turned into a lie.

TWENTY-FIVE

SIMI

My truce with Rupi feels precarious, but also precious. We've taken to watching movies together again, and that seems to comfort her. Last night we watched our favorite classic comedy from the sixties, *Padosan*, where a man who can't sing to save his life enlists the help of a music teacher to woo his music-obsessed neighbor. The scenes where he lip-synchs to the other man's singing as she watches and listens from the window across the street were still every bit as funny as they were in our childhood. We huddled over my laptop with chai and popcorn and laughed so hard that at one point, I had to thump Rupi's back to keep her from choking on her laughter.

I haven't seen my sister laugh like that in too long. I haven't laughed like that in too long.

This morning, she sewed a broken button back on my blouse, and I made her pancakes.

We kept our conversation on movies and Chandni's hair art and N&N's obsession with anime. All the things that aren't our personal land mines. No mention of our mother, green cards, Prem, or wedding shopping with his mom.

At least Karina is no longer a land mine. I did tell Rupi that I did as she said and called Karina's bluff. Threatening to quit got the doctors to sign the papers. I haven't told her I caved first. I haven't told her about the dead cop either.

I'm not going to. What difference does it make? PK Sharma may not be lying in wait to hunt her down, but everyone she knows is lying in wait and armed with judgment. I cannot imagine her having to go back to that kind of public shaming. Truth is that I also cannot imagine living without her again. The thought of her leaving brings an edge of panic, and I'm not ready to face it.

While I made pancakes, she sketched a drawing for me. Two sisters huddled over a laptop, their bodies filled with laughter and love.

I told her that if I ever got a tattoo, this was the one she was giving me. She didn't respond. She just smiled, but her eyes went sad. So, tattoos were also out as a topic of conversation.

I put the picture on my fridge and told her stories of the triplets' poop-related disasters to perk up the mood again. Rupi laughed until tears ran from her eyes. I forgot how much she enjoyed potty humor.

Now we're on our way to see Saj at his office. He has something important to discuss.

One part of me doesn't want to go. For one, I don't know what kind of news he has for us, but even more importantly, the idea of upsetting my peace with Rupi makes my belly cramp. Her emotions seem to pop right up to the surface around Saj. Right now, she's leaning extra hard into nonchalance, which means she's wound tight about the meeting too.

Prem is traveling again. It's been a week since I saw him last. The distance between us is starting to grow thorns. I'm starting to feel hopeless. But I might have my sister back, and that's what matters right now.

We get out of the car outside an impressive steel-and-glass building in the trendy Gulch. In the four years I've been here, Nashville has grown at such an alarming rate, sometimes I barely recognize it.

The lobby is all white marble. The receptionist with the bluest eyes walks us to a waiting area and lets us know that Mr. Rawal will be with us soon.

The white fabric couches are so bright that sitting on them doesn't feel like an option.

When we first walked into the building, Rupi looked uncomfortable, but now she's smiling. "What a perfect place for cyborgs. Do you think there's a pod in his office where he gets charged?"

"Why don't you come in and find out for yourself," Saj says, walking up to us.

A laugh bursts out of me, but neither of them cracks a smile.

Saj leads us into his corner office overlooking the river. It's like an office in one of those high-powered big-city movies. Rupi widens her eyes at me behind Saj.

"Thanks for coming. Can I get you something to drink?"

"Like what?" Rupi asks, walking up to a wall covered in framed newspaper and magazine articles. They're all high-profile cases Saj was involved in.

He watches her study the wall. "Like tea, coffee, water, soda, beer, wine . . ."

She turns away from the articles and looks at him. "Really? Fancy." She whistles.

"So?" he asks.

She looks confused.

"Can I get you anything?"

"No, thanks."

Then, in the most out-of-character way, she sashays past him and drops into the couch. She gives a little bounce. "Seriously fancy. I had no idea immigration attorneys do so well."

"They don't. It's my dad's practice. Intellectual property and patent lawyers do so well."

"Ah," she says. "So, the rich kid is taken up with lost causes."

"Actually, the rich kid believes that no cause is a lost cause," he says.

Before she can say something even ruder, I ask for a soda. I think I'm going to need some sugar for this.

He gets me a Sprite from a fridge tucked into a bookcase lined with leather-bound books.

I walk up to the impressively tidy mahogany desk. My eyes stop on an Indian passport in a zipper bag sitting on the leather liner.

I look up to find Saj watching me. "Is that—?" I can't keep the excitement out of my voice.

He nods, but he doesn't seem to share my excitement. His gaze is worried as it slides to Rupi, who's checking out the breathtakingly lovely view from the floor-to-ceiling windows.

"Rupi," I call out. "I think you need to see this."

She saunters over, then stops in her tracks when she sees the passport. Every bit of nonchalance leaves her body.

Saj takes a step closer to her, then steps back.

She looks at him with her whole heart in her eyes. "That's my passport."

He nods.

"How . . ." Rupi is never at a loss for words. She picks it up and takes it out of the bag and looks like she might cry.

I do cry. I can't remember the last time I was happier.

Saj hands me a tissue, looking as somber as ever. His eyes keep straying to Rupi.

"My gosh, Saj, this is amazing," I say. "I can't believe you did it!"

"I did," he says, but there's a distinct lack of jubilation in the words.

"What's wrong?" I ask.

His eyes on Rupi are so intense, I don't know how she can bear it.

She blinks up at him. She's confused by his behavior too. Then she examines the passport again. "Did you change your mind and get a fake made?" She opens it and looks through it. "Nope. This is my passport photo. Then why are you looking at me like you expect me to bite your head off?"

The strangest expression passes over his face. "Because you might do exactly that." He looks genuinely afraid of Rupi decapitating him.

Rupi seems to read something in his face and steps back. "My god. Tina knows where to find me. You told her." Her gaze slides to the door. "Are they coming for me?" She starts pacing.

"Can you sit down, please? I'll tell you everything."

She spins to face him. Her cheeks are blazing. "I don't want to fucking sit. Am I going to be sitting in jail? What did you do?"

"I told you I won't let that happen," he says in the gentlest voice. "You're safe. I've already applied for an extension for your visa. That's not what I want to talk about."

"Can you spit it out already?" she says. "Please."

"I hired a private detective to investigate Tina and Ron's businesses before I went to LA to meet Tina." He takes a breath. "You weren't the only girl Ron took advantage of. He was running an escort service out of Curry with undocumented South Asian women."

He pulls pictures out of an envelope and holds them out to her. She doesn't take them. Obviously she already knew this. I take the pictures from him. They're heartbreaking. Night shots of young women dressed in tight, glittery Indian dresses getting in cars and entering hotel rooms with men of all ages. They look even younger than I am. It's their eyes that catch me. Dead eyes.

I drop into a chair.

"Most of them are graduate students and tech workers who've lapsed their visa status because of lost jobs and constantly changing immigration policies," Saj says.

I press a hand to my chest. "That's terrible."

Rupi hasn't said a word. Her jaw is clenched tightly enough to crack teeth.

Saj is watching her with so much focus, it's like I'm not even in the room.

Finally Rupi looks back at him. "What does Tina want?"

"She wants to get out of the business. She wants to go to the authorities and ask for immunity in return for turning into a witness. Obviously the operation runs deep and wide. Apparently she's in trouble. The documents you took had some crucial information. Codes to safety-deposit boxes and accounts. She's being threatened. She's scared for her life."

"Good," Rupi says. "But I don't have the file anymore. You know that."

"She knows that. That's not what she wants."

"Just say it, Saj," Rupi says.

"She asked for my help."

Rupi starts laughing. "Wow. She wants you to be her lawyer. I did not see that coming."

"Or she wants me to help her find one."

"And you promised to do that in exchange for the passport."

"I told her I'd think about it in exchange for the passport."

"You asshole," she says. "I trusted you."

"Rupi," I say. "He hasn't done anything. He got your passport back."

"Can you for once be on my side?"

"I am," I say.

"We both are," Saj says.

"He's not going to help Tina," I say.

Another laugh spurts from Rupi. "Of course he is. Didn't you hear him before. There are no lost causes." She squeezes her temples, then turns to him, a new realization in her eyes. "I'm such an idiot. I knew it." She gets up and goes to the wall covered in interviews and articles about Saj's cases. "I was right. You don't actually care about my case at all, do you? You never did." She points to the framed news pieces. "This was always about the trafficking. You were just using me to get that case. Helping me doesn't get you an article in a magazine." She starts walking toward the door. "Let's go, Simi."

"I hate those frames," he says as Rupi reaches the door. "My dad's the one who had them made. He likes to show them to his clients."

Rupi stops at the door but doesn't turn around. "Is he also the one who gave all those interviews?"

Saj walks up to her but leaves a few feet of distance between them. "Rupi."

"Don't say my name like you're my friend."

"Please turn around and hear me out."

"No. I did that once, and you used me."

He takes another step closer. For a moment I think he's going to take her arm and turn her around. But he doesn't touch her. "Do you know how many people knowingly abuse and threaten immigrants who have no legal recourse to protect themselves? Too many. Do you know how many Americans care about what happens to people stuck in the mess of immigration laws? How many people give a shit what happens to hardworking, well-meaning people lost because some policy changed in the middle of them living their lives? Too few. The only way to get them to care is to talk to the media. Every time I win a case and someone covers it, someone sits up and takes notice of the fact that something is broken. So yes, I do the interviews."

She turns around and looks at him. Her eyes are blazing with anger, but she's listening again.

"And yes, from the time you told me what happened to you in LA, I've wanted to burn that place to the ground. If Ron were alive, I'd want nothing more than to throw his ass in jail. And if I have a chance to lock up the other shits who worked with him, then yes, I want that chance. That doesn't mean I don't care about yo—about your case."

They're staring each other down again, and I'm holding my breath.

"Then don't abandon me." She swallows. "I mean, don't abandon my case."

"I'm not. I was never going to. Working with Tina doesn't mean not working with you. And I'm not working with Tina unless you tell me you want me to go after the operation. But I want you to think about it. Those women need help, Rupi."

"I was almost one of those women," she whispers. "Not everyone has a sister to run away to and a hotshot lawyer who befriends her. They have nowhere to go."

"But they have us. We can help them. You can help them."

For a long time, she says nothing. They stand there, watching each other, their breathing expanding and contracting their chests in matching rhythms.

Finally Rupi speaks. "What happens to the girls when the ring is busted?"

"I'm not sure yet."

"Then find out. And ask me again when you know."

With that, she lets herself out without waiting for me to follow. But before I jog after her, I see the most goofy smile on the face of the most serious man I've ever met.

TWENTY-SIX

SIMI

"Is it okay if we don't go straight home?" I ask my sister. It feels like we have something to celebrate. Now that Rupi has her passport, the visa stamp extension should come through pretty fast. It also means she and Prem can apply for the marriage license and provisional green card, but I can't think about that right now.

"Only if you buy me ice cream," Rupi says.

"Sure, I'll buy you ice cream and take you to my favorite spot in Nashville."

We drive to the Parthenon, the full-scale replica of the one in Athens. We park the car, then pick up ice cream from my favorite creamery—a triple scoop for Rupi, and a single scoop for me—and follow the trail to the pond. It's where my favorite view of the monument is, across the water.

"Very dramatic," Rupi says, taking in the pillared building. "When you said the Parthenon, I was expecting a ruin." She snaps her fingers. "But just like that, the building is whole again. Like us, move it from one country to another and boom! Fixed!"

I have to laugh at that. "Very symbolic, didi. If only we humans could rebuild ourselves that easily."

She takes a giant bite and squeaks as the cold fills her mouth. "You know what, Chipku? I think you have."

I stare at our reflections in the water. Two silhouettes jiggling on the surface, the ripples moving us closer, then pulling us apart, the sunlight dancing at our edges.

"You think I've rebuilt myself?"

"Yes. Beautifully. Look at you. You never have to rely on anyone. You stand tall on your own feet."

"You sound proud."

"Of course I am. I'm incredibly proud of you. I've always been."

Tears push at my eyes, but I control them. I don't want to ruin the moment. "Thanks, that means a lot."

She pats my cheek. "Sheesh, we'd better be careful, or we'll turn into the Guptas before we know it."

"I mean, you are about to actually turn into a Gupta," I say without thinking. But I realize how bitter I sound and apologize.

"Thank you *and* sorry all in the same day. Let's not get carried away," she says, but she doesn't seem angry, and I relax.

Something about her is different. She's been oddly Zen lately. As though all her time with the Guptas has injected a tranquilizer into her veins. Even with Saj just now, I can't believe how they both laid it all out like that. The entire time they were talking, I was waiting for Rupi to blow up and walk out of there and slam the door in Saj's face. But she stayed and listened and told him how she felt. Since when did my sister get so comfortable with being vulnerable?

For a while we stand there, watching the sun going down over the beautifully balanced structure, then we start walking along the circuitous path.

"This is nice, isn't it?" I say, wary of disturbing the peace but hungry for the connection of being able to talk to her.

"Not the best vanilla I've ever had. But yeah, definitely nice."

I laugh. "I've missed you, didi."

"Fine, it is nice. I like it when we're nice to each other."

"Me too. I can't believe that we're living in the same home again," I say. "I never dared to hope that we would. And I hate fighting with you. I'm so tired of all the ugly feelings."

Same here, baby girl, her eyes say. She takes another bite and savors it. "But you still have them, the ugly feelings?"

I should have known she wouldn't let that go. I have the same feeling in the pit of my stomach I had when she forced me to take bitter medicine or made me study for exams. I could take my time, but there was no getting away from it. "Not as ugly as they were. But you are marrying the man I love."

Again, I regret saying it the moment it leaves my mouth.

"I'm sorry. I shouldn't have said that," I say.

She takes another bite of her ice cream and pauses before turning to me. "Why? I practically forced you to say it. You don't have to keep buying peace by suppressing what you're feeling, Simi. Maybe it's time to stop doing that."

"That's not what I'm doing," I say a little too quickly and far too defensively.

I expect her to call me out, but she doesn't.

We walk in silence for a few minutes, pouring our focus into the ice cream until we reach the monument. Light filters through the columns behind us as we drop down on the stone steps. Rupi quietly finishes her cone. Her three scoops gone before I've made a dent in my one.

"Fine," I say finally. "Maybe you're right. Maybe that is what I'm doing. Maybe I don't know how not to."

She turns the full force of her newfound calm on me. "Then learn. You've learned a whole new way of life here." She looks around at the families out for a stroll, the office goers out with friends after work. "You didn't back down from Karina. You're taking care of me like you're the older sister. Surely you can learn to say what you're feeling."

Can I? I want to.

"It's been hard," I say before I can stop myself. There's a dam in my throat, and there's a flood behind it. Rupi watches me with a challenge in her eyes and waits.

"It's been brutal, in fact." I let the words out. "You're living all the moments I've dreamed of for myself with Prem. Being embraced by the family, how you've bonded with each one of them, planning the details of the wedding. I know you think it's not real because the marriage is not. But these things are real. You're in their hearts now, Rupi. This was supposed to be my life. It's not going to be the same when it's me after you get divorced. You'll have already broken their hearts. Everything will be tainted by then. And Prem's dad. Prem worships him, and I may never get to meet him as his daughter-in-law if something happens to him." I stop to catch my breath. Tears are running down my face.

Rupi leans over and wipes my cheeks. "There, was that so hard?" She throws a look at the ice cream melting in my hand. I hand it over. I'm done with it anyway.

"Yes. It was awful." The hardest words I've ever said. And now that they're dug up, I feel gouged out. Like I should be bleeding from the wounds.

She starts on my cone. "You weren't wrong earlier. When we were growing up, I was so used to thinking for the both of us that I steamrolled you when you expressed your opinions. I didn't mean to, but I did. Maybe that's why you didn't know how not to suppress what you're feeling. I'm glad you got that out."

"Why? What good does it do us?"

She tucks a loose lock of hair behind my ear. "It helps us come up with a plan. If we're going to live this lie, we have to be able to talk about how to do it. You can't just keep focusing on all the things you're losing because I'm marrying Prem. We can't do anything about that at this point. Let's figure out how you're going to continue your relationship without all this sulking both of you have been doing."

My first instinct is to deny it. *We're not sulking* I want to say. "We're trying," I say instead.

She laughs. "Wow, that's you trying? Is this how you guys communicated before I came along?"

That stings. Maybe we've had enough communication for a day. "Our relationship was perfect. A situation like this would throw any relationship for a loop." I purse my lips and swat away the fat tear that leaks out of my eye even as I try to stop it. "I don't know why you keep trying to undermine my relationship."

"I'm the one undermining your relationship? When this supposedly perfect guy is dealing with things by running away every chance he gets?"

"You're being unfair. I know you think he somehow doesn't deserve me. But how can you think that when you've seen the person he is and what he's done for me, and for you, at every step."

"That's not what I'm saying at all. I did think he didn't deserve you at first, but I was wrong. I know that now." She throws me a look that tells me I'm not going to like what's coming. "But I don't think you do. What I'm saying is that you're the one who acts like you don't think you deserve him."

I stand up. I guess this letting-my-feelings-out thing isn't all it's cut out to be. "I don't know why I even try with you."

She pops the last piece of my cone in her mouth and wipes her hands on her jeans, then she stands. "You try with me because I'm your sister. You try with me because I'm all the family you have and you wouldn't be here without me." She says it calmly, but there's nothing calm about how those words land on me.

"And I'm all the family you have too. You wouldn't be here without me either. You'd never know what it's like to live in a big house and be fawned over by a loving family without me."

That elicits a smug smile. "See. Already you're getting good at saying what you mean. Well done." She's trying to make some sort of point, and I wish she'd just spit it out. She goes right ahead and does. "So, that's the charm. It's the big house and the fawning family. That's why you love him." She starts walking down the steps without waiting for me to follow.

The calmer she is, the more restless I get. "You know that's not why I love him. But that is what you're falling in love with, aren't you?"

Now she stops and turns to face me. "I am not falling in love with a damn thing." She takes a breath. I guess I'm not the only one who has trouble facing my feelings, after all. "But if it's not the family and the house, what do you think it is?"

"That sounds like a rhetorical question. You're dying to tell me what *you* think it is. So, just tell me."

"Could it be how easy it is to get your way? How he never pushes back or makes you work to make him feel loved? He lets you drive every single thing in your relationship."

"You know what's funny? That sounds exactly the way you've always loved me."

That stops her. She turns to me, her eyes wide with the pain of the accusation. But she doesn't punch back. Maybe it is possible to truly change. Maybe I'm not the only one who's rebuilt myself.

She takes my hand. "You're right. I already admitted that I felt like I had to make all the decisions for both of us. I'm the one who taught you how to love someone. It's no wonder you think that's the only way to do it."

She's right. She is the one who taught me how to love. Could it be that I'm doing just that? Loving Prem from a place of struggling to retain my power?

She squeezes my hand. "We were children, Simi."

"I know. And that's on me. What we learn from our circumstances is based on who we are."

"We're both responsible."

I laugh. "But I'm the one who's messed up my relationship with the best man in the world because of it."

She pulls her hand out of mine. "See. There. That's the problem. He's no better a person than you are! This is why you act like a damned spineless fairy princess around him. Around all of them."

"I do not!"

"You do." She looks so sad, my heartbeat speeds up. I recognize the look in her eyes. She's the old Rupi again, and she's about to drive a dagger into my heart with what she says next. "And do you know why it bothers me so much? Because that's exactly how Mom was when she was in love. Like she'd won the lottery. Like all she had to do was hide who she was, and she'd get to keep the jackpot. Untrusting but wildly performative."

"Go to hell, Rupi!" I run down the steps and start jogging to the car without waiting for her. I guess this sisterly communication thing isn't for people like us. We're too broken for that.

She follows me and gets in the car wordlessly, and I back out a little too fast. For an inordinate amount of time we just drive, sitting in this hurtling metal box as though the anger gathered inside us is propelling us forward.

"I'm sorry," Rupi says finally. "I shouldn't have brought Mom into it." And there it is—the reason why we will always feel broken.

"We're never going to be rid of her, are we?"

"When did we ever have her?" she says. "Isn't that funny? We keep trying to get rid of something we never had."

That is funny, but I can't bring myself to laugh. "Do you ever miss her?"

"Not even a little bit. All I feel is relief that she's gone. And sadness that she was who we got."

"Same. Can you imagine what the Guptas would think if they knew how much we hate our mother?"

She goes quiet again.

"I've never told Prem how I feel about Mom." I don't mean to say it, but it comes out.

"I know. It's not an easy thing to share with anyone. But that doesn't mean everything else inside you can't be shared either."

I hate that I want to cry again. I hold it in. "How can it be both those things? Either I run this relationship, or I'm a spineless fairy princess. How can I be both?"

"We're talented, I guess," Rupi says. "Our damage is pretty complex, Simi. I don't think there are easy answers. Maybe someday we'll be able to afford therapy, and then everyone around us can have some peace."

I can already afford therapy, but the idea is terrifying. "Do you really think I don't show him my real self?"

"Well, has he ever seen you not dressed for company?"

I shift in my seat, and my chin goes up. "We usually meet at the Johnsons', or outside the house. It's not like I can be running around town in a nightie."

"What about when he stays over?"

I don't answer. I can hardly admit to making sure I'm all dressed up before he wakes up.

"You hate his family pizzas. Does he know that?"

"Everybody else seems to love them, so that might just be me. Why hurt his feelings?"

"Fair enough. What about the fact that you're terrified of having kids? Does he know that?"

Growing up, that was one thing Rupi and I always said—that motherhood wasn't for us. "Actually, I've changed my mind about that. I think it was TASha. Or maybe it's Prem. I can imagine being a mother with him."

For the first time she looks at me like I've taken her completely by surprise.

"Prem's not like anyone else I've ever met." I let out the saddest smile. "And if you say that's because he's a rasgulla, I will smack you."

She smiles sheepishly. Obviously that's exactly what she was going to say. "But motherhood?" So many emotions flash through her eyes. This is the thing she can't get past?

"Ma wasn't the one who taught me how to be a mother, Rupi. You were."

She presses a hand to her mouth. I think she might cry. She doesn't. She just looks at me like she's seeing me for the first time.

It takes her a long time to speak again. "Tell me something," she says finally. "Why hadn't you ever met Prem's family? You were together for a year. If you're so sure of your love, why were you not already engaged when I got here? I'll bet he'd already asked you to marry him."

How on earth could she possibly know that?

"He did ask me. And I would have said yes eventually, but then you showed up."

"But why did you say no in the first place?"

"Because I work for his sister. I was afraid of losing my job."

"John wasn't the one you were in love with. Why would you lose your job?"

She's not wrong. Preeti and John never led me to believe they didn't want me to be with Prem. Now that I think on it, Karina might have been more inclined to sign my papers if I were engaged to Prem. Then why did I use that as an excuse?

I haven't said that out loud, but Rupi still hears it. "You know, it would be entirely impossible for someone who saw what we saw growing up to not be afraid of marriage. It's actually amazing that you're brave enough to love someone. Maybe you knew that you couldn't get married until you were able to show him all the parts of you, even the ones that feel too ugly to be loved. I'm sure it didn't help that you had a sister who taught you that loving someone means giving up control to them."

It's a good thing we're home and I pull into my parking space, because my heart is racing in my chest. I wish we'd had this conversation long before this. Because now it's too late.

"None of this matters anymore. Because I think I've already lost him."

"Lost him? What are you talking about? We're not actually getting married, Simi. He has no interest in me."

"I know. But he hasn't talked to me—really talked the way we used to—in months. He's never in town." I press a hand into my chest to quell the ache there. "I love him so much, Rupi. He's everything that's good in this world. He's everything I've ever wanted. The things everyone else believed that we never could . . . He makes it easy to believe those things. I wish I hadn't been afraid, because he's gone, and I miss him so much it hurts."

"Oh, baby girl," she says. "Then let him see all of that. Let him see you. He's already met me. What could you possibly show him that could scare him away after that?"

"Don't say that. You're the best part of me. Now that he's met you, how can he ever love me?" My shoulders are shaking. Sobs are erupting from my chest like little earthquakes. There's a monsoon on my face.

"For the love of god," Rupi says. "You're such an idiot." But she reaches over the armrest and pulls me close.

I fall into her. And for the first time in a million years, I sob in my sister's arms.

TWENTY-SEVEN

RUPI

I must've fallen asleep again while reading to Baba, because when I come awake, I sense a presence.

Before I can startle, Saj speaks, the rumbly, calming voice sparking under my skin in a way I hate, because I realize I've been waiting for it.

"Morning. Didn't mean to scare you." He says it softly because Baba is sleeping, and the net impact of that voice leaving his body softly is spectacularly unfair.

I turn around and meet his gaze. "Then why are you sneaking up on me?"

He laughs. Gosh, how can making someone laugh be this satisfying?

"Are you here to take your girlfriend out?"

This time he groans. "Can you please help me out with that?" He's standing in the doorway, leaning against the doorframe. His arms are folded across his chest, and he's wearing a suit. Oh, and he's completely unaware of what a meme he's being.

How has this man not killed anyone yet?

My heart does some sort of weird racing, and I ask it to stop being idiotic. I'm not the Count Dracula type.

I stand up and walk to him. "You need my help with asking my sister out?"

"Not funny."

I pinch my thumb and forefinger together. "A little bit funny."

His eyes flare with something. I think I like his robotic eyes better.

I've spent the past weeks trying not to think about him telling me how he wanted to burn down the place where I was trapped and throw Ron in jail if he were alive, and the fact that he didn't take Tina's case without asking me, and the fact that he navigated my terms without once shaming me for them.

"It would really help if you asked Prem's mom to lay off the matchmaking. She's getting quite insistent, and she listens to you."

She hardly knows me I want to say, but I'm acquainted with this man's bullshit meter. "Maybe take your best friend on your date. He needs to be spending some time with"—I check to see if Baba is still asleep—"her. Win-win."

"Is he still gone a lot?"

"He's home today. But yes, pretty much all the time. She's not doing well."

"Are you going to ask about an exit strategy again?"

I was thinking it. "No."

That's when I notice that he's carrying a folder, and he's here on a Wednesday evening. "Are you here to try and push me about Tina again?"

"No. I'm still finding you your answers for that."

"Then are you here for another reason?"

"Yes." He pauses a long second as he looks down into my upturned face. "I think you're going to like this much more than our last meeting."

Dude, I already like this a little too much. "Is this you withholding pleasure from me?"

He blushes, of all things. Then gives another unnecessarily hot laugh. I just flustered Saj Rawal, and it's unexpectedly sweet. Need cramps low in my belly.

Our gazes hold. He seems to forget what he was about to say.

"Saj?"

He blinks.

"You have news for me?"

"Yes." He straightens up and squares his shoulders as though bracing himself for my reaction.

"What is it?"

"Our petition for an extension of your tourist visa came through."

"Are you serious?" Joy explodes inside me, and relief and disbelief. "That's . . . that's really good, right?"

"It's a best-case scenario. Yes."

Oh my god! I throw my arms around him. "Thank you!"

His body jolts. Then goes very still. Not a muscle moves. His arms hang by his sides.

Embarrassment blooms inside me. What was I thinking? I'm not even a hugger.

I start to pull away. His arms come around me. In the space of a single breath, his body warms and melts and pulls me close. So close. It's like he's gathering me into himself. His hands are big and steady and his chest more solid than anything I've ever experienced. And his smell, the feel of the suit, the rhythm of his breathing. Every piece of me is swallowed whole in that hug.

Dear god, who hugs like this?

When I pull away, my legs are wobbly. His hand on my elbow gives me back my bearings.

For the briefest moment, his eyes hide nothing. They lay him bare. They're defenseless, helpless, fathomless. Everything. I see everything.

Behind us Baba clears his throat, and I spin around.

He's watching us with his signature curiosity and kindness.

"My visa extension came through," I say, going to him. My voice comes out louder than I expected, and I temper it. "This is going to make applying for a green card so much easier. It's going to make everything so much easier, isn't it, Saj?"

I wait, but Saj says nothing, so I turn to him.

"It is," his gravelly voice says. "This is going to make everything so much easier." The way his eyes fight those words makes me tremble.

Please, can he go back to being a robot?

Baba smiles and raises his hand to make his favorite gesture, the thumbs-up.

"What's going to make things easier?" Prem asks, coming into the room. He's carrying a plate with pizza cut into sample-size pieces. He's back in town and has been working on his beloved family pizzas all day, as though it will somehow set him free. He's lost weight in the past two months and is looking one hundred years old. How does his family think he's happy?

Saj updates him on the visa situation. We're two weeks away from the wedding. This is really good news. For me. I have to keep my mind on that. I can't think about my sister crying in my arms. I certainly can't think about the sadness dragging at Prem. They'll still have each other.

Prem makes the effort to smile. "I just made some family pizza. Want to taste?" He tries to feed a piece into Baba's mouth. Baba stops him. He takes a piece from the plate and moves his hand, with all his focus, to his mouth, by himself.

Prem turns to me. There is such incredulousness in his eyes. "Did you see that?" For the first time since I met him, he seems awake and alive. His eyes shine with his father's success. Maybe I do see what my sister sees in him.

"Baba's been doing that more and more. It's pretty amazing, isn't it?" I say, pride filling me.

Baba grins and points at me.

"What? She did it? How?" Prem says.

I feel Saj's eyes on me.

"I didn't. This was all him. I think his body is getting stronger. It's natural progression in his healing. He's worked so hard on it."

Baba rolls his eyes. I wonder if he learned that from me.

"Mamma was saying you spend all your time here and you've been getting him to do some movement or the other continuously."

"Again, it's all Baba. He's the one doing all the work."

Prem squeezes his shoulder. "That's fantastic, Baba."

Baba looks at me and then at the window. It's something we've been talking about.

"Actually, Prem," I say, "I need help with something. Do you think we can take Baba out of the house?"

Prem looks at me like I've lost my mind, then at his father. What he sees there gives him pause.

"His wheelchair is state of the art. And his muscle control is better than it's ever been since the stroke. I talked to his doctor. She thinks it's a good idea."

"You want to do this?" he asks his father and gets a nod, a strong nod, in return.

The light is back in Prem's eyes. "I'll talk to Mamma." Then he turns to me. "Rupi, I don't know how to thank you. This is . . . this is fantastic. Thank you."

"Well, umm, what's on the pizza?" I ask instead of responding.

"It's charred eggplant."

Baba makes a face and a sound that's close to "yuck."

"Like bharta?" I ask. I love bharta, but why would anyone put bharta on pizza?

Prem nods, and I take a bite.

He waits.

"It's . . . well, it's not great." Surprisingly, it's not terrible either. "But there's something there. There's potential."

Prem looks a little too thrilled with that bare praise. He holds out the plate to Saj, who takes a step back and raises a hand. "You know I don't eat eggplant."

"You don't eat eggplant?" I ask with utter horror. "Who doesn't eat eggplant?"

"Anyone with taste buds," Saj mumbles.

"Are you listening to this guy?" I ask Prem.

For the first time in my life, I see Prem grin with his whole heart. His entire face comes into play, and ugh, I totally get what my sister sees.

"It's no use casting pearls before swine," he says, eyes twinkling.

"No kidding," I say. "You know what? We're going to fix this, and then Saj is going to taste it, and he's going to admit to being wrong."

Baba gives a jubilant grunt and, you guessed it, a thumbs-up.

"No, I'm not," Saj says.

"We'll see about that," I say. "Come on."

Prem follows me out, and Saj trails behind us.

For the next hour, Prem and I figure out what the eggplant topping was missing. He's really good at flavors. We reduce the amount of cumin, remove the coriander. Add a dash of garlic and experiment with both feta and parmesan. Eggplant goes well with both.

Much to everyone's surprise, Saj stays. It has nothing to do with me. Neel and Nathan, probably his favorite humans on earth, have been in a war of the worlds with their grandmother about doing math homework since they got back from school, but the minute their uncle offers to help, they get on it like it's one of their video games.

He takes off his jacket, loosens his tie, and rolls up his shirtsleeves. Basically, he's showing off, because what is it with those forearms? And where the hell does one find shirts that fit like that?

Mamma joins Baba in their room, and they turn on an old black-and-white Hindi movie on full volume. Every fifteen minutes a song breaks out, and I want to hum.

Obviously, I don't.

Because the urge to hum is as alien to me as the rest of this circus. Be that as it may, I'm here now. So, I might as well teach this boy to trust his flavors.

The pizza turns out spectacular. Prem even tweaks the dough with some fennel seeds.

Saj does not take a bite.

Talk about stubborn. I set Neel and Nathan on him. They challenge and goad and call him chicken and run around him, flapping their arms and making clucking sounds. Finally he takes a nibble. It's mostly dough and feta, but he's tasting it.

"Yumm," his mouth says even as his eyes say he's gagging. He hates it.

I haven't laughed like this in my life.

He watches me, his dark eyes stripping me to my soul.

I thank him for his service and courage.

He thanks me for testing his limits. Apparently every man has them, and his are eggplant. Then he drops kisses on his nephews' heads, lets them climb all over him for hugs, and leaves. I do not wonder what it might be like if we were the kind of people who hugged goodbye. I am not thinking about his hug or letting the warmth of being wrapped up like that dance across my skin, across every fiber of my being.

Mamma and Baba eat their pizza, which they love and praise as though Mount Everest has been scaled. The boys, having earned their video game time, get to it. Their parents are working late.

So, my fiancé and I share the rest of the pizza at the kitchen island by ourselves.

"How are you so good at this?" Prem says, taking a bite.

"I did work at a restaurant for years. Our chef in Mumbai made sure we knew what everything tasted like. And his description of flavors and ingredients made a lot of sense." I'm not used to talking about the past without pain, and it's strange to have a memory so clean of bitterness.

"Now that the visa extension has come through and everything is on track, maybe once the green card comes through, you can help at the restaurants?"

"Maybe."

He leaves it at that and takes another bite. "But this is really good. Thanks for helping me with it."

"It's okay," I say.

"Do you mean the pizza is okay, or was that for me thanking you?"

"Both." I bite into the flaky, buttery crust. "Fine. It's delicious."

"Even though Saj hated it?"

"I mean, are there things Saj likes? Also, eggplant is a polarizing vegetable. Have you ever thought of putting these pizzas on the menu at the restaurants?"

"What? No!" He's totally lying, and I narrow my eyes at him.

"Nah, we're a franchise. We have to stick with the recipes."

"But you don't. Mamma told me you tweak."

He looks surprised. "She told you that?"

"Of course. Why would she not trust her future daughter-in-law?"

His face falls into a pout. Gah! Is the guy actually bordering on cute? When did this happen?

"It's only two years, you know. I've already spent three months here, and those went by fast, didn't they?"

Shock flashes in his eyes. Great. They were the longest months of his life. Just like they've been the longest months of my sister's life.

"This isn't long term, you know that. You'll marry her after two years, and then it won't matter. And well, you know you can be with her that entire time, right? As long as no one finds out."

He's studying his fingers.

"What?"

"I'm not so sure she wants that."

Excuse me? "Why do you say that?"

"Simi." His voice breaks on her name. I want to laugh at that, because it's hilarious, but I can't, because also it's not. It's heartbreaking and beautiful. He rubs a hand into his chest. "She's been avoiding me. And she's been so angry with me. I'm . . . I don't know what I've done."

Oh dear. "Have you asked her?"

He looks at me like the thought never occurred to him. "Simi, she . . . sometimes she needs her space, and if I push her, she'd never push back so, I . . . I don't. And I don't . . ." A fat teardrop leaks from his eye, and he swats it away.

Can you believe these two?

"You don't what?"

"I don't want to force her to be with me."

Wow, he's full of surprises today. And just as much of an idiot as Simi is.

"Prem, are you doing this . . . marrying me, because you were afraid she'd leave you if you didn't?"

He looks genuinely surprised, as though that thought, too, never occurred to him. "No! Well, I'm doing it because she can't do anything herself to help you, and it would destroy her if she couldn't help you. And well, you . . . what you've been through. It's not fair."

My hand presses against my mouth. The boy is actually angry on my behalf.

"That's really sweet, Prem," I say. "Thank you."

He looks all alert, as though I'm softening him up so I can stick a knife into his side. I want to tell him to cut it out, but he's not wrong. In fact, it's a bit disturbing that I'm not reaching for the proverbial knife and plotting his stabbing.

"Then why do you think she'd leave you?" I ask.

He studies my face, his nails, the kitchen, the empty pizza stone. He pushes the crumbs on his plate around. I consider poking him and asking him to hurry up.

"Even before you showed up, I don't think she was ready for marriage. I wanted to ask her to marry me months after meeting her, but . . . but when I tried, she was just so, so scared. I'm not sure she wants to be with me, at least not all the time. And well, I sometimes wonder how someone like Simi is with me in the first place."

"Someone like Simi?"

He looks at me like I'm being deliberately obtuse. "Someone that smart and kind and gorgeous."

Oh my god. It's official. He just crossed over the line of cuteness to frickin' adorableness. "You think Simi is gorgeous?"

"Doesn't everyone?"

Everyone except her. "I'm not sure she does."

He sits up and looks like he just thought of something for the first time.

"What?" I ask.

"Is that why she's with someone like me? Because she has no idea that she's gorgeous?"

Great. These two are exactly alike. How will they survive this big, bad world together?

"No," I say. "It's because she has terrible taste in men."

He's about to pout again, but then he has yet another realization. "You're joking. Ha!"

Indeed I am. "Well, maybe instead of avoiding her and running away to the far reaches of the tristate area, take some time to tell her all this."

"I have."

"Obviously she hasn't heard you. Tell her again. And demand that she listen. She's asked you for something bigger than the realm of a normal relationship demands. Maybe demanding your time and attention in addition to that feels like too much. But trust me, she needs to hear everything you just told me. And she needs to hear it soon."

Maybe then I can stop this absurd wave of guilt and have some damn peace.

TWENTY-EIGHT

RUPI

"There's going to be no time for a bridal shower," Mamma says with some regret. "And Rupi wants only two events for the wedding, just the ceremony and the reception. No sangeet, no haldi, no mehendi. No nothing. So, I thought a small family party would be fun." She turns to Simi. "What do you think, Simi, beta?"

It's strange how tongue-tied Simi gets around a woman who emanates such kindness.

I widen my eyes at Simi. *Say something. The woman just asked you a question. Show her who you really are!*

It's a lot to communicate through eye contact alone, yet I do a pretty solid job. Simi just sits there, speechless.

Mamma pats her shoulder. "You are Rupi's sister." She tries again. "I want to know what you think."

"I think it's a good idea?" Simi says finally, turning it into a question like a teenager. "If that's what you want?"

We are drinking chai in the kitchen while Prem and Saj go over some paperwork for the new restaurant location. I widen my eyes at her again, for all the good it's doing.

"It's a done deal, then," Mamma says, then throws a loaded glance at the table, where Saj and Prem are sitting. "Saj, beta, is the law practice not going well these days?" she asks, tongue firmly in cheek.

"It's going fine, Auntie-ji." He slides me a glance. "Why do you ask?"

"I've seen more of you these past few weeks than I've seen you in the past year."

Saj's color heightens the tiniest bit. I hate that I notice.

Before he can answer, Mamma winks at me. "What do you think, Rupi? Aren't we seeing a lot of Saj these days?" My cheeks are starting to warm when she throws a suggestive glance Simi's way. "Has Saj asked you out on a date yet, Simi, beta?"

I focus hard on taking a sip of my chai without choking.

My stupid sister grins at me, as though the joke is suddenly on me instead of her.

"Rupi, did you talk to Saj about it like I asked you to?" Mamma asks.

Saj is watching me across the kitchen with those black-on-black eyes instead of being a good lawyer and watching those papers. "I did, and he's excited." I smile my sweetest smile.

"Of course he is. He might be a hotshot lawyer, but how is he going to find a wife on his own if he frowns that much? He needs help."

"You're right, Auntie-ji. I'm told the assassin vibe doesn't work for everyone." Saj raises a brow at me, and my cheeks warm.

"What do you think, Simi?" I ask, then turn to Mamma before she answers. "My sister is so sweet and shy and so hardworking, she seems to have no time for dating. I don't know what to do with her. I think she needs to spend some time with you, so you can teach her how to dive into the moment."

Mamma grins and pats my cheek. "You're right. Simi is too sweet and shy. Not at all like girls these days." She walks to Prem and ruffles his hair. He's looking even more distraught than usual. "But don't worry. I used to feel like that about my Prem too. So old-world like. But see, he found your sister. Opposites can attract. You think Saj is nice, don't you?"

"I think he's really nice," Simi says pointedly. "I actually don't see the assassin thing at all." She throws me a look that's neither sweet nor shy.

"You're exactly right!" Mamma says with some jubilation. "And he's Prem's best friend. The four of you can do everything together. Have a foursome."

Simi's eyes dance with laughter. "I think that's what Rupi is hoping for."

I kick my sister under the kitchen island. My cheeks are well and truly flaming, and my stupid sister's shoulders are shaking with laughter.

Prem and Saj are also cracking up.

I point a finger at Simi. "Shut up," I mouth, making her perk up even more.

"Hah," she whispers to me. "So much for not complicating the situation more."

"I have no idea what you're talking about," I say, then turn to Prem's mom. "Mamma, Simi's saying she'd love to go out with Saj."

This time Simi kicks me under the table.

Mamma claps her hands. "I have an idea, why don't the two of you go for a walk? The weather is lovely! When Pankaj came to see me for the first time, our parents sent us on a walk, too, and look at us now. What do you say, Saj?"

"That's a great idea," Saj says. "Actually, Pankaj Uncle wanted to go on a walk. Why don't the four of us take him out?"

My heart does the oddest squeeze. The last time we spoke, I asked Saj to take Prem on his date with Simi. He was also there when I talked to Prem about taking Baba out.

Mamma deflates a little. "Oh, you know Pankaj doesn't like to leave the house."

"Actually, he did really well with the wheelchair on TASha's birthday," Prem says. "And he wants to. Ask Rupi."

Mamma wrings her hands together. "Rupi?"

"He's been asking for a week now. I talked to his doctor. She's fine with it. Just a short one. Just to the park."

"And Simi is here." Prem looks at Simi. "We have a nurse with us. In case something goes wrong."

Mamma turns to Simi.

"I can take his vitals before we go. I'll stay with him the entire time." For the first time, Simi sounds like an adult around Mamma. Like a professional.

Mamma hurries to Baba and demands to know if we're telling the truth. Baba's excited grin is a thing of beauty.

As promised, Simi takes his blood pressure and pulse and listens to his lungs. Baba lifts his hand and pats her cheek when she's done. Then Prem and Saj put Baba in his wheelchair. I wrap a shawl around him, and he gives me my favorite thing in the world: his thumbs-up.

We take the ramp out of the house and make our way to the sidewalk. Prem pushes the wheelchair, and I walk next to him. Saj and Simi walk in front of us. For the first ten minutes, no one says much. The neighborhood is lush with flowers, black-eyed Susans and cornflowers rising from waves of petunias. The Kentucky sky is a blazing blue.

When we get to the park, Saj leans over and picks up the front of the chair so he and Prem can carry Baba down the stairs that lead to the path edging the pond. As Simi and I follow, my foot hits some gravel, and my ankle twists. I'm about to go flying face forward when Saj leaps up and catches my fall. Strong hands grip my arms even as I fall bodily into him, finding my balance as I fist his shirt in my hand.

It takes a moment for the world to reorient itself as Saj helps me find my footing.

"You okay?" he asks, still holding me. His breath is warm against my temple. His heartbeat fast beneath my fist. He smells like spring rain on parched earth—fresh and clean, and so familiar and comforting, my entire body leans into it.

Prem clears his throat, and I look up to find Prem, Simi, and Baba watching us.

We're still holding each other.

I pull away.

"I'm fine," I say. "Just clumsy. Sorry."

"Did you twist it?" Saj is still holding my hand. "Put weight on it first."

I do as I'm told. Mostly because I don't want to argue in front of an audience.

My ankle is fine, although for the briefest moment I consider pretending it's broken to see what Saj will do. I imagine him sweeping me up in his arms. I can practically feel him pull me close as my arms go around his neck.

I take a step away from him, and he lets me go, an inch at a time, as if in slow motion.

I look up. I've forgotten again that we have an audience. It's Baba's eyes that I find first. There's curiosity there. Then his gaze moves to Prem and Simi, who are looking at each other instead of us. They're standing so close, their bodies are touching. Their bodies are so comfortable with each other, they haven't even noticed.

Baba's lips purse together.

"Let's go. We're blocking the path," I say, and we start walking.

"I can push the chair." I go up to Baba, but he shakes his head and looks at Prem. For the first time since I've met him, his eyes are inscrutable.

"Simi, why don't you walk with Saj," I say. I'll give Prem company.

Baba makes a sound and looks from Prem to Simi.

"He wants Simi," Prem says, and his voice trembles on her name.

Simi throws me a look and then starts walking next to Prem as he pushes the wheelchair.

I stand there, frozen, watching them go. Saj's hand lands on the small of my back, then pulls away as though burned. The imprint stays on my back.

"This was a bad idea, wasn't it?"

"The walk or the whole scheme?" Saj asks, and his hand flexes behind his back.

I start walking without answering.

"Rupi." He falls in step next to me, and my name sounds like a plea on his lips. "There's something I needed to tell you."

"They were both a bad idea," I say, cutting him off. "The walk, the whole scheme, even what you did back there. That can't happen again. Baba knows something is wrong."

"How can he possibly know?"

I point a finger at his face. *Because you won't stop looking at me like that.* But I can't say it.

"You wanted me to just let you fall?"

I stop and turn to him. His eyes are so intense they sparkle like a starlit night sky.

"I'm fully capable of catching myself when I fall."

"I know." It's a whisper.

"The wedding is in two weeks," I say, because that's what this moment needs.

"I know," he says again. "That's what I wanted to talk about. I probably won't see you before the wedding. I'm going to California tomorrow to get you your answers."

And there it is. The white knighting is what he's here for. I'm not stupid enough to not see that he's started to care for me, but what he really cares about is those women at Curry and his poor broken justice system.

"It's just as well," I say.

"Yes. Yes, it is. Because . . ." He looks so tortured, I almost reach out and cup his jaw. "I can't have any kind of relationship with a client, Rupi."

That lands on me like a shove. I stay standing. I pull my hand back and fold my arms across my chest. "Is there a client who wants to have a relationship with you, Saj?"

He squeezes his temples. Then smiles. It's a painful smile, but it's there. I made him smile. This time I can't find any joy in it.

I start walking again. "Since we are putting our misconceptions out there, there's one I'd like to clear up too."

"We don't have to do this," he says. "That wasn't me saying goodbye."

"It was. It has to be." Baba might know, but no one will call him in to give testimony. The rest of the Guptas will not be spared. They cannot find out. "That first time we met. When you saw me naked. I didn't know I was opening the living room door. I thought I was opening Simi's closet." I don't know why I need to clear this up, but I do. Now it's done.

"Of course I know it was something like that."

"Is that why you didn't react at all?"

"You didn't either."

"I didn't?"

"Nope. No horror, no fear, no embarrassment. Nothing."

"I think I was dead inside." I think I still might be.

He takes a step closer to me. "You weren't," he says. "You were more alive than anyone I've ever met. You've always been."

"Thanks," I say, and I hope it covers everything. This time I do stroke his cheek. It's quick, and I regret it the moment I do it. His skin is warmer and softer than I expected, despite the stubble starting to darken it. Sparks tingle from my fingers down my arm, and an electric pulse slashes my chest.

We're back at the Gupta house. Simi and Prem have taken the wheelchair inside.

"I think you should leave from here," I say without meeting his gaze.

He watches my face for a long moment. "You're right," he says finally. "Goodbye, Rupi." And with that, he's gone without a backward glance.

TWENTY-NINE

SIMI

My sister has slid back into being this huge presence in my life. Just the way she was when we were kids. Not where she's telling me what to do and running my life, but where I feel completely enveloped in her presence. Comforted by it. I don't think it's just me who feels that way.

She's letting everyone see her softness, as though someone turned her inside out like a fleece-lined sock. What I've always seen is now exposed, unguarded.

The Gupta home vibrates with Rupi magic.

I love it and hate it in equal measure.

I still struggle with feeling trapped inside a shell. I want to reach out of it, be as brave as her, but I just can't seem to sustain it. Except with Baba.

Ever since we took Baba on a walk for the first time last week, he seems to know what's happening with Prem, Rupi, and me. When we got home, he sat the three of us down and gave Prem one of those piercing looks. Prem cried. That was it. And Baba put a hand on my head. Then he pointed to his chair and to me. So, I've been coming over a little earlier in the morning to drop Rupi off and take him for a walk in his wheelchair by myself.

I tell him my day's plan, and we pluck flowers from the park and bring them home for Prem's mom. It's only been a few days, but it's been such a balm to my heart. No wonder Rupi essentially spent the past three months here in his room.

I have the day off today, and I'm supposed to be helping Prem's mom with wedding stuff, which is hard because I can still barely talk in front of the woman.

Tanuja, Rupi, and I are having chai in Baba's room.

"I have a huge favor to ask you, Simi," Tanuja says just as Prem walks into the room. He goes straight to Rupi and ignores me. I know his mom is sitting right here, but my heart still pinches.

Then he looks over at me, and I forget what I was mad about.

"Prem," Tanuja says. "Can you take Rupi and go check on the swatches I left in your room for the remodel?"

Rupi stands, and Prem says something near her ear, and they both giggle. He gives her a worshipful look. I have no idea why that hurts so much, but it stings like a fresh burn. So much for my shell. Prem, like the rest of them, has fallen completely under Rupi's spell.

They roll their eyes, pick up the empty cups of chai, and leave.

"I sent them off on purpose," Tanuja whispers conspiratorially.

Very subtle I want to say. But don't.

"I was wondering if you could help me with something. In private," Tanuja says.

"Anything," I say with a little too much enthusiasm. She doesn't even notice. She's watching Prem and Rupi leave.

"You know the whole wedding dress fiasco?"

I nod. After Rupi and Tanuja staged a walkout on a local dressmaker for throwing shade at Rupi's tattoos, they tried ordering online, but something has gone wrong with each order. Which means there's no wedding dress yet.

Preeti and Chandni both offered to let Rupi pick something out of their closets, and she jumped on that option with great relief. So, I thought the matter was closed.

"I think I have an idea. Come with me." She leads me into her closet. Some fifty saris are hanging across one side of the giant walk-in closet. It's a veritable wonderland of color, texture, and warmth.

"I was wondering . . ." She reaches up and pulls down a cloth sari bag, then places it on a shelf and unzips it, exposing the most gorgeous red silk woven entirely with gold thread. My heart gives a cramp of longing. This is exactly the kind of sari I've always imagined myself getting married in.

"Do you think Rupi would mind me asking if she wants to wear my wedding sari?"

My eyelids burn. My throat constricts. I absolutely cannot cry right now. My eyes tear up, and I turn away and pretend to cough.

"I'm so sorry, is it dusty in here? Do you have allergies?" She starts studying the shelves for dust.

"No, sorry. Just a tickle in my throat." God, how can this be happening? Why can't I stop feeling this way? Why didn't I just jump on it when Prem asked me to marry him? Why was I such a coward?

I thought I made peace with this. I promised my sister we're going to make it work. Everything is as it should be. But it's not. It's not. I touch the silk of the sari. The way it slides between my fingers feels like pure, irreversible loss. I know in this moment that things will never be okay. I'll never be able to do this. No matter how much I love my sister, I am not her. I cannot make a sacrifice of this magnitude. Not even for her. I'll give her a kidney, but this feels like actually dying.

"You okay, beta?"

"She'll love it," I say, pulling my hand away and clutching it against my chest. "This is so incredibly kind of you." It is, and Rupi is going to die of joy.

"You girls are so lovely. I can't imagine Preeti or Chandni being okay with wearing hand-me-downs for their wedding." As soon as the words leave her, she slaps a hand across her mouth. "I didn't mean to say that. Don't tell them I said that, okay?" She winks at me and hands me the sari.

"Let's take it out and surprise Rupi." She's as excited as a kid who's discovered a hidden stash of her favorite cookies.

My heart is racing as I follow her, clutching the sari like I'll die without it. My stomach is in knots. I don't know how my legs are working.

She calls out to Rupi and Prem, and they come back down.

I let the sari go. I watch the scene play out as Tanuja offers it to Rupi.

Rupi cries. My sister, who never cries, throws her arms around Tanuja and sobs. Tears stream from my eyes, too, but they aren't the kind of emotional tears Rupi is crying. They're my heart breaking. Prem's mom pulls him into a group hug with Rupi, and he wraps his arms around them both.

When he looks up and catches my eye, the pain I feel is so intense, I might throw up. I turn away.

I have to get out of here.

I can't drive away. Leaving will attract too much attention, but I have to be alone.

I'm not thinking when I leave the kitchen. The only room I've been in upstairs is Prem's, so I head there without thinking.

Big mistake. Because his room is infused with him. His clothes, his shoes, his smell, his essence. It's everywhere.

I turn back around. I can't be here either. Yet another place I can no longer belong in. The throw I made for him is lying on his pillow. I snatch it up and am about to throw it across the room when he enters. He shuts the door behind him.

The throw slides from my fingers. For a few moments we just stand there. Looking at each other.

"Simi." That's it. He says my name. Then stops.

The silence sucks the air out of the room. It sucks the life out of me.

"Say something," I whisper. "Please."

He looks flustered. If he were holding something, he'd drop it. I want him to. I want him to stumble. I want him to show me some feeling. Anything.

"Did you . . . did you need something?"

I laugh. I can't help it. I laugh, and I feel like my sister used to be. Mean.

"I need you to tell me what's going on," I say.

"I . . . What? What is that supposed to mean?"

"That means, your mother just gave your fiancée her wedding sari. I want to know how you feel about that."

He blinks. "My mother just gave her wedding sari to your sister and not to you. How do you think I feel about that?"

"I don't know anymore. Suddenly you seem to be quite comfortable with all this."

"You think I'm comfortable with all this?"

Repeating my questions is not an answer.

"Aren't you? Haven't you . . ." I clasp and unclasp my hands. I don't know what to do anymore. What to say. "Prem, have you developed feelings for Rupi? Because . . . because you're acting like she's really going to be your wife."

He looks at me like he doesn't know who I am, like I'm the one being unfair. The dark hit of emotions I'm feeling is so overwhelming, I can't think around it.

"You think I've developed feelings for her? Like romantic feelings? Are you for real, Simi?"

He starts pacing. And naturally he trips over a footstool. I don't help him, and he corrects himself and pushes the stool out of the way.

"You're the one who forced me into this situation. You're the only reason I would ever consider something like this. How can you ask me such a thing?" He looks so incredulous, deep shame slides through me, taking away my ability to come up with a response.

"I'm sorry," I say, close to tears. "It's not like I wanted this. It's not like any of this came with a manual. I couldn't think of another way to help my sister. All I knew was that she deserved my help. I had to help her."

He looks at me funny. "I know, baby. Of course she does. But, Simi, what you're accusing me of right now is absurd. How can you not know that I'm only doing this for you? It's an act. An act you demanded of me."

"Since when did you become such a good actor, Prem?"

"You think I'm a good actor?" His foot is about to get caught in the rug, but he catches himself before it happens. My body still lurches to help him. "Do you know how I even did all this? How I pulled off the act when we first started it?" He takes a step closer to me. "All I had to do was pretend I'm talking to you, pretend that I'm talking about you. That I'm looking at you. The only way I could do this was if I made myself see your face in place of your sister's face."

I know he means everything he's saying. What I don't know is why I still can't believe him. My heart is racing so fast, it's a miracle I'm not gasping for breath.

"I know that's how it was at first. But recently, in the past few weeks, something has changed. But even before that, you've been avoiding me for months, Prem."

He runs his hand through his hair, pulling it back so tight, the skin of his forehead stretches. "You're the one who's been avoiding me. You've been working so much, it's like I haven't seen you. And it hurts. My time, my life, everything has revolved around you this past year. It was the best year of my life. Not getting to see you, having you avoid me . . . The only way I knew how to deal with it was to leave, to find work away from home."

"But even when you're here, you're not the same. You know how you're clumsy when you're nervous? You're only that way around me. You're never that way around your family. You're never that way around Rupi."

"So?"

"So, I make you uncomfortable enough to trip over your own feet and knock things over, but they don't. She doesn't."

"Are you trying to say that the way I feel about you is different from how I feel about everyone else I love? How's that news, Simi?"

"Are you telling me nothing has changed since you first met Rupi? Your feelings for her haven't changed?"

He looks surprised. "Of course they have. She isn't at all what I thought she was. You know how we were afraid she'd hurt the family. We were so wrong. She's . . . she's fit into the house like my dad's favorite adage: Always enter any place like sugar in a teacup. She's dissolved into this home and made everything better. I've never met anyone else who can put others at ease so very much without even trying. In fact, while trying to do the opposite." He smiles.

"Oh god, you sound like you're in love with her."

"What are you talking about?" Suddenly he's looking at me differently, as though he's seeing something for the first time. "What I'm saying is that I get why you did this. I get what you said about how she raised you at the cost of her own childhood. I can see her doing that now. I think she's fantastic. I'm glad she's going to be my family, but only because she's related to the woman I love."

He's standing really close to me now. He tucks a lock of hair behind my ear, then cups my cheek. There's an odd determination in his eyes. "She's not you, Simi. No one is. No one will ever be. She's not the one who makes my entire body come alive when she's in the room. She's not the one who makes me feel electric sparks in my belly. She's not the one who makes my palms sweat because I want her so badly. She's not the one I lie awake in fear of not loving me back the way I love her."

I lean into his hand. My chest hurts so bad, I don't know how I can bear it. "So, you're telling me the only reason you love me is because you're physically attracted to me?"

He steps back. Why do I keep ruining the moment? Why am I pushing him away again?

Our damage is pretty complex. No kidding, didi!

He comes back. Steps closer again but doesn't touch me. "It's not just about physical attraction. It's not like Rupi isn't beautiful."

"You think my sister is beautiful."

He looks up at the ceiling like someone up there can save him from what I'm putting him through. "God, Simi! Everyone thinks your sister is beautiful. You're both blessed with the kind of beauty poets write poetry about and artists paint portraits of. I can't stop thinking about the exact brown of your eyes, the curl of your lashes, the way your mouth curves upward at the edges, the softness of your skin. I've daydreamed about those things from the first time I saw you. But there are a lot of beautiful women in the world. I used to feel that way about every actress I ever had a crush on. This is not that. Looking at you brings me to my knees, and that has nothing to do with your beauty. It has everything to do with who you are. That's what lights you up. It has everything to do with what it feels like just to be with you. Simi Naik, I am madly, irreversibly, and wholly in love with you and only you."

I'm speechless. A trembling starts deep inside me. I'm shaking. He's not done.

"But I hate feeling like it isn't enough. I hate feeling like you're going to walk away from me because I don't know how to show it. Because I never know how much to show it so I don't scare you away."

"You're afraid I'll leave you?"

"That's what I'm trying to say, yes. I've been terrified of it from the very beginning."

This time I reach out and cup his cheek. He leans into it. "And I live in fear of you leaving me."

"You do?"

"All the time."

"Why do you think that is? Why do you think neither of us can believe that we found each other?"

"Rupi thinks it's because we found each other so easily. Because loving each other is so easy, we don't value it."

"Well, she's full of shit about that." He wraps his arms around me and pulls me close. "What we're doing for her is not easy. What you've done for her is the most generous darned thing I've ever seen anyone do.

Staying away from you in public, it's the hardest thing I've ever done. Keeping my hands off you has been pure torture, Simi."

I reach up and thread my fingers through his thick curls, and that electric spark he speaks of nearly splits me in half. "I don't want you to keep your hands off me," I whisper. "I want your hands everywhere." I kiss the edge of his mouth. He has stubble now, and it's a whole new sensation. His jaw is also sharper.

He pulls me into himself and strokes his hands up and down my back, cupping my butt and lifting me close. "Like this?" he asks.

Exactly like that. "I've missed you so much," I say as I make my way across his jaw to his lips, searching for everything that's changed and finding everything so familiar that it's an extension of myself.

He waits. Pressing into me with his entire body, caressing me with his hands, but waiting, waiting for me to find his mouth.

I do. It's like coming home. It's like coming undone. It's like the dam breaking. His hands, his mouth . . . They're everywhere, all at once. My hair, my lips, the column of my throat . . . He takes it all, slow at first, then hungrier and hungrier. Sucking and nipping, peeling away everything I've been feeling. Consuming me. Inhaling me. Reaching all the way inside. I wrap my legs around him, pressing and pushing, wanting it all, wanting it to never stop.

Just as his tongue is deep in my mouth, my fingers deep in his hair, our clothes halfway off, my legs around him, clutching and reaching, the door opens.

A scream crashes through the mindless haze wrapped around our bodies.

"Prem! What are you doing!"

It's his mother's voice. Oh god. His mother is here, and my legs are wrapped around his waist. His pants are unzipped, and my underwear is halfway down my thighs. Oh, and my buttons are off, and my bra is on full display.

I think I'm going to die.

"Mamma!" Prem says. But he does not drop me. He keeps me in his arms.

"I . . . I . . ." Words stutter on my tongue. Shame swallows me whole. I haven't stuttered since I was ten years old.

"It's not what you think!" Prem says. He keeps holding me even as I let my legs slip down him and he spins around so she doesn't see what's happening in his pants.

She lets out another shriek. "That's because I could never think such dirty things."

The last time I wanted to die of shame, a neighbor had declared that a whore's daughters could only ever be whores. Rupi had run at her and scratched her face, then gotten punched and had her nose broken in return.

"Can you wait outside, Mamma, please," Prem says with utmost calm. "I can explain. I promise."

Without another word, she leaves.

I'm shaking. Prem zips his pants and then helps me put myself together.

"Simi, it's—"

"N . . . N . . ." I swallow. I count. I breathe. I do everything I'm supposed to do to get my tongue to start working again. He waits.

"N . . . No. I . . . I can't. Please. J . . . Just go."

"We have to talk about this."

Except I can't fucking talk.

"I have to tell her the truth."

"N-no!" I go deep into my gut, and I dig up my voice. "No. We can't tell her, Prem. Not until we've talked to Rupi. Please." I can't screw my sister over.

"Okay. Fine. I won't tell her yet, but we have to tell her once we've talked to Rupi. And Saj. Saj will know what to do."

I nod. "I can't face her right now. Your mom."

"I know. It's okay. Wait here. I'll go talk to her."

He walks to the door, then turns around and comes back to me and pulls me close. "I love you, Simi. Please don't ever doubt that. It's going to be okay."

He kisses me.

Nothing is ever going to be okay.

"Baby?" he says.

"I'm fine. Go."

He does, and I follow him to the door but stay inside the room, where I can hear them but they can't see me. I cannot face anyone right now.

"What is wrong with you?" she says to him. The disgust in her voice cuts through me. "Is this how I raised you? You're cheating on your fiancée a week before your wedding." Here her voice turns into a hiss. "With her *sister*. Oh god, oh Krishna. What kind of girl is this?"

"Mamma, please, it's not her fault."

"You're right. You're right! It's your fault. Oh god, oh Krishna, what kind of man did I raise? What did I do? Rupi, oh my god. That poor child."

"What's the matter?" Good, my sister is here. She's going to take care of this. Rupi is going to take care of this. Relief washes through me.

"Nothing. Nothing is the matter." Tanuja says. "I, uh, let's go down and steam the sari. Oh god, the wedding." Prem's mother is going to hate me forever. Everyone in the family is going to hate me forever.

"Mamma, what's wrong?" my sister says. "Prem? Tell me what happened."

"I will. Just give me a minute. Mamma, please, can you give us some space?"

"You're asking me to leave? Really? So Rupi is alone when she finds out? I'm not leaving her to face this by herself."

"Can you trust me for one second, please?" How is he so calm?

"Prem, it's okay, just tell me. Whatever it is, you can tell me in front of your mother. We have no secrets."

Really?

"I will tell you when my mother leaves."

"What's in the room?" Rupi asks.

"Don't go in there, beta," Tanuja all but shrieks. Which is the surest way to get Rupi to walk straight to the door where I'm standing, hair askew, eyes swollen.

She startles. "Simi!" Her head pivots from me in the room to the corridor outside. "What . . . what are you doing in Prem's room?"

And that's when I know what it feels like to be thrown under a bus by your own flesh and blood.

THIRTY

RUPI

My sister looks at me like I just pushed her off a speeding bus. "Did you come up here to find my earrings?" I say, trying to give her an out because she seems unable to make words. "They're not in Prem's room, silly. They're in the guest room." I turn to Prem's mother, who looks so guilty, it's like she's the one—not her son—who cheated on me.

"Or, Mamma, maybe I put them in your room? Can you check for me, please?"

"Yes, yes, let's go down," she says. "I need your help with something too."

Great. Now we're both trying to take each other away from the crime scene.

"I'm right behind you," I say, but she doesn't budge. "I'm fine, really. I'm just going to check if they're in the guest room."

Time hangs while she decides if I'm being brave or stupid. Finally she turns and leaves with enough reluctance that I know I have just moments to turn this capsizing ship around.

"Why the hell didn't you lock the door?" I hiss at my sister. Then turn to Prem. "Call Saj right now."

"Why?" both Prem and Simi say together.

"Because we can't tell Mamma the truth without making her an accomplice. And we can't keep lying to her anymore."

"Oh god," Simi says. "You're right. We can't do that. We can't tell her."

"Can't tell me what?" Great. She's back. How fast does this woman move?

Simi looks up in horror. Then swallows, squares her shoulders, and steps in front of Prem and faces his mother. "I'm sorry you had to see that, Auntie. But there's something you should know. This isn't his fault."

"Simi," Prem says.

"No, Prem. Your mother deserves the truth. Let me talk," she says. Great, now she decides to be assertive with him. She turns to his mother and dives in. "I've always been in love with Prem. I met him when I started taking care of the girls, and well, it was instant. I'd never met anyone like him, that gentle, kind, smart." Her eyes are shining. "For a long time, I didn't say anything. I couldn't. I mean, look at him. What would someone like him ever see in me? But we did become friends, and it just got worse. He's everything I've ever dreamed of. I kept wanting to tell him, but before I could, he met my sister. You know the rest. He fell so hard. I was heartbroken. I was also angry."

She turns to me. "Rupi's always had everything I've wanted. I shouldn't have been surprised. Then you all met her, and not just Prem but all of you fell in love with her. I was left out. For these past few months, it's felt like my life is over. Today when I came up, looking for her earrings, I ran into Prem in his room. We started talking, and I realized once again what I had lost just because I didn't tell him how I felt when I had the chance. I lost all sense of right and wrong."

I squeeze her arm. "Simi." I try to stop her.

"No, let me finish. You've always sacrificed for me." She throws my hand off with so much force, I stumble back. "You've been through so much, and I've still been jealous. I threw myself at him. I was the one who kissed him. I practically attacked him. He was trying to push me away when you came into the room."

Prem groans. "Simi, don't."

"No, Prem. Stop trying to protect me. I know you're doing it for Rupi. But stop."

She turns to me again and takes both my hands. I grip her tightly and widen my eyes. *Stop it!*

"I'm sorry," she says, then she yanks her hands away even as I struggle to hold on.

Prem's mother's gaze pings from Simi to me to Prem, then back again all the way. "Is she telling the truth, Prem?" she asks her son. The woman is too smart by half.

Prem looks at Simi with so much helplessness, I don't know how she can stand it. "No, she isn't." He squeezes his forehead with a shaking hand. "Simi is one of the best people I've ever met." He takes a breath. "She . . . she had a weak moment." Simi sags in relief. Is it relief? "If you hadn't come in right then, everything would have been okay. I would have managed to push her away."

It's amazing how good we've all gotten at telling these curated truths in a way that they're essentially lies.

And it's one person's fault. Mine.

"So, if you'd been able to push her away without Rupi finding out, that would have been okay? So, just because Rupi doesn't know that her sister is betraying her, that means everything is okay? Is that how truth works for you now, Prem?"

"Well, who does it help if the sisters lose each other?"

"It helps her." Mamma points at Simi and gives her a scathing look. "She gets away with cheating her sister, who doesn't deserve it. She gets away with violating her sister's relationship."

"You're correct. I'm . . . I'm so sorry," Simi says.

Mamma turns away from her.

Simi bites her lip, turns, and heads toward the stairs.

Prem looks like he wants to follow her, but no one wants this to blow up in the family's face and hurt them. Supporting immigration marriage fraud is a criminal offense. There can be hefty fines, even jail time. To say nothing of the scandal it would cause in the community.

That's never happening.

"Simi, wait," I call after her. "Come back."

Simi turns to me, her eyes filled with tears but also warning. She wants to be the one to make the sacrifice, to be the one to protect me. But to hell with that. It's not a contest. It never has been.

Only one person can fix this. Just like only one person could fix the shit that was our childhood. It's not Simi's fault that she never got to be that person.

"Simi wasn't the one violating her sister's relationship." I look away from her and turn to Prem's mom. "She wasn't the one who was betraying her sister."

"What are you talking about, beta?" Tanuja says with all the gentleness that made me imprint on her like a baby chick.

I soak up the way she's looking at me, because it's the last time she ever will.

"Simi hasn't betrayed anyone," I say. "I have."

THIRTY-ONE

SIMI

After a lifetime of witnessing my sister blow shit up, watching her telling Prem's mother the truth is one of the saddest, dumbest, bravest things I've ever seen anyone do.

As for the aftermath, I'm not sure what I was expecting, but it wasn't watching Tanuja Gupta turn into someone straight out of the soaps Rupi and I grew up watching. She's totally and completely losing her shit.

"I never want to see your face again," she says to Rupi, pressing both hands into her temples as though it will keep her head from exploding. "Who does this to their own sister? And to think I was starting to make you my favorite. Everyone is right about me. I'm too trusting." She turns to Prem. "How could you deceive me, Prem? You were the child I never had to worry about, and you're the one who lied to me. You let these girls you met yesterday make you lie to your own family."

In the face of conflict, every family's dysfunction comes out, I guess.

Even more tragic than Prem's mom's anger is Rupi's reaction to it. After admitting to pulling Prem and me into this arrangement, she's just sitting there and gathering up Prem's mother's rant as though her anger is precious, albeit heartbreaking. As though she's waited all her life for someone to love her enough to lose their shit over her. There's not even a hint of responding anger in her.

I want her to push back, but what can she possibly say to make this better? That's never stopped her before. Making a bad situation worse if she can't control it has been who she is for so long, this feels like losing her. All I want to do is take her away from here and figure out what to do next, how to make sure she's safe.

For my whole life, whenever I've seen Rupi in crisis, she's been coiled up like a spring, filled with the potent force of trying to get away and finding an out. A cornered animal. Now there's no hint of that. She's completely and totally still, as though there's a deep knowing inside her that whatever happens is going to happen. She is currently an observer in her own life, and she's okay with it.

I sit down next to her on the couch in the sitting area on the upper floor. We're surrounded by walls plastered with the Gupta family's joy.

"Everything I said before about how I feel about Prem is true," I say to Prem's mother, who's pacing. "But you're right, I took advantage of him. The only person I've ever been able to rely on before I met Prem was my sister. I could think of no other way out but to ask for his help. I should never have put him in that position. I wish I could go back in time and undo things. I never meant for it to hurt you. Prem would never lie to you if he had a choice. He wanted to tell you the truth, but we were all scared."

"I'm not a puppet, Simi," Prem says. "I was never, not even for a moment, not aware of the choices I was making or the risks involved. Even if we did go back in time, I would do exactly the same thing again. I would do anything to keep you from being hurt."

His mother presses a hand to her mouth. I press one to my chest.

I try to telegraph both my gratefulness and a warning to Prem. "Please, can we not do this right now?" I turn to his mother. "You've done so much for Rupi and me. You took us into your family." My gaze strays to the smiling pictures we're surrounded by. "Showed us for the first time in our lives what that feels like. Thank you. I truly am so sorry we put you through this."

Tanuja doesn't respond.

I take Rupi's hand and pull her up. "Let's go, didi."

For once in her life, Rupi follows without a word.

Prem grabs my other hand. "Hang on a minute, Simi."

I try to pull away, but he holds on.

"I lied to you too," he says to his mother. "Do you never want to see my face again either?"

She gasps.

"Don't do this," I say. "Don't say things to hurt your mother. She's right. I forced you to lie. I took advantage of your love. I gave you no choice."

"Didn't you hear me? I knew exactly what I was doing," Prem says. "That old cliché is true. You always have a choice. I chose this."

"Neither one of you chose this," Rupi finally chimes in. "This was just the easiest choice for me to make, and I made it. I took the easiest path."

"You took the only path," I say. "The choice of going back to India and facing what awaits you there isn't a choice. You are not going back. But you are coming home with me now."

"I'm going with the two of you," Prem says.

Tanuja's eyes widen with shock. "You're leaving home over this? After lying for this girl, you're leaving your family for her?"

"Can we please not be so dramatic, Mamma. I'm not leaving home. But from now on, I will be where Simi is, always. Everything I've done is on me, not on Simi and Rupi. I can't believe you, of all people, are blaming them. What happened to 'I'm not like other mothers'? They asked me for help. They didn't even know you. They had no commitment to you. I'm the one who did."

She sticks out her chin. He's managed to wound her even more. "You are correct. This is on you. Why did you do it?"

"Because I love Simi." He pulls my hand to his lips and drops a kiss on my knuckles. "And now I love Rupi too. They're my family, too, now. Look at them, Mamma. Didn't you just see them throw themselves in front of each other so the other didn't take the blame and look bad in front of you? You've spent months saying how loving and strong and generous they are. You were absolutely right, they are, and no one gave them that. Their values and strength and love weren't taught and modeled by a family like ours was. They've had nothing their whole lives that they didn't create themselves. Not even love. All the things you've taught us about life, they are models of it, and no one taught them. They just are."

"They lied to all of us, Prem! They made my son lie to me. They turned the love we gave them into a lie."

"No, Mamma, they returned your love tenfold. Baba can use the remote control by himself. He held my hand by himself the other day. He leaves the house! Is that a lie? Did any one of us spend months working with him on that? Neel and Nathan, they grow vegetables and draw and take showers without being bodily forced into it. Is that a lie?"

He throws me a worshipful look. "Even before Rupi came into town, Simi was having trouble with Karina at work. I was already madly in love with her and asked her to marry me. She could have married me, gotten her green card, and then found another job. But she didn't because she didn't want to turn our love into a lie. She could have left Preeti to her own devices with TASha to placate Karina, but she didn't because she loves those girls so much. Is that a lie? Do you know the thing that broke Simi's heart today? It was losing the chance to wear your forty-year-old wedding sari. Simi and Rupi love you and this family, and you know it."

Tanuja's shoulders descend a few millimeters. "Then why not tell us? Why not trust us? Do you not think your mother, your family, would have supported you and helped you?"

"We do trust you," I say. "But we already put Prem in jeopardy, we couldn't drag the rest of you into this mess with us too. At first we were just afraid, but once we got to know you, the idea of exposing you to legal action became impossible. Telling you the truth would have made you accomplices."

Rupi has been eerily quiet until now. "I'm sorry," she says, gaze on her hands. Even the most heartless person would see the effort it takes her not to let the words crack on her tongue. "There's no excuse. I shouldn't have done it."

Tanuja folds her arms across her chest.

We wait for her to respond, but she doesn't. There isn't much more we can do, so we take her silence as goodbye and leave the house. I can't seem to let Rupi's hand go. She doesn't pull away, but her heart's not in it. She's letting me hold her hand because she doesn't have it in her to fight me. All the fight inside her is gone.

THIRTY-TWO

RUPI

Seeing the purpose on Saj's face when he walks into Simi's apartment wrecks my hard-won peace.

He strides toward me and doesn't stop until he's standing too close, our bodies almost touching.

I think of myself telling Simi and Prem to get a room. Prem and Simi do not pay me back in kind. They watch us.

"We will figure this out." It's the first thing Saj says.

He got on the first flight back from LA as soon as Prem and Simi filled him in on the full crash and burn of my plans. I have several missed calls and messages from him, but I haven't read them. I can't be on my phone right now. It feels like too many eyes on me, and all I need right now is to be invisible. To disappear somewhere, so I can think.

Saj does not oblige my wishes with those seeing eyes.

I take a step away from him. "You take this magic wand thing too seriously."

"Why do you sound like this?" he demands.

"Like what?"

"Like you've given up."

Because I have. "It's not so much that I've given up as I've come to my senses."

"Can I have a moment alone with her," he throws at Prem and Simi without looking away from me.

"You good?" Simi asks.

No. "I'm not going to run away, Simi. Stop being such a chipku."

Prem drops a kiss on my cheek. "Listen to him. Annoying as it is, he really is as smart as he thinks he is." With that, they leave Saj and me alone in the apartment.

I pour us chai, and we take our cups to the open window, where the sound of the freeway ebbs and flows like the ocean, and the breeze has the weight and heat of home.

"Tell me what happened in LA," I say.

He's about to argue, but he doesn't because I must look really pathetic when I say, "Please, Saj. That first. Did you find out how we can help the girls in LA?"

He takes a breath and looks at me like he can't believe that's what I want to talk about, but he gives me what I want.

"Yes." He fills me in. There's an organization that provides legal counsel to women and girls who are out of legal status and have been trapped into sex work. The USCIS issues special visas that let victims of human trafficking stay in the country and find a pathway to rehabilitation, but they have to cooperate with law enforcement to put away the perpetrators. Which is terrifying, because the threat of violence is real. Sometimes the known devil feels safer than the unknown angel.

"I'm working with the organization to find safe houses and ensure protection," he says. "But earning the girls' trust is going to be the main concern."

"And Tina? She'll get away with it?"

"She might have to disappear and go into witness protection. But if those women get their lives back and others don't get trapped in it, isn't it okay to let karma do the rest and take care of her?"

"Wow, I didn't take you for fatalistic."

"I'm not. We're going to work pretty hard to bring her to fate's door. She's going to lose all of her assets. She'll have to start over with nothing." The way his eyes shine with purpose might be what I love most about him.

"Okay."

"Okay what?"

"You can go after them. I'll give a statement, be a witness, do whatever you need me to. But you have to make sure the girls are safe. You have to make sure not one of them gets hurt."

"Do you even need to ask?" He's looking at me like my trusting him is the most important thing in the world.

"No." I reach out because I so badly want to touch him, to cup his jaw and test if it cuts my hand. Wipe the worry creased into his forehead. But he's my lawyer, and he's already told me that means he's off limits. So, I take my hand back and keep it where it belongs—on my side of the line between us. "Can you do me one more favor?"

"Anything."

"Tell Tina the Om on her butt is upside down and that it's really bad luck."

The smile he gives me is awfully sad and sweet, which is no longer surprising, which in itself is quite a shock.

"Done. Now can we talk about the rest of it?"

"Sure. You can also tell her that I slept with her husband in their bed. But that might be a little too mean, even for me."

"Rupi." I hate how he makes my name sound at once like a warning and a prayer and a storm that's brought him to his knees.

"What?"

"This is not over."

"I know. It's the beginning of the rest of my life."

He doesn't like that. "Don't be like this."

I laugh. "It's really annoying how much I get that."

"Then stop. Because you're out of control. You need to stop." He looks like he's drowning.

"Fine. I'll stop. How would you like me to be instead? I'm so darned tired of being me. I really am. I just want someone to tell me who to be. Tell me. I'm listening, Saj. I swear."

"Good. Then listen to this. You're not going anywhere. So, stop acting like you are." His eyes are whirlpools of intensity. They tug at every cell in my being. "Let's figure out what to do next."

Fine. "Tell me, then. What are my options?" I try to make myself sound interested.

"We can stay the course. We've already applied for your marriage license. I know it's what Simi and Prem want. Your green card application is ready to go as soon as we have the license. Nothing has to change."

"But everything has already changed." There's the little issue of the Guptas hating me now. "The only people who are going to get married are Prem and Simi. At this point we need to focus on making sure the Guptas don't blame Simi for my mess."

"They won't," he says with complete confidence.

"I hope you're right. And you were right before. They are good people. You know, in Indian culture—at least, in movies and TV shows—a parent's most sacred duty is to get their daughter married into a good family. And I'm Simi's parent for all practical purposes. So, I did good, ha?"

He doesn't respond. But the oddest expression falls over his face.

"On second thought. That's a crap sacred duty, isn't it?"

He laughs. His eyes shine with a bitterness I haven't seen there before. "No kidding."

I point a finger in his face. "Wow. That's not the reaction I was expecting. Is this about the 'hurt on both sides' in your divorce?"

He raises that beautiful, gruff brow. "It is."

"Do these short answers mean you don't want me asking what happened?"

"No." He smiles, and I want to high-five someone. Will that ever go away? "These short answers mean I don't know why I want to answer all your questions when I've never wanted to answer anyone else's."

I press a hand to where that lands on me. Straight through the heart. "Do they teach you how to wield words like weapons in law school?"

"That's pretty much the entire degree."

"She hurt you." I can't make it a question.

He shrugs.

"Will you tell me what happened?"

"Our parents introduced us. I found out three years into the marriage that she'd been forced into meeting me because her parents didn't like the guy she was in love with. She never stopped being in love with him." He gives me the saddest smile. "I guess a robot like me seemed like a good option for someone who thought her heart was taken. She never complained about my working sixteen-hour days. I thought I'd gotten lucky and found someone who understood me. I just wish I'd known, you know, so I could have known to try harder, known what I was working with."

I've never wanted to kiss anyone so badly in my life, never felt this raging need to comfort another human being. "So, you never got to fight for her?"

"Actually, fighting for her meant not fighting for her. At least I got to do that."

"My god, Saj. Please tell me you didn't help her get back together with her ex when you found out."

He shrugs. "They really were in love, and they seem very happy." He gives me one of his state-of-the-art meaningful looks. "I'm a fan of being wanted by the person I fight for."

Well, yet again you're out of luck, buddy. "And I'm a fan of how good you are at helping people get out of trouble."

"I haven't helped you yet."

I point a finger at him. "In that you're wrong."

Our gazes have done that thing again, where they've snapped together like magnets. Connection sizzles between us.

Suddenly his eyes fill with a strange intensity. "You know how I said I cannot have any sort of relationship with a client?"

"You said that?" I ask. "When?"

He laughs.

It's a good thing he laid that out like that. It's not like the idea of marrying him hasn't crossed my mind. All this eyefucking can turn a girl's head. Marrying him would solve everything. Problem is I'm not stupid enough to believe that anymore. Or try that particular path again. You know what I do want to try? Learning from my mistakes.

But there's something else. Something bigger. I've always believed that destroying something to save yourself is just the way the world works. For the first time in my life, I have something I can't risk destroying.

"I'm going to find you another lawyer," he says, and I blink up at him.

"That's not an option!" I shake my head with so much force, my hair flops over my forehead. "I need you to be my lawyer, Saj. I need you to be in my corner. That's all I need from you." I sound desperate, because this is nonnegotiable.

With the gentlest finger he pushes the hair off my face and finds my eyes again. "I am in your corner, Rupi. I will always be." Then his hand curves around my jaw.

All by itself, my body rises up on its toes. His bends closer. There's his smell again and the sweetness of his breath. Our lips are so close, it makes my knees weak.

I can't be weak right now.

I drop down on my heels. Pull away. "Then please don't take that from me." My heart is racing. Sparkles tingle where his skin is touching mine. "I've never had this before. Someone I can trust. Someone who's acting on my behalf." I step back and away from his hand.

"None of that will change if you get another lawyer." He reaches for me again.

"No!" I say with all the finality I can muster. "I have to do this my way, Saj. It's taken me a long time to get where I am, and using our friendship to marry you would destroy that."

"That's not how it would be." He takes my hand, and it's just such a bloody bummer how that feels like being picked up and held close. "I want to be with you. You already know that."

I laugh. I love a good irony. But does this have to hurt quite so much? "We barely know each other. And this is not how I want to get to know you. Not with a green card–shaped gun to our heads. I can't. Not with you. You don't understand what my life has been like. What getting to have you . . . have all this has meant. Please. Don't take that from me."

That stops him. I'm begging, and I don't care. "I won't change my mind about this," I say. "Please." A stupid tear leaks from my eye.

He squeezes the bridge of his nose.

I've been with a lot of men for a great many reasons, but I've never seen longing coiled inside one of them like this. He wipes my cheek and steps back. He steps back. And he gives me what I've asked for. He does exactly what I need him to do, even though I can see how very much it isn't what he wants. He listens to me.

"Fine," he says. "I'm sorry. Tell me what you need." He's back to being a robot, but, honestly, it doesn't work as well if his heart's not in it.

"Well, first, let's get my statements and whatever else you need from me to go after Ron's operation. Then we'll figure out the rest."

THIRTY-THREE

SIMI

It's been close to twenty-four hours since my stupidity put my sister in the path of danger again. Ever since Rupi quietly let Prem and me bring her back to my apartment like someone who's had the life force sucked out of her, we've barely heard a word come out of her. I thought Saj's visit would change her mood. It did a little. She's excited about going after Ron's operation now, but she won't talk about anything other than that.

Prem and I make chai in our pj's. Rupi is drawing on her sketch pad on the living room rug, completely lost in the world of what she's creating.

Prem wraps his arms around me from behind and places his chin on my shoulder. "You smell good enough to eat," he says. "Like spun sugar and hugs."

I press into him as he nuzzles my neck. It's weird to have him see me like this—in the liminal space between leaving behind the night and not yet dressed for the oncoming day. He's squeezing me like he wants to soak this unguarded me up, like this is the me he's always seen.

We stand there like that for a moment, watching Rupi. I can feel my worry reflected in his breathing. Somehow having the concern in both of us merging like this feels like purpose.

"She's plotting something, isn't she?" he says. "Do you think she'll run away again?"

"She's definitely up to something," I say. "But I have no idea what. She isn't following her usual patterns of behavior." But neither am I.

We take the chai to Rupi. She shows Prem the sketch she's working on. A sleepy-eyed girl in pajamas with waist-length hair and bare feet.

"Almost as beautiful as the real thing," he says, and Rupi makes a gagging face, even though they're both looking smittenly at the paper.

After chai, Prem kisses me, hugs Rupi, and leaves for work. He's going to work the first half of the day, and I'm working from afternoon to evening. We don't want to leave Rupi alone. The fact that she broke and told Prem's mother the truth means she's already chosen a path, and I just know that the path is going to involve removing everyone else from danger. Especially Prem's parents. And doing something incredibly stupid.

I'm not sure if she's feeling reckless enough to run away and go back to India, but I can't think of any other option, and there's a good chance she can't either. So, I'm not ready to leave her alone and take that chance.

How can she think about leaving me now, when we've found each other again? When we have access to everything we've ever wanted. The comments from our neighborhood group keep running in my mind. I would do absolutely anything to keep her from those vultures.

"There's something I haven't told you," I say.

She looks up from her sketch and meets my gaze warily. She's been avoiding eye contact. It's telling that she doesn't ask me what it is.

"Remember the blackmailer cop?"

That makes her sit up a little. So, she isn't quite as insulated as she wants me to think.

"I googled him."

She sighs and puts the sketchbook down. "That's really smart."

"Well, he's dead. He died of COVID. In jail."

She blinks. "Google told you all that? How come?"

"Because the case got a lot of coverage."

"Really?" I can tell her brain is racing. "Why? It's just another corrupt cop."

"Because your recording was leaked, and it went viral. He was famous, or infamous."

She rubs at the ink on her arm and chews hard on her lip. "So, everyone knows what happened."

"Everyone."

"How do you know?" She's working hard to hide her horror, but her skin is turning pink under her thumb.

I pull her hand away and squeeze it. "I went to the neighborhood social media group."

Her eyes pick up the rage inside me. "It's that bad, ha?"

I nod. "Going back home is not an option, didi. Please."

Suddenly the way she's looking at me changes. "How long have you known?"

"I just found out."

"Simi? I thought we weren't lying to each other anymore. How could you not tell me? How could you keep going with our plan when you knew everything had changed?"

"Because nothing has changed. You are not going back. How does it matter how long I've known? What matters is that you know how vicious those people are."

She pulls my hand to her chest. She's barely shown any emotion since we came home from the Guptas'. Now her eyes fill with tears, and she looks at me funny. "No. That's not the part that matters." She drops a kiss on my knuckles. "And I can be a hundred times more vicious than they are. You know that. They're just people."

I'm about to argue with her, but she wipes her eyes and gives me her first real smile in the past twenty-four hours. "Dead, ha? And jail! I guess you were right, sending the video was pretty badass."

I pull her into a hug. "Have I told you how lucky I am to have you for a sister?"

"Not lately. But you were enough of a chipku that I do know that."

I pull away and study her face. "We're going to make this work, okay? I'm not letting you go back."

She turns away and then lies down with her head in my lap. It's been a while, but this used to be our favorite way to talk. Only it used to be my head in her lap as she asked about my day.

"You and Prem should go over to his house today," Rupi says. "His mother is going to worry if Prem doesn't go back and reassure her that he's not angry. You should go with him. Present a united front."

"But he *is* angry."

"Why? It's not his mother's fault. She has every right to be upset. Make sure she understands that you know that."

"Fine, let's go over there now and visit."

"I've been wanting to work on some sketches. You know how much I miss it. But you should stop over on your way to work. And anyway, I don't want to deal with Tanuja's drama. You don't have a choice but to deal with it."

I know Rupi too well to fall for this. She's just being her stubbornly sacrificial self again. She wants me to use this crisis to bond with the Guptas.

"I'm a little fed up with you patronizing me, Rupi," I say.

Despite her best efforts, she looks so crumpled, so defeated, lying there. I want to shake her but also squeeze her tight. I stroke her hair.

"I don't know what you mean," she says.

"I don't need you to lock yourself away from the Guptas for them to like me."

"Oh, I don't think there's any danger of them liking me more than you right now. It's more like separating yourself from the shadow of evil."

I smack her shoulder. "Stop it! Pathetic is just as bad as patronizing, and it suits you even less. Don't think I don't know what you're thinking."

"What am I thinking?"

"You're thinking the 'sometimes loving someone means letting them go' thing. And it's nonsensical."

"You know what's even more nonsensical? The 'you only hurt those you love' thing."

"I'm sure there's a balance between those two things, and we're going to find it together. Remember how you used to always say we're a package deal? Well, we are, and the sooner the Guptas know that, the better."

Turns out we shouldn't have worried, because as I sit there stroking my sister's hair, a knock sounds at the door.

Prem's mother, Preeti, and Chandni march into my apartment. They're riding on a mighty cloud of apology and bluster.

"I am a terrible person," Tanuja opens with and then throws her arms around Rupi.

"What you are is a dramatic person, Mamma," Preeti says and throws her arms around me. "I knew it! I knew I couldn't have been wrong about you and Prem."

"I'm sorry I didn't tell you," I say.

"Obviously you didn't tell me. Such a mess of complications going on around here," Preeti says.

"No kidding," Chandni says, then offers to make a piece for the empty wall in my living room.

Apparently, everyone knows all the sordid details of our arrangement.

Also, apparently, they don't care.

"What kind of person makes a sacrifice like this for her sister?" Prem's mom says, throwing her arms around me and kissing my cheek with some force. She smells like lemons, jasmine, and chai. Everything comforting in the world. Something as soft as a fuzzy blanket wraps around my heart. Rupi is right. This woman is potent. I feel like I've been injected with a dose of liquid maternal warmth.

She wipes my eyes with the edge of her scarf in the most movie-mom gesture ever. "It's too much. You girls are too much." She's miserable, and her misery feels so much less complicated than any misery I've ever experienced, it makes me feel lighter. "I said such awful things to you. I'm so sorry."

"Please, please don't say sorry, Auntie."

"What is all this Auntie-Shantie business?" she says. "You will call me Mamma, yes?" Then she looks at Rupi. "But maybe in private for the next two years?"

Confusion clouds Rupi's face.

"Rupi, beta, we have to make one change to the wedding plans. You will have to pick a different sari. I think I want to save my wedding sari for Simi. If that's okay with you, Simi, beta?" She turns to me, and if I weren't so confused, I'd already be crying.

"What are you saying?" Rupi says.

"What does it sound like we're saying?" Preeti says. "There is absolutely no reason to change any of our plans. The wedding is next week. Everything is already paid for. Why cancel now?"

"Why cancel?" Rupi says, eyes wide with disbelief. "Because this was never meant to be a group fraud project."

"What fraud?" Chandni says, studying other walls in my home to hang hair on. "All we know is that Prem loves you, and we can't wait to welcome our new daughter-in-law"—she throws a look Rupi's way—"and her sister into our home."

Identical smug smiles cover all three of their faces. Rupi looks too stunned to make words.

"It's the perfect solution," Mamma says. "If both you and Rupi move in—you know we have plenty of extra bedrooms—no one needs to know who does what."

Now I'm too stunned for words. That's exactly what we were planning ourselves, but from her mouth it sounds too preposterous to wrap my head around.

"That's . . ." Rupi looks at me. She's thinking the same thing I am. A month ago, she'd said darned near the same thing. Now she folds her arms across her chest and looks at everyone like they've collectively lost their ability to think.

She opens and shuts her mouth a few times. Then instead of arguing the point, she settles on "That's very generous of you."

Which is the thing that strikes terror in my heart, because I know that look and I know that she's made up her mind about something, and it's far worse than the rest of this mess.

THIRTY-FOUR

RUPI

Saj's apartment is as beautiful as he is, and like him, it feels as safe as a fortress.

Which is why I can let neither the apartment nor the man lull me into safety.

It's been two days since I called him to get me from Simi's apartment in the middle of the night. I had to leave like a thief while she and Prem were asleep. Because I'm not stupid. I know when I'm on runaway watch. They were never going to leave me alone in the light of day.

Saj didn't ask a single question. I asked him to get me, and he did. I asked him not to tell anyone I'm with him, and he didn't. I didn't doubt he'd do either of those things even for a second.

I signed the papers with my testimony statements for the trafficking case. He worked really hard to get that done and out of the way so I could leave, even though he doesn't want me to.

"I've done what you asked me to do, Rupi. Can you at least listen to me about this one thing?"

"Alas," I say, "that one thing isn't just one thing. It's the whole thing."

"Fine, don't marry me. But you can't go back to India."

"You know that's the only thing I can do."

"You're a witness. We can apply for asylum."

"I don't want to seek asylum. I don't want to be a victim. I don't want to count on people's charity. Not even a country's. I've told you why it's important to me."

I throw a look at my bag sitting by the door. We've discussed this over and over, and I don't want it to be the last conversation I have in this place I got to love for too short a while.

Last night he asked me what happened with the cop, and I told him. Even the parts that I thought I'd never be able to tell anyone, not even Simi. The parts that break my heart for the girl I was then.

His reaction destroyed me. Rage, and sadness, and pride all rolled into one. This guy is definitely the angel of death, because more and more every day he's killed me. And strengthened my resolve to leave.

"Why doesn't it matter that I have feelings for you?"

Those feelings are the reason I have to go. I can't risk them on holding him in a hostage situation. The two days I've spent in his home we've talked endlessly but also sat silent by each other for hours. I will take our silences and our conversations with me and hold them close forever.

"It does matter, Saj. But what our circumstances will do to those feelings matters more. Ever since we met, you've fixed everything for me. That can't be our dynamic. I wish I wasn't out of time, but I am. I want to fix this myself. I've learned so much here. I want to honor that and face what's waiting for me." I step close to him. He hasn't touched me once in his home. Probably some sort of ethics thing that I hate but I'm also deeply grateful for. "You know how very grateful I am, right?"

Instead of acknowledging that, he walks past me and grabs my bag. "Since you have made up your mind, we don't want you to miss your flight."

For the first time in a long time, he's stiff and shut off. Distant in a way that hurts, but it's just as well. If that's what he needs to get through this, then that's what he needs.

He puts the bag down again, and I want to groan. Why won't the guy give up? But instead of more pushing, he disappears into his room with "I need to grab my laptop. I might as well go into work after I drop you off."

For the entire drive to the airport, Saj doesn't say one word to me. When we get there, he pulls my bag from the back seat, then we walk across the airport parking lot to the terminal. We get into the elevator, where he tries to step back and give me space. Unfortunately for him there isn't any, and our bodies are almost touching. The elevator is huge but filled to bursting with people and luggage. Not a surprise, given the world has a stuff problem. Even when they travel, people insist on lugging all their stuff everywhere they go. I twiddle my fingers, hating the restlessness in that gesture. All I have is a duffel bag, and Saj won't let me carry it.

The elevator stops, and I step out and start walking.

"Rupi. God. Wait. I can't let you do this."

I liked it so much more when he was having a silent tantrum.

"Are you really not going to talk to Simi and the Guptas before you go?"

"I told you. I can't."

I can't believe they're all on board with going through with the wedding. My insides hurt when I think about it. How they're ready to take on the US government for me. I can't let them do that. I just can't.

I'm well acquainted with Gupta stubbornness. They think it's just a matter of convincing me. Which is why there is no way I can tell them that I'm going back to India. I can't deal with the tsunami of resistance. They will use bodily force to get me to stay if they have to. The only way I can stand up to it is to leave without telling them.

As for Simi, she should be focusing on Prem and his family. Because of course they love her and feel bad for her and want to heal the hell out of her.

Of course leaving without seeing them hurts. Other than that, going home doesn't feel that terrible anymore. I feel strong, but in a completely different way than I ever have. Getting to tell the Guptas the truth did something to me. Seeing my sister and Prem together did something to me. Being with Saj in his home did something to me. I want to go home and see how this new Rupi fares in the place where she was such a mess.

My visa extension expires in a week. I want to leave while everything is still good and legal. I want to be able to come back someday and see my future nieces or nephews.

Saj stops before we enter the terminal. "Rupi." That's it. Just my name, and I want to fold in half.

I can't do that.

I turn to him. "Actually, there is one more thing I need from you. I need you to let me do the rest of this myself. You don't have to come into the terminal. Thanks for the ride. Thanks for everything you've done. Thanks . . . How have I not thanked you yet?"

"You have. I don't want your thanks."

"Okay. And . . . um . . . Can you send me the receipt for the ticket. I'd like to pay for that myself. I'll send it as soon as I have the money."

"Don't do that. Don't be like this."

"Like what?" It comes out a whisper. "Don't be strong?"

"That's not what I'm saying. You are strong. Do you even know how not to be strong?"

I laugh. Maybe that's what I'm doing wrong. "Will this be easier if I cry? I'm not great at that. But I've had a little practice recently. I can give it a try. Then again, that's more Simi's skill. Sorry."

I turn away from him and start walking again. I have to, or I really might turn into a Simi-like watering can.

I expect him to grab my arm.

I expect him to turn me to himself.

I expect him to pull me to himself.

To kiss me. Ravish me. Soothe the longing coiled within me just as tightly as it is within him.

Unfortunately this isn't one of the soaps I grew up with.

This isn't a rom-com. Because he doesn't.

Not any of it.

And me? I care for nothing except the fact that I know, really know, how badly he wants to.

That has to be enough. I keep walking. Why does the walk from the parking lot to the terminal have to be miles and miles?

"Rupi."

Gah, can he stop saying my name. "What now?" I turn to him. He's holding out a brown paper bag. Where did he pull that out of?

"It was in my pocket. I've had it for a few weeks now. The opportunity to give it to you just never came up."

"I don't want anything from my lawyer. You'll just bill me for it."

He laughs. It's a sad thing, that laugh, but just as satisfying as all the other laughs I've ever squeezed out of him. "I didn't get you anything. I can't take more from you, Saj."

He groans. "Fine. Don't take it." He starts stuffing it back in his pocket.

He looks so destroyed, I snatch it out of his hand.

I open the bag and look inside. It's a Mast Tattoo tattoo gun. The best in the market. Wireless, in bright pink.

It's pink. *I hate pink* I want to say. I want to give it back. But I pull it to my chest.

"You've had this for weeks?"

"I bought it the day after your visa extension came through. I just . . . I'll take it back." He tries to take it from me, and I twist away.

"Don't even think about it." I unzip my duffel and stuff it inside. He stands there, watching me. He left his suit jacket in the car, and he's wearing another of his absurdly well-fitted shirts. His cologne wafts around me and makes me lightheaded. I take my time shoving the gun in and zipping it back up. Then because he's looking at me like that again, I go up on my toes and drop a kiss on his cheek.

"Thank you," I say. "Can you stop doing nice things for me now? It's messing with the robot vibe."

"You're welcome," he says. "I hope it will help you forgive me."

"For what?"

He looks over my shoulder, and I spin around.

"Rupi!" seven voices say at once. It's all the Guptas, every one of them.

"Oh god." Saj called them. The traitor. "I'm going to kill you," I say, and yet again I make him laugh.

It's a good thing that we got here early, because they try every trick in the book to get me to go home with them. I can't. I am, however, incredibly grateful to get to say goodbye.

"When will I see you again?" Simi says.

"At your wedding," I say. "Don't make him wait too long, he might find someone else."

"I did," Prem says, hugging me. "But she didn't want to marry me."

Simi pushes him away and grabs me. My chipku.

"India is still on this planet. You'll come see me," I say, but I hug her back for so long, I can't figure out where she ends and I begin.

"You're my person, didi," she says. "My everything."

"Right back at you, Chipku," I say and kiss her cheek and stroke her hair and then let her go, which might be the hardest thing I've ever done.

"You're leaving without saying bye to your baba," Mamma says.

"How could I ever do that?"

"You told him."

I nod. Saj sneaked me into the house yesterday when no one was home.

"See, you're not allowed to make me love you more." She has tears in her eyes.

"Thank you," I say. "For everything. Will you come see me in Mumbai?"

"You're leaving me, so I guess I have to. I hear you have a flat. Hotels in Mumbai are very expensive."

"And you'll get a tattoo?"

"Only if you give me one. I want one that says *Pankaj*. Can you design one?"

"On it." I try to be nonchalant, but when I hug her, tears spill from my eyes.

I wipe them and hug the others. Preeti, her babies (who, it turns out, aren't that hard to tell apart), John, Pawan, and Chandni. Neel and Nathan hold me for so long, I don't think I can ever let them go.

I try to stop myself, but I can't help but throw Saj one last look and wave. I can't say bye to him in front of this audience. He doesn't push the issue. We've said all there is to say.

They watch me until I disappear through security.

When I get to the gate and hand my boarding pass to the gate agent, he looks at me with some surprise. "You're in the wrong line," he says. "Business class is that way."

Shit, I'm going to have to send Saj a business class fare. I can't afford that. Except I know that no invoice is ever going to come from him.

I hold back my tears until I'm in my seat. Then the dam bursts.

A flight attendant comes and asks me if I want my duffel bag in the overhead bin. I tell her I want to hold on to it for now.

I hug it to my chest. I need something to hold. I try to remember the woman who hugged her backpack on a seemingly endless series of trains and buses as she ran for and from her life. She's still inside me, but she isn't running anymore, even when she is. I thank the person who stole my backpack. I hope the theft changed their life, too, the way it changed mine. I hope it led them to what they were looking for, too, the way it led me there, even when I didn't know what that was.

The tattoo gun pushes against my hand through the fabric of the bag. I stroke a thumb across it. He bought me a darned tattoo gun. The one thing I missed when I had so much more than I ever had before. Who does that? I lean my head into the bag and close my eyes. Mostly I'm just working hard not to get up and get off the plane. I should marry Saj. God knows I want to be with him. Then why can't I?

Because I can't. Because I love him too much to do it like this. Because I want to, for once in my life, choose the thing that's the right thing to do, not what feels like my only way out. And because sometimes fighting for someone means not fighting for them.

I will see Simi again. Tanuja will visit me. I know they've been meaning to bring Baba to India because he wants to go.

I'll see them all again. Maybe even Saj. But, god, leaving him hurts in a whole different way.

"Is this seat taken?"

My eyes pop open. "What the hell, Saj! What are you doing?"

He lowers himself into the seat next to me. "Several things. But first, I'm trying to get a client to fire me."

I grin like an idiot. I can't help it. "You have no luggage."

"I'm told there are stores in India."

"You can't be serious."

"I'm told I am. Serious in an angel-of-death sort of way."

My heart is doing things no human can survive. "What about your work?"

"Good thing I grabbed my laptop and my passport on the way out."

"You've been planning this since we left home?"

"*Planning?* What's that? From the moment I first laid eyes on you, I've had absolutely no control over anything. All I've known from that moment is the need to be near you. And when you disappeared into that security line and the Guptas asked if I was coming home, I knew the only home I wanted to go to was you."

I close my eyes. I'm 100 percent sure I'm swooning, but I smile. "So, the Guptas forced you on the plane."

"Well, my sister's mother-in-law has been trying to set me up with her daughter-in-law's sister. I broke."

Was he always this funny? My cheeks hurt. I was right—smiling is a cheek workout. "Are you really going to India with just a laptop bag?"

"Nope, I'm going to India with the most incredible woman I've ever met, because I might be hopelessly in love with her."

My smile stretches across my face. I look around. "You are? Where is she?"

He leans close to me. "I'll show you. But first I need you to do something."

"What?" I lean close too.

"Fire me, Rupi," he says, his lips hovering over mine.

"You're fired, Saj," I say, and then I kiss him.

ACKNOWLEDGMENTS

If I had ever imagined that I would write twelve books, I don't think I could have imagined that the twelfth one would take just as much out of me as writing the first one. If anything, it might have needed more of a community, more cheerleading, and more faith from loved ones. All things I find myself incredibly lucky to be blessed with.

My first and biggest thanks goes to my editors Nancy Holmes and Alicia Clancy, who wield both the shovel and the chisel with equal skill and grace. Thank you for trusting me enough to push me and see the tree when I could barely see the seed, and for holding strong while I thrashed about. And to my agent, Annelise Robey, for giving me exactly what I needed exactly when I needed it and for being such a timely and brilliant flashlight on this often-muddled path. Thank you!

As always, wanting to tell stories is like having a kitchen full of ingredients. To make anything meaningful from them takes recipes and utensils and gadgets. Which is a bad metaphor for all my writer friends who take my hand every day and tell me I can do it, and when that is not enough, proceed to show me how. Barbara O'Neal, Virginia Kantra, Jamie Beck, Priscilla Oliveras, Liz Talley, Tracy Brogan, Sally Kilpatrick, Kristan Higgins, Susan Elizabeth Phillips, Shirlene Obuobi, Annika Sharma, Ali Rosen, Naina Kumar, Alisha Rai, Nisha Sharma, Robin Skylar, Melonie Johnson, CJ Warrant, Stephanie Jayne, having you in my corner is to never be lost, no matter how hard things get.

Every story requires experts to bring authenticity to it. To my Kentucky girl, Vibha Ancha, this story (much like my life) is more fun because of you. Thank you for sharing your home, your family, and everything really, with such generosity. To Subodh, the brother of my heart, thank you for patiently answering even my hardest, most insensitive questions. I am so grateful for your presence in my life. And to Evelyn Irani, Nurse Extraordinaire, for sharing your experience and expertise, and of course, for doing the hardest job in health care.

Once the work of making the story is done is when the real hard work begins. The work of taking the book to the reader. Thank you to the tireless design, editorial, marketing, and publicity teams at Lake Union: Kimberly Glyder, Rachael Clark, Bella Roberts, Brenna Bailey-Davies, and Elyse Lyon. With you, I always feel like I'm handing my book baby into the most capable hands.

There can be no stories without a life that feeds them. To my friends and family for not just letting me mooch off your lives and keeping up the shenanigans, but also for acting like deadline behavior is normal, for providing wine, snacks, and shoulders to cry on, and for showing up for me no matter where I am on this roller coaster. Gaelyn, Rupali, Anita, Swati, Ira, thank you for the endless conversations and for getting stuck in whirlpools with me and leading me out of them. Mamma, Papa, Mihir, Annika, and Manoj, you are the reason all this happens and the reason any of it means anything at all.

Last but not least, thanks to all the librarians, booksellers (especially Anderson's Bookshop in Naperville), bloggers, podcasters, and all the book evangelists who work tirelessly to connect readers with stories. And of course to you, my readers, who let my stories into their hearts and take these journeys with me, thank you a million times over for letting me do this work I love.

BOOK CLUB QUESTIONS

1. Simi and Rupi embody strength in very different ways. Which sister did you connect with more?
2. The sisters are bound by sacrifice, betrayal, and love. Do you think one sister "owes" the other more? Overall, do you think it is possible for familial relationships to be equal?
3. Rupi constantly reinvents herself in order to survive. Simi craves healing and works as a nurse. Discuss how their trauma factors into their career choices.
4. Rupi and Simi believe that the fake marriage is a matter of survival. How did you feel about them putting Prem in that position?
5. Prem's family offers the sisters a home filled with love and safety. What role do chosen families play in the novel? How do they impact the blood ties?
6. Both sisters' fates hinge on immigration law and the people who control their paperwork. What does the novel reveal about the balance between the right to dream and work for a better life, and laws and bureaucracy?
7. The green card marriage forces everyone into deception. Do you believe lies told for survival are justified? What would you do in a similar situation?

ABOUT THE AUTHOR

Photo © 2025 Chandra Wicke

USA Today bestselling author Sonali Dev writes stories that explore the experience of being a woman in today's world. Her novels have been named Best Books of the Year by *Library Journal*, NPR, *The Washington Post*, *Cosmopolitan*, BuzzFeed, PopSugar, and *Kirkus Reviews*. Dev has won the American Library Association's award for best in genre, the *Romantic Times* Reviewers' Choice Award, and multiple RT Seals of Excellence. Other honors include being named a RITA finalist and being listed for the Dublin Literary Award. *Shelf Awareness* calls her "not only one of the best, but one of the bravest romance novelists working today."

Sonali lives in Chicagoland with her husband, two visiting adult children, and the world's most perfect dog. Find out more about the author and her work at https://sonalidev.com.